81-23328

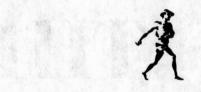

THE

WINNERS

Part II of
Joyce Haber's
The Users

by
DOMINICK DUNNE

SIMON AND SCHUSTER

NEW YORK

Copyright © 1982 by Joyce Haber
All rights reserved
including the right of reproduction
in whole or in part in any form
Published by Simon and Schuster
A Division of Gulf & Western Corporation
Simon & Schuster Building
Rockefeller Center
1230 Avenue of the Americas
New York, New York 10020
SIMON AND SCHUSTER and colophon are trademarks
of Simon & Schuster
Manufactured in the United States of America

1   3   5   7   9   10   8   6   4   2

Library of Congress Cataloging in Publication Data
Dunne, Dominick.
Winners: part II of Joyce Haber's The users.
I. Haber, Joyce. Users. II. Title.
PS3554.U492W5   813'.54   81-23328
ISBN 0-671-24978-9   AACR2

Acknowledgment is made for permission to quote from "That Old Black Magic" by Harold Arlen and Johnny Mercer, copyright 1942 by Famous Music Corporation, copyright renewed 1969 by Famous Music Corporation.

For
Griffin, Alex and Dominique

THE
WINNERS

Chapter 1

A BLACK MERCEDES 600 LIMOUSINE rolled to a stop in front of the fashionable restaurant on Melrose Avenue. A uniformed chauffeur leapt out and opened the rear door. The autograph hunters who always waited outside, and the photographers from the fashion and social press, turned their attention away from the society women, film stars, and moguls who were the regulars of the lunch bunch to see who was arriving in such classic splendor.

A woman got out of the car, spoke briefly to her chauffeur, and proceeded down the walkway to the entrance of the restaurant, oblivious to the photographers who took her picture, ignoring the autograph hunters who knew her by name. She wore dark glasses. She wore a black turban. She wore a wide-shouldered smartly cut black dress. There were pearls around her neck, earrings at her ears, and an immense diamond ring on the fourth finger of her left hand.

"Who's that lady in mourning?" asked an out-of-towner.

9

"Oh, my God," said an in-towner, seeing who the out-of-towner was referring to. Other people in the restaurant were beginning to notice her as she stood in the entranceway waiting for Patrick to seat her, and a buzz went around the patio.

"Who is she?"

"That's Mona Berg."

"Isn't she the one who—?"

"It was an accident."

"But I thought—"

"She was cleared by the Grand Jury."

Although her figure was almost slender, there was a sense of largeness about her, as if there had once been more of her than there now was. What hair showed beneath the confines of her turban was blond and luxuriant and combed into a turned-under pageboy. Her teeth were beautifully capped. Her nose was perhaps a trifle too small for the size of her face, although exquisitely shaped, or reshaped. She was neither beautiful nor unbeautiful. She was noticeable. She was a presence.

Patrick, the owner of the smart restaurant, the arbiter who knew who was who, who separated the riff from the raff, broke off in mid-sentence with Cary Grant and rushed to her side. She held out her hand to him. He took it, lifted it to his lips in courtly fashion, bowed his head. "Congratulations, Miss Berg," he said.

"Thank you, Patrick," she answered.

"It's good to see you out again."

"Is Marty Lesky here yet?"

"At the center table, waiting for you."

He preceded her through the crowded patio to Marty Lesky's table, aware, as she was, that all eyes were upon her.

"Congratulations, Mona," said Cary Grant as she passed his table.

"Thank you, Cary," she answered.

"Congratulations, Mona," said Warren Beatty as she passed his table.

"Thank you, Warren," she answered.

"Congratulations, Mona," said Diana Ross as she passed her table.

"Thanks, Diana," she answered.

"What are they all congratulating her for?" asked the out-of-towner. "Didn't she kill the guy?"

"Shhhh," said the in-towner, embarrassed at his guest's lack of decorum. "I told you it was an accident."

"Even so," said the out-of-towner.

"That's not why they're congratulating her."

She arrived at the center table, Marty Lesky's table, and Marty Lesky rose, as did the seven men who were also seated there, to welcome her. Marty Lesky kissed her on each cheek.

"Who's he?" asked the out-of-towner.

"Marty Lesky. The head of Colossus Pictures."

"Who are the guys in the gray flannel suits?"

"The board of directors of Colossus."

"What's going on?"

"Didn't you read the trades?"

Marty Lesky took Mona Berg around the table and introduced her to each member of the board. Patrick himself opened the first bottle of Dom Perignon champagne, poured a bit into Marty Lesky's glass for him to taste. He gave his nod of approval and Patrick filled Mona Berg's glass, and then Scotty Warburg's glass, and then Abe Grossman's glass, and on and on around the table.

"I'd like to propose a toast," said Marty to the board. "I

would like you to join me in welcoming Mona Berg to Co-lossus Pictures."

The seven rich and distinguished men rose and held their glasses to the new studio head. Every eye in the restaurant was turned toward the table. Then the people at the other tables rose also, in tribute to the lady, and an ovation swept through the tables on the patio of the restaurant.

"Thank you, thank you," said Mona Berg, first to the board of directors and then to the people at the other tables. There were tears in her eyes. It was the moment of her life that she had always felt she was born for.

Chapter 2

IT WAS NEARLY five years earlier that the events of a single day changed forever the course of Mona Berg's life. It was a day that began in an ordinary enough fashion within the exotic confines of the world of film and fame and fortune. . . .

Warren Ambrose, the famous agent with the famous client list, started off his day the way he started off all his days when he was in residence in the film capital—which was all of the time he was not making deals or visiting clients on location in other capitals—by reading Dolores DeLongpre's column. It was a well-known fact among those who knew him, like his secretary Mona Berg, that no one enjoyed reading about himself in the columns more than Warren Ambrose did, especially Dolores DeLongpre's column, where his name appeared with great regularity, for having brought to fruition this big deal and that big deal involving glittering names from the film and literary worlds.

It was a beautiful Southern California morning, and all was right with his world. His grapefruit was sectioned just the way he liked it to be. His bagel was toasted just the way he liked it to be. His raspberry preserve and his breakfast tea were English. The napery on his bamboo tray was sparkling white, as was the jacket on the Japanese houseboy who served him on the terrace of his Los Angeles home, in the exclusive area known as Bel Air. His telephone was at hand for his early calls to New York, with the synopses of several new properties nearby, prepared for him by his secretary, the same Mona Berg whose job it was to read for him. If Dolores DeLongpre were at hand to describe his dress, she would have written, in her rococo style, that he was sartorially splendid, and the description would have pleased him, because he gave a great deal of thought to the matter each morning.

The telephone rang. It was Mona Berg, as he knew it would be, the endlessly efficient Mona Berg who telephoned him every morning at the same time to tell him what his appointments were to be for the day.

"Good morning, Warren," she said. "Did you see your name in Dolores DeLongpre's column?"

"No, what's it say?" replied Warren, who, of course, had seen his name but liked to appear as if it were of no import.

"It's about the *Green Hat* remake," said Mona, who knew that he had already read it, just as he knew that she knew, but it was a performance they played out.

" 'Warren Ambrose sets English writer Lambeth Walker to write screenplay of studio topper Marty Lesky's personal production of—' " read Mona from the column.

"Don't eat on the telephone!" barked Warren. It was a thing about her that drove him mad. It sounded moist to him, like a jelly doughnut.

14

She paused a moment, hurt, and then proceeded reading from the column in a more remote manner. " 'I put together more deals at my parties than I do in my office,' said the ten-percenter."

"Swallow it, for God's sake," Warren said to her impatiently. He knew her habits. He knew she was holding the jelly doughnut in the back of her mouth and trying to talk as if there were nothing there.

They went on to other things, the business of the day, where he would lunch, where he would dine, what time he would be at his office, the calls he would return, the calls she would return.

"What else?" he asked.

"Burns Harrison called," said Mona.

"What did he want?"

"He said he didn't like the size of his name on the cover of his book," answered Mona.

"What's wrong with the size of his name?" asked Warren.

"He said it's so small you can't read it," said Mona.

"Tell him he's lucky to have his name on it at all," said Warren.

"He's in town from New York for a few days and wants to have dinner with you on either Tuesday or Wednesday," said Mona.

Burns Harrison was the kind of writer you hired to write the sequel to someone else's best-seller and not worth an evening in such a busy social schedule as Warren Ambrose's.

"He's lunch," said Warren in the dismissive kind of voice he used for people of that echelon.

Warren Ambrose, at sixty, sixty-something—he engaged in vagaries about his age—was a man whose time had come. He had been a friend of the celebrated for four decades of Hollywood life, and the mantle of celebrity that he now wore was a tribute to the persistence of his pursuit of the powerful. As a very young man, he had pursued both daughters of Louis B. Mayer, the legendary head of MGM Studios, but that powerful man had far grander plans for his daughters' wedded life than the diminutive and pushy Warren Ambrose. He was called into the great man's office, treated as an upstart, and told in no uncertain terms to cease and desist his pursuit of either daughter, or he would be barred from the lot permanently, a fate somewhat akin to banishment.

He accepted his snub, as he would many others over the early years from the first families whose daughters he attempted to court. If he felt hurt, he did not let it show, nor did he cease to venerate the very families who had sent him packing: the Mayers, the Warners, the Goldwyns, the Meyers, and later the Zanucks and the Steins. That he would not settle for less than a bona fide Hollywood heiress became such an oft-repeated Hollywood story that, with the passage of the decades, it changed in the telling from indignation to amusement to admiration.

The snubs that would have felled a feeling man he somehow re-energized into a formidable ability to outstare and outnegotiate in business matters the most hardened studio chieftain. He became the ally of the artist against the studio, the little guy who wasn't afraid to talk tough to the tough guys; and the elite of the creative ranks flocked to him for protection and representation. Pushy little Warren Ambrose, formerly Warren Ackerman, prospered; and the talent agency that bore his name, the Ambrose Agency, acquired a reputation for "class," the very thing the first families had thought Warren most lacked.

When it finally dawned on Warren that he was making it

16

on his own, he abandoned forever his pursuit of an heiress wife, and married a bland creature called Alice who arranged his home and his meals and otherwise remained in the background of his life, closing her eyes and ears to his numerous infidelities. When she made a quiet and unobtrusive exit from his life and her own, expiring from cardiac arrest in her dentist's chair during the removal of a bothersome molar, there were those, particularly young ladies, who were surprised to read in the obituary columns of the *Hollywood Reporter* and *Daily Variety* that she had even existed. Thereafter he turned to starlets, on a far less permanent basis than marriage and, in the long run, a far more agreeable arrangement for himself, in that it left him free to make his personal life available to the glamorous clientele he served.

Like a great art collector who acquires and discards and hones his collection to perfection, Warren Ambrose, in time, let go of all but a dozen clients, but those twelve, as Warren was fond of telling interviewers, were among the highest-salaried people in the world.

He was the earliest practitioner in Hollywood of what has since come to be known as packaging, a practice of putting together from his own clients a combination of writer, director, and star in a package so dazzling in box office prospects that studios often vied to outbid each other. That Warren had rarely read the novel or screenplay from which the package originated attested to the persuasiveness of his selling technique. He had a gift for saying the right thing to the right person at the right time that put a project into motion and then brought it to fruition. He enjoyed an intimacy with the industry hierarchy that gave him access to their private time and private thoughts, and it was in these circumstances of acceptance that Warren Ambrose, who once had doors closed in his face, operated to his greatest effectiveness. To share this intimacy with anyone else he took to be a diminishment of himself, and so he built his agency into the most famous one-man operation in the world.

Warren Ambrose was of a nature that made working for him unbearable. The charm and wit that so captivated his clients and made him a favorite dinner guest of industry hostesses he denied his associates, just as he denied them partnerships when they sought advancement. The Ambrose Agency was his and he guarded it jealously from the succession of young men who had assisted him over the years and left when he refused them the recognition they felt their tenure deserved. He wanted them to be lieutenants, no more, to deal in detail, to back him up, but to leave the driving to him.

And then the young lady named Mona Berg entered his life with a bump, a six-hundred-dollar bump, when her Ford backed into the side of his Rolls-Royce in the parking lot of Schwab's, the famous drugstore on Sunset Boulevard where Lana Turner was discovered for films or so the legend goes. Along with his Braques and his Jacuzzi, Warren's Rolls-Royce was a prized possession, and the dent to the passenger side rear door filled him with a diminishment of self, as if the car were a part of him. A bump. An expensive-sounding crunch. Followed by appropriate obscenities from both cars. And then sobs from the Ford, which was very old and very run-down.

"Oh, Mr. Ambrose, I'm so sorry," said the girl tearfully as she got out of her car to survey the dent. She was a large girl, more than inclined to heavy, wearing thick glasses in a harlequin-shape frame. The fact of the matter was, and they both knew it, that the accident had been as much Warren's fault as it had been Mona Berg's, but for reasons best known to her at the time, she assumed full responsibility.

"I was looking out my rearview mirror, but I didn't see you, Mr. Ambrose. It's all my fault. I probably should have honked," she went on in apology, and the tears continued.

"What are you crying for? Did you get hurt?" asked Warren.

No, she told him, she was crying because she didn't know how she would be able to pay for the damage she caused to his car, because she was driving without insurance.

"Maybe I can work it off," said Mona hesitantly, as if it might be a solution to the problem.

"What do you mean, work it off?" asked Warren, not quite sure whether she was offering him herself, an offer Warren felt to be inadequate.

"As a secretary. I was number one in my class at Fairfax High in typing and shorthand. I'll work for half salary until that's paid off," she said, pointing to the six-hundred-dollar dent. Even then she understood about taking advantage of a situation, turning a minus into a plus. She knew that, after several weeks of doing the caliber of secretarial work she was capable of doing, shame would keep Warren Ambrose from holding her to the half salary he rapidly agreed to that winter afternoon in the parking lot of Schwab's Pharmacy.

Mona was a find right from the beginning, and none knew this more than Warren Ambrose, but Warren possessed a certain meanness of character that prevented him from ever admitting that to Mona. He let it be known that her efficiency was what was expected of her in this fortunate position he had given her, and there were lots of other girls out there ready to step in if it got to be too much for her. He recognized in her, though still subdued, that lust for advancement that he once possessed, but he did not fear her as in the past he had feared several of the bright young men who had worked in his office and dared to have ambition.

She took dictation and typed at an alarming speed, and his clients remarked to Warren about her charm and efficiency on the telephone that never overlapped into familiarity. In time she learned to read and write contracts with the speed of a lawyer, adapting into her business vocabulary words like "pari passu" and phrases like "favorite nations clause." She read and synopsized for Warren all the novels and manuscripts and screenplays that he never had time to read.

"Gimme the plot in one or two sentences," Warren would say to her about a six-hundred-page manuscript.

"Story of a factory worker who loves a wealthy girl and has an affair with a working girl, with tragedy resulting," Mona answered.

An hour later at lunch, at Ma Maison, Warren Ambrose would say to Marty Lesky, or Robbie Slick, or Myron Kahn, or whomever the executive might be, "I read Edwina Calder's new book last night and I couldn't put it down. Best read I had in a long time. It's about this handsome young guy, be great for Warren Beatty, a factory worker who falls in love with a beautiful rich girl, could be Candy, could be Jackie, whose father owns the factory, only Warren's having an affair—"

Before the lemon mousse had been cleared, a deal would have been made, a deal in seven figures, Warren Ambrose would report to Dolores DeLongpre, who in turn would reveal it in her daily column in the Los Angeles *Record,* and ninety-six other papers across the land, a reportage of life in the film capital.

Warren came to rely on Mona more and more. She prepared him for his life, just as she prepared him for his meetings. She took his suits to the cleaners and his Rolls to the carwash. She wrote the checks for his houseboy and scheduled the succession of starlets who visited his Jacuzzi. He rewarded her with gift certificates from the fashionable boutiques on Rodeo Drive in Beverly Hills, tax deductions all, but he never included her in his life, other than allowing her to sit at the door and check the guest list at his annual party at Chasens restaurant on the night of the Academy Awards. He believed her to be content, and for a certain number of years she was.

It was Mona who suggested to Warren that the rather belittling stories that were always being told about his early years ("Did you ever hear about the time Sam Goldwyn kicked him off his croquet court for cheating?" "Do you remember the time Bogart got into a fight with him at Mocambo?") would be better told if Warren told them about himself. The suggestion became the passkey to his own celebrity. "Tell about the time Louis B. Mayer kicked you out of his office," Amos Swank, the talk show host, asked Warren on his program. The once wounding episode, retold with the perspective of time, with affection replacing anger, humiliation transformed into humor, made his reputation as a Hollywood historian.

The longtime friend of the famous deeply loved the spotlight in which his diminutive figure now stood as an acknowledged celebrity himself. His picture began appearing in newspaper columns with tall young beauties, and his stories were quoted by chroniclers of Hollywood life. His one regret in the entire matter was that the honor had not befallen him earlier; and in an effort to recreate that circumstance, a round-the-world trip to visit clients on various far-flung locations resulted in a secret face-lift from the noted Brazilian plastic surgeon Dr. Ivo Pitanguy, the administration of youth-rejuvenating serum at the Rumanian clinic of the celebrated Dr. Anna Asalan, and the application of a red toupee by the remarkable Siegfried Geike of the San Fernando Valley. ("No one will ever know," Siggie assured him.)

During the long sojourn, Warren ran the office from Rio or Rumania with daily telephone calls to Mona, who for the first time became the direct intermediary between Warren and his clients and Warren and the industry figures he had always managed to keep remote from his associates. During one of the multiple emergencies that are part of the everyday life of people in demand, Mona handled with dispatch a certain matter involving the film star Marina Vaughan and the Malibu police; and on another occasion, when Warren's eyes were still too purpled to return, she sat in for him on a contract negotiation in the office of Marty Lesky at Colossus Pictures. Heady stuff. Little wonder that a certain resentfulness crept into her attitude when Warren returned, re-youthed, from his round-the-world trip and relegated her back to the ranks. ("Would you get some coffee for Mr. Diller, Mona?")

If Warren Ambrose was aware of the discontent that was brewing beneath the ample breast of Mona Berg, he chose not to notice it. He was aware that the latest belt or buckle or bag from Gucci or Vuitton no longer had quite the magical effect of bringing contentment that it had had for six years, but Warren reasoned, and reasoned correctly, that the cachet of his name, now that he was a media personality of equal rank to any of his clients, would outweigh other considerations, and her moment of restlessness would pass. And Mona, no fool, knew that to dissociate herself from this power at this time would be a serious miscalculation; and the resentment she felt for the nonrecognition of her capabilities she buried as she typed contracts and fetched coffee and drinks for meetings that she was not asked to attend.

*　*　*

At that moment, then, there, at the house in Bel Air, on the lovely California morning, when all was right with his world, Warren Ambrose walked along on his terrazzo floors, in his Lobb shoes from London, straightening his Van Dongen by an eighth of an inch, telling his houseboy his plans for the evening, how he wanted it all arranged for later, the Jacuzzi, the towels, the white wine in the silver cooler, and, oh, yes, he could take the evening off. There was the anticipation of romance in the air. A certain Miss Laurel Leigh, a former drum majorette from UCLA, barely turned twenty, had become a presence in his existence.

Outside in the circular driveway, his Silver Cloud Rolls-Royce waited to take him to the office. He was struck by the perfection of the picture of his life.

"Here," he said to his houseboy with a magnanimous gesture. "You can have these seats to the premiere of the new Rebecca Kincaid picture at the Plitt." He forgot he had already promised them to the enormously efficient Mona Berg, who by that time had been hard at work for several hours at his office on Sunset Boulevard.

Chapter 3

DURING WARREN'S ABSENCE for renovations, his Sunset Boulevard office had been renovated also, the last word in chromium chic, and rushed to completion in anticipation of a layout in *People* magazine. The single economy agreed on between Warren and the fashionable decorator Perry Rifkin was the elimination of the once-considered private office for Mona. She sat now in the outer office—itself stark and smart, a muted version of the more elaborate inner sanctum—with the second secretary, a pleasant young fellow called Bill, within whom the lust for advancement did not exist. That he was thoroughly agreeable was of secondary consideration in the friendship that Mona shared with Bill to his disarming lack of competitiveness.

During the Ambrose sojourn, Mona grew to rely on Bill to accompany her to the screenings of new films that she went to on Warren's tickets. It was a ritual that they both loved, the "being there" with stars and producers and directors, and the exclusivity of seeing a film that no one in the world had yet seen. Heady stuff again. At first they whispered out of the side of the mouth to each other the names of the celebrities they spotted. Then Mona picked up that it gave you dead away for the outsider you were if you stared, so she let Bill stare and whisper to her.

"Why don't you try doing your hair like Streisand's?" Bill said to her one night when that great star and her friends sat a few rows in front of them at the Directors Guild screening room.

"You mean frizzy?" she wisecracked just an instant before she realized how right it would be. Bill was usually right about things like that, and Mona, who was sensitive about her appearance, usually took his advice.

On this lovely California day, Warren Ambrose sat behind his meticulously neat desk a contented man. He was reading with great delight an article about himself entitled "Warren Ambrose, Agent Extraordinaire" in the current issue of *People* magazine. He looked up and caught sight of himself in the Lucite-framed Art Deco mirror, one of a pair that Perry Rifkin had bought from the old Dolores Del Rio house, and he liked what he saw. He rubbed his little finger (he had long since stopped saying pinky) across the tight, almost translucent skin under each eye and patted in verification the red toupee that Siegfried Geike had so ingeniously placed beneath and between his own thinning red locks. He decided he looked "about forty-nine," gave himself an approving wink, and read again the five-page article, delighting in the pictures of his perfect life, his favorite being a double-page photograph of himself on the telephone in his Jacuzzi, at the same time dictating to a secretary who was nearly out of focus in the foreground, a detail that eluded Warren as he buzzed for this same secretary. "Do you want to come in for a moment, Mona? I have a surprise for you."

"A surprise?" There was a note of anticipation in her voice.

"You got your picture in *People* magazine."

"*What?* I'll be right in."

And she was. And Warren magnanimously handed her the magazine across the desk, and Mona enthusiastically grabbed it. Just as Warren had noticed only himself in the photograph, Mona noticed only herself, and she was clearly disappointed with her out-of-focus debut in print. "Oh," she said, but Warren did not seem to notice.

"Where do you suppose they got that stuff about me being worth—how many million do they say I'm worth?" said Warren, with a bit of self-deprecation in his voice, orchestrating the moment away from her.

Right-out-of-your-mouth-is-where-they-got-it, was what Mona wanted to say, but, of course, she didn't.

She read the caption beneath the picture and gasped. "They called me Minna instead of Mona," said Mona, dejection, disappointment, defeat in her voice. "Didn't you give them the right name?"

"Of course I gave them the right name," said Warren. "They goofed, that's all."

How she had waited for that moment, counted on it, knowing at some level within herself that it would change her life, having her picture in a magazine for all to see, showing that she was someone other than the lump that life had always taken her for. Oh, how gladly had she posed for that picture, steno pad in hand, efficiency herself, the right hand he couldn't do without.

The article hadn't just happened. It was part of a public

relations campaign set in motion by Warren himself, with the aid of skilled practitioners in that craft, to perpetuate his newfound celebrity as host, wit, raconteur, social figure, and agent extraordinaire to some of the fanciest talent in the world. To be included meant everything to her. It was she who had suggested the picture to Grace St. George, the public relations woman Warren had hired for the job. She suggested it in such a way that Grace St. George thought the idea was her own.

"Wouldn't it be *marvelous*, Warren, to have a picture of you *in* the pool *on* the telephone, work-work-work-every-minute sort of thing, and this marvelous girl standing here in the foreground taking dictation," Grace had said at the time. The weeks had seemed like months as she waited for the article to appear.

"I'm going to have my picture in *People* magazine," she had said to her mother when she visited her at the home for the elderly where she lived, not sharing the moment in anticipated joy with her, because they did not have that kind of relationship, but showing off with it, another step away from her mother's kind of life.

"I'm going to have my picture in *People*," she had said to Bill, the other secretary, and to a variety of other people, including a hustler Bill had fixed her up with, as if that knowledge about her made her more attractive, or more important, or more something than what she was. And then the picture was out of focus, not Warren in the pool on the telephone in the background, just her with the dictation pad in the foreground, blurred lump of blurred lumps.

She was the kind of girl who had always been left out, the one who didn't receive a valentine when everyone else in the class did, the one who didn't get invited to the girl next door's birthday party. She had gone through life being snubbed, but no snub ever wounded her more than being denied this moment in the sun, out of focus and misnamed.

"Say, you might pick me up a dozen copies over at Schwab's," said Warren.

"I'll do it when I pick up your suits over at Don Cherry," said Mona quietly. Her body was hot with the hate that she could not give vent to. A litany of mockery was pent up within her. She had the ability to mutilate a carcass with the viciousness of her tongue, but she withheld directing her litany toward him. She had an inner instinct for timing.

They went on to other things. It was the Reade Jamiesons' wedding anniversary, and did he wish to send flowers? Rex Vaughan was coming back from Europe, did he wish to send caviar? She gave him a plot of a screenplay about face-lifts that might be a good vehicle for Faye Converse's comeback picture. She told him that Grossman-Dragonet, the immensely successful television production company, was thinking of doing a revival of the old television series *South Sea Adventures*. She told him that the Marty Leskys' daughter, Cecilia, the Hollywood heiress, was coming back from Europe to live with her parents.

"What else we got? I got an important appointment up at the house at four o'clock," said Warren, looking forward to having done with the office for the day and getting on with the more pleasurable aspects of success.

"If you mean your four o'clock with Miss Laurel Leigh," said Mona, not about to let him get away with that bit of business bluffery, at the same time staring at his wig, squinting at it even, with her petite eyes behind her tinted spectacles, knowing how uncomfortable it made him, "she's going to be half an hour late."

She could never understand why Warren Ambrose could never come clean with her on the matter instead of inventing business appointments. After all, she talked to the girls half the time when they called to break appointments or change the time, or when they misplaced the piece of paper with the address on it, or when they got lost in Bel Air. ("I've been driving around for half an hour and I can't find the fucking house," one of the girls had said.) It was the same Miss Laurel Leigh, a drum majorette she was, an aspiring starlet she was, who told her in her adorable kind of way that Warren had a dick like a Tampax. Still the masquerade persisted. He never acknowledged to Mona what Mona already knew. He never opened a door of himself to her that wasn't business, as in the old officers-don't-mix-with-the-enlisted-men theory, to which he adhered.

"Did you finish the manuscript of Edwina Calder's new book?" asked Warren, irritated that she should be aware of his Jacuzzi date.

"It's four hundred pages, Warren. You only gave it to me last night," answered Mona in a tone that indicated there was a limit to even her efficiency.

"Can you finish it tonight? You don't have anything to do, do you?" Mona rarely had anything to do nights, and he knew it.

"I was just going to one of Sylvia Lesky's parties, that's all," replied Mona.

"Sylvia Lesky's having a party?" Warren was one of those people whose life was temporarily ruined if he heard of a party he hadn't been invited to.

"Don't have a heart attack, Warren. I was only kidding," said Mona. "That is my ambition, though. To go to a Sylvia Lesky party."

"The next time she's having a big party, I'll ask her if you can sit at the door and check the guest list," said Warren in his second magnanimous gesture of this encounter.

"That's not what I meant, Warren," replied Mona evenly.

Whatever showdown between the two the conversation was heading for was averted when the door to the outer office opened and the film star Marina Vaughan stuck her head into the room.

"Young Bill out here says you're busy, but what's the point of being a movie star if you can't walk in on your agent without an appointment," said the beautiful movie star, with the assurance that any interruption from her would not be unwelcome. She was twenty-eight, marvelous of figure, marvelous of face, with the derring-do kind of personality that made her such a darling of the tabloid press.

She had made her first movie when she was eleven, costarring with her father, the film star Rex Vaughan, in a comedy-tearjerker that was hugely successful at the box office, for which she received a best-supporting-actress nomination. It was what they used to call box office magic, and the praises of Warren Ambrose were widely sung at the time as the architect of the idea, Warren having been the agent for Rex Vaughan, as he would be henceforth for Marina, about whom he felt fatherly affection.

She always led a well-publicized life. Who had not read about the movie-star-daughter-of-movie-star-parents? Even her godparents were celebrated. Montgomery Clift, her father's great friend, was one, and Faye Converse, the legendary star, was the other. And yes, the story was true that Monty Clift in a tipsy moment nearly dropped her at her christening and Faye Converse caught her. A lot of name-dropping in those two sentences, yes, but that's the way it always was in her life.

When she was twelve, she discovered her mother's body after her mother committed suicide in the predictable vodka-Seconal manner, but by that time her mother and father weren't married anymore, and her mother had moved to Palm Springs. She dropped out of movies for her high school years and attended the exclusive Westlake School, where Candice Bergen was a year or so ahead of her and Cecilia Lesky was a couple of years behind her; but she didn't fit into that kind of privileged all-girl existence, having been a child celebrity. She was always in trouble with her escapades involving marijuana and boys, and eventually was asked to leave, which bothered her not a whit. She returned to films at eighteen, that world being her natural habitat and, under the guidance of Warren Ambrose and the protection of her father, made a couple of good films and a couple of so-so films, and married a couple of times, and divorced a couple of times, and had a lot of romances with this star and that star, or so they always said about her.

"Marina! What a surprise!" said Warren, delighted to see her, delighted as well to have done with the discontent of Mona Berg. They performed the ritual of the double cheek kiss, Warren and Marina, so popular in the circles where they lived their lives. "I read in Dolores DeLongpre's column that you were in Acapulco with, uh, who was it now? I can't keep up with you."

"Mick Jagger," said Mona, who was always a mine of information on the comings and goings of people whom she did not know.

"Yeah, that's right, Mick," said Warren, annoyed with her interjection.

"Listen, darling," said Marina. Marina called everyone darling. She called herself darling when she talked to herself in the mirror, and she called God darling when she prayed, which was when she wanted a part, or wanted a romance not to end. "In the last year DeLightful DeLicious DeLongpre has had me involved, engaged, or married to Jack Nicholson, Warren Beatty, John Travolta, and Ryan O'Neal. I'm beginning to sound like the town tramp, and only about sixty percent of it's true."

They all laughed. It was Marina Vaughan who gave Dolores DeLongpre the nickname DeLightful DeLicious De-Longpre after singing the revised lyric to the Cole Porter song It's DeLovely at an industry charity event, and the name stuck, to the great displeasure of the powerful columnist.

"How was Travolta?" asked Mona.

"To die!" answered Marina, and the two girls laughed.

"You know my secretary, Mona Berg, Marina," offered Warren, clarifying positions.

"Of course I know Mona Berg," said Marina. "She got me out of the Malibu jail one night when you were cavorting around the world and couldn't be reached."

"I heard about that," said Warren.

"A little revelry that got out of hand, nothing more, but your Mona Berg was the very soul of efficiency. No fuss. No bother. No press. Mona, I thought you might like this more than a bread and butter letter." Marina took from her bag a gold bracelet and handed it to Mona.

"Miss Vaughan!" said Mona, thrilled with the attention she was getting from the famous star.

"It's Marina, please. Your initials are on the back. I hope you don't have a middle initial; if you do it's not there."

"It's beautiful, Marina," said Mona, clasping it to her wrist. "Look, Warren."

"Beautiful. You're spoiling the help, Marina," said Warren in a mock chiding fashion.

"Well, she deserves it," said Marina. "Everyone says she does all the work around here, anyway. Oh, only joking, Warren. Now, darling, sorry to break in on you like this, but there's a part coming up that I've got to talk to you about."

Marina's remark about Mona doing all the work did not sit well with Warren, joke though it may have been. "Would you excuse us, Mona? Miss Vaughan and I have a few things to talk over."

"Oh, sure," said Mona, her face reddening and her body assuming the clumsy pose it sometimes assumed when she felt herself left out in a social situation.

"Would you like anything, Marina? Tea? Coffee? Perrier?" asked Warren.

"I'll have a beer," said Marina. "I have a terrible hangover."

"A beer for Miss Vaughan, Mona. And after you pick up my suits and get me the dozen copies of *People* magazine, will you drop them up at my house? Say, did you see this piece about me in *People*, Marina?

"I don't know where they got that stuff about me clearing ten million dollars a year," he said in his self-deprecating voice as Mona left the office, having been sent on her way.

"Darling, tell her to get rid of some of that Gucci. She looks like a walking alphabet," said Marina about Mona when the door had closed, not looking up from the article she was reading.

"Mona's just fine the way she is," answered Warren.

"One of these days she's going to walk right out on you, Warren. That girl could be the highest-paid executive secretary in town. Any studio would want her." Marina, star daughter of a star father, had a tendency to lock people forever in the category in which she first met them.

"I love the piece," she said to Warren, looking at him at last, and for a terrible moment Warren thought she was talking about his hairpiece rather than the magazine piece she meant. "It makes me know I'm in the right hands. Warren, I want to play Iris March in the musical remake of *The Green Hat.*"

When Mona returned to the outer office, she found Bill in the high state of excitement that any encounter with a film star called forth, only more so, because the film star in this case was Marina Vaughan. She was a great favorite of Bill and the circle of friends in which he moved, a circle of young men who dressed alike and danced away most of their nights together in a discotheque in West Hollywood.

"Marina Vaughan looks great," enthused Bill. "I told her I saw her dancing at Studio One the other night, and do you know what she said?"

"No," answered Mona, her mind elsewhere.

"She said next time to cut in if I was a good dancer."

"That's an intimacy I wouldn't share with Warren if I were you."

"What's the matter?" said Bill, sensing her gloom. "You sound down."

"Same old crap," said Mona. "Do all the work and then he treats me like a stewardess when any of the clients come around. One of these days, so help me—"

"—you're going to really let him have it. Right?"

"Just as sure as there's an alligator on your tit." Mona flicked a glance at his sport shirt, one of thirty he owned in the identical style. "By the way, your dancing partner wants a beer. I'm going out to do errands. Take the calls, will you?" She gathered up her things—keys, wallet, telephone book,

34

statused all—and tossed them into the Louis Vuitton tote bag Warren had given her for Christmas.

"Your mother called from the home," said Bill quietly, knowing it was not what she wanted to hear. He was right.

"Later," answered Mona.

"She said you haven't been to see her for three weeks."

"I said later."

"Did you ask him if you could use his tickets to the premiere tonight?"

"He gave them to his houseboy," said Mona, and she went out the door.

Chapter 4

SO FAR, the day had been a bummer for Mona Berg. She was driving along the Sunset Strip in Hollywood toward Schwab's Pharmacy, on the last of several chores for her employer. God, how she hated to do chores for her employer, personal chores, that is, like taking his Rolls-Royce to the carwash, or his Gucci shoes to be resoled, the cheapskate, or to pick up his new suits, tailored to his new slimness, as she had just done. And now to Schwab's for his magazines, she was thinking, and then up to his house in Bel Air to drop off everything, and then home to Laurel Canyon to read a four-hundred-page manuscript so she could fill him in on the plot before his lunch date tomorrow with Marty Lesky, the head of Colossus Pictures.

The magazine article had bummed her out. Imagine having your picture in *People* magazine, and having the picture out of focus and the wrong name under it. Getting the bum's rush at the Marina Vaughan meeting had bummed her out too, even though she should be used to that by now. And hearing from Bill that her mother had called from the home bummed her out the most. She wished her mother wouldn't telephone her at the office, just as she wished her mother wouldn't write her at the office. She didn't know which she hated more, her mother's accent or her mother's handwriting, still immigrantlike after thirty years. She felt guilty when she felt ashamed of her mother, and she was always amazed that Bill never made any cracks about her mother's accent or handwriting, both of which filled her with unpleasant rushes of shame for the obscurity of her birth.

She didn't hate her mother. She only hated her mother's acceptance of the circumstances of their life, as if it were their lot in life to be poor. Mona hated everything about being poor, the sights and sounds and smells of it. She knew early that she wouldn't marry out of it, her looks were not the type that attracted eligible men, so she applied herself to the secretarial arts and speed reading offered in her high school, becoming the fastest and the best, so expert that the teacher suggested she teach, but the typewriter was not an end for her, only a means to an end. The end was movies. That was what Mona had in mind for herself, somehow, someday.

During high school she started going to Schwab's Pharmacy in the afternoons after school, on her way to her part time job, to read the movie magazines and the trade papers and fantasize about which among the young actors drinking coffee at the counter were "destined for stardom." She never read a bit of junk news about a film star that she did not retain at some remote level. She could remember such trivia as the name of Rock Hudson's ex-wife or the names, in order, of all Elizabeth Taylor's husbands when, for some reason, it became important to know that kind of information.

Every time she drove into the parking lot of Schwab's, she remembered the time that she had backed her car into the side of Warren Ambrose's Rolls-Royce, a bump that changed the course of her life, in that it resulted in her first step away from the home and neighborhood and background that she despised so much. Sometimes she wondered just how accidental that accident was. Certainly she was aware who Warren was and had seen the sleek silver automobile other times, but she preferred to think of the incident as the intervention of fate.

The trouble with Schwab's these days was that you could never get a place to park, all those people taking up space who were only in there reading movie magazines and the trade papers. Mona honked her horn impatiently, to no avail. She never stopped to think that the offenders were doing no more than she used to do herself every afternoon not too many years ago, but once Mona moved on from a situation she never went back, looked back, or remembered back. With a quick glance to the left and right, and the assurance that no one was looking, she pulled her old Ford into a space marked "Reserved for the Handicapped" and rushed into the pharmacy, not even noticing the Volkswagen with the wheelchair tied to its roof that couldn't find a place to park.

"Is the new issue of *People* in yet?" asked Mona, a trifle imperiously, of the cashier, a faded beauty in her middle years for whom the Hollywood dream had not been realized.

"Just being unpacked in the back," replied the cashier.

"I want a dozen copies. It's a charge to Warren Ambrose."

"Oh," said the cashier, brightening up at the illustrious name. "How is Mr. Ambrose? He's such a darling."

"Read about him in *People*."

"Well, I can't wait. What a success story that is," the cashier, whose name was Flo, said, "and he's just as nice as any-one you could ever hope to meet."

What Mona Berg did not wish to engage in at this time was a duologue with a dyed blonde about what an old sweetheart Warren Ambrose was, the prick, and she continued moving on to the counter before this woman could relate her Warren experience.

"Excuse me, I think I'll have a cup of tea while I'm wait-ing," she said. She knew she wasn't going to order tea even as she said this. She knew she was going to sink her face into something on white bread with extra mayonnaise, the better to deal with the disenchantment that had finally set in with Warren Ambrose.

Watching this dispirited woman from the magazine rack, where he was reading in the *National Enquirer* an article about the latest romantic entanglement of the film star Ma-rina Vaughan, was a remarkably good-looking young man. He was dressed in the manner of many remarkably good-looking young men, of whom there are a great number in this part of the world, in blue jeans and a tee shirt. His name was Frankie Bozzaci. He didn't have much background and he didn't have much education, but his perceptions were keen and there was something about him that was crying out to be noticed. The young man moved to the counter and took the stool next to Mona Berg. He had not followed her, as a man follows a woman, for the purpose of romance, but because that particular stool happened to be empty at the moment he decided to have a cup of coffee.

"A cup of coffee," he said to the waitress.

"Coffee's sixty cents here, with only one refill," replied the waitress. Her name was Fay and she had been working the counter for enough years to know who didn't have the price of a cup of coffee in his pocket.

"I didn't ask the price. I asked for coffee," said the young man quite pleasantly.

"Just wanted to make sure we all understand each other," said Fay, pouring his coffee. She looked at the copy of the *National Enquirer* that the young man had picked up and read aloud the headline about the film star Marina Vaughan. " 'This-time-it's-for-real,' says Marina," read Fay, another of the endless commentators on Hollywood life. "Sure, Marina, true love at last. With a ballet dancer."

"Would you check to see if my order's ready," said Mona. "I'm in a hurry."

When Fay started on one of her commentaries, she didn't like to be interrupted, so she went right on with her thoughts on the latest romance of Marina Vaughan. "That girl's going to go right down the drain, just like her mother before her, you mark my words," said Fay before moving on to pick up Mona's order. If Mona had not been so downcast, she could not have resisted showing the waitress the gold bracelet that the very same Marina Vaughan had just given her, thereby establishing her credentials. "Look what Marina Vaughan gave me," she would say, holding out her wrist, but in other circumstances than these.

"Egg salad san on white. Double mayo. And a chocolate shake," announced Fay as she placed Mona's order in front of her, each fattening word a reminder that she'd already had lunch and was going to have dinner and this was a trip that wasn't necessary. She was furious with the waitress and furious with Warren Ambrose as she put her face into the soft white bread and the soft yellow filling, comforting somehow the demons of unrest inside her. She bit and swallowed almost simultaneously, her concentration total, interrupting herself only to suck on the straws that brought up the chocolate that comforted more. Once she had eaten a dozen jelly doughnuts, right out of the box, in the ladies' room of the bakery where she had bought them after an argument with her mother.

"You gonna eat your pickle?"

She was so deep in thought that it was a few seconds before she realized that someone was speaking to her. She caught sight of the source of this voice in the mirror opposite the counter, stifled the smart-ass answer she was about to give, and turned to look directly into the face of Frankie Bozzaci. Zing went the strings of her heart, as the old song goes.

"Be my guest," she said daintily, sliding her plate toward him. "It's much too much food for me anyway."

"Thanks." He ate the pickle like he was hungry. She couldn't think of anything to say and went back to her sandwich. There was silence except for pickle noises.

"Refill?" asked Fay, and he pushed his cup toward her.

"You wouldn't happen to know how I could get extra work on *Love Boat*, would you?" he asked the waitress about the television series, acknowledging her expertise on matters of show business. "I read somewhere you get to go on a two-week cruise to Acapulco and get paid all at the same time."

"Is that what you are, an extra?" asked Fay.

"Not yet."

"Is that what you want to be?"

"Sounds better to me than delivering telegrams. Or parking cars. Or cleaning swimming pools. Or a few other things I could mention."

"Well, hang around Schwab's. Lana Turner got discovered here. About forty-five years ago."

"Maybe lightning will strike twice," said the young man.

"Check," said Mona Berg, sitting up to leave. She wished she hadn't eaten the food. She wished she were more attractive to men. In this maze of maudlin thought, she knocked over her Louis Vuitton tote bag, the contents of which scattered on the floor. The young man hopped off his stool and picked up her belongings for Mona, her Gucci key ring, her Gucci wallet, her Gucci address book, the double G's everywhere.

"Lemme guess your name," he said, handing her each item. "Gloria? Grace? I hope not Gertrude, I hate the name Gertrude. Gertrude?"

All these prized gifts from Warren seemed less valuable to her as she put them back into her bag. "It's Mona."

"You're sure this is your bag?" he said, referring to all the G's.

"I'm sure."

"I'm Frankie."

"I'm late," she said. She gazed into his deep brown eyes, and her heart dropped twenty stories inside her.

"I have your *People* magazines, miss," the cashier called over, and the moment between them was broken. "My God, your picture's in it."

"Out of focus," said Mona.

"Out of focus-schmokus. Your picture's in *People* magazine! Congratulations, Minna."

"It's Mona."

"It says Minna."

"It's wrong," corrected Mona, but the awe in the woman's voice perked up her spirits for the first time. She signed for the magazines and then reached over and picked up Frankie's coffee check. "Thanks for your help," she said, indicating the check. At the door, Mona looked back at Frankie for a second and left. The cashier was still deeply engrossed in the Warren Ambrose article. "It says he's building a private discotheque in his basement," she called over to Fay at the counter.

"Imagine, at his age," said Fay, admiration in her voice, loving conversations about successful people being successful.

The young man looked out the glass doors after the woman whose pickle he had eaten, whose bag he had picked up, who had paid for his coffee, whose picture was in a magazine, out of focus-schmokus. He watched her walk in a huffing and puffing manner, with a dozen magazines under her arm, to a nondescript car in a space reserved for the handicapped. When the car pulled out of the parking lot and headed west on Sunset Boulevard, he turned and walked back to the cashier, who was still absorbed in the glamorous life of the agent Warren Ambrose.

"May I have a copy of *People* magazine?" he asked.

Chapter 5

"DID YOU HEAR about the deaf mute with the speech impediment?" asked Warren Ambrose, assuming the expectant look he had when he told a joke.

"One arm was shorter than the other, you already told me," said the delicious young lady, in an I-already-heard-it voice.

"When?"

"Last time I was here."

"I forgot." She was poolside. He was in. "Did you hear the one about the Polish lesbian?"

"I don't want to hear any more jokes, Warren."

"She fell for every guy she met." He slapped the water as he roared with laughter at his punch line. Warren loved his jokes. "Picked this one up from Jessel," he used to say in the old days, Jessel being the comedian George Jessel, giving credentials to his joke, as if somehow it were better or funnier for having come from an illustrious source.

"You promised me you'd call Robbie Slick and get me a

reading for his picture," she said. There was a trace of petulance.

"I don't want to disturb him during his tennis game," said Warren.

"You promised, Warren, and I'm not going into that Jacuzzi until you call him." The girl was almost, but not quite, complaining. She knew how to say something serious and keep the tone of voice pleasant at the same time, and she had let it be known that if he wanted his nooky she wanted her reading. The barter system at work in Hollywood.

Laurel Leigh was an aspiring starlet, young and blond and beautiful in an of-the-moment sort of beauty. When he took her places where she could be seen, like a premiere or a fashionable restaurant or a party at the Marty Leskys', the excitement of the externals and the close brush with success made her more abandoned when he claimed his rewards at the end of an evening. However, a one-to-one evening, starting with a Jacuzzi in the fading afternoon sun, promising dinner on a tray in front of the fire, the houseboy being off at the premiere, was a less attractive prospect to a twenty-year-old starlet than it was to a sixty-something-year-old roué, freshly rejuvenated from Rio and Rumania and the San Fernando Valley.

"What's it like to ball an old guy like that?" her roommate, Jeanine, had asked her. "Hard work," replied Laurel. "He's got a dick like a Tampax." The girls, who regularly compared notes on romantic matters, had a good laugh over that one, and Jeanine, more practical than Laurel in economic matters, explained to her friend the rules of the barter system in Hollywood, that respected American custom of exchanging one commodity for another, goods for goods instead of goods for money.

"He gets real sensitive if he thinks you're after something

rather than just him. He thinks he's enough," complained Laurel.

"Well, what you've got to do is let him know in a very nice way he's not, and I don't have to tell you how to do that," replied the ever practical Jeanine.

"Right," said Laurel, "then what?"

"Let him open some doors for you, to start."

"What time do you suppose Robbie Slick finishes his tennis game?" asked Laurel. Her instincts about him were not incorrect. Like a miser reluctant to part with a buck, Warren was hesitant about making this call to his old friend Robbie Slick. It was not that he begrudged arranging for her a bid for stardom. Instead it was the age-old doubt of the older successful man: Is it me she wants or only what I can do for her?

"You kids want everything handed to you on a silver platter these days," he said, dialing the telephone and asking for Robbie Slick. "In the old days, when studios were studios, the kids trained and studied and took small parts and learned their craft. You kids today don't know about hard work."

You think fucking you isn't hard work? is what Jeanine would have said under the circumstances, but not Laurel. She was thrilled that he was talking to Robbie Slick and saying such nice things about her, how he'd seen her at a workshop production at a little theater on Melrose. "That's where you see the real talent, Robbie, not at all these damn parties," he said. Once Warren started to sell, he always began to enjoy himself. It was one of the things that he did best. He hadn't been to a little theater on Melrose Avenue for twenty years and he'd never seen Laurel Leigh perform, other than as a drum majorette, but at the moment he honestly believed he had, and he nearly had Robbie Slick believing it too.

"I know you're practically set to go with Farrah Fawcett,

Robbie. I understand that the studio would like you to set Farrah Fawcett, Robbie," he was saying, stating the facts, acknowledging the odds, impressing her, "but I think you will regret it for the rest of your life if you don't meet this lovely young actress before you arrive at a final decision. Her name is Laurel Leigh."

Such nice things he was saying about her, and her talent, and her looks, and her potential.

You sure know the way to a girl's pussy, Jeanine would have said under the circumstances, but not Laurel. She loved hearing Warren talk like this about her.

"No, not L-e-e," he spelled, "it's L-e-i-g-h, like in Vivien. . . . That's right, Robbie, a very classy name and, may I add, a very classy young lady." He looked over at her and made a magnanimous gesture, as if to say, You see how easy it is?

The moment had turned lovely and they were both savoring it. His enjoyment of her admiration equaled her enjoyment of his power. Date and time and instructions were handled with dispatch. "Three o'clock Monday. At the studio. Thank you, Robbie. You're in for a big treat. Sorry to interrupt your tennis game. Bye, kiddo.

"All set. They'll give you the script there."

"You're wonderful, Warren."

"You're not so bad yourself."

She reached behind her back and untied the string that held up the bra that covered the nipples of her lovely breasts. Warren was entranced as she touched them, bringing up her hands gracefully from underneath, holding them up for his admiration, enjoying his enjoyment of their beauty. She stood up and pulled down her briefest of bikini bottoms, kicking it toward him. He was standing, elongated some, at the steps of his Jacuzzi, holding out his hand in courtly fashion to lead her into its bubbling heat. It was a performance that he had played many times, with many young ladies. The stage had been set: the giant-size towels were neatly stacked, the white wine was in the silver cooler, cigarettes and poppers were in the white pigskin box, and a multibuttoned telephone was at hand. An exotic setting, surely.

If only it were Warren Beatty instead of Warren Ambrose, she was thinking as she closed her eyes to conjure up this picture.

They were standing in the churning hot water. His face was buried between her breasts. His hands were meeting between her legs. He was rubbing his penis against her thigh. His absorption was total. He did not hear the buzz of the intercom that buzzed insistently from the poolside telephone.

"Warren!" It was Mona Berg calling to him from the house, where she had just delivered his suits from Don Cherry and his twelve copies of *People* magazine.

"There's somebody calling you, Warren," said Laurel to the busily occupied agent. "Kind of a big lady."

"Oh, for God's sake. What is it, Mona?" Warren yelled back.

"Marty Lesky's on the phone." Marty Lesky. The head of Colossus Pictures, as well as its largest stockholder. Winner of the Jean Hersholt Award at last year's Academy Awards. A person of consequence in the film hierarchy, for whom even such a sophisticate as Warren Ambrose would delay an orgasm.

"He's returning my call about Marina Vaughan," said Warren, torn between desire and obsequiousness.

"Don't stop now, Warren. You got me going," said Laurel, not wanting to prolong this sexual activity any longer than necessary.

Under the circumstances, Jeanine would pop one of those poppers in the white pigskin box and get his mind back to where it was, and that was exactly what Laurel did at that moment, breaking the yellow vaporole under Warren's nose, first things first, and then taking a few sniffs herself of the intoxicating fumes before lowering it again to Warren's nose.

The quickened heartbeat. The already reddened face reddening. Mindless desire. Gutter language. "I'm gonna eat your cunt, baby," said the sixty-something-year-old roué, sliding down her beautiful body to busy his face within her beneath the water.

"Warren, do you want to speak to him or not? It's about Marina Vaughan," Mona Berg yelled from the house, impatience in her voice.

The massive heart attack that racked Warren's body at that moment was mistaken by Laurel for a mercifully premature ejaculation. It was a moment before Laurel realized that something else had happened.

"Get up, Warren. Warren." She reached into the foamed and bubbling water, pulling him up by his hair. The red, uh, thing, that surfaced in her hand was the carefully concealed, never before revealed, red toupee made for Warren by the remarkable Siegfried Geike of the San Fernando Valley. Warren was no longer attached to it.

"Warren! *Warren!* Somebody help! *Help!*"

Chapter 6

WARREN AMBROSE'S heart attack was Mona Berg's ticket to the big time, the event that focused on Mona Berg the attention that he had so long denied her.

She had arrived at his hilltop estate in Bel Air, with his suits and his magazines, as Marty Lesky, the head of Colossus Pictures, was telephoning him, a call that Warren could not hear, being otherwise engaged, necessitating her to step out on the terrace at almost the exact moment of his massive heart attack.

Had she not been there, there would have been no one to hear the screams of Laurel Leigh, the houseboy being off at the premiere, and Warren most certainly would have ended his life in murky circumstances at the bottom of his Jacuzzi.

However, she was there, and a rush of adrenaline flooded her system into action of a magnificent nature. She was a young woman who recognized her opportunities as they were happening to her, an ability that more than compensated for the lack of advantages that she sometimes decried in her life.

She pulled Warren out of the water, calmed and got rid of the hysterical Laurel Leigh, notified his doctor, the Bel Air Patrol, 911, Rescue 8, and Dolores DeLongpre, the gossip columnist. She dried him, covered him, and reattached his red toupee.

By the time the screaming ambulance screeched to a halt in the emergency entrance of the Cedars-Sinai Medical Center, a television news crew was there to record it, and word had started to spread throughout the industry that Warren Ambrose was "near the end."

No one came forward to take over. There was no wife, no child, no family of any kind except a sister, nearly eighty and senile, in a nursing home in Omaha, Nebraska. The friends, and they were "legion," as Dolores DeLongpre reported, were people he made deals with and went to parties with and played backgammon with, but communication never exceeded that level, and there was a hesitancy among them as to which was more qualified, or had sufficient time, to make certain medical and economic decisions in their friend's behalf.

Mona wasn't hesitant about anything. She ordered the best of everything, knowing the money was there to pay for it. A world-renowned heart specialist was flown in from Texas to confer with the excellent team of surgeons assembled by Warren Ambrose's general practitioner.

"Who's the physician in charge of the case?" asked Marty Lesky, the head of Colossus Pictures, when he arrived at the three-hundred-dollar-a-day room Mona took as a refuge for the friends of Warren to congregate in during the long hours of the surgery.

"Dr. Denniston," replied Mona, naming the well-known

general practitioner, more a social than medical celebrity, who had arrived in surgery wearing a dinner jacket. "He was wearing a tux," Mona said about him sometime later, discrediting his physicianship, when he sought to interfere with her handling of Warren's case.

"Typical," said Marty Lesky under his breath to his wife. He meant typical for Warren, who often bragged he'd never had a sick day in his life, to have entrusted his medical affairs to the local society doctor, a favorite extra man of industry wives, adored by them as the dispenser of Valium, "for nerves," the prescriptions read, or Eskatrol, "for appetite suppressence," or Quaaludes, "for sleep," or Amyl Nitrite, that which was in the white pigskin box, locally known as poppers, "for chest pains."

"I've sent for Dr. De Bakey, on a consultation basis," Mona Berg said to Marty Lesky, referring to the famed Houston heart specialist.

"That's exactly what I was going to suggest," said Marty, his apprehension lessening, looking at her. "Tell me your name once more."

"Mona Berg. I went to a meeting in your office on the Berkowitz contract when Warren was delayed in Rio last month," she said, identifying herself.

"Of course. This is Mrs. Lesky," he said, bringing forth the elegant woman Mona already knew to be Sylvia Lesky, the reigning hostess of filmland society, as Dolores DeLongpre called her in her rococo style. Only that morning Mona had told Warren, not totally in jest, that one of her ambitions was to go to a Sylvia Lesky party.

"You deserve a lot of credit, Miss Berg," said Sylvia Lesky in her refined manner, with her refined voice, and Mona Berg blushed at the approval of this lady about whom she had read every word in the magazines and newspapers.

"Tell me how it happened," said Marty Lesky. "Was there any warning?"

It struck Mona at that instant how exceedingly sordid the circumstances of Warren's heart attack actually were, how badly the story would repeat to people like these: naked in a Jacuzzi with a twenty-year-old aspiring starlet and a box of poppers, the tacky little Warren Ackerman of forty years ago reverting to type, an unclassy smirch on his classy business. At that moment she became the keeper of his flame.

"I was up at his house taking dictation," said Mona. "He'd been dictating his autobiography, *Big Deal*, to me after office hours, and all of a sudden, right in the middle of one of his sentences, he just keeled over, and I said, 'Warren?' and—" Mona was very good at telling elaborate stories. She had an eye for the kind of detail that gave verity when none existed. "I had your husband on hold," she went on to Sylvia Lesky, "because I wasn't sure at first, and the ambulance—"

Mona gave a dignified, and literary, reversal to the circumstances of Warren's heart attack to Sylvia Lesky, which became thereafter the way that it had happened.

The thing to do over the next twenty-four hours was to drop in at the Cedars-Sinai Medical Center and get the latest bulletins on Warren's condition. Everybody came: studio heads, producers, directors, writers, movie stars, the friends by the legion that Dolores DeLongpre wrote about in her column "People Like Us." "How is he?" they would whisper on entering, and Mona gave them the latest information. "He's still in surgery," she would say. Or, "At the present time, Dr. Denniston says he has better than a fifty-fifty chance." Or, later, "They've inserted a pacemaker." Or, much later, "He's out of surgery and in intensive care."

She was at the center of everything and, if the truth were known, had never been so happy. She recorded all the telephone calls. She signed for all the telegrams. She found water for the roses sent by Cary Grant. She knew everybody's name, everybody's drink, and everybody's latest project, when the conversation turned from Warren to the picture business, which it invariably does when picture people get together, no matter what the circumstances.

She knew unlisted telephone numbers by heart. ("I should let Paul Newman know, but I can't remember his number," said Marty Lesky to his wife. "It's 457-9226," offered Mona, right off the top of her head.)

She knew what rough cuts were being shown in what projection room in Beverly Hills that night. ("Barry Diller's screening the Coppola picture tonight," said Robbie Slick to Marty Lesky. "Tomorrow night," corrected Mona. "Abe Grossman's screening it tonight.")

She knew the particular thing to say to the particular person that made the moment particular. ("I loved your picture in *Vogue* this month," she said to the social figure Mrs. Reade Jamieson. "Thank you, Miss Berg," said Elena Jamieson, with a trace of her adorable stutter. "My husband thinks I get too much pubpubpublicity." "I don't think there's any such thing as too much publicity," replied Mona, and they both laughed.)

And she spoke quite sharply to a reporter from *The New York Times* who questioned the optimistic prognosis on Warren's condition that she gave to the press.

"I like the way you spoke to that reporter from *The New York Times*," said Marty Lesky to her as she squeezed by him carrying a dark brown drink to Marina Vaughan.

"He acted like he was writing an obituary," said Mona with a slight degree of moral indignation.

"He probably was," said Marty, looking at her. She could

feel that he was noticing her, that he was looking past the efficient secretary of her, seeing more, and he was. He knew a good piece of manpower when he saw one. "There's not many secretaries around like you, Miss Berg. Pray God it won't, but should something happen to Warren, I could always use someone like you on my staff."

"Oh, Mr. Lesky," said Mona, reddening. Lovely rushes of good feelings flooded her system, the bliss of praise so long denied her. "I could never leave Warren."

"I've been around this town for a long time," said Marty, "and it's a tough town. You may be getting all these messages of love from Warren's clients tonight, but if he's not up and around by the time their next deal comes up, they're going to move on to other agents."

"They'll never leave Warren," said Mona, not quite believing what she was saying as the truth of what he said began to register on her. "He's friends with all his clients. His business life and his social life are all the same."

"He never trained anyone to take over," said Marty, watching the thoughts in her head. "Think about it." He turned to say hello to the gossip columnist Dolores DeLongpre, who had just arrived in her usual state of disarray, having first written her column to make her deadline, most of it about Warren, her friend of many years, she called him.

"Why don't I take that drink, miss," Dolores said, reaching out and taking Marina Vaughan's drink out of Mona Berg's hand. "This old woman's wrung out." She drank it down, half of it at once, eyeing the room, noting who was there, ever on the alert for movie news, even in moments of sadness.

"I'm Mona Berg, Miss DeLongpre," said Mona. "We've talked on the phone."

Their eyes met, these two women from different generations, the secretary and the gossip columnist. So this was the one who had called her with the scoop, the heart attack scoop, in the midst of ambulance sirens arriving, a girl after her own heart, to be sure, providing Dolores with a box on the front page, hard news that it was, in addition to her column. Dolores didn't mention the telephone call in front of Marty Lesky. She knew an informer when she saw one, and she understood the rules of that relationship. She knew there would be more stories to come, in other areas, now that the lines of communication were open between them.

Dolores DeLongpre reigned supreme as the foremost pillarist of the activities, both business and social, of that part of filmland society known as the crème de la crème, as Dolores called it. Although trained in the art by no less a personage than the celebrated Hedda Hopper during the declining years of that long-deceased lady, Dolores disliked the term gossip columnist, and preferred to think of herself as a chronicler of life at the top. She even went so far as to describe her understanding of the intricacies of the relationships of the participants as Proustian, although she had never read Proust. What she meant was that she was the only one of them, columnists that is, who was invited to dine in the great homes of the city, and her daily account of life therein was a part of the morning ritual at every breakfast table. To have one's name in Dolores DeLongpre's column—as having been here, there, and everywhere—was thought to be proof positive that one had arrived.

"Everyone says you're doing such a wonderful job, Miss Berg," said Dolores DeLongpre, complimenting her in front of Marty Lesky, on this her day of compliments.

"It's Mona, please, not Miss Berg," said Mona. Demure, self-effacing even, were the adjectives that applied to her manner.

"Then you must call me Dolores," said Dolores. "Now listen, dear." She drew close. "Pray God it won't, but if something should happen to Warren, I'm going to need all the eight-by-ten glossies you can lay your hands on of Warren and all his famous clients over the years for my Sunday piece. I thought I'd do a photomontage of his whole career."

"Warren's not going to die, Dolores," said Mona. There was in her tone of voice a determination that Warren Ambrose was not going to die, as if she were going to will it. "Excuse me, there's something arriving that I should sign for."

A telegram from Henry Kissinger. A telephone call from Switzerland from Faye Converse. A cymbidium plant from Dom and Pepper Belcanto. The Kirk Douglases in tennis clothes rushed in from their tennis court, having just heard; and the Myron Kahns in evening clothes tiptoed out on their way "somewhere," Delphine Kahn having told the story again about Warren and Louis B. Mayer in the old days. Marina Vaughan told a funny story about Warren and Princess Grace of Monaco at a party at David Niven's house on the French Riviera. Sylvia Lesky told Pearl Silver that her daughter Cecilia was returning from Rome, after several years, to live with them; and Pearl Silver said she had read about it in Dolores DeLongpre's column.

Drinks were passed. Food was brought in. People came. People went. Robbie Slick told Saul Berkowitz that Warren had always promised to leave him his Vlaminck, and Saul Berkowitz said he usually ended up with the cuff links. People who did not normally speak to each other spoke, and the chauffeur of one of the daughters of Louis B. Mayer brought roses from the garden of that lady.

Mona opened the bathroom door at just the moment Marina Vaughan was taking a large hit of cocaine from the tip of her long red fingernail.

"It's called caught in the act," said Marina.

"Oh, don't worry about me," said Mona. "I just wanted to get some water for these flowers."

"Listen, darling," said Marina, "I'd appreciate it if you didn't say anything to those squares out there. They think it's bad for you."

"Just call me tight lips," said Mona in her new friend-of-the-star voice.

"I've got this playgirl reputation that's going to ruin me," Marina went on, combing her hair and fixing her lipstick, but not seeming really concerned.

"You're one of the most famous actresses in the world!"

"All of a sudden I'm famous for all the wrong reasons. I'm more famous for my love affairs than I am for my last picture. Listen, Mona, what's going to happen to the agency if Warren dies?"

"He's not going to die. He's going to be back on his feet in no time!"

"No, he's not. It's going to be months and months, if at all," said Marina who, like the reporter from *The New York Times*, discounted Mona's cheery prognosis of Warren's condition.

"You're not thinking of leaving the agency, are you?" said Mona, her heart sinking.

"What agency?" asked Marina. "Without Warren, there is no agency. That's the trouble with these one-man operations. One day the man gets old and dies. I'm at a point in my career where I need someone out there fighting for me. I feel terrible talking like this, with Warren up there fighting for his life. He was my mother's agent, my father's agent, and he's been my agent since I did my first picture when I was eleven. Do I sound like I'm on a talking jag?"

The door burst open and Dolores DeLongpre walked in. "Ladies, you're hogging the facilities! This old woman needs the toilet," she said, keeping Marina from formulating her thoughts on the subject and giving Mona time to formulate hers.

"Come in, Dolores," said Marina. "I've got a bone to pick with you. In Acapulco with Mick Jagger indeed!"

"Marina's been telling me stories about Warren," said Mona.

"Now who sent those flowers?" asked Dolores. It was the sort of thing she liked to know.

"Cary Grant," said Mona, loving to be able to use the name.

"Cary and Warren go way back," said Dolores.

After Mona closed the door, Dolores said to Marina about her, "She's the one who bears watching."

"What do you mean?" asked Marina.

"She has success written all over her. Isn't it typical of Warren to have kept her hidden?"

"Promise you won't tell Gloria Steinem this, Dolores? I prefer to do business with men," said Marina, preparing to leave.

"Darling, you prefer men, period," said Dolores.

It's DeLightful. It's DeLicious. It's DeLongpre, hummed Marina, without actually saying the words, of course, as she left the room.

The exchange with Marina Vaughan, directly following the almost prescient warning by Marty Lesky about the

59

length of time Warren's clients would remain with the ailing agent filled Mona Berg's mind with a thousand thoughts as she met with Dr. Denniston, Dr. Karlin, Dr. Levinson, and the consulting Dr. De Bakey from Texas. It was after one in the morning. Most of the friends had gone. Their lives started early every day. The doctors told her that Warren's heart had been severely damaged and that a slight stroke he had suffered during the six-hour operation could possibly result in a partial paralysis of his left side. But he would live. There was that to be said.

In the parking lot, Marty Lesky walked the exhausted Mona Berg to her car. "Robbie Slick showed me your picture in *People* magazine," he said.

"Out of focus," said Mona.

"I shouldn't think for long," said Marty.

Chapter 7

MARTY LESKY was right, as Marty Lesky was usually right about such matters. Mona Berg wasn't going to be out of focus for long. Not for long at all. It was as if a new life force entered her at precisely the moment it exited, for all practical purposes, the water-logged body of the diminutive Warren Ambrose.

Bill—Mona's secretary Bill, good and faithful Bill, born to follow not to lead, whom she used to tell everything to—noticed the new life force within her as early as the following day. She told him she felt the moment had been orchestrated for her when they discussed the event that had happened.

"What about the chickee?" Bill asked her, meaning Miss Laurel Leigh. "How did you get rid of her?"

"I gave her an extra two hundred and fifty out of Warren's wallet, and told her that the whole thing would be a smirch on her reputation as an actress if word got out that she was breaking poppers into the nose of an old man in a Jacuzzi," said Mona. "She got the message and got lost."

"I couldn't believe it when I saw you getting out of the ambulance on television," said Bill. "How did they know the ambulance was coming with Warren in it?"

"I called Dolores DeLongpre while I was waiting for the ambulance to come," she answered matter-of-factly.

"Now let me get this straight," he said. "You pulled him out of the Jacuzzi. You dried him off. You stuck his wig back on. You put him in a terry-cloth robe so they couldn't say he was naked. You threw away the poppers. You got rid of the wine. You got rid of the chickee. You called the police. You called the ambulance. You called the doctor. You called the columns. I thought you hated his guts."

"If this hadn't happened, I was going to quit him," said Mona. "If he were already dead, I probably would have left everything just as it was, Miss Laurel Leigh and everything. It would have served him right. But he wasn't dead. Just almost dead. And alive-and-ailing all of a sudden presented an infinite variety of possibilities to me."

"Like what?" asked Bill.

"Like last night at the hospital Marty Lesky offered me a job at his studio. Marty Lesky himself! He was impressed with the way I was handling things."

"Are you going to take it?"

"If he asked me yesterday morning, after *People* magazine came out, I would have said yes and left without giving a day's notice. But not today. I'm all of a sudden in a high-visibility position."

"What are you going to do?" he asked.

"Stay tuned for station identification," she said.

In the week that followed, she almost never left the hospital, and her devotion and loyalty were much commented upon, as was her efficiency, by the steady stream of visitors of high rank. She knew what she wanted. Within days after the sad event, her plan began to take form, and her plan had nothing whatsoever to do with becoming the executive secretary to anyone. She wanted to take over the running of Warren's agency. She wanted to be made a partner in his agency. She knew that Marina Vaughan was going to be her ticket.

"The natives are restless," said Bill to her one afternoon after reading her the list of people who had called the office that day.

"What do you mean?" asked Mona, but she knew what he meant before he told her. It was what Marty Lesky told her was going to happen.

"Lambeth Walker said he hasn't heard anything from the studio about his script," said Bill, "and wasn't there someone here who could call Marty Lesky to see if there's been any reaction to it; and Faye Converse said she liked the face-lift script, but who's going to talk to Robbie Slick in her behalf; and Sam Roth thinks he's a natural to direct the *Green Hat* remake, but he doesn't think he should be the one to call Marty Lesky; and Rebecca Kincaid said—"

"Yeah, yeah, yeah," said Mona.

She herself could feel the first glimmer of change in priority of subject matter in the daily telephone calls from the clients of the Ambrose Agency inquiring as to the condition, medically speaking, of their dear friend and agent, Warren Ambrose. What they were starting to wonder was What about us? although no one had actually said the words. She covered such a moment with Marina Vaughan by saying how touched Warren had been by a note she had sent, and added as garnish that her yellow roses were what he wanted right next to his bed.

When the moment came to speak her piece, she knew all

her lines. She had rehearsed her speech over and over in the bathroom mirror while brushing her teeth, and in the car mirror while driving to the Cedars-Sinai Medical Center each day since it happened, so that she would be ready, when he came to sufficiently, to make Warren Ambrose aware of a very grave problem.

"Listen, Warren, I know you can't talk, but I want you to listen," she said to him, pulling her chair close to his bed. "You can hear me, can't you? Blink your eyes or something if you can."

He did—blink his eyes—thinking it was going to be condolence messages she wanted to regale him with perhaps.

"We have to be totally practical about your situation, Warren. You're going to be all right, all the doctors say so, but it's going to take a long time, and by the time you get back on your feet, it's just possible there could be no agency left."

The electrocardiograph on the television screen that monitored the pacemaker that accompanied the heart of Warren Ambrose took a bright green leap. His agency! His! Even in the face of death, which had been a presence, he had seen nothing that took top billing over his agency; his Tiffany product, his life, his reason to live.

Death be damned. Mona had hooked his attention. She was succinct. She had a way with words, of using the right ones, that said the most in the least amount of time. It was just a matter of time before they left him, all his Tiffany product, she said, making Tiffany-product sound oh so slightly tarnished. Another bright green leap from the electrocardiograph on the television monitor. She could have gone further; she could have told him the rumor that Marina Vaughan, his favorite of favorites, was seen lunching at the Bel Air Hotel with Stan Kamen of William Morris, a rival agency, but she didn't. Call it forbearance, or call it knowing when you've been dealt a trump card and didn't need to press to make a point.

"Now don't get yourself all upset," she went on. "That's what Mona's here for. I don't have to tell you, this is a tough town, Warren, and unless we do something quick to show you're still in business, all your clients are going to drift away or be lured away by William Morris or ICM." It was a practicality that he understood and he feared, even in intensive care, that without his agency he was nothing.

He never trained anyone to take over, that's what was being said all over town, she told him, and the speculation in the industry was that Warren, in order to save his business, would have to offer a full partnership to the aforementioned agent from William Morris, or another of similar stature from ICM, stars both of the agency business, no less luminaries than Warren himself, but younger and with healthier hearts. They both knew, Warren and Mona, that it was a practical and sound solution, either of the two mentioned, but they also knew, Warren and Mona, for different reasons, that it was impossible.

They would want their names ahead of his on the letterhead. They would want more than 50 percent of his agency, that was what Mona was thinking, for them to give up the lucrative pension plans and stock options that their own agencies had showered on them. Warren was thinking about some papers in the office safe that pointed to transgressions of a financial nature, having to do with double commissions, that he would not want them, or anyone else for that matter, to see.

By the time Mona got around to proposing herself to be

made a partner—not a full partner of course, at least not at this time, she knew how far to go in a negotiation—Warren was ready to listen. It surprised her that it was so effortless. She was not sure if he was sicker than she thought or if he admired her ability more than she had realized.

"The fact of the matter is that I've been doing all the work and you've been getting all the credit since your male menopause set in three years ago. What I think you have to do is make me a partner and announce to the industry, through Dolores DeLongpre, that I'm going to hold down the fort until you return in a few months. Otherwise, I guess I'll have to take the position that Marty Lesky offered me at Colossus Pictures."

There was a whimper from Warren. He needed her, and they both knew it.

"The first thing I have to do is get Marty Lesky to agree to see Marina Vaughan about the lead in the *Green Hat* remake. That should hold her tight for a while. If I can make her happy, all your clients are going to feel safe and protected until you're back to take over the reins again. Now you just don't worry about a thing, Warren, except getting your health back. Mona's going to look out for your business."

Chapter 8

To CONVINCE Warren of the feasibility of the idea was one thing; Warren didn't think of her as a threat. To convince his client list that she was capable of negotiating in their behalf was quite another thing. But she was operating, and she used her time well in the moments of one-to-one intimacy she had with Warren's callers in advancing the best interests of his client list. It thrilled her to be in direct contact with the men who made the decisions in the industry, the kind of people who could say yes or no to an idea, and that was it. Power. It was what she always wanted to be near. It was what she knew, when she got hold of it, was going to make everything all right in a life that had never been all right. She hated her body. She hated her background. Unlovely and unloved, the words gnawed at her innards. She realized early on that the paths of life were easier for girls with pretty faces and rich fathers, but she had never ceased believing that her pathway would be shown to her.

When her moment was presented to her, she was ready to take control.

She told the head of Liberty Studio, Robbie Slick, that she knew of a great vehicle for a comeback film for Faye Converse, about a society woman who has a face-lift to save her marriage. When he was only politely interested, she sweetened the package by saying she thought she could deliver Marina Vaughan, Faye Converse's real life god-daughter, for the cameo role of Faye Converse's daughter, a possibility Robbie Slick found more interesting, for the publicity value of the idea and the fact that he was known to have a crush on the irrepressible Marina.

She told Jess Dragonet, of Grossman-Dragonet Productions, the television conglomerate that was a subsidiary of Colossus Pictures, that she thought he should conduct a nationwide talent hunt for a newcomer to play the lead in the proposed revival of the television series *South Sea Adventures*, in the manner of the search for Scarlett O'Hara in *Gone With the Wind* all those years ago. Jess Dragonet liked the idea and passed it on to Abe Grossman, who had a nose for publicity and put the idea in the works by phoning it in to Dolores DeLongpre for her column.

Mona was cooking. She was saying the right thing to the right person at the right time, in the darkness of a hospital room, in the whispered kind of conversation that takes place in the presence of the unconscious, creating concurrent comment for both her business acumen and her tireless devotion to Warren. The other thing she did was to put Marina Vaughan in the running for the role of Iris March in Marty Lesky's personal production of the remake of *The Green Hat*, although Marty was known to have other ideas on the subject. Mona knew it was what Marina wanted, and by dangling the possibility of same, she hoped to forestall the predicted exit of that star from the Tiffany ranks.

"Marina? It's Mona Berg. I have some glorious news for you." It was nine o'clock in the morning, not the hour to call a movie star between pictures, especially a movie star who went out every night and drank a lot of champagne and snorted a bit of cocaine and sometimes woke up with men whose names she couldn't remember.

"Can't it wait, Mona? I had a late night last night," said Marina Vaughan, not without a trace of annoyance in her tone for the earliness of the hour and the fact that her private line had been used, an impertinence that fitted into the picture she was beginning to formulate of Mona Berg.

"I'm sorry to use your private line," said Mona, understanding what Marina's tone was implying, that she was being pushy, "but Marty Lesky wants to have lunch with the two of us at Colossus today. It's about *The Green Hat.*"

"What about *The Green Hat?*" said Marina, coming to life.

"He wants to talk to you about playing Iris March," said Mona, measuring her words.

"How did that come about? I thought he didn't want me for the part," said Marina, now fully awake and totally involved in the conversation.

"Trust your new friend Mona to remedy that situation. It's called being in the right place at the right time. Marty Lesky showed up at the hospital late last night, and we got talking. There were only the three of us there in the room, Marty and Warren and me, and Warren was totally out of it. I thought to myself, Mona, you're sitting here with the most important man in Hollywood, all by yourself. Do something to make him remember you, and perform a service at the same time for an about-to-abort client called Marina Vaughan who's only able to visualize you changing typewriter ribbons and not making deals with studio biggies."

"Oh, darling, I've just become your biggest booster and most devoted client. Tell me everything," said Marina.

"He said you always seemed a little bit drunk or a little bit stoned to him," said Mona.

"That son of a bitch," interrupted Marina.

"And I said you only seemed that way, you weren't that way at all, you were a very dedicated artist, and that anyway, those very qualities, that little-bit-drunk-little-bit-stoned quality, were what were just right for the role of Iris March, that it only added to the sense of glamorous doom that is indigenous to the character," said Mona, who loved nothing more than to recount step-by-step the levels of her persuasiveness in business matters.

"Mona, I didn't know you were so literary," marveled Marina.

"Who do you think has been reading all the scripts and all the novels all these years, and has been telling all the plots to Warren Ambrose, who never read anything through to the end in his life? Mona, that's who. Besides, I'm not literary, I just know how to sell a client. I figured if I could make you happy right off the bat, I could make the other clients happy too, and with a little bit of praise from you hang on to them and keep this agency going until Warren is back on his feet," said Mona.

"Oh, darling, if this all comes through, I'll be tootin' your horn all over town," said Marina.

Marina looked beautiful and starlike as she made her way across the crowded commissary at Colossus Pictures, only a few minutes late, stopping to kiss Warren Beatty at his table, stopping to kiss Jack Nicholson at his, giving Marty Lesky, whom she'd known nearly all her life, a double cheek kiss when she arrived at the alcove where his table was.

Marina's father, the great star Rex Vaughan, had been under contract to Colossus Pictures when he was a young actor starting out and old Marcus Meyer, who founded the studio, was still running things. Years later, after a number of dire years, Rex Vaughan had made his comeback film under Marty Lesky, and a friendship had developed between the families. Privately, Marty Lesky felt there were a few chinks in Marina Vaughan's stardom, but they weren't discernible that day, and the impression was, from the lunch and from what Dolores DeLongpre reported in her column about the lunch, that Marina Vaughan had the inside track on the role that Dolores called the most sought-after of the year, the part of Iris March in Marty's personal production of the remake of *The Green Hat.*

While no commitment was actually made, the luncheon was thought to have gone well, with Mona Berg being very persuasive once again in pointing out the similarities between her client and the character she wanted so much to play. Any doubts that Marina may have had about the capability of the recent secretary to handle her representation were dispelled, and she was heard to sing her praises far and wide, giving assurances to other clients that they were in more than capable hands until Warren returned to the helm, an impression that Mona continued to foster until her hold on things was inviolate.

There was about Mona not a bit of hesitancy as she took over the office where she had only very recently considered herself no more than a serf. The once pristine desk of Warren

Ambrose, behind which she now sat, was covered with scripts and papers. She was able to do several things at once, talk on the telephone, sign papers, read scripts, and give orders to Bill.

"Company rule," she said to him on her first morning in the office after Warren had returned to his home in Bel Air for the long recuperative period. "No one gets in to see Warren, no matter how good friends they used to be. If the word gets out that one side of him is paralyzed and he's only got a partial return of his speech, it's not going to take long before there's no agency left. Tell anyone who wants to visit that he'd be embarrassed to be seen without his wig but that he's running all their affairs from his bed. They all know how vain he is."

"You're moving pretty fast, Mona," said Bill. She wasn't sure if there was admiration or criticism in his voice, or if it fell somewhere in between.

"It's called knowing your moment," she said. "This is my moment, and I'm not going to miss it. I'm sick of being on the outside looking in. This is my chance to get noticed."

"Well," said Bill, "I'd say you're being noticeable."

"Listen," she went on, as if he hadn't spoken, "check out leasing me one of those Mercedeses that all those people drive, the kind where the roof comes off."

"Where are you getting all this money?" asked Bill.

"Warren insisted I have a new car and the office pay for it," said Mona. "I can't go to meetings at movie stars' houses driving that old crate of mine, can I?"

"How did Warren insist?" asked Bill. "With his feet?"

Just as it had been with Warren before her, one of the first orders of the day was to read Dolores DeLongpre's column, where her name had started to appear. Also, just like Warren before her, it always put her in a lovely mood to see her name in print. There was nothing she enjoyed hearing more than someone saying to her, "Hey, I saw your name in Dolores DeLongpre's column this morning."

Later, people said about Dolores DeLongpre that it was she more than anyone else who created the legend of Mona Berg. She was the first one to prefix to her name the word superagent. She was the first one to call her Ms. Mona. The fact of the matter was, however, it was Mona who created the legend of Mona Berg, for it was she who realized the value of the constant repetition of her own name. The tit for tat of it was implicit and unspoken. Mona was one of those people who always knew whose marriage was in trouble, whose picture was a disaster, who was gay, who was having an affair with whom, and she shared these secrets with Dolores, covering her tracks, of course, so they couldn't be traced to her, even about her own clients and friends. The most popular feature of Dolores' column, "People Like Us," was the blind item, in which sometimes scurrilous information about the famous was revealed without mentioning the person's name.

An item appeared in Dolores' column:

> My old friend Warren Ambrose, dean of Hollywood agents, is on the mend at his Bel Air estate after a long siege following the massive heart attack he suffered several weeks ago. Meanwhile it's business as usual at the Ambrose Agency, whose Tiffany catalogue of clients includes such luminaries as Rex Vaughan, his daughter Marina Vaughan— I could go on and on. Holding down the fort until Warren's return is his former assistant and new partner, Mona Berg. Industry insiders are impressed with the wheeling-dealing Ms. Mona.

"Ms. Mona! Hey, I like that," said Mona.

"That's the second time this week she mentioned your name," said Bill.

But there was more. There was the blind item at the bottom of the column. "What famous movie star locked herself in the men's room of Miss Garbo's, the mostly male discotheque in West Hollywood, with six of her dancing partners, to the dismay of the management?"

Right off, Bill knew that Mona had given Dolores the story, because Bill was the one who told it to Mona.

"That's the story I told you," he said to her in an accusing manner. "What did you do? Tell it to her? Is that how your name keeps getting in the paper? You give her the dirt on everyone and she keeps mentioning your name?"

Bill admired Marina Vaughan inordinately and was upset by the item. The part of the story that was not mentioned was that the boys were only showing Marina the graffiti on the walls, but Dolores' item—subject unnamed but unmistakably Marina—would have you believe that she and the six boys were locked in the men's room for reasons more carnal. Bill was ashamed that he was the carrier of a story that got twisted so far out of shape.

"You didn't tell me not to tell anyone," said Mona, as if shifting the blame over to him.

"I didn't think I had to," he said. "I'd like to point out, Mona, that you're changing. And not for the better."

There was a long pause. "You've had the curse for about a week now," she said, measuring her words. "Get over it. Either get off my back and get on my bandwagon or get out, because I'm on the move."

There was a long silence, a strained moment between the two friends. Out of it their future relationship was defined. She was the boss. He was the employee. The telephone rang on the extension they used for their personal calls.

"I bet that's your mother," said Bill quietly. "She always

calls when your name's in Dolores DeLongpre's column."

"Say I'm not here," said Mona. "Say I'm at a meeting at Marina Vaughan's house."

"Mona Berg's office," said Bill, answering the phone. "Hello, Mrs. Berghof. No, I'm sorry, she's not here. She's out at a meeting at Marina Vaughan's house. . . . Yes, I read her name in Dolores DeLongpre's column. . . . I'll tell her, Mrs. Berghof. . . . How's the new night nurse treating you? Good. Oh, I know she'll be down to see you soon. Take care. What? No, I don't know who the movie star was who locked herself in the men's room. Bye." He hung up the telephone. "Your mother said to tell you she's proud of you."

"I want you to check out getting me a license plate with MS-MONA on it. I want you to order new stationery with the Ambrose-*Berg* Agency instead of just the Ambrose Agency on it. I want it engraved on gray stationery with red printing. And send some flowers to Dolores DeLongpre. Take this down for the card. 'Dear Dolores. Thanks for the lovely things you've been saying about me.' Sign it Ms. Mona. She'll get a kick out of that."

Chapter 9

IN ANOTHER PART of the town, in the area known as Holmby Hills, where the houses were vast and the living was gracious, the heiress Cecilia Lesky, a stranger to the hustle and bustle of deals and advancement, was about to return home from a long sojourn on foreign shores, most recently to Italy, to take up residence again in the Palladian villa of her parents, Marty and Sylvia Lesky.

Anyone who knows anything about Hollywood knows who the Marty Leskys are, just as in the old days anyone who knew anything about Hollywood knew who the Louis B. Mayers were, or the Jack Warners were, or the Sam Goldwyns, or the Darryl Zanucks, or any of those families who made up the ruling class. Sylvia Lesky came out of one of those families to begin with, being the daughter of the Marcus Meyers, and had the extra added attraction, as Dolores DeLongpre once wrote, of being second generation at the top. As for the Lesky daughter, Cecilia, there were those who thought her lineage almost royal, especially Dolores, who almost never did not mention her name without the word heiress preceding it, a matter of dismay to her father, who feared fortune hunters nearly as much as he feared kidnappers.

Old Marcus Meyer, who had founded Colossus Pictures, and his wife, Belle, also had a son, Markie, who hanged himself at Yale, for reasons never divulged. They lavished their love and attention on Sylvia and brought her up in a hothouse atmosphere, not intending to stultify, but stultifying nonetheless. She had a governess who taught her French. She went to finishing school in France. Old Marcus Meyer would have liked nothing better than that she connect with one of the Barons Rothschild, but there was about Sylvia a certain rigidity, caused perhaps by her aloneness or her aloofness, that made her a not-sought-after girl in that sort of marital sweepstakes, as if the Hollywood in her was somehow a taint.

Then Sylvia Meyer met Marty Lesky on a blind date arranged by Faye Converse, an actress under contract to Colossus Pictures. Nowadays Dolores DeLongpre always wrote about Marty Lesky that he was the most powerful man in Hollywood. That may or may not be. Dolores sometimes dealt in superlatives to make her points, and she was always reverential in her dealings with any of the Leskys. Certainly he was one of the most powerful men in Hollywood. When he wanted to get a picture made, it got made. He didn't have to check it out first with the board of directors, or anyone else for that matter, and any agent will tell you that that is the best indication of power. So firm was Marty's hold on the reins of power that it was easy to envision him as having sprung forth full-blown as the head of Colossus Pictures, but such was not the case. He had humble beginnings, just as

Warren Ambrose had before him, and Mona Berg had after him. Marty's was the old poor-boy-marries-rich-girl story; but the switch in the Lesky version was that the poor boy became richer than the rich girl's rich father, who, people said, must have turned over in his grave at the time of the nuptials, so inappropriate would he have considered his daughter's choice.

At the time of the courtship, people said about Marty Lesky that he was pushy, that he was a social climber, that he was a fortune hunter, that he was using Sylvia as a stepping-stone. Nonetheless they wed, in an elopement sort of wedding, old Marcus not having been dead a year, and old Belle maintaining that he was turning over in his mausoleum.

All the things they said about Marty were true. He was pushy. He was a social climber, and a fortune hunter, and he did use her as a stepping-stone, but all that was more than a quarter of a century ago, and the marriage endured, and continues to endure, and probably will continue to endure until death do them part. That is not to equate endurance with happiness, however. They celebrated their mounting anniversaries with dancing parties under striped tents on their tennis court, and they gave each other gifts of art, or race horses, but they spent less and less time together as the years went on, except for the frequent ceremonial occasions where they found it was easier to laugh and chat together than it was when they were alone, giving constant assurances to the myth of their happiness. There was a desert house in Palm Springs, a beach house in Trancas, an apartment in New York at the Sherry Netherland, and a chalet in St. Moritz, to all of which Sylvia repaired, depending on the season, for increasing lengths of time. They said about Marty that he saw other women in the afternoons, but no one said it very loud, at least not if they wanted to keep working at his studio, or any other.

They brought their daughter, Cecilia, up in splendid isolation in the vast Palladian mansion in Holmby Hills. Her playhouse was built by studio craftsmen with the same loving attention to detail that David O. Selznick once put into the building of Tara, the MGM back lot home of Scarlett O'Hara, from which it was copied in ⅞ scale. On Christmas mornings the south lawn of her parents' estate, where the sculpture garden now was, was transformed into a winter wonderland with snow brought in from Lake Tahoe by studio teamsters. On the rare occasions she played with other children, she was delivered and picked up by a chauffeur and a governess. On some afternoons she was brought to the studio lot to visit her father, and his secretaries vied to take her for walks to the stages, or toss a ball with her on the lawn outside the Administration Building that had been built by her grandfather nearly half a century before.

Warren Ambrose used to say about Cecilia Lesky that one day she would be worth sixty-five million dollars, including, as Warren put it, what was on the walls, meaning the art collection. When people would say to Warren, "I thought the Leskys would have more money than that," meaning the sixty-five million, as *Fortune* magazine listed them in the one-hundred- to two-hundred-million-dollar category, Warren would explain that the rest of the money was going to the Lesky Foundation for medical research and art enhancement and the film department of the University of California.

Money was the thing about Cecilia Lesky that set her apart. When a stranger at a party asked who she was, "heiress" was how she was described, even by people who loved her. Heiress. She had no close friends. The kinds of girls she might have liked she was told were secretly jealous of her, and the kinds of boys she might have liked she was told were only interested in her money. She spent more time riding her horse, in the English manner, than she did with children of her own age, whom she only saw, outside of school, at her elaborate birthday parties.

It was a curious fact of the family that they were not close to each other, even before the event occurred, in Cecilia's seventeenth year, that would render them asunder on a permanent basis. Marty's life was his work. There was never anything in it that interested him more than running the studio that Sylvia's father had founded, bringing it to an eminence, and holding it at an eminence, that would have flabbergasted old Marcus Meyer had he lived to see it.

He lavished presents on Cecilia on the appropriate days; but the shy and quiet little girl who was his daughter never fascinated him sufficiently for him to develop a relationship that was ever more than dutiful. Between mother and daughter there was a lifelong tension, based on an early fear on the mother's part that Cecilia was going to be fat. Scales and diets and cross words about sweets and starches were part of their daily conversation until the young girl was shipped off to her boarding school in Connecticut. There, in the spartan simplicity of that exclusive academy she slimmed down of her own accord. She made friends with girls who had names like Gillian and Venetia and Antoinette and saw for the first time other alternatives than her parents' kind of life for her own future.

In the summer that followed her graduation year, there appeared on the scene, as an extra man at one of her mother's dinner parties, a young fellow from another city called Cheever Chadwick who had all the right credentials. He danced well, played tennis well, and was amusing. From the beginning, Sylvia doted on him, especially when he took an interest in Cecilia. Although Cecilia had no real commitment to a higher education, she was scheduled to return to the East in the fall to attend a college in New York. She never got there, because she married Cheever Chadwick instead. Her mother didn't push her into the marriage. She simply fostered it, because of his suitability, after she suspected that Cecilia might be showing too avid an interest in a young Italian boy who worked at the stable where her horses were boarded. It was a plan that simply fell into place. It seemed to suit everyone.

"I think Cheever Chadwick is a very nice fellow," Sylvia said to Cecilia one day, "and he seems *mad* about you."

"You just like him because he's goy and social," said Cecilia.

"That's not true, and don't say goy," said Sylvia.

"He doesn't *do* anything," said Cecilia.

"Your father can get him a job at the studio," said Sylvia, in her simple-as-apple-pie voice.

"Perfect!" said Cecilia, meaning imperfect of course.

Nonetheless, the seed was planted. Cheever was twenty-five and had friends in Pasadena and Santa Barbara and San Francisco, and they went to polo matches and parties, and Cecilia saw a California life that was removed from the industry kind of life that her parents lived, and she fell in with it and accepted his proposal of marriage when it came not long after they met. Of course he wanted to work at the studio, and of course a job was arranged for him to have there when they returned.

Sylvia Lesky was ecstatic. So was Marty, although he found conversation with the young man difficult. Sylvia liked the kind of schools that he had gone to and the kind of WASP

81

look that he had and the kind of people that he knew. The tensions of the family were relieved in the two months of preparation. The planning of the elaborate wedding became almost a full-time job.

Having eloped herself twenty-five years earlier, Sylvia had always dreamed of having her daughter, in bridal white, descend the lovely staircase of the Palladian mansion. It was a dream they all became involved in—mother, father, and daughter—and the two months of preparation for the event were probably the closest they ever were as a family. Cheever Chadwick had repaired to his own city to close out his affairs at the time.

On the night before the wedding, while driving home from the bridal dinner in the upstairs private dining room of the Bistro in Beverly Hills, Cecilia became increasingly concerned with the remoteness of the man she was about to marry. Since his return a week before, there was about him a different attitude, which she first attributed to wedding nerves and then to a decrease in ardor toward her.

"What's the matter?" asked Cecilia. They were in Cheever's new car, a wedding gift from Marty and Sylvia.

He looked at her as if there were things on his mind that he wanted to say, but then returned his gaze to Sunset Boulevard and his attention to the oncoming traffic. "What do you mean?" he asked.

"There's a certain elation missing for a man about to be married," said Cecilia. "You were the only one in the wedding party who didn't give a toast tonight, and that's not like you. Are you upset because your parents didn't come?"

"My father's not well, and my mother didn't want to leave him alone."

"I know. You told me that. What about your sister? Why

didn't she come? Or your brother? Is it because we're movies?"

"Of course not."

"What then?"

He gripped the steering wheel tighter and kept his eyes on the road ahead. When they came to Delfern Drive, where the Lesky estate was, he didn't make the turn-off.

"You missed the turn," she said.

"I have to talk to you, Cecilia," Cheever said.

"Don't you love me?" she asked.

"Yes, I love you," he answered.

"I'm feeling very fearful."

"My divorce didn't come through. That fucking bitch wouldn't sign the papers. I'm still married." He started to cry.

"What fucking bitch are you talking about?"

"My wife."

"You never told me you were married, Cheever." Her heart was beating wildly. She did not know yet what her feelings were. "My God, my mother. My father. Six hundred wedding guests. Eight bridesmaids. How could you do this to me, Cheever?"

"It was supposed to have been final. That's why I went home."

"You better take me home."

"I'm sorry, Cecilia."

"That doesn't do it, Cheever. How do you tell six hundred people there isn't going to be a wedding?"

She knocked on the door of her parents' room. It was one o'clock in the morning.

"Are you asleep?" she asked.

"Come in," said her mother. "You shouldn't have stayed

out so late. You'll have circles under your eyes tomorrow. Don't wake up your father. Have you been crying?"

"Yes."

"What's the matter?"

"Did you know he was married before?"

"No."

"He was. He still is. There was supposed to have been a divorce, but it didn't come through."

"What?"

"You better wake up Daddy."

"What's the matter?" said Marty, waking up, looking at his wife and daughter, sensing there was something wrong.

"There's not going to be a wedding, Daddy," said Cecilia.

"What are you talking about?"

"He's married."

"Who?"

"Cheever."

"What are you talkin' about?"

"I thought you checked him out?" screamed Sylvia.

"You're the one who said he had all the right connections," yelled Marty back.

"He was getting a divorce. He thought it would come through by the time of the wedding, but it didn't."

"Jesuschrist."

There was a silence as each absorbed the catastrophic social situation that they were in.

"How can I tell all that St. Moritz crowd?" said Sylvia. "They skipped Grace and Rainier's gala in Monte Carlo to come to this wedding."

"My whole board of directors is out here from New York. Oh, Jesus, and Scotty Warburg," said Marty.

"Who's Scotty Warburg?"

"From the brokerage house who's bringing out the new stock issue for the studio."

"What are we going to do?"

"We're going to go through with it. That's what we're going to do."

"What?"

"That's bigamy."

"We're going to go through with it as if nothing is wrong, and in a week's time you can separate, and we'll get the marriage annulled," said Marty.

"What about Cheever? He'll never go through with that," said Cecilia.

"That little prick will do just what I tell him to do, or I'll have Dom Belcanto's boys break every bone in his body. I might have them do it anyway after this whole thing's over and done with. Now let me get that prick on the phone, and if he's skipped town, God help him."

They went through the entire pageantry, with smiles on their faces. Marty brought Cecilia, veiled by Galanos, down the winding stairway, past the weeping maids, across the atrium to the terrace where six hundred people made a path through the sculpture garden for father to escort daughter to a bogus husband and a mock ceremony. It was a decision they wished they never had made. If it were a moment of their lives they could have relived, they would have played it differently. But they couldn't. The marriage was annulled a week later.

Like the suicide of Markie Meyer at Yale all those years before, Cecilia's wedding to Cheever Chadwick was an event of their lives that they never discussed, either between themselves or with their friends. Marina Vaughan, who had been a bridesmaid, along with Cecilia's school friends Gillian and

Venetia and Antoinette, was one of the few people who knew of the deep hurt and embarrassment that Cecilia felt, and she urged her to leave the city and begin a new life elsewhere.

First Cecilia went to New York and attended for a term the college where she had been enrolled, but she was no longer interested in going to school and dropped out. Then she went to London and shared an apartment with Antoinette and made plans to open a kindergarten, but Antoinette married Vyvyan Kingswood, and the kindergarten never came about. Then Cecilia moved on to Rome and shared an apartment with her friend Venetia and began to enjoy her life again, especially after she met a young Italian boy whom her parents would have loathed, and had her first affair.

Then her father called her home to live, for the first time since her wedding—the marriage that never was.

The flight from Rome arrived on time at the Los Angeles airport. Cecilia Lesky, carrying several coats and a piece of hand luggage in each hand, waited in line with the other passengers to have her passport checked. She was tired after the long flight, and there was no sense of joy in her demeanor as she returned to the town where she was born.

She was twenty-four years old, almost pretty, with an only-child, sheltered-life look about her. Her hair was short and strawberry blond. Her eyes were gray-green. She had a shy elfin smile that could be terribly winning. She looked as if she played tennis well, and she did. She looked as if she rode a horse well, and she did. She looked as if she didn't belong in Hollywood, and she didn't. It was one of the few things about herself that she understood perfectly, although her roots were planted deeply in its soil.

"Welcome home," said the friendly immigration officer, stamping her passport and handing it back to her.

"Thank you," Cecilia answered.

"Will you be staying long?"

"I'm going to be living here."

She picked up her passport and went to collect her luggage, dreading the tedious and tiresome affair that she knew it to be. In the baggage area she saw a man holding a piece of cardboard with her name written on it in crayon.

"I'm Cecilia Lesky," she said to the man.

"Welcome home, Miss Lesky," said the man. "I'm Tom Stout. Public relations. Your father asked me to help you with your luggage. May I have your baggage checks?"

"There's a flock of them," said Cecilia, almost in apology for the inconvenience that she might be causing him. "I've been away for years." She handed him the baggage checks that were stapled to her ticket.

"Why don't I pass you through customs," said Tom Stout, "and then I'll come back for your bags and have them sent over to your father's house. You must be tired after that long flight."

"That would be bliss," said Cecilia.

"You have a friend waiting," he said.

"Who?" asked Cecilia, surprised, expecting only the chauffeur.

"A surprise, she said," he answered.

She saw Marina Vaughan as she cleared the customs barrier, in what Marina always called her movie-star-anonymous outfit, huge dark glasses and a turban completely covering her hair, which only made her more noticeable. She was signing an autograph when she noticed Cecilia.

"Cecilia! Cecilia!" she called out to her and waved.

The two ladies hurried toward each other, gave each other a hug and a kiss on each cheek.

"Let me look at you," said Marina. "You look beautiful."

"No, no, *you* look beautiful," said Cecilia. "I look almost pretty." They laughed the way old friends laughed, as if they were repeating a conversation from an earlier time.

"I like your hair cut like that," said Marina.

"You always did make me feel good about myself," said Cecilia. "How's the movie star business?"

"I'm up for a picture with your father. I'm afraid to talk about it, I want it so much. Listen, I'm sure you were expecting your father."

"No, I wasn't," said Cecilia.

"Or your mother," said Marina.

"Actually, I was expecting the chauffeur," said Cecilia. "This is awfully nice of you to come all the way out here and meet me."

"I saw your parents at a party last night, and they told me you were coming home today, and I couldn't bear it that no one was meeting you after all the time that you've been away," said Marina.

"I'm sure my father's at Ma Maison making a big deal with Warren Beatty, and I'm sure my mother's having her hair done by the latest hairdresser who's all the rage," said Cecilia, laughing. "First things first, you know."

"Close," answered Marina. "She's at a committee meeting for the AFI dinner." The girls laughed again. "They let me ride out in their Rolls. Yang is downstairs, and he'll take care of all the luggage."

"How is my father? Busy, busy, busy, I expect."

"Busy, busy, busy," repeated Marina. "That says it. Are you glad to be back in California?"

"Not really," said Cecilia. "I liked living in Italy. No one ever heard of Marty Lesky. No one gave a damn about Colossus Pictures."

"Why'd you come back then?"

"Same old rich-kid story. Daddy was afraid of kidnappers again. From the day I was born, my father has been afraid of kidnappers. Some day I think he's going to wish it into being."

"I guess I'm supposed to say, 'Don't say that, Cecilia. You don't mean that.' But I'm not going to. I know what your life is like. I saw that wedding of yours close up."

"You're the first person who's mentioned the wedding to me. They act like it never happened."

"Listen," said Marina.

"What?" answered Cecilia.

"I'm glad you're home."

"Thanks."

Later, when they were seated in the back seat of the Rolls-Royce, Marina turned to her friend. "What about you?"

"What about me?" asked Cecilia, knowing what Marina meant, beginning to feel uncomfortable, as she always felt when the conversation was directed at her, when she felt that she was being asked to give an accounting of her life, or how she felt about it.

"You know what I mean," said Marina. "What are you going to do with your life now that you're back? You're not just going to sit in that big house, are you, and wait for the next marital candidate to be hand-picked by your parents."

"I don't have talent like you," said Cecilia defensively. "I can't go in the movies and act."

"Now don't get defensive," said Marina. "I'm trying to be your friend. You've got to participate. Give a little. Get a little."

"Oh, Marina," said Cecilia, "I don't know what to do. I don't know what I want. All I know is what I don't want. I don't know what I'm good at. I won't be in that house five minutes when they'll be telling me, especially my mother, how fortunate I am to have the kind of life I have."

"Honey, that's life style. That's not life," said Marina.

Tara was gone, her playhouse with its soda fountain having been donated to the John Tracy School for the Deaf, to make room for the Henry Moore sculpture that Sylvia gave Marty for his fifty-fifth birthday. There was a new croquet court, croquet having come back into fashion, with lights for night playing. There was a new gate at the entrance, of the ducal variety, that only opened after identification of oneself had been made over a call box to the main house. There was closed circuit television hidden in the gates for further verification. And to make the point about staying out if you didn't belong there, in case it hadn't already been made, there was a guard with a gun and a Doberman Pinscher attack dog on duty, or rather, three guards on shifts of eight hours apiece.

Outside of those things, everything was pretty much the same. They were a family estranged. They found it difficult to converse with each other. Sylvia was forever picking on Cecilia, the habitual sort of picking-on. Sylvia was a perfectionist in matters of fashion and style and entertaining and running vast houses. That her daughter's interests in these pursuits were minimal was a great source of annoyance to her. She was forever pointing out to Cecilia her advantages. She had always had social ambitions for her daughter, and even after the Cheever Chadwick affair she purred a bit inwardly when she heard Cecilia was seeing a member of the nobility during the time she was sharing the apartment in London with Antoinette. Between father and daughter, there existed also a complicated relationship. Once, at the Grand Hotel in Rome, Cecilia walked in on her father with an actress only a few years older than herself. It was an incident that neither had ever mentioned to the other, as if the moment had simply not existed.

When they sat together at a meal, the three of them, which was not frequent, because of social activities, they made each other nervous. Conversation was never easy among them. They talked like people at a dinner party, about the kinds of things people at a dinner party talked about. They kept the conversation going until the dinner was over, and then they ran a movie, and after the movie was over, they had it to talk about, if all three of them had stayed awake till the end.

Right off, Cecilia started talking about getting a job. Her problem always was that she never knew what kind of job she wanted to get. Sylvia Lesky didn't approve of "people like us," meaning her and her daughter, getting jobs. She thought they had a responsibility to work on committees that did good works for people less fortunate than they.

"What I don't want to do," said Cecilia, as if it was one thing she was definite about, "is to be on the junior committee of the Cedars-Sinai Women's Guild, and I don't want to work for the Colleagues, and I don't want to be a docent at the Los Angeles County Museum, just because half your art is going there when you die."

"What do you have in mind?" asked her mother, trying to be patient on a subject she had very little patience with.

"I'd like to work at the studio," she said as a sudden thought, "but Daddy won't hire me at the studio—nepotism, you know—and the only kind of people in the business who are willing to hire me are the ones who are sucking up to Daddy."

"Don't say that," said Sylvia, with her fingernails-on-the-blackboard shudder.

"Say what?" asked Cecilia.

"Sucking up," said her mother. "I *hate* the sound of that expression."

"Oh, Mother, *listen,*" said Cecilia.

"I am listening. Don't say I'm not listening. They'll all resent you."

"Who?"

"All of them. They always think you're taking bread out of their mouths." Sylvia Lesky always talked about *they* and *them.*

It didn't have to be decided right then, in the first week. There was time, and the living was easy, what with a swimming pool and a tennis court and the new croquet court and a sculpture garden and a greenhouse full of orchids right in her own back yard, not to mention the brand-new thirty-five-thousand-dollar white Porsche that awaited her in the courtyard on her arrival, a welcome-home gift from her parents that was supposed to get everything off to a good start. Even Cecilia could see why people said about her, "I should have her problems."

Chapter 10

MONA BERG was hypnotized by the glamour of Marina Vaughan's life. For a brief period the two became inseparable. Mona told people Marina was her best friend, which was probably true at the time. The thing was that they had different notions of what friendship meant. It was a thing that Marina gave too freely, and it was a word that Mona was never to understand. She was always to have a new best friend. That year it was Marina Vaughan. Except for a tendency to repeat almost everything that was told to her in confidence to prove her familiarity with the great, her commitment to the friendship was total until she had exhausted each of the possibilities it opened up to her. Friendship was a stepping-stone, and Marina Vaughan was the stepping-stone of stepping-stones.

"Marina Vaughan lives the way you hope movie stars are going to live, but never do," was what Mona Berg said to Bill, her secretary Bill, who never got sick of hearing Marina

Vaughan stories. The word that best fit her life style was glamorous. She lived in a beach house in Malibu with a swimming pool on the Pacific. She drove her white Rolls Corniche with the top down and smiled at people who recognized her. She kept champagne on ice at all times and on rowdy nights drank it from the bottle. She loved to dance in nightclubs and loved to go to parties. Her name was in the columns every day for having been here and there with this one and that one. She had lunch with beautiful young actresses who were her kind of friends, and dinner with movie and rock stars who were her kind of lovers.

Not a bad life. Not a bad life at all, for as long as it lasts. At its core and root were her stardom and fame, and it would last as long as they would last. Only a year ago that had seemed forever. Then she lost the lead in a picture she wanted to be in because she'd shown up at a breakfast meeting at the Beverly Hills Hotel in an evening gown, on her way home from the night before. They said it was a conflict in schedules, why she couldn't do the movie, but it wasn't. The director whom she was to meet, an Englishman wary of the ways of Hollywood, didn't want an actress who came to breakfast in an evening gown. Nothing more. It had never occurred to her that she wouldn't get the part. It was her first rejection as a star, and her first glimpse of her own mortality as one. Then another picture came along, and the incident was forgotten. Her father and friend, the movie star Rex Vaughan, who never criticized the things she did in her life, just as she never criticized the things he did in his life, told her to think of the experience as a lesson, Rex having had his share of glimpses of his own mortality as a star.

So much did Marina want to play the role of Iris March in Marty Lesky's remake of *The Green Hat* that she dropped out of the party set and nightclub life that she loved so much and spent more and more evenings at home, wanting to keep her name out of the gossip columns. Mona never had anything to do nights, and Marina was having an affair with a rock star who was on the road and didn't like her to go out when he wasn't there. So they spent a lot of nights at the beach house, eating dinner, smoking grass, laughing, talking girl talk, waiting for Rick's nightly call. Rick was the rock star. Sometimes after Rick's call, she and Marina would go out to a late movie, or a beach bar for a couple of drinks. Marina told her a lot of stories about people in the town, the backstage kind of stuff that you only knew if you were really in it. The thing about Mona was that she never forgot even the most trivial piece of information about people who were on a higher rung up the ladder than she was.

Mona would never have known, for instance, that the socially impeccable Sylvia Lesky, whom she idolized from afar, had talked her daughter into going through with her wedding, bigamous though it was, in order to save face in front of the assembled guests, if Marina Vaughan hadn't told her. Nor would she have known that Robbie Slick, the studio topper, as Dolores DeLongpre called him, who had a well-established reputation as a lady killer, was oftentimes less than adequate in his sexual performance, if Marina hadn't told her. Nor would she have known that there were those in the crème de la crème who thought that Dolores DeLongpre might have a slight kleptomania problem that they all overlooked. Marina told her things like that in the first flush of their friendship, thinking they were safe.

A lot of people didn't like Mona. She wasn't the type you warmed to. When Marina heard these complaints, she always came to Mona's defense. "Listen, I know exactly what you mean," Marina would say, "but she's really not like that at all. Once you get to know her, she's really a wonderful person. I think there's a lot of goodness in her."

"That's only because you're a movie star, Marina," said Juanita one night. Juanita was Marina Vaughan's maid, and friend.

"What's because I'm a movie star?" asked Marina.

"I mean she sucks up to you because you're a movie star and introduce her to all your friends and tell her all your gossip. You ought to hear what the answering service says about her," said Juanita.

"What does the answering service say about her?" asked Marina.

"They say she's a cunt," said Juanita.

Marina Vaughan was awfully upset when it appeared in Dolores DeLongpre's column that she was having an affair with the rock star. Among other things that made the item inopportune was that the rock star was married, and Marina had already had her share of bad notices for having affairs with married men.

"I have something I want to ask you, Mona," said Marina on the telephone.

"What's that?" asked Mona, a wary note in her voice.

"Did you tell Dolores DeLongpre about me and Rick?"

"I swear to you, Marina, as God is my judge, I would never repeat anything you ever told me in confidence," said Mona.

"You're the only person I told," said Marina.

"I didn't. I swear to you I didn't. I value our friendship too much. How about Juanita? Or your answering service? I hear they listen in and then tip off the columnists," said Mona.

A few weeks later, Marina said to Mona, about the studio topper Robbie Slick, "Say, you didn't by any chance tell Robbie what I told you, did you?"

"Tell him what?" asked Mona.

"That he couldn't get a hard-on and then came too quick," said Marina.

"I swear to you on my mother's life, Marina, I would never repeat anything you told me in confidence. How could you even suggest a thing like that?" asked Mona in her aghast voice. When Mona lied, she was at her most sincere. The mother whose life she swore on was the one she never visited in the home.

"He snubbed me at Chasens last night," said Marina. "Cut me dead when I spoke to him."

"Will I be seeing you at the Kahns' cocktail party tonight?" Mona asked Marina one day when they were on the telephone together. It had been in Dolores DeLongpre's column that morning that Myron and Delphine Kahn, who were always entertaining visiting nobility passing through the city, were having the crème de la crème to a party in honor of a famous French viscountess.

"Yes, I'm going," said Marina, who was always invited everywhere.

"Do you suppose you could take me?" asked Mona. "My Mercedes is in the shop."

The Kahns thought Marina had brought Mona to the party, and Marina thought the Kahns had invited her. It was not until later that the ruse came to light.

"She's so pushy, darling," said Marina's friend Babette Navarro.

"She's using you, darling," said her friend Pearl Silver.

"You don't understand her," Marina said back. "Underneath all that pushiness is a very good person."

The thing about Marina was that she'd gone so far out on a limb for Mona—as her booster and backer in the early days after Warren's heart attack when she was trying to establish herself—that it took a long time to pick up on the fact that Mona was passing her by, having exhausted Marina's possibilities and the doors she could open for her.

Marina was extravagant, always buying clothes or things for her house, always coming up short at the bank.

"I told them not to take any withholding out of your salary for *The Day Before Lent*," said Mona one day.

"Why did you do that?" asked Marina, who was always vague about money matters. It was a thing she always left in the hands of other people.

"You'll have more money to spend," said Mona. "You can make it up out of your salary for *The Green Hat*," said Mona.

"Is that legal?" asked Marina.

"Everyone does it," said Mona. "Declare ninety-nine dependents."

Everyone didn't do it. Nor would Marina have done it if Mona hadn't come up with the advice. It was the beginning of Marina's problems with the IRS.

"I *insist* you fire your answering service," demanded Mona Berg to Marina Vaughan one day. She was in a fury, out of control with rage.

"Why should I fire my answering service?" said Marina. "I've had Pat for ten years."

"He hung up on me when I was trying to leave a message for you that the first draft of *The Green Hat* was finished," said Mona.

"I don't think he'd hang up on you, Mona," said Marina. "Tell me about the first draft of *The Green Hat*."

"I want you to fire that service," said Mona, raising her voice. The matter of the answering service took priority over the matter of the first draft of *The Green Hat*. "After you fire him, call me back and we'll talk about *The Green Hat*. I have to call Robbie Slick and Rita Belcanto. They use the same service, and I'm going to get them to fire him too."

The operator from the answering service, whose name was Pat, told Marina that Mona Berg had been rude and abusive to him when she called to leave the message. He said he only hung up on her after she said to him, "No wonder you're only an answering service operator."

Mona was always getting operators on answering services fired, or waitresses in coffee shops fired, or chauffeurs of limousine services fired, if they did not respond to the importance of her. A slight from anyone in a service capacity called for instant revenge.

She took a day out of her life to get even with the operator from the answering service. She called every person she knew who used the answering service and got them to threaten to take their business elsewhere unless the offending operator was fired. She told Benny Doberman, who was involved with a business scandal at the time, that the operator listened in and tipped off the papers on all his calls. She had never seen the operator. He was faceless and nameless to her, no more than a voice, but she hunted him down for his affront to her, for not accepting her abuse, which she saw as a mere show of her authority, and he vanished forever.

Then, in a grandstand play, when the first draft of *The Green Hat* looked as if it had been written especially for Marina by the English screenwriter Lambeth Walker, so perfectly did it suit her talent and personality, Mona exceeded by two hundred and fifty thousand dollars the asking price that Warren Ambrose would have set Marina for. It was a show-off tactic that backfired. Had it worked, Marina would have been the recipient of a million-dollar salary for the first time, and Mona would have been the heroine of the hour, but it didn't work. Instead it angered Marty Lesky, and he directed his anger at Marina Vaughan, assuming it was she who was behind the ploy. He ordered screen tests to be made of Rebecca Kincaid and Gloria Morgan, stars both themselves; and Marina Vaughan, who would have played the part for scale, so much did she want it, became the victim of Mona's misplaced strategy.

Eventually the fight came, as it had to come. The weeks had gone by—four, five, six of them—and there had been no further word from Marty Lesky on whether or not the part of Iris March was hers. Then she read in Dolores DeLongpre's column that the director Sam Roth had tested Rebecca Kincaid and Gloria Morgan for the role. She always knew that other actresses than herself were under consideration for the part. That was part of the business she was in—too many stars, too few parts—but Rebecca Kincaid was also a client of the Ambrose-Berg Agency, and she understood for the first time why Mona had been hesitant over the weeks about calling Marty Lesky to see where she stood.

She asked Mona to come out to her house in the Malibu Colony, and then kept her waiting for half an hour while she chatted on the phone with Babette Navarro about a shopping expedition they were planning. Then she took a call from her father. Then she took a call from her pusher. When she walked into her living room, Mona was looking at the framed photographs of famous people.

"I always loved Montgomery Clift," said Mona, putting the picture back in place.

"He was my godfather," said Marina, cool and distant, establishing the difference between them. "He's supposed to have dropped me at my christening."

"I think I read that in his biography," said Mona, a little nervous about the cool reception she was getting.

100

"Did Juanita make you a drink?" asked Marina.

"Yes, she did," said Mona. "I'm fine."

Marina went to the bar, made herself a drink, walked back to the sofa, sat down, and lit a cigarette from a Rigaud candle that was burning on the table, taking her time in each separate act, as if she were interviewing a new maid.

"I'm going to leave the agency, Mona," she said.

"If it's about that item in Dolores' column, don't give it a thought, Marina. You still have the inside track," said Mona. There was a note of anxiousness in her voice. She was too recently in charge to risk losing a name as big as Marina Vaughan's.

"Don't give me any of your agent double talk," said Marina. "I've had it up to here with you. I haven't minded you using me to advance yourself, but I do mind when you start to get more out of it than I do."

"What do you mean, agent double talk?" asked Mona.

"How about agent lie? Does that make it clearer?"

"When you say agent lie, you don't mean me, do you?" asked Mona, with a grievance in her tone.

"Mona, you're the biggest fucking liar I ever met in my life," said Marina. "You'd lie when the truth would sound better."

"This is my big chance, Marina," said Mona, ignoring the words.

"You know, Mona, if I were a young actress starting out, I'd probably feel lucky to have you. But I'm not a young actress starting out. I'm a star. Let's go so far as to say I'm a big star. A big star beginning to get in trouble. I need a different kind of agent than you. I need an agent who has access, socially as well as professionally, to the studio heads and the top producers and directors. No offense, darling, but you were still changing typewriter ribbons three months ago.

101

Warren Ambrose made most of his deals at parties, but no one seems to want you at their parties, Mona. Too pushy is what they're saying about you."

Of all the ugly things that were said, it was that, the social slight, that she felt the most. More than anything else, Mona wanted to be accepted in the society of the industry, as if acceptance therein would eradicate the shame that she felt for her background.

"We couldn't all have it handed to us on a silver platter, Marina, the way you did," said Mona in retaliation, zeroing in on what she knew was a sensitive point. "Daddy a star. Mommy a star. Every door open to you from the day you were born." She spat the words out in a way meant to minimize every accomplishment.

"Don't give me that have-and-have-not crap," said Marina. "I'm not where I am by accident." There was the slightest note of uncertainty in her voice, as if Mona had hit on a thought that was hidden within her.

"You know of course that this is going to kill Warren," said Mona in a voice meant to inspire guilt. "I mean literally kill him."

"Don't lay a guilt trip on me, Mona," said Marina. "You've been lying about Warren's condition the way you've—"

"I swear on my mother's life I did not lie to you about Warren's condition. You have no idea how much improved he is."

"That's not what Dr. Denniston has to say."

"You mean Dr. Denniston who arrived in surgery in a tux?" said Mona, minimizing his medical credentials.

"Dinner jacket, not tux, darling," said Marina. The snub again. "Listen, it wasn't my intention that this meeting take a low turn like this, but there's something about you that brings that out in me."

"You're upset, Marina. When we both calm down from this, we'll both be friends again."

"No, we won't," said Marina. "A friend to you is someone who can help you get ahead. That's not one of my criterions for friendship. Now I think you better leave."

There was a silence while Mona registered that she had been dismissed, like a fired maid, both as agent and guest. She felt embarrassed and rejected and clumsy, the way Warren Ambrose used to make her feel. As Mona rose to leave, her Louis Vuitton tote bag knocked over the silver-framed photograph of Montgomery Clift. The glass smashed on the floor.

Chapter 11

IN A DARKENED screening room of the Administration Building of Colossus Pictures, Marty Lesky and the director Sam Roth and the writer Lambeth Walker ran for the second and then the third times the tests made by the actresses Rebecca Kincaid and Gloria Morgan for the part of Iris March in Marty's personal production of the remake of *The Green Hat*.

"She doesn't have the class for the part," said Lambeth Walker about Gloria Morgan. "That little turned-up nose is all wrong."

"What about Rebecca?" asked Marty.

"Maybe we should run it again," said Sam Roth, not wanting to commit himself.

"She's all wrong too," said Marty, answering his own question.

"Where does that leave us?" asked Kip.

"Did you check out Diane Keaton's availability?" Marty

asked a casting director who was seated in the back of the room.

"She's making a picture in Paris," said the casting director.

"How about Faye Dunaway?" asked Marty.

"She's making the Crawford picture at Paramount."

There was silence.

"Okay," said Marty finally.

"Okay what?" asked Lambeth Walker.

"Okay we go with Marina Vaughan," said Marty.

"How about the money?"

"We pay it."

"Shall I call Mona Berg?" said the casting director.

"No, I'll do it," said Marty. "I think I'll call Marina herself. For old times' sake. She always said it was the part she was born to play."

If Marina had been home and had answered her telephone, there would have been a different tale to tell, but she wasn't, or so her maid Juanita said. But, there was always a but with Marina Vaughan. Madcap, irrepressible Marina Vaughan. That's what she was, up to a point. Then she went further. When she was unhappy, there was a tendency in her to self-destruct, on liquor or drugs or sex, either singly or in combinations. She liked anonymous sex, with men she didn't know and wouldn't see again. Tricks. One-night stands. One-hour stands. Even some twenty-minute stands, if gossip was to be believed, behind the set with grips and gaffers, or in the bathroom at parties with waiters and bartenders. It was a surcease for her, to quiet the demons of self-doubt that sometimes stirred within her. What Mona said to her, that she was only where she was because of who she was, struck a nerve. She was afraid for the first time in her career, that without Warren Ambrose to guide her, as he always had, she might be left behind.

Into her garden on the morning following the fray walked a substitute pool man of astonishing beauty.

"Pool man," he called out, identifying himself, carrying the implements of his temporary trade.

Marina was on the telephone, lying on a chaise by her pool, talking with her father, with whom she maintained a close relationship. She was dressed in a beach robe, with a large sun hat and dark glasses. "I wish you could see what just walked into my garden," she said to her father, at the same time acknowledging with a wave across the length of her pool that he could enter and go about his business. He was not wearing a shirt, and his jeans, unbelted as they were, fell a few inches beneath his navel. Marina continued to talk to her father about Mona, about the blind item in Dolores' column, about the things they talked about, at the same time watching the handsome tanned pool man vacuum the water and apply the chlorine.

When she hung up, she called out to him across the pool, "Where's Rusty?" Rusty was her regular pool man, with whom she sometimes dallied.

"He's off today," called back the young man. "He has an interview for *South Sea Adventures*. I'm just filling in."

She liked the sound of his voice. It matched the look of his body. "What's *South Sea Adventures*?" she asked.

"It's a new series they're going to do. They're looking for a leading man," he answered. He was efficient at his job.

"You an actor too?" she asked him.

"Hoping to be someday," he said. "Sounds better to me than delivering telegrams, or cleaning swimming pools, or a few other things I could mention." For the first time he looked at her and recognized who she was. "My God, you're Marina Vaughan!"

106

"Didn't Rusty tell you that?" she asked.

"He just said, 'Vaughan—Malibu Colony.' He probably thought I'd bring my autograph book, and I probably would have too." They both laughed. "This is a real pleasure, Miss Vaughan. This is a beautiful place you have here."

"Thanks," said Marina, and they looked at each other with a look they each understood, as a rush went through their loins. It was exactly the kind of situation she liked. It was exactly the kind of situation he liked as well. No fuss. No bother. No dinner first. No pretext of courtship. Just sex for the sake of sex. With drinks, of course. And cocaine, of course. And poppers, of course. And no obligations afterward or desire for continuance, a one-time thing.

"What's your name?" she asked, enjoying the moment.

"Frankie," he answered.

"You look like a Frankie," she said. "Frankie what?"

"Bozzaci."

"You feel like a drink, Frankie Bozzaci?"

"Sure," he answered.

"Let's go inside."

"Maybe I should jump in the pool first," said the young man. "I might be a little sweaty after working out in the sun like this."

"That wouldn't turn me off," she said.

"You sound like a lady after my own heart," he said.

"I always had a thing about pool men," she said, and they went into the house.

"I always had a thing about movie stars," he answered.

"Get out of those jeans, why don't you?" she said.

"Drop that terry-cloth robe, why don't you?" he said. She liked that he wasn't intimidated by the movie star of her, that they were equals in their promiscuity.

She picked up the telephone on her bar and buzzed the kitchen. "Juanita," she said, "answer the telephone if it should ring. I don't care who it is, say I'm out, and you don't know where I am."

Mona Berg was in a vile mood on the morning following her dismissal by Marina Vaughan. Bill, her secretary Bill, who was watering the cymbidium plants, tried to get her to talk about whatever was bothering her, after his steady stream of gay gossip failed to cheer her up.

"You're Gladyce Glum today," he said. "Did something go wrong with Marina Vaughan last night?"

"Miss Vaughan is no longer a client of this agency," said Mona.

"What?" said Bill, putting down the watering can, shock and amazement in his voice. Marina Vaughan was one of the mainstays of the Ambrose Agency.

"You heard me," said Mona sourly.

"Does Warren know?" asked Bill.

"No, Warren doesn't know. No one knows. Yet."

"What happened?"

"When I arrived, she kept me waiting while she talked on the telephone, first to her pusher to order some coke, and then to Babette Navarro about shopping, as if my time counted for nothing."

"Yeah?" He wanted to hear the story in detail.

"And then she fired me."

"Why?" he asked. He was shocked and disappointed.

"She said, 'I'm a big star and I need someone to represent me who has access to the studio heads and the big producers and directors.' "

"Was it about Rebecca Kincaid doing the screen test? You should have told her that, Mona."

"And then, do you know what that bitch said to me?" she asked, ignoring his question about Rebecca Kincaid. "She said, 'No offense, darling, but you were still changing typewriter ribbons three months ago.' How do you like that? Do you know what she is? She's a spoiled brat who had everything handed to her and never had to work for anything."

The more she talked, the more of a fury toward Marina Vaughan she worked herself into. " 'Montgomery Clift was my godfather,' " she went on in a deadly accurate imitation of Marina's very specific vocal inflections. " 'He's supposed to have dropped me at my christening.' Right on her stoned head is where he dropped her. What do you expect? Her mother was a drunk and her father's a fag."

"You're a real winner today," said Bill quietly. As he got up to leave, the telephone rang.

"I don't care who that is, I don't want to talk," said Mona. "Say I'm up at Warren's at a staff meeting."

She could hear him in his outer office, where she used to be, answering the telephone. "Miss Berg's office . . . I'm awfully sorry. Miss Berg is away at a staff meeting. . . . May I ask who's calling? . . . Oh, Mr. Lesky . . . yes, Mr. Lesky, I'll tell her."

Marty Lesky himself. She grabbed the telephone out of Bill's hand, snapping out of the lethargy the fight with Marina had left her in. "Hello, Mr. Lesky," she said. "I was just on my way out to a staff meeting at Warren's. But Bill was able to stop me."

"What I'm calling you about is Marina Vaughan," said Marty Lesky.

"Marina?" answered Mona after a slight pause.

"I called Marina first, for old times' sake, because of Rex and all, to give her the good news, but she wasn't home," said Marty.

"What good news?" asked Mona, aware that he didn't know that Marina was no longer represented by her.

"We're prepared to meet Marina's price and make an offer for her to play the lead in *The Green Hat,*" he said.

There was silence from Mona. She realized that she had pulled off her grandstand play and now could not deliver the client.

"You seem awfully silent," said Marty Lesky, "for the agent of the actress who's just been offered the lead in a movie."

"Listen, Mr. Lesky," she said, having impregnated her pause to give her time to wave Bill out of the room so she could be alone to deal with the situation in her own way. "I have to talk to you. My conscience won't let me close this deal without making you aware of a few facts that I think you should know about."

"What sort of facts?"

"Warren would kill me if—"

"Warren's sick."

"It's about Marina."

"What about Marina?"

"She's in terrible shape, Mr. Lesky."

"*Marty.*"

"She's in terrible shape, Marty. She's taking a lot of cocaine. I mean a lot. Even that night in the hospital. She was doing coke in the bathroom when Warren was in the operating room. She looks terrible, and she's drinking a lot. She's not in a reliable frame of mind. I mean, I don't think you could count on her. Sam Roth could give her a set call, and she might fly to Paris for a party. It's like that," she said, her voice agonizing at her revelations.

His pause matched her earlier one. Then he said, "Jesus.

What's wrong with everybody today?" His disapproval of drugs was well known. She suspected, however, that it had more to do with production schedules and going overtime than it did with moral conviction on the subject. "Why are you telling me all this?"

"Because I think there's such a lack of integrity in so many of the deals that are made in films today. So many of the stars hold up production because of lax behavior, and I don't think it's fair to the guys who run the studios."

"You have no idea how appreciative I am for this information, Mona," he said. "This picture had a tight schedule, and she's in every scene."

"That's why I wanted to warn you," said Mona, a grievous tone in her voice, as if her integrity had exhausted her.

For the favor she had done him, Marty Lesky took Mona Berg to lunch at Ma Maison, the most celebrity-oriented place to be seen any Monday through Saturday at lunchtime. Each knew that her being seen there with him in business conversation was a form of knighthood in the film community.

When she arrived, a sense of panic overtook her that she would be snubbed. Tales of the snobbery of the restaurant were regularly told. Remember who you're meeting, she said to herself over and over again.

"Yes?" said the maitre d', without a hint of welcome in his voice.

"I'm, uh, meeting, uh—"

She saw him look over to the unfashionable side of the room where the nobodies sat who came to look at the somebodies. She could tell it was where he pegged her for.

"Marty Lesky," she went on, finishing her sentence.

"Oh," he said, looking at her again, reassessing her, changing his attitude. "Right this way. Mr. Lesky's already here."

Marty Lesky rose to greet her and shook her hand warmly. When she saw that he was drinking Perrier water, she ordered the same.

"This is the first time I've ever been to Ma Maison," said Mona, looking around the restaurant, knowing she was being looked at, loving the feeling of importance it gave her.

"I thought when you suggested coming here, you must be a regular," said Marty.

"I've always been afraid Patrick wouldn't give me a table, or else he'd give me a table over there in Siberia," Mona said, pointing to the unfashionable side of the room. "I don't know which would be worse."

"Oh, Patrick," said Marty Lesky, beckoning over to his table the owner of the restaurant. "This is Mona Berg. I'd like you to take good care of her whenever she calls in for a table. Miss Berg is Warren Ambrose's partner."

"I'll be happy to look after Miss Berg," said Patrick in a charming manner. "Tell Warren we miss him. How is he?"

"He's doing beautifully, all things considered," said Mona.

"I recommend the striped bass today," Patrick said and went on his way.

"Thanks for doing that, Marty," said Mona.

"You scratch my back, I'll scratch yours. Old Hollywood expression," said Marty. "I have a feeling we're going to be doing a lot of business together, Mona."

"You're the first person I've told this to, and I hope you won't repeat it until she's had a chance to make other arrangements for representation, after all she is our friend, but I've had to discharge Marina from the Ambrose-Berg Agency," she said, concluding that subject. It was the beginning of Marina Vaughan's downfall. Blackball was the word for it, a whisper in the ear, just the right ear, that suggested

that production could be held up because of some sort of lax-
ity, and the word was out, and moral indignation came into
play.

She looked around the restaurant again, pleased to be
where she was, pleased to be with whom she was. "I understand Benny Doberman got a standing ovation when he came
in here after he beat his kickback rap," said Mona.

"Is that what you'd like, Mona? A standing ovation?" asked
Marty, amused by her.

"Yeah, someday," she said. "Someday I'd like a standing
ovation at Ma Maison."

"Stranger things have happened," said Marty.

"Look, there's your wife," said Mona excitedly as the fashion-plate Sylvia Lesky, followed by a young lady with a re-
luctance in her walk, made her way over to a center table
where a group of more fashion-plate ladies greeted her enthusiastically.

"My wife and my daughter," said Marty. "Excuse me. I'll
go over and say hello to them."

Later, when she went over the lunch with Bill, giving him
all the details, she described the arrival of Sylvia Lesky in the
restaurant. "She had on this little hat and an Adolfo suit and a
ring this big," said Mona, who knew about herself that she
was wrong, but didn't know what to do about it. "I wonder if
I could get away with a hat like she had on."

"Don't copy the society ladies, Mona," said Bill, shaking
his head no to her fashion suggestion. "You're never going to
be one. You're more Joan Crawford in *Mildred Pierce.*"

"Is that a crack?" asked Mona. She hated her bigness.

"No, it's not a crack," said Bill. "You're the girl from the
wrong side of the tracks who's making good. That should be
your image."

"I gotta get myself invited to their parties," said Mona.

"That's where the big deals get put together. You know something? When Marty Lesky went over to say hello to all those ladies, he didn't take me along to meet them. Should I interpret that as a snub?"

The luncheons at Ma Maison between Marty Lesky and Mona Berg became a weekly thing. The deals Mona made with Marty were reported faithfully in Dolores DeLongpre's column. It was said of her in more and more places that she was a young woman to watch.

"How's Sylvia?" she would ask from time to time, about his wife, whom she admired inordinately for the social figure she was.

"Oh, she's fine," he would answer and drop the matter at that.

"Send her my love," Mona would persist, wanting him to talk about her in the confines of his Palladian villa, where she longed to be invited, hoping to make a wedge there.

One day he said to her, in an unguarded moment, about his wife, "I love Sylvia, but I'm not in love with her."

She said to him, in the way that she had of never allowing an opportunity to pass her by, "Listen, uh, Marty . . ." letting it trail off.

"Yeah?" said Marty.

"If, uh, you should, uh, ever want to borrow my house in the Hollywood Hills, you know, uh, for whatever, you're welcome. I know it must be hard for someone as well known as you are to find a place where you wouldn't be recognized, or gossiped about. Any afternoon. I could have a key made for you."

"Well, that's quite an offer, Mona," said Marty after only a moment's pause. It was true what she said, about being well known, being recognized, being gossiped about, all things he was concerned about.

"I always remember what you said to me the first time we had lunch here," said Mona.

"What was that?" asked Marty.

"You said, 'Old Hollywood custom, you scratch my back, I'll scratch yours.'"

So began his afternoon trysts with some of the loveliest starlets and models in Hollywood, away from prying eyes and gossipmongers, some of the assignations arranged by Mona herself as a way of currying favor.

However, she was never invited to the Lesky home to any of the evenings that she read about in the social columns of the city.

Chapter 12

"DON'T FORGET to put Tuesday in your book," said Sylvia Lesky to her daughter Cecilia. Sylvia was arranging flowers, an occupation at which she excelled, tiny yellow orchids and white violets, exotic and rare and scentless. She was always doubly occupied during family conversation. Sometimes it was needlepoint. Sometimes it was driving her Rolls-Royce. Sometimes it was arranging place cards.

"What's Tuesday?" asked Cecilia, who had been home from Italy for several weeks.

"It's the AFI dinner, Cecilia, in honor of Rex Vaughan, as I've told you three times now," said Sylvia, patience in her voice, trying hard as she was to achieve a sense of harmony in family life that matched the harmony of her floral arrangement.

"Do I really have to go?" asked Cecilia.

"Yes, Cecilia, you really have to go," said Sylvia. "I'm the chairperson. It's in honor of Rex Vaughan. Rex Vaughan is one of your father's closest friends. And besides, everyone's dying to see you."

"Who's everyone?" asked Cecilia. "Babette Navarro? Pearl Silver? Delphine Kahn?" She refrained from calling those fashionable ladies clones of her mother, which is how she thought of them—ladies who confused life style with life.

"Faye Converse. You always liked her," said Sylvia, ignoring the reference to her friends Babette and Pearl and Delphine. "And Elena Jamieson, and lots of people you'll enjoy. Not to mention just about every star in Hollywood. Most people wouldn't find that such a chore."

"I'm being a brat, aren't I?" said Cecilia. "A twenty-four-year-old brat, and you and Marty are trying so hard to have us look like a family united. Of course I'll go."

"I wish you wouldn't call your father Marty," said Sylvia. "It sounds so tough."

"Daddy, Dad, Pop. None of those words fit him," said Cecilia. "Why doesn't anybody like my father?"

"What a ridiculous thing to say," said Sylvia.

"Everybody's afraid of him," said Cecilia. "That's not the same thing as liking him."

"You sound like you've been talking to Marina Vaughan," said Sylvia.

"Why are you and Marty so down on poor Marina?" said Cecilia. "She's the only friend I have in this town."

"Hmmm," said Sylvia, shifting the position of an orchid.

"She'll be at the dinner, won't she?"

"She's supposed to sing."

"Great. The evening's starting to sound better."

"Your father says she's on drugs."

"Marty thinks everyone's on drugs."

"She didn't get that picture because of that."

"What picture?"

The Green Hat."

"That's the one she always wanted to play."

"They said it was a conflict of schedules, but that was the real reason."

"That looks pretty," said Cecilia about the floral arrangement.

"Ask Theodore to put it on the console table in the hall, will you?" said Sylvia. "Perry Rifkin's coming by for a drink, and you know how he notices everything."

"You won't believe who called me today," said Babette Navarro to Pearl Silver. Babette Navarro was the wife of Nando Navarro, the producer of the Amos Swank show, the late-night and nightly entertainment that kept the nation awake past its bedtime. Pearl Silver was the widow of the late film producer Irving Silver. Indefatigable hostesses both, they enjoyed being photographed by the fashion and social press on their way in and out of whichever of the three or four restaurants they regularly lunched at when they weren't entertaining in their own homes.

"Who?" asked Pearl Silver. They were at the Bistro, having been photographed in their Adolfo suits on entering, having been seated at their favorite table in the corner, having waved and thrown kisses at their friends at other tables, having ordered their white wine and cheese soufflés, getting down to conversation.

"That pushy what's-her-name," said Babette. It was a way they had of not being able to remember the names of people who functioned at a less exalted level socially than they did.

"That could be almost anyone out here," said Pearl, laughing, in her inside-looking-out voice. "What pushy what's-her-name?"

"With all the Gucci. Who works for Warren," said Babette.

"Oh," groaned Pearl. "You mean Mona Berg. What did she want?"

"She was trying to push her way into my table at the AFI dinner. She said Warren Ambrose asked her to call. She was using Warren's illness to push her way right into our table. I said, 'Well, I'm awfully sorry, Miss, uh'—whatever her name is—"

"Berg. Mona Berg," prompted Pearl.

" '—but I've already given what would have been Warren's places at the table to Dom and Pepper Belcanto.' That shut her up. Imagine! The nerve of her."

"Did you hear what she did at Delphine and Myron's?" asked Pearl.

"Marina told me," said Babette.

"Sylvia Lesky said that Marty says she's supposed to be a good agent," said Pearl.

"But you'll never see her at Sylvia's house," said Babette. "I can guarantee you that." The two friends laughed.

Mona Berg had not been invited to the glittering society event that the American Film Institute dinner in honor of Rex Vaughan was, and her several attempts at maneuvering her way in had not been successful. It was not that Mona did not have the price of tickets, formidable though it was, for the agency would have paid for them as a necessary business expenditure, nor that the sale of tickets would have been denied her, charity being charity, one person's buck being as good as the next. It was the seating that counted, being seen with the right people at the right table. Mona was of the opinion that it was better not to go at all than to have people like Marty and Sylvia Lesky or Dolores DeLongpre see her at the nondescript kind of table she knew she would be assigned by the society ladies in charge.

Another consideration, of course, was that she had no one to take her except Bill, her secretary Bill, and Bill, dear though he was, simply didn't fit in with that kind of crowd. She spent the whole day in the kind of mood she got into when she felt that she had been socially slighted. Gladyce Glum is what Bill called her when she got in one of her moods, and he wasn't surprised that she scheduled a meeting with Warren Ambrose at his marbled aerie in Bel Air that afternoon. "Gladyce Glum was on the warpath today," he would tell whatever trick he went dancing with that night. She usually took it out on Warren, and ended up with a few more privileges or concessions or advances in his beloved agency, which was becoming more and more her agency.

"Cecilia, have you given any thought to what you're going to wear tonight?" said Sylvia Lesky to her daughter. Sylvia was having her nails done by Blanchette, her manicurist, who came to her house three mornings a week. The fact was that Cecilia hadn't given it a thought until that moment, which Sylvia knew, and it was her oblique way of bringing up the subject without starting an argument. "I have a new dress from Adolfo I haven't even worn yet which you're perfectly welcome to wear," she went on, at the same time wondering if the new color Blanchette was using would work with the rose-colored Galanos she was going to wear that night.

"You're too best-dressed-list for me," said Cecilia. "I thought I'd go into Beverly Hills and put a dent into our fortune with some new clothes." The idea just occurred to her and seemed logical enough.

"Would you stop by Van Cleef and pick up my pearls,

which they've-been-restringing-for-exactly two-and-a-half-months," said her mother.

"Okay," said Cecilia.

"And would you take this piece of moire down to Perry Rifkin's showroom, and tell him *this* is the color pink I want for the new lampshades in the bedroom," said Sylvia.

"Okay," said Cecilia.

"And, darling, the studio's sending a limousine, and we have to leave this house at seven o'clock *promptly.*"

"Okay," said Cecilia.

"Yushi will be here at five, if you want him to do something about your hair," said Sylvia.

"Okay," said Cecilia.

"Blanchette, you're going to kill me. I think I'd like it darker."

Chapter 13

IN A LESS opulent part of the city, the young man called Frankie Bozzaci, who appeared at the counter of Schwab's to ask Mona Berg if she was going to eat her pickle, and who appeared later at the swimming pool of Marina Vaughan in Malibu as a substitute pool man and one-shot lover, was having his own kind of problems. His were of the economic variety. The rent was due the following day, and he didn't have it. The problem went deeper than the rent. What he was feeling was a discontent with the way his life was not shaping up for him.

He wanted to be more than he was, the odd-job man, but he didn't know what it was he wanted to be, or what the steps were to get there. "Something will happen," he always said. Now he wasn't so sure.

Marina Vaughan had given him a hundred dollars after the several hours they spent together, and he knew that that was a way that was always open to him; but he wanted that to be a means to an end only, not the end, as if there were no more to him than the sex of him. He lived in a one-and-a-half-room apartment over the garage behind a building on Havenhurst Drive in West Hollywood. It was his. He liked it. He didn't want to lose it.

His telephone rang. It was his friend Rusty, the pool man whose substitute he was when Rusty went to read for acting parts.

"How'd your reading go?" Frankie asked him.

"Same old shit," said Rusty.

"What?"

"I balled with one of the producers and still didn't get the part."

"You shouldn't ball with them until *after* you get the part."

"*Now* you tell me."

"What's up, man?"

"There's a bartending job at a party in Bel Air this afternoon. You interested? Sixty bucks for the first three hours, then overtime."

"Yeah, I'm interested. My rent's due."

He didn't tell Rusty that the battery was dead on his Volkswagen. He said he'd be there. He needed the money. He said thanks.

A little bit of her mother's kind of life went a long way with Cecilia Lesky. On Rodeo Drive she ran into old Delphine Kahn, her hair freshly blued, her walk slightly unsteady, being helped into her Rolls by her ever faithful Chauncey, her chauffeur of thirty years. They talked about Rome, and old Delphine wanted to know about this countess and that princess, and was it true that everyone was afraid to wear their jewelry over there? Then she saw Pearl Silver, who asked her to one of her luncheons the following week. Then she saw Babette Navarro, who everyone said liked to shop nearly as much as she liked going to parties, and Babette told her about an evening dress that would be perfect for her at Giorgio's. Coming out of Van Cleef and Arpels, where she picked up her mother's pearls, she ran into Marina Vaughan, nearly bumping into her.

"Cecilia," said Marina.

"Marina," said Cecilia. They looked at each other fondly. They had known each other all their lives, more or less, but they had never really been close friends until recently, when Marina came to the airport to meet her, a gesture that had touched Cecilia enormously. Marina was five years older, which had made a lot of difference in their lives previously, and her early celebrity and subsequent reputation for wildness had made her a not ideal candidate for best-of-friends for the sheltered Cecilia, at least as far as Cecilia's parents were concerned.

"How's it going?" asked Marina.

"Oh, you know," said Cecilia.

"What are you doing now that you're home?"

"Right now I'm picking up my mother's pearls, which have been restrung. Get the picture?" asked Cecilia, and they both laughed. "And then I'm taking this piece of pink moire to Perry Rifkin's showroom for him to copy for the new lampshades in my mother's bedroom." They laughed some more. "Want me to go on?"

"You and I have to have a little talk one of these days," said Marina. "You're a big girl now. You have to get a job. You have to have your own place to live. You've got to start seeing some fellas that they wouldn't approve of at all."

"It's so good to see you, Marina," said Cecilia, and the two girls hugged.

"Same here," said Marina. "I'm pissed off at your old man anyway."

124

"I heard about the picture," said Cecilia. "I'm sorry."

"Sore subject still," said Marina. "I really wanted to play that part. I suppose they told you I was a drug addict."

"Words to that effect."

"T'ain't true."

"I know that. How'd he get that in his mind?"

"That's a long story, and I still have to get my hair done. I'm singing tonight at the AFI dinner," said Marina.

"I know you are, and I'm going. I'll see you there. I'm on my way to buy a dress for my re-entry into filmland society, as Dolores DeLongpre calls it," said Cecilia.

"Well, spend a lot," said Marina. "They can afford it."

The hitchhiker on Sunset Boulevard in the tight jeans that showed a basket, as the expression went in the circles in which he moved, was the handsome Frankie Bozzaci, on his way to the bartending job in Bel Air that his friend Rusty had arranged for him as a means of paying, at least in part, his rent that was due the following day.

The girl in the thirty-five-thousand-dollar white Porsche, with the dress box from Giorgio at her side, was the shy and almost beautiful Cecilia Lesky, on her way to her parents' Palladian villa in Holmby Hills to have her hair done by Yushi, in preparation for the AFI dinner in honor of Rex Vaughan, the father of her friend Marina Vaughan, of which her mother was the chairperson.

If the light hadn't turned red at the stoplight under which he was standing, her car would have gone right by him, and they wouldn't have met. But it did turn red, and she did stop, like the obedient girl she was, instead of racing through it, as if the expensiveness of her car gave her extra privileges, like Mona Berg would have done.

A boy. A girl. A stoplight. Like a lyric to a love song. He

saw her before she saw him. Actually, he saw her car before he saw her. It was the car he liked best of any car, he who was hitchhiking because the battery on his Volkswagen, fifth-hand and dented, was dead. He whistled a whistle of admiration that could have been for it, or her, or both. At any rate, it caught her attention. She had lived in Italy. It wasn't the first whistle she had ever heard. She turned and looked at him. Zing went the strings of her heart.

"My, my. What a beautiful, uh, young lady," he said, seeing her, smiling at her, showing good white teeth, undulating his thumb westward, in the direction they were both heading.

She looked at him, and from the safety of her car she smiled back at him.

"Aren't you going to give this weary traveler a ride?" he asked her.

"My daddy told me never to pick up hitchhikers," she said, flirting, or at least matching his flirt, intonation and all.

"Why don't you make an exception to your daddy's rules?" he asked her, opening the door of her car and hopping in. "My name's Frankie. What's yours?"

"Hey, I wasn't kidding about picking up hitchhikers. Out of this car," she said. There was the first note of alarm in her voice.

"Oh, come on, rich girl. Give this poor boy a ride. I'm going to be late for work," he said. "My, this sure is a pretty car. I'm just going to the west gate of Bel Air."

The light turned green. "The light turned green," he said, pointing.

"I'm not moving until you get out of this car," said Cecilia.

"Come on," he said. "You got nothing to be afraid of. You look beautiful angry." He reached over and put his foot on the gas pedal and his hand on the steering wheel, and the Porsche moved forward. Cecilia slammed her foot on the brake, and the car stopped abruptly, her head hitting the steering wheel.

"Oh, my God," he said. "Did you hurt yourself?" He reached over and put his hand on her face.

"Hands off, hitchhiker, and back on the boulevard where you belong," she said, angry and scared, jerking her body away from his touch, the tone of her voice stinging.

"Hey, I'm sorry," he said, meaning it, understanding by the tone of her voice that she was somebody and he was nobody. "I'm sorry. Really I am. I thought the way you met my eyes before, you meant business."

"Well, you thought wrong," said Cecilia, her fright ebbing at the gentleness of his tone. She put her hand to her right eye where she had struck it against the steering wheel. Their eyes met, and there were tears in each.

"You're going to get a black eye," he said, backing out the door.

"That's going to make me real popular at home," she said.

"I'm sorry," he said once more, closing the door behind him, deeply troubled by what had happened. The white Porsche took off.

In the minutes that followed the young man felt wave after wave of shame flood through his body. Like a video tape that would not erase, he kept seeing himself as he thought she must have seen him. Even though the look in her eye had belied the tone of her voice, his feeling of shame would not settle. He was no one, and he never felt it more than at that moment. A part-time jobber, no more than that, a deliverer of telegrams, a parker of cars, a server of drinks, a cleaner of pools. And, on occasion, a seller of his flesh.

Shortly thereafter, the yellow Mercedes-Benz of Mona Berg, with the tape deck and the telephone and the license plate MS-MONA, headed west on Sunset Boulevard, with Mona at the wheel, on her way to Warren Ambrose's house for the meeting she had scheduled on agency business when her last-minute efforts to secure placement at the AFI dinner in honor of Rex Vaughan had failed. Her offer of herself in Warren's stead, trying to place herself where he would have been had he not continued to be incapacitated, had not been accepted.

Her mood was not pleasant. "Oh darling, if only I'd known last week, I'd have been able to arrange something," Dolores DeLongpre, who had known last week, had said to her, at the same time accepting some gossip of the prurient variety from her for her column. Grace St. George, the society publicist, the one who came up with the idea for the photograph in *People* magazine of Warren in the pool and Mona in the foreground, said she thought she could get Mona seated at Bonnie Rapp's table, Bonnie Rapp being the executive assistant to the vice president in charge of creative affairs at Atlantis Pictures, but Mona didn't want to sit at the table of the executive assistant to the vice president in charge of creative affairs at Atlantis, thank you very much, so she had a few hot words with the waitress in the coffee shop at the Beverly Wilshire Hotel when that unfortunate lady erred by bringing a sandwich on whole wheat rather than white, and she had a few more hot words for the parking boy in the garage of her office building when he did not give her priority over the people who were waiting ahead of her for their cars.

"I'm on my way, Warren," Mona said to Warren Ambrose on the car telephone. "I should be there in about fifteen minutes. So be ready and don't keep me waiting like last time."

Behind his back, she called him the veg, as in vegetable, which he wasn't, but it was hard for him to talk, and he had a tendency to moan out long sentences, which she had taken to finishing for him.

"I *am* in a bad mood. You're quite right," she said when she got the gist of what he was saying. "Everybody in town's going to the AFI dinner in honor of Rex Vaughan tonight, and I didn't get invited."

She always talked on the telephone when she drove. She liked the picture it presented of her to passing cars. When Warren was moaning on to her about what real troubles were, she spotted, sitting on a bench at a bus stop, the handsome young man she had met once before at the counter of Schwab's.

"Goodbye Warren," she said, hanging up right in the middle of one of his slow sentences, cutting across two lanes and pulling up to the curb.

The young man was so deep in thought that he seemed unaware of her for a moment. "Hey," she said. "Remember me? I gave you my pickle."

"Oh, yeah, Ms. Mona," he said, brightening up for the first time since the girl in the white Porsche had driven off. "I saw your picture in *People* magazine, and I read your name in Dolores DeLongpre's column a couple of times. I didn't realize you were such a big shot."

"Are you loitering or would you like a ride?" asked Mona. She loved to be thought of as a big shot.

"Sure, I'd like a ride," he said getting into her car. "I gotta bartend a party in Bel Air."

"You're a bartender now?" she asked.

"You name it, I do it," he said. "Jack of all trades. That's me." The car took off.

"I thought you wanted to be an extra," she said.

"You can't be an extra unless you're in the union, and you can't get in the union unless you've worked as an extra," said the young man, shrugging his shoulders at the illogic of it, at the same time looking over her car, the tape deck, the telephone, the luxury of it. "I like your license, Ms. Mona, and I sure do like this car."

The people Mona was always trying to impress already had what she had and didn't respond to the paraphernalia of success that she had acquired. It soothed her that he did. He stretched his hands behind his head, and leaned back into the new-smelling leather of the bucket seat.

"I sure do like that hair below your belly button," she said, matching his cadence about her car, looking him over, wanting to reach over and put her hand there.

He was used to having people saying things like that to him. There was something about him that said sex, that said he was available. He liked it that he turned people on. When they got that look on their face that he recognized so well, he almost always responded to what they wanted. It was his natural asset. It was what he had to give, or sell, as the case may be.

"I think I may have found myself a lady who likes to talk dirty," he said to her. "My name's Frankie, Ms. Mona, and dirty talk's one of my specialties."

Actually Mona was no stranger to hitchhikers. It was her way of meeting men. She only picked up the young ones who were peddling it, and it worked out most of the time. The aggressiveness that turned men off in her work life worked in her favor in these hitchhiking situations. Sometimes, if the trick didn't pick up right away that he was with Somebody Big, she would telephone her office and tell her secretary,

Bill, who was onto her ways, that if Miss Minnelli called, or Miss Vaughan, when she was still in the picture, that she could be reached at home, and it was all right to give out the unlisted number, but only to Miss Minnelli, or Miss Vaughan. Mona found it to be unfailing. More often than not, the encounters were once-only situations though. Mona had long since discovered about herself that, once the sexual curiosity was over, she had no curiosity at all about people who were not successful. A few bucks changed hands, and a fake telephone number, just the one digit off to make it useless, if the trick asked if she could arrange for an interview with a casting director.

"Did anyone ever tell you you're beautiful?" asked Mona.

"Yeah," said Frankie. "But it's not something you get tired of hearing. Thanks."

"How much do you get paid for bartending?"

"Sixty bucks for three hours, plus tip, usually, plus overtime. Why?" He looked at her as if he didn't know what she was going to say next.

"How about calling in sick?" said Mona, looking over at him, meeting his glance.

"What have you got in mind?" he asked.

"My place in the Hollywood Hills. I've got some good grass, some nice wine. I'll give you a check for what you're losing out on the job. Plus tip. How's it sound?"

"Sounds fine," said Frankie. Then he added, almost as an afterthought, "Except for the check. I'm not in that kind of business."

Mona made a U-turn on Sunset Boulevard, just at the West Gate, in the midst of late afternoon commuter traffic, oblivious to the horns and swearing that were aimed at her from other cars, and headed back to Hollywood.

"Excuse me," she said as she picked up her car telephone and gave the necessary numbers to the operator. "I have to call my office. Give me the number of that party where you're working. . . . Hello, darling, any messages? . . . Well, if Miss Minnelli calls back, it's all right to give out the private number, but only to Miss Minnelli. . . . And will you call the veg and tell him I can't make it this afternoon, that something has come up."

She looked over at Frankie and smiled.

"And call this number I'm about to give you and say the bartender can't make it."

Sylvia Lesky's dressing room was mirrored and marbled and splendid. Her clothes were catalogued and coordinated in such a way that her maid, Mae, who had been with her since before Cecilia was born, could tell at a glance what shoes, bag, and jewelry went with each of the dresses that hung on the department store racks in department store space behind the mirrored doors. Sylvia Lesky spent a lot of time in her dressing room. She was not vain in that she had illusions about her beauty, because she did not. Her looks were a disappointment to her and she learned early to make the most of them by never being less than perfect in matters of make-up and grooming and dress. Her style was something that was always commented on. When her name appeared in society columns, which it very often did, it was with adjectives like best-dressed and elegant and perfectionist, and to a certain kind of people in a certain kind of society those words had a special kind of beauty. Many of her friends, like Babette Navarro and Pearl Silver and Delphine Kahn, said about her, "I think Sylvia's beautiful," but their husbands didn't think so. "I think Sylvia Lesky gives the most superb dinner parties in this town," said Nando Navarro to his wife Babette, "but beautiful, no, I don't think she's beautiful."

Sylvia Lesky never liked to have more than one person working on her at a time. It made her nervous, she told Babette, when Blanchette was doing her nails at the same time Yushi was doing her hair, so Blanchette came in the morning and Yushi came in the afternoon. Yushi always knew who was going to wear what that evening, and conversation of that sort was about all she could cope with when she was distraught, which she was in the beginning stage of being. Cecilia had not returned from shopping.

"What's Elena Jamieson wearing tonight, Yushi?" she said.

"Yellow. Yves St. Laurent. . . . Copy," said Yushi, and they both laughed. Yushi was a Japanese, and the fashionable hairdresser of the moment, mostly because of Sylvia Lesky's devotion to him.

"Don't tell me that little old dressmaker in the Valley has come back into the picture," said Sylvia. "I could have told Elena how tight Reade really is. . . . Why don't you comb that back a little. Over the ear. Perfect."

Her maid Mae always knew when she was nervous about something, and usually knew what she was nervous about. She was hanging up the rose-colored Galanos she had just finished pressing. "Maybe she's playing tennis at the Bakers'," said Mae, who sometimes covered for Cecilia when relations were strained between the generations.

"I never understand why she prefers to play tennis at the Bakers' court when she has a perfectly good tennis court right here," said Sylvia, who knew she wasn't playing tennis at the Bakers'. "Did you call Giorgio's?"

"She left there at four," said Mae.

"I hope she at least bought a dress. The car's going to be

133

here in twenty minutes. Her father's going to be furious," said Sylvia, letting her nervousness show.

"You sound like you took a diet pill," said Mae.

"Careful. I'm not in the mood to be criticized. Call Van Cleef and see if she picked up my pearls," said Sylvia. "You don't think it's too Eva Peron, do you?" she went on to Yushi, about the hairstyle, cupping her hand around the chignon at the back of her neck, knowing it looked perfect.

"It looks perfect," said Yushi, but he saw her mind had gone on to something else. "What are you thinking?"

"I was wondering what to wear instead of the pearls. Where *is* she?" said Sylvia, the first suggesting the second to her again. "Her father will have the National Guard out."

Then Cecilia came home. They could hear the car in the courtyard outside. She had a remote control in her car so that she could open the gates from the car without having to announce herself over the security system speaker or wait for the guard with the gun and the Doberman Pinscher to open the gate for her.

"I hear her car. That's her," said Mae, who was as relieved as Sylvia, the fear of kidnapping having been instilled into the family and retainers as a very distinct possibility "in the lives of people like us."

"Where have you been, Cecilia?" said Mae to her, when she opened the front door. The limousine from the studio was pulling in. "Your father's on the warpath, and you're turning your mother into a nervous wreck. Why, Cecilia baby, you have a black eye!"

She did indeed have a black eye, although it was mostly masked by a pair of dark glasses, which masked also that she had been crying.

"Black eye!" called Sylvia from the top of the stairway. "Cecilia, come up here!" Cecilia walked upstairs, past her mother, into the dressing room, took off her dark glasses, and looked at herself in the mirror.

"Oh, Cecilia," said Sylvia, disappointment in her face and voice.

"What happened?" asked Mae.

"I fell down the stairs at the Bakers' tennis court," said Cecilia.

Marty Lesky walked into the dressing room through the door that connected with his dressing room. His black tie hung untied around his neck. He brought with him a sense of chill. "A likely story," he said to his daughter.

"It's true," said Cecilia, afraid of her father because of the circumstances.

"Mae, would you tie this?" said Marty about his untied tie, giving a signal to Sylvia to get rid of the hairdresser. Never talk in front of servants, except Mae of course, was one of the cardinal rules of the Lesky household.

"That will be all for tonight, Yushi," said Sylvia to the hairdresser. "I'm going to need you tomorrow. We're going somewhere, I don't remember where."

"Good night, Mrs. Lesky. Everybody," said the little Japanese hairdresser as he exited the room. When Mae finished tying the tie, she also left the room. There was a family silence, an estranged family silence.

"I hope that little Jap can keep his mouth shut," said Marty.

"Keep his mouth shut about what?" said Sylvia. "She fell down the stairs at the Bakers' tennis court. What's to gossip about that?"

"Shut up, Sylvia," said Marty.

"Don't tell me to shut up," said Sylvia. "Honestly, Cecilia, for a girl who's had every advantage."

"A little advantage goes a long way sometimes," said Cecilia.

"How did you get your black eye, Cecilia?" asked Marty, in a tone of voice that said game time was over.

"A hitchhiker I smiled at got into my car," said Cecilia.

"What?" said Sylvia, in a shocked tone.

"You heard me, Mother."

"Go on," said Marty.

"He gave me a black eye."

"I seem to have missed something here, Cecilia. What happened between the time you picked him up and the time he beat you up?"

"Not what's on your mind," said Cecilia.

"Do you think we should call the police?" said Sylvia.

"*No,*" said both Cecilia and Marty.

"Did he rape you?" asked Marty.

"Oh, my God!" said Sylvia.

"No he didn't rape me. Now back off," said Cecilia, with the same kind of quiet authority that her father had. "I'm a twenty-four-year-old woman, with an annulled marriage behind me, and I don't like being spoken to as if I were still playing in Tara behind the soda fountain."

The annulled marriage was a subject they rarely discussed, having collectively participated in a wrong decision. Gears changed when it came up, and each retreated.

"If I ever come face to face with that son of a bitch, I'll kill him," said Marty.

"You won't," said Cecilia. "N.O.C.D."

"What are we going to do about the AFI dinner?" said Sylvia. She had been brought up to think it was ladylike, aristocratic even, to never show what she was feeling.

"We're going to go. That's what we're going to do," said Marty. "Get someone to take her place," he went on, meaning Cecilia, who couldn't go with a black eye, and who never had really wanted to go anyway.

"For God's sake, Marty, who am I going to get at seven o'clock to be at the Century Plaza Hotel in evening dress in forty minutes? I couldn't even get *Yushi* to do that," said Sylvia Lesky, in the tone of voice she got with Marty when he asked her to do the impossible. "Oh, wait a minute. I have an idea. I know exactly who."

"Who?" asked Marty.

"That pushy what's-her-name," she said.

"What pushy what's-her-name?" asked Marty, who knew perfectly well who she meant as soon as she said it.

"With all the Gucci. Who works for Warren."

"Oh, Mona Berg. Perfect."

Chapter 14

MONA BERG took the handsome young man to her little house in Laurel Canyon in the Hollywood Hills. It was a house that she had grown ashamed of since her newfound success in the agency business. Other than Marty Lesky, who sometimes used it in the afternoons for assignations with starlets, she never brought any of her clients to it. It was an inexpensively built redwood and sliding glass structure, more undistinguished than ugly. Much of it was flashy in interior design, but it had, like Mona herself, a certain something that made it not unnoticeable. It wasn't that it was so bad as that Mona didn't think it was good enough. More and more she had started to talk about getting a new house one of these days in Beverly Hills.

"This is a nice place you got here," said Frankie, looking around.

"I'll be looking for a bigger place soon. So I can start to entertain," said Mona. In an exact imitation of Marina

138

Vaughan's elegant gesture, she lit a cigarette from her brand new Rigaud candle and settled back into the cushion of her chair. She was nervous. He could tell that right away, far less brash when they were out of her Mercedes and in her living room. The cigarette was marijuana, already rolled. She inhaled it deeply and handed it to Frankie.

"Think Liza Minnelli will call?" asked Frankie.

"Why on earth would Liza Minnelli call?" she asked, taking back the joint from him.

"You told your secretary to give her the unlisted number," he said.

"Oh, sharp ears, in addition to all his other attributes."

"I get turned on hearing about people like that," he said.

He could tell from the way she moved when she poured some wine that she didn't like her body and was holding herself in positions that would mask it. He was right. He was always right about things like that. She hated her body. She hated the excess of it. She always kept her slip on during sex. She explored the man's body, taking the aggressive role, because she felt that her body didn't invite exploration.

"You got any music?" he asked, taking a deep toke from the joint.

"Over there," she pointed.

He put on a Rod Stewart record and started to boogy to the music. He was graceful and sexy, and he knew it, and she knew it. He understood a lot about sex. The advantages that life had dealt him were minimal in regard to home and family and education, but there was a sexual availability about him that made his looks and body irresistible to a great many of those with whom he came into contact. He looked on it as his natural asset in life, and he always knew that it was going to take him to wherever he was going. He had never met the person to whom he could not respond sexually if there was something in it for him.

"Think I could ever be a movie star?" he said in a half-joking way as he continued to dance.

"What makes you think you could be a movie star?" she answered in a half-joking way also, feeling the marijuana, enjoying the sight of him dancing.

"Wait'll you see this body," he said. The white LaCoste shirt went over his head in one graceful pull, with an extra few seconds while the shirt covered his face for her to see the fantasy that he was creating. He dropped the shirt at her feet.

"Oh, yeah, take it off," she said, encouraging him.

"It gets better. Do you want to see more?" he asked.

"Oh, yeah," said Mona, completely engrossed in the scene before her. He took off his clothes in the kind of way that people have who take off their clothes several times a day to do just what they were soon going to be doing. He unbuttoned the fly buttons of his jeans with two hands, then pulled them down until they were at his feet, and then kicked them off. He wore white jockey shorts.

"Jesus," said Mona, marveling at his beautiful body.

"You ain't seen nothin' yet," he said.

He sank back into the sofa next to the chair where she was sitting. His legs were bent at the knees and spread apart. She was mesmerized.

"This is like the first scene of a porn film," she said.

"Funny you should say that," he said. He rubbed one hand on his private parts through the jockey shorts and twisted one of his nipples with the other.

"Jesus," she said again. When the head of his erection extended out of the top of his jockey shorts, Mona, in a frenzy, reached over, involving herself at last, and pulled the shorts

140

off him. She stared at the beauty of him. "My God," she said, kneeling into it. "It's a masterpiece." She was beside herself with ecstasy. It was the kind of adulation that he responded to.

"Let's go into the bedroom," he said, leading the way into her room, at ease in his nudity. He pulled down the covers, lay back on her sheets, hands behind his head, offering her the feast that she thought he was for her consumption. She was down to her slip. She started with his armpits, and went over to his neck, and kissed his throat and chest and nipples. She kissed down the front of him to his belly button and buried her face in the hair of his stomach.

"Take that big dick in your mouth, baby," he said to her, understanding that it was the way she liked to be talked to in this kind of circumstance. She did what he told her to do. She was proud of her oral accomplishments and liked to be complimented for the pleasure she was able to provide.

Then he reached out to her, pulled her down on the bed, and started to rub his hands on the inside of her thighs. It was the sort of thing that never happened to her. Usually she masturbated herself while the man lay back and she brought him to his pleasure. His big hand worked its way up her thigh and then started to play in the area of her moisting wetness. She was ecstatic with pleasure. She realized that she was having the greatest sexual experience of her life. He put his fingers into her. He put his tongue into her. He put his hands behind her knees, and lifted her up. Just as he was about to put his enormous penis into her, the telephone rang.

"I'm not going to answer it," she whispered. Her eyes drank in the sight of him mounting her. The telephone rang again.

"The service will pick it up after the third ring," she whispered. There was the left-out in her, as in being left out of things, that made it impossible for her to allow a telephone to ring, as if she might miss something. The telephone rang again. Even in the land of plenty, which she was then in more than she had ever been in her life, the lure of the ring was irresistible to her. He knew she was going to answer it.

"Say 'Hi' to Liza for me," he said.

"I'll get rid of who it is fast," she told him, "and then I'll take the phone off the hook. Hello?"

"Mona?"

"Yes?"

"It's Sylvia Lesky," said the deep-toned society woman voice. It was the kind of voice that thrilled Mona, for the sense of belonging that it conveyed.

"Oh," said Mona, unhinged at the turn of events.

"Have I caught you in the middle of something?"

"Oh, no, uh, Mrs. Lesky."

"Please call me Sylvia," said the voice of Sylvia Lesky, "especially as I'm about to ask you a favor."

"I hope I can help," said Mona on her end, her ear glued to the telephone, her eyes glued to that which had been about to enter her.

"Now I know this is terribly late notice," Sylvia Lesky went on, with the assurance in her voice of one who knew she was going to get what she wanted, "but Marty and I were wondering if you'd be a *marvelous* sport, and come and sit at our table tonight at the AFI dinner in honor of Rex Vaughan."

"Oh, is that tonight?" asked Mona, stalling, stalling the moment that was happening to her.

"You see," Sylvia went on, as if she were unaware of a hesitancy in the other's voice, taking her into her confidence,

142

"our daughter has had a little car accident and—"

"I hope it's nothing serious," said Mona.

"Well, actually, it's more embarrassing than serious. She has a black eye, and she can't go tonight, and that leaves an empty place at our table, and Marty's such a great admirer of yours, and the *marvelous* job you're doing for poor Warren, and we thought we'd take a chance to see if you'd join us at the last minute like this."

"The only thing is," said Mona, not sure what to say, "that I, uh, sort of—"

"It'll be Faye Converse, who's flown in from Rome especially for the night, and Amos and Marianna Swank, and some business friends of my husband's, Abe and Taffy Grossman, and the Navarros, and, oh yes, Warren Beatty," said Sylvia.

"Why, sure," said Mona, "I'd, uh, love to go." The Leskys, the Swanks, the Navarros: it was the group she longed to be in, the crème de la crème, as Dolores DeLongpre called them, a one in a million chance that might not come her way again.

"I knew I could count on you, Mona," said Sylvia.

"What time?" asked Mona.

"It's eight o'clock, at the Century Plaza Hotel, long dress. We're at table number one, right in front of the dais. If they give you any trouble at the door, just tell them you're at Marty Lesky's table. You are a darling, Mona, and I won't forget this," said Sylvia, signing off, having talked right through any objections that might have been lurking in Mona's mind, a woman who understood exactly the power of her position in the town, and the lure that it was to people on the make, no matter what they happened to be doing at the time.

"I'm sorry," she said to Frankie. "Something's come up."

"Something's gone down, too," he said, wounded that he had not been her priority at such a moment.

"Let me explain," she said, reaching out to touch him, but he pulled away from her.

"What are you going to do? Lay some big names on me to make it all right?" he said. He walked back into the living room for his clothes. "What's the number for the taxi?"

"That lady happens to be the wife of one of the most important men in Hollywood, and it's a big deal for her to ask me. It could make a big difference in my career. Her daughter got a black eye in a car accident and can't go out in public," Mona went on, offering explanations that would have seemed logical to her in his place.

"Spare me the problems of the very, very rich," he said, angry at the rebuff, not connecting the connections.

He was angry. The whole day had been a rotten one for him. He didn't have rent money. He'd behaved in a way that had shown him at his worst in front of a young girl in a white Porsche, whose sense of class and breeding overwhelmed him. He'd tossed over the bartender's job that would have given him enough money to meet his rent, at least in part, because he thought something better came along, in the person of Miss Mona Berg, and he'd performed like he was in a porno flick for that large lady, thinking of his betterment, only to be thrown over at the moment of entry by a telephone call that superseded him in importance.

"Can't we get together tomorrow?" Mona asked him, not understanding his not understanding.

He lifted his leg, orphan asylum fashion, and let a fart in her direction, of the short raspberry variety. Mona was street too, a different kind of street, but street nonetheless, and she understood the meaning of his fart. He thought he was a bigger draw than the Leskys' table at the AFI dinner, and she wasn't *ever* going to get another chance with him. He didn't say the words—the-fat-lady-blew-it—he let his fart say it for him.

"Are you an actor?" she said, formulating an idea, wanting to have her cake and eat it too, wanting to go to the party, and wanting to have him stay there and wait for her.

"You going to offer me a movie, is that it?" he said in the tone of one not wanting to deal with any more bullshit. "Kick me over that pair of jockey shorts."

"No, I'm serious. Are you an actor?"

"Why?"

"Do you know about *South Sea Adventures*?"

"Nation-wide-search-for-a-new-young-star, you mean?"

"The guy who's the executive producer of that is going to be at my table tonight, right now, at the Century Plaza Hotel, and I'll get you a reading. That's not a bad make-up present, is it?" she said.

"You didn't let me tell you if I was an actor or not," he said. "Would you give me my jockey shorts please."

"I don't want to give you your jockey shorts."

"Come on," he said, snapping his fingers, sick of her game.

"Don't snap your fingers at me. I'll buy the fucking shorts from you."

"Hundred bucks."

"Sold."

"Cash only."

"You didn't have to say cash only. You already won the point."

"I was in a fuck flick once, and they told me I had star quality. If that means I'm an actor, yeah I'm an actor."

"That's not what they're looking for on the back of an eight-by-ten glossy."

"My friend Rusty had a reading for *South Sea Adventures.* He tricked with someone, and they gave him a reading," said Frankie.

"Not with Abe Grossman he didn't trick!" said Mona.

Frankie shrugged.

"What about it?" he asked.

"What about what?"

"You want me to stay and wait for you?"

"Yes, I want you to stay and wait for me."

"And you're going to get me a reading for *South Sea Adventures?*"

"Striking a bargain, are we?"

"You bet your ass, Ms. Mona. I want the reading."

"I'll speak to Abe Grossman."

"That doesn't give you any discount on the jockey shorts."

"That's class."

"Look who's talking about class!"

"There's something about you, Frankie, that's very attractive."

"So I've been told."

"What's your last name?"

"Bozzaci."

"We're going to have to do something about that."

"You got food in the ice box?"

"There's a steak. Help yourself."

"Where's the thing for the TV?"

"Right here. And the grass is here. And the ice is there. And in case I didn't say it before, I think you're the most beautiful man I ever saw in my life."

Chapter 15

IT WAS THE PLACE TO BE. The grand ballroom of the Century Plaza Hotel, on the Avenue of the Stars, in Century City. There were all manner of charity events in the film community in the course of the year, but the American Film Institute dinner was the one that year after year commanded the attendance of the establishment. The American Film Institute's Life Achievement Award went every year to an individual "whose talent has in a fundamental way advanced the film-making art; whose accomplishments have been acknowledged by scholars, critics, professional peers, and the general public; and whose work has stood the test of time," as Charlton Heston said in his introductory remarks before Rex Vaughan entered the mobbed ballroom. High praise indeed for Rex Vaughan and his fifty-two films, elevating him to the ranks of filmland nobility, as Dolores DeLongpre called it, of such previous recipients as James Stewart, Orson Welles, Bette Davis, Henry Fonda, James Cagney and Dom Belcanto.

"Hello Audrey," people said to Audrey Hepburn. "Hello Fred," people said to Fred Astaire. "Hello Ingrid," people said to Ingrid Bergman. "Hello Elizabeth," people said to Elizabeth Taylor. "Hello Greg," people said to Gregory Peck. "Hello Barbra," people said to Barbra Streisand. Hello Cary. Hello Kirk. Hello Ronnie. Hello Nancy. Hello. Hello. Hello.

"They're all here tonight" was a line said over and over again, from table to table, with pride in the voice saying it, for being in the right place at the right time with the right people, and for only five hundred dollars a ticket.

"There's Billy Wilder." "There's Vincente Minnelli." "There's George Cukor." "There's Dick Zanuck." "There's Lew Wasserman." "There's Marty Lesky." "There's Barry Diller." "There's Ray Stark." "There's Robbie Slick."

"They're all here tonight."

"For Rex Vaughan, you know. Everyone loves Rex."

"I'm so glad they're giving it to Rex Vaughan when he's still young enough to appreciate it."

"Remember poor Hitch that year. More dead than alive."

"When does Rex come in?"

"Not until everyone is seated."

"Look, there's Princess Grace."

"Everyone loves Rex."

"There's Robert Redford. He never goes anywhere."

"For Rex Vaughan. Everyone turned out for Rex Vaughan."

"Where's Cecilia?" people asked Sylvia Lesky over and over, about her shy and elusive daughter whose appearance had been promised by her mother at the glittering event.

"Oh, she wanted to come *so* much," Sylvia said over and over, "but she had a car mishap this afternoon and bruised her eye." She couldn't bring herself to say that her daughter had a black eye. "I managed to get Warren Ambrose's new partner to fill in. She's called Mona Berg and she'll be along soon."

"The tables look marvelous, Sylvia," people said over and over about the silver lamé tablecloths and the rubrum lily centerpieces that had been her idea.

"Thank you, darling," said Sylvia over and over.

"Nobody does it like you do, Sylvia."

"Thank you, darling." It was one of the things she was good at, planning this sort of evening, and she liked it when her details were noticed. She enjoyed social life and was better than her husband at concealing the annoyance they both felt with Cecilia for the affront her behavior was to the picture of family solidarity they would have liked to present.

"Congratulations, Sylvia, the room looks beautiful," said Marina Vaughan.

"Thank you, Marina," said Sylvia Lesky.

"Where's Cecilia?" asked Marina.

"She had a slight car mishap this afternoon."

"I just saw her this afternoon."

"It must have been later."

"Is she all right?"

"She bruised her eye."

"Give her my love."

"Hello, Marina," said Marty Lesky, offering his hand, observing the amenities, as if *The Green Hat* episode was not a factor in their lives.

"Hello, Marty," replied Marina, observing the amenities in turn.

"Where's your father?"

"He's still upstairs. They bring him in with fanfare when we all sit down."

"Is he nervous?"

"You know Daddy. He's never nervous. I'm nervous. I have to sing."

For Marina Vaughan it was the night her life started to fall apart in Hollywood. She had on a new white dress and wore gardenias in her hair, and people complimented her on the smartness of her look. It was her first time out since the story had circulated about her that she had lost the lead in *The Green Hat* because she was taking too much cocaine, and she wondered if people were talking about her. It was an evening she would have skipped gladly if the recipient of the award had not been her father. She would have treated herself to two weeks in Oregon, and licked her wounds, and then come back and gone into action again. But it was for her father, whom she loved, and with whom she shared a complicated and deep relationship. She co-starred in a movie with him when she was eleven, and she called him when she found her suicided mother when she was twelve. She knew about what he did in his private time, and that was all right with her, and he knew what she did in her private time, and that was all right with him. They were adults together, albeit Hollywood movie star adults.

"Hello, Marina."

"Hello, Robbie," she said, kissing the studio head Robbie Slick on the cheek. "Do you find it as hard as I do not to keep running into old lovers at all these parties?"

They both laughed. They had had a well-publicized affair a few years before. "The other night I was somewhere where there were three at the same table." They laughed again.

"Maybe you should move to the Valley," said Robbie.

"Probably wouldn't help."

"What are you working on?"

"Maybe I'll do a picture in Morocco," said Marina.

150

"What picture?" asked Robbie.

"Uh, the King of Morocco's brother told me they'd finance any picture I wanted to do there," she said.

"Not bad auspices," said Robbie.

"Of course, we'd had a couple of stingers at the time," said Marina.

Mona Berg stood at the entrance of the ballroom, dressed in a caftan that Bill, her secretary Bill, had picked out for her at Lane Bryant on her last birthday, surveying the dazzling sight of over a thousand rich and famous people.

"May I see your ticket?" said an attendant to her.

"I don't have a ticket," said Mona. "I—"

"I'm sorry," said the attendant, not knowing he was about to be withered. "This is a private party."

"I'm a guest of Mr. and Mrs. Marty Lesky," she said in measured tones, as if she were saying, I'm a guest of Mr. and Mrs. John D. Rockefeller. It had the same effect, as she knew it would.

"Oh, of course, excuse me," said the flustered young man. "The Leskys are at table number one. That one there, where Marina Vaughan is standing."

She made her way through the room, looking at this one, looking at that one. The stars. The moguls. The society ladies. The dresses. The jewels. Past Bonnie Rapp's table, where she had declined to sit. Past Grace St. George's table. Past Dolores DeLongpre's table. Deeper into the center of the room. Her heart was beating fast. She was arriving at where she always wanted to be. The vortex.

"Oh, my God," said Marina Vaughan.

"What?" asked Robbie Slick.

"What's she doing here?"

"Who?"

"Mona Berg, that's who," said Marina. As she turned away abruptly, so as not to have to speak to her, she collided with a waiter who spilled a glass of red wine on her new white dress.

"Damn," said Marina.

"I'm sorry, ma'am," said the waiter.

"My fault," said Marina. "Waiter?"

"Would you like a wet towel, Miss Vaughan?"

"No, I'd like a martini."

"Uh, Sylvia?" said Mona, arriving at the table where Sylvia was engaged in conversation with Babette Navarro.

"Oh, hello Mona," said Sylvia Lesky. "I'm so glad you were free to fill in like this. Marty, Mona's here."

"This is awfully nice of you, Mona, coming on such short notice," said Marty.

"I've never seen so many famous people in my life," said Mona.

"Let me introduce you to all these people. This is Perry Rifkin," said Sylvia, who had a knack for introducing.

"Oh, the famous decorator," said Mona to the tall, slender, epicene man who did not bother to look at her when he shook her hand.

"And Mr. Beatty, Miss Berg. And Babette Navarro. And Amos Swank. May I present Mona Berg. And this is—"

"How could Sylvia Lesky invite that woman to sit at her table?" said Marina Vaughan. "Pour some of that vodka in here, will you, Robbie?"

"You're drinking too much," said Robbie.

"Shut up and pour, darling."

Mona Berg had never been one who agreed with the old adage that flattery will get you nowhere. If she had heard it at all, she would have substituted everywhere for nowhere. It was a thing she was good at, paying compliments to people, but a shrewd observer like Sylvia Lesky would have noted she paid compliments only to important people. Sylvia, who had been born at the top, knew a climber when she saw one, and she watched her last-minute fill-in work the table and then work the room during the social part of the evening, before the speeches and the film clips and entertainment. She saw a little bit of the early Marty in her, and she saw a lot of the early Warren Ambrose in her. "Only more," she said to her friend Babette Navarro about her.

Mona told Babette Navarro she thought she was one of the best-dressed women in Hollywood, which is what Babette Navarro wanted to hear. She told Perry Rifkin she loved the pictures of the house he'd decorated for Jaclyn Smith in the new issue of *Architectural Digest,* which is what he wanted to hear. She told Pearl Silver she was an admirer of her late husband's films. "No one could make movies about rich people the way Mattie Silver could make movies about rich people," she said to Pearl, and Pearl was visibly touched. She told Sylvia Lesky that the freshly restored commissary at Colossus, which restoration Sylvia had supervised to make it look the way it had been during her father's reign there, should be in every textbook on the history of Hollywood, "so important a room do I think it is." She told old Delphine Kahn that she thought her dress was the prettiest in the room, after overhearing Babette Navarro tell Perry Rifkin it was "that same old blue Balenciaga Delphine's been wearing for the last twenty years." She told Faye Converse she thought she was the quintessential movie star. She told Taffy Grossman, the wife of Abe Grossman of the Grossman-Dragonet Grossmans, that she had the most beautiful hands she'd ever seen. And she told Abe Grossman she thought he was the finest producer in television, and Abe Grossman, who was surely the most successful producer on television, having created an empire, controlling hours of prime time, never received a compliment on quality, only quantity, and was absurdly flattered, as she meant him to be. It was he, together with his partner Jess Dragonet, who was producing the series *South Sea Adventures* that she promised Frankie Bozzaci she would get him a reading for.

"Did you read the plug I gave *South Sea Adventures* in my column, Abe?" asked Dolores DeLongpre, table-hopping as she was, picking up items for her column on life in the film capital. "I said it was the biggest talent hunt for a new discovery since Scarlett O'Hara in *Gone With the Wind.*"

"I think every actor in America read it, Dolores," said Abe, almost wearily. "We've had to stop seeing people. They all start to look alike after a while."

"Then put me on your selection committee, Abe," said Dolores. "I never get tired of looking at beautiful young men."

The cue. The perfect cue. As if it had been rehearsed.

"*Speaking* of beautiful young men," interjected Mona, who had ears in every direction, and who minutes before had established her credentials by telling Abe she thought he was the finest producer in television, "I just signed a new actor today who would be *perfect* for the part."

"It's too late, Mona. We're only going to test ten actors out of the thousand we've interviewed, and we've already decided who the ten are going to be," said Abe, putting an end to the matter, sick to death of the topic.

She wasn't going to be put off, and persisted with her entreaty. "Just meet him at least," she said.

"Ladies and gentlemen, the recipient of this year's American Film Institute's award, Rex Vaughan," said Charlton Heston, at the podium, over the public address system, and it was a signal that the festivities were to start.

"She don't let up, that one," whispered Abe Grossman to Pearl Silver about Mona Berg.

For Rex Vaughan, it was a night of laughter and tears, kisses from former leading ladies who came up to the podium to tell their stories about him, and bear hugs from former directors who did the same. It was an occasion of *hommage* to a film star, popular in the industry, in recognition for the totality of the accomplishments of his career.

Throughout it all, the several hours of it, Mona never let up for a second in the let-your-presence-be-known interpretation of life. She was the first at her table to identify each film clip, no matter how remote the film was, and some of them were very remote, especially from Rex Vaughan's down-and-out period before his spectacular comeback in one of Marty Lesky's pictures. She knew the name of the picture, the director, and the year. She was the first one on her feet to lead the crowd in standing ovations for Faye Converse and Audrey Hepburn and Ingrid Bergman, clapping with her hands far out in front of her for the film buff she wished to establish herself as being. It was a source of almost continual annoyance to Marina Vaughan when the wide-figured lady in the Lane Bryant caftan leapt to her feet, and occasioned more drinking.

"They'll think you're on cocaine if you don't eat anything," said Rex Vaughan to Marina. They were sitting side by side at the center of the horseshoe table.

"I don't like to eat before I sing," said Marina, taking another drink.

"You used not to like to drink before you sang."

"Oh, Daddy, don't you start. If it weren't for her, I'd be playing the lead in *The Green Hat.*"

"It gives that woman power for you to allow her to upset you that much."

One of the delights of the evening was the surprise appearance of Faye Converse, all silver-foxed and black-satined, wearing diamonds from her turban to her toes, back in the town where she had started, after years of living abroad, for her old friend Rex Vaughan. There was always excitement about Faye Converse. She was a much loved star. Her fifth marriage had ended, the one she once told Dolores De-Longpre was the one that was going to last, to Sir Adrian Bailley, the Irish actor, and the AFI dinner was the excuse that she needed to bring her back to Hollywood, to stick her foot in again to see if she liked the temperature was the way she put it to Sylvia Lesky. Sylvia decided then and there, at the table, to give a party for her on the thirtieth, to welcome her home properly. Faye gave a speech for Rex Vaughan, her old co-star in several pictures, with whom she'd been under contract in the old days at Colossus, when old Marcus Meyer was still running the show.

"And now here's my old friend and god-daughter, Marina Vaughan, to sing for us," said Faye Converse from the podium, having given her speech, having told the story about Monty Clift dropping Marina at her christening, and there was great applause. "With special lyrics written especially for the occasion by Marina herself," Faye Converse went on, and there was more applause. "Marina, where are you?"

As Marina rose from her seat, a spotlight picked her up and followed her as she moved through the tables to the stage, where her accompanist sat at a piano. As she ascended the stairs, she missed the top step and almost tripped. There was a murmur in the crowd, and a feeling of relief as she collected herself and proceeded to the microphone. It was apparent that she was drunk.

"That's what I meant," whispered Mona Berg to Marty Lesky, happy at the proof positive that Marina was beginning to act out in front of them some of the things that she had told Marty about Marina. Things often worked out that way for Mona.

The accompanist played the introduction to the song entitled "Rex" for Marina to sing to her father. She made a false start and then began again, and then faltered again shortly into the verse.

"I can't see the damn TelePrompTer," said Marina, holding her hands to shield her eyes.

"What's that on her dress?" whispered Babette Navarro.

"That light's right in my eyes," said Marina.

"She spilled red wine all over herself," whispered Mona Berg.

"Would you roll it back please," said Marina.

"She's drunk in front of the whole industry," said Robbie Slick.

"Do you remember when her mother did this at the Academy Awards?"

" 'He's the man of the moment, the star of the year, the face of the decade, but he's my daddy dear,' " sang Marina, in a faltering start.

"If Marty ever does a remake of *The Razor's Edge,* she'd be great for the Anne Baxter part," whispered Mona. "Wouldn't have to rehearse."

"God almighty," said Rex Vaughan.

"I've lost my place," said Marina, a note of panic in her voice. "I don't know where the hell I am. Can you start back at the beginning of the verse? Harold, give me a note."

The room was in silence. No one knew what to do. There were tears in Rex Vaughan's eyes. Then Faye Converse appeared at Marina's side. She put her arm around Marina's waist to steady her and with the other hand pointed to the TelePrompTer.

"Now there it is there, darling, do you see?" said Faye, pointing to the lyrics on the TelePrompTer. "Now come on, Marina, you can do it. 'He's Rex to the masses. And Rexy to some. His name is on billboards. But to me—'"

Marina got hold of herself and joined Faye Converse in completing the song, for the moment turning the incident into an act of show business recovery. At the completion of the song, the entire audience rose in relief, and the applause was deafening. Faye continued to hold her arm around Marina's waist and acknowledged the applause and blew kisses to Rex Vaughan.

"Thanks for saving my life," said Marina to Faye.

"What are godmothers for, darling?" she said, waving to the audience. "I think you should see Mercedes McCambridge."

"About what?" asked Marina.

"AA," said Faye.

"I just didn't have any lunch today. I'm not—"

The evening was over. People were leaving, gathering up programs, kissing good night. Babette Navarro couldn't find her gold minaudier and wondered if Dolores Delongpre had taken it. Taffy Grossman took home a centerpiece of rubrum lilies. Old Delphine Kahn drained her glass of scotch.

"It was nice of you to fill in on such short notice," said Marty Lesky to Mona Berg.

"I had a wonderful time," gushed Mona.

"Let me know if I can ever do anything for you," said Marty.

"Like what?" said Mona, quick on the uptake.

"Open any doors, that sort of thing," said Marty.

"There is something," said Mona.

"You don't waste any time, do you?" said Marty, surprised that she took him up so quickly. "What is it?"

"Abe Grossman told me your studio's going to test ten actors next week for the lead in *South Sea Adventures*," said Mona.

"That's right," said Marty.

"Test eleven," said Mona.

"We can't do that."

"Why not?"

"Because we can't."

"You said to let you know if you could do anything for me," said Mona.

"But that's all decided on," said Marty.

"It's not going to cost any more. The set's built. The director's hired. The crew will be standing by."

"Who's the guy?"

"Somebody brand-new. Just arrived from New York. I have a gut instinct about this guy, Marty," said Mona.

"What kind of gut instinct?"

"Star."

"Do you know how many times I've heard that one, Mona?"

"Not from me you haven't."

"I'll meet him. What's his name?"

She couldn't remember his name, so she pressed on. "I want you to do more than meet him, Marty. I want you to test him."

Shades of his early self were what he saw in her. "Okay. We do eleven tests," he said, smiling. "What's this guy's name? You got me fascinated."

"Yang ran over my Basset hound," said Sylvia Lesky to Pearl Silver, about her chauffeur and her dog.

"Bassett. Frankie Bassett. Franklyn Bassett, actually, l-*y*-n," said Mona, leaping at the name.

"Call me tomorrow. We'll set it up," said Marty.

"When's your party for Faye Converse?" said Pearl Silver to Sylvia Lesky.

"On the thirtieth. I'll send you a reminder card," said Sylvia.

"Good night, Mona," said Marty.

Chapter 16

MONA BERG wasn't at all the sort of person who used words like yoo-hoo to announce that she was home, but yoo-hoo she used when she returned to the little house in Laurel Canyon that night.

The newly named Franklyn Bassett, with just a towel around his waist, was watching Joan Crawford and John Garfield in *Humoresque*, right at the end, where Joan Crawford was walking into the sea to drown, scored by a hundred studio musicians. His attention was total. Joan Crawford was Mona Berg's favorite movie star, so she postponed for a moment taking over the scene, her announcements of great import not taking priority over Joan Crawford's suicide over unrequited love.

"What's Joan Crawford crying about?" said Mona.

"She's this rich lady who helps out this musician from the slums. She falls in love with him, but he doesn't fall in love with her," said Frankie, recounting the plot.

"No wonder she's taking a late-night dip," said Mona, flicking off the set. "Hi darling. Ms. Mona's home."

"You're in a good mood," he said. "How was the party?"

"Well, as Dolores DeLongpre said, all the glitterati were there."

"Like who?" he said. "I like to hear about famous people."

"Shall we start with Marina Vaughan?" she said, with anticipatory relishment.

"I love Marina Vaughan. You know, I once cleaned her . . ." started Frankie, but he let it drift off. He already knew it, and what she was going to tell him he didn't know.

"She was sooo drunk."

"No."

"Singing her drunk little heart out," said Mona, getting into the story that she would perfect with subsequent tellings into a classically funny drunk story that did nothing but diminish further the declining fortunes of Marina Vaughan. " 'I can't see the damn TelePrompTer,' " she mimicked, with acute accuracy taken a few steps further to the funny side of ridicule, so that even the former pool cleaner, who'd once fucked her brains out, as he later told his friend Rusty, had to laugh. " 'The light's right in my eyes. Take it from the top, will you, Harold? Oh, Rexy,' and then she tripped and fell, I swear on my mother's life. You can read all about it in Dolores DeLongpre's column tomorrow."

"I'd like to go to places like that," said Frankie after she listed the names of all the famous people who were there. "I'd like to see all those people. I bet I will someday."

"Maybe sooner than you think," said Mona, having saved the best for the last.

"What do you mean?" said Frankie. "Did you get me a reading?"

162

"No," said Mona, playing out her moment.

"No?" said Frankie, this not being the first disappointment he'd ever had to contend with.

"No. I got you a screen test."

"A screen test?"

"You heard me, a screen test. Ever since I worked in Holly-wood, I've been hearing how the biggies put together deals at parties. They all know each other. They've all got the goods on each other. And they all do business together, like a private club closed to outsiders, like a goy trying to get into Hillcrest. So I decided not to waste my debut in high society on mere chitchat. And I got you a guaranteed screen test! I went right over the head of Mr. Abe Grossman to Mr. Marty Lesky himself," said Mona, hands out in mime, as if presenting him with an enormous gift-wrapped package.

"How do you know I can act?" he asked, his body relaxing into the good feelings that were flooding it.

"I just have this feeling about you," she said, looking at him, stretched out on her sofa, hands behind his head. "I have from the minute I first saw you." The towel around the middle of him began to lift in the air from the erecting penis beneath it, from the words of recognition that she spoke. "Well, what have we here?" she asked, lifting the towel, exposing the presence.

"It's what's called a token of my appreciation," he said, taking hold of it in his hand, fondling it for her viewing pleasure, as he said.

"Jesus, Frankie," she said, wet with desire to touch it.

"Why don't you get out of the muumuu?" he whispered.

"Why don't you stop calling it a muumuu? It's a caftan," she said, shy about her imperfect nakedness in the presence of his perfect nakedness.

"Why don't you get out of it, whatever you call it. I want to thank you for my screen test."

Later, after she had reached her contentment for the first time in her life, she lay back in her bed and watched him as he dried himself after a shower.

"How immodest," she said, covering her eyes in mock Jane Austen fashion.

"I like to be naked," he said. "I feel good naked."

"You look good naked," she said.

"You know something, Mona? I always knew something like this was going to happen to me. I've been waiting for it."

"It hasn't happened yet."

"An arrangement for a screen test for me has happened. Where I've been, that's big progress, or my name isn't Frankie Bozzaci."

"Oh," said Mona, snapping her fingers as if remembering something.

"What?" asked Frankie.

"Your name. It isn't Frankie Bozzaci. At least it isn't anymore."

"What are you talking about?"

"I couldn't remember what your name was tonight, after I got you the screen test, so I made up one."

"What?"

"Bassett. Franklyn Bassett—l-y-n Franklyn."

"That sounds classy. How'd you think of that name?"

"Don't ask," she said.

Later, when he was scrambling some eggs in her kitchen, he said, "Wait until they hear about this at St. Joe's," meaning about what was happening to him.

"What's St. Joe's?" asked Mona.

"St. Joseph's Home for Boys, in Chicago. That's where I grew up."

"Wayward boys?" asked Mona.

"Some wayward. Some from broken homes. I was a little of both," he said.

"That's not what they're going to want to hear on the screen test," said Mona, all business again. "In addition to a new name, I'm going to have to give you a new history."

"We got a lot of work ahead of us, Ms. Mona."

Franklyn Bassett was a quick study. He was into any kind of improvement, and Mona Berg seemed to know just what to do in order to bring off what she had in mind for him, in the way of image to project. The secret of their relationship was that she saw in him a potential that he wasn't really aware of, except as an unfocused kind of muffled thunder. She changed his hair; she sent him to Little Joe, the barber of the stars, to get just the right look. She changed his clothes; she sent him to Dorso, the tailor of the stars, to get just the right look. She got him an acting coach. She had him take sailing lessons and tennis lessons. She renamed him and she rehistoried him. The only thing that he wouldn't do was cap his teeth. He said he didn't want to look like Erik Estrada. What he didn't want to do was monkey around, as he put it, with the way God had put him together. She knew he was right the minute he said it and conceded the point. She got her teeth capped instead, which was probably what she had in mind in the first place. She had fallen hopelessly, madly, in love with him.

The day after the AFI dinner she wrote Sylvia Lesky a thankful thank-you note for having included her at such an illustrious occasion, as she put it, on her brand new stationery that had just arrived from Tiffany's with her name engraved across the top.

"What's the point of spending all that money for engraving

if you cross a line through your name?" asked Bill, her secretary Bill.

"That's what all those people do," answered Mona, not particularly interested in the whys and wherefores of the customs of polite society, only in conforming to what was established. She included the note in a floral arrangement that was too expensive for the circumstances, but noticeable enough to elicit comment.

"Who sent *that?*" said Cecilia Lesky to her mother. "It looks like something for a gangster's funeral."

"Mona Berg, that's who, your replacement for the evening," said Sylvia, "and, oh, God, she wants me to have lunch with her," she went on, using her give-those-people-an-inch-and-they-take-a-mile voice. "Don't you *hate* red and white carnations?"

"Why don't you give them to the watchman? His wife's in the hospital," said Cecilia.

Mona became a great writer of notes, of the condolence or congratulatory variety, to people whose attention she wanted to attract. She wrote to a studio head whose brother had died in a fire. She wrote to a famous director whose picture had flopped, saying she'd loved the film, as if she saw in it the director's vision that the critics missed. She was put out when the famous director ignored her note.

"Why actually did you write to him that you loved the movie when you told me you thought it was a piece of shit?" asked Bill.

"What do you mean?" asked Mona, knowing perfectly well what he meant.

"You know perfectly well what I mean. What did you want to get out of the letter? Did you want Eddie Dietrick as a client?"

166

"Of course I don't want that old grouch for a client. He hasn't had a successful picture for ten years."

"Then why did you write the letter?"

"I wanted to get invited to one of his Saturday night beach parties I'm always reading about in Dolores DeLongpre's column."

"Did you ever stop to think he might have figured that out, beneath all your adoration for his film?"

"At least Robbie Slick sent me a fire detection unit when I wrote him after his brother died in the fire."

When she was snubbed, she didn't recognize it, and spoke to the people who had snubbed her as if they might not have seen her. One day she passed Pearl Silver on the street, and Pearl pretended she didn't see her.

"Hello, Pearl," she called out after Pearl feigned interest in something in a shopwindow.

"Hellohowareyou?" Pearl said, all as one word, and didn't call her by name.

Later she worked it into a conversation that she'd run into Pearl Silver that day on Rodeo Drive as if it had been a pleasant encounter. She knew about the art of persistence. She knew it would pay off.

After her teeth were capped, she got a new hairstyle and went on a diet and began to pay more attention to her clothes. She worked just as hard and just as tough, but there was a glow about her that had not been present before. She injected a note of humor into her dealings that took the sting out of her toughness.

"Listen, Laddie," she said on the telephone one day to the head of a production company about a new star she was representing, "I'm asking two million, take it or leave it, plus ten percent of the gross, take it or leave it, plus six round-trip first-class tickets to Paris on the Concorde, for the nanny and the children . . . And goodbye to you too. He hung up."

"A little piggish, weren't you, Miss Piggy?" said Bill, who was fascinated by the progress his old friend Mona was making in her life.

"It makes them talk about you when they yell and holler and hang up the phone," said Mona.

"He must be having plenty to say right now," said Bill.

"He'll call back. I've got an instinct about these things. And meet Jane's price. Besides, there's nobody else available. Now, listen, sis," said Mona.

"Don't call me sis," said Bill. "I don't like to be called sis."

"And I don't like to be called Miss Piggy. Get it?" said Mona.

"Got it," said Bill. "I'm sorry, Mona."

"Okay. Now, who called?"

"Dolores DeLongpre called while you were on the telephone to see if you had any dirt for her, and to tell you that Marina Vaughan got busted for drunken driving last night, and they called from Dorso to say that Frankie's new clothes are ready, and your mother called from the home again, and said you haven't been to see her, and Patrick said he wouldn't be able to let you have the table you asked for because it's already booked but he has a nice table for you on the other side, and—"

"You call him back, and you tell him that my luncheon guest is Mrs. Marty Lesky, and he'll make it available. Who else called?"

"Jess Dragonet's office called to say the screen test for *South Sea Adventures* is going to be Thursday, and he's sending over the test scene today, and Frankie called—"

"Why didn't you put him through?" interrupted Mona.

"You were talking to Marty Lesky at the time," said Bill.

"What do you think of Frankie, Bill?" asked Mona.

"He's beautiful."

"Do you like him?"

"Yeah, I like him. Do you love him?"

"I can't stop thinking about him. I can't stop looking at him. Every inch of his body fascinates me. I never had this feeling in my whole life," said Mona.

"I think you could call that love," said Bill, "with a heavy overtone of lust."

"I never had a lover before. Only tricks. Guys run away from tough girls like me," said Mona.

"How does he feel?" asked Bill.

"I don't know. He's fun, and he's sexy, but I'd be kidding myself if I didn't admit that it's the screen test that's turning him on," said Mona. It was rare that she was so open about herself. If the telephone hadn't rung, she might have talked more.

"Miss Berg's office," said Bill. "Just a minute please." He pushed the hold button. "It's Laddie."

"Laddie?" she said.

"As in two-million-dollars, take-it-or-leave-it, Laddie," said Bill.

"*That* Laddie. I told you he'd call back."

Frankie and Mona. Mona and Frankie. She was right, of course. It was the screen test that was turning him on. Her inner feelings told her that she could not hold on to him if it was just the two of them, in a one-to-one relationship. She took him to screenings to see new films. She took him to the kind of restaurants that he had only read about. She did everything she could to impress him with the importance of her, and the things she was going to do for him. It was the only way she could think of to hang on to him.

Mona Berg and Sylvia Lesky were at the good table at Ma Maison, the one she wanted in the first place, the one that Patrick told Bill wouldn't be available, the one right near the entrance where everyone could see her. Sylvia Lesky was used to being used, and allowed it to happen in certain cases, like this one, to pay back a favor.

"I don't usually go out to lunch," said Sylvia, as if saying that it was a first-and-last-time event that they were participating in, "but I was so appreciative to you for filling in at the last minute the other night, that I couldn't say no. My chef gets awfully angry when I go out to lunch."

"Well, any time," said Mona, overlooking the distance that was being placed between them. "It was a wonderful evening, except for Marina, of course. It's really tragic what's happening to Marina, isn't it? Marty must be thanking his lucky stars he had the good sense not to use her in *The Green Hat.*"

Sylvia Lesky had had plenty to say on the subject of Marina Vaughan, to Babette Navarro and Pearl Silver and Delphine Kahn, but she withheld any negative comment on Marina in front of Mona Berg, not wishing to be quoted by her. She only said, "I've known Marina all her life. Her father was a contract player at the studio when my father was still running it. Rex was so good-looking in those days. Tell me, Patrick, how is the bass?"

Sylvia didn't laugh when Mona referred to her friend Perry Rifkin, the decorator, as she and her and Miss Rifkin, as Mona thought she would, and she abandoned that avenue of conversation as well as Marina Vaughan. She told Sylvia she loved the way she did her hair and found out that her hairdresser was a Japanese called Yushi. She found out that her manicurist was named Blanchette. She found out that Las Floristas was the right florist to use, or Bruce and Barry, as Sylvia called them, and not the one she had sent the eighty-dollar red and white carnation arrangement from. She found out it was Nino you called to get a good table in the Polo Lounge, and Kasper you called to get a good table at the Bistro, and Ronnie you called to get a good table at Chasens. She got the feeling Sylvia Lesky thought Gucci luggage was tacky. She heard about sheets called Porthault, and crystal called Baccarat, and china called Lowestoft, and each name and person registered in her status computer. And then, much too soon, skipping dessert, Sylvia Lesky said she had to go. She was having a dress fitted at Danny Damask's, and then had a board meeting at Cedars-Sinai, and then a tennis game with her daughter, Cecilia.

"It's a wonderful picture of Cecilia in *Interview* this month," said Mona, wanting to prolong things a bit, not having gotten around to what this lunch was really about.

"Her father hates her to have her picture in magazines," said Sylvia, adjusting her earrings, blowing a kiss to Pearl Silver across the room.

"It says she's the latest of the Hollywood heiresses to come into social focus," said Mona.

"That's exactly why her father hates her to have her picture in magazines," said Sylvia, preparing to leave.

"I love the word heiress," said Mona.

"Goodbye. Thank you so much. And don't forget to give my love to Warren when you see him, and tell him we all miss him," said Sylvia.

"Don't make any plans for the thirtieth," said Mona, jumping in with both feet, now or never, knowing perfectly

171

well the Leskys were having a party for Faye Converse on the thirtieth, having heard Babette Navarro, or was it Pearl Silver, mention the date at the AFI dinner. "I'd like to take you and Marty to the Bistro that night."

"I'm afraid we're not free that night," said Sylvia, with her so-that's-what-she-wanted look in her eye.

"Is it anything you can get out of?" asked Mona, persisting.

"No, I'm certain we can't," said Sylvia.

"Well, whoever it is you're going to, would you like to bring them? I could easily expand the table," Mona went on, a left-out girl not wanting to be left out any longer.

"That's awfully nice of you, but these are plans that can't be changed," said Sylvia, meeting Mona's eye, holding it, letting her know what was what.

"Sure, I understand," said Mona. "Who's having the party?"

"As a matter of fact, we are, Marty and I. It's just a small dinner. It's not a party."

"What's the occasion?"

"We're just having some old friends in to meet Faye Converse while she's in town."

"Wasn't she great the other night, the way she came to Marina Vaughan's rescue?"

"We'd love to have you sometime, but this is more of a family night, not business. Faye was my bridesmaid when Marty and I were married twenty-six years ago."

"It doesn't make me feel real good to know I'm the type you only invite at the last minute, after somebody backs out," said Mona.

"Really, Mona, you're assuming an intimacy between us that I don't think exists. I don't like to be manipulated," said Sylvia. There was a silence.

"It would mean a great deal to me to be seen at a party like that," persisted Mona.

"You never let up, do you? I can see why Marty says you're such a good agent. You never get embarrassed. My mother used to call it thick skin."

"It got me from where I was to where I am."

"Where are you from, Mona?"

"I wasn't a Hollywood heiress. Let's put it that way."

"All right, Mona," said Sylvia, giving in, not wanting to hear the born-with-a-silver-spoon-in-your-mouth routine that she felt would be coming next. "It's on the thirtieth, as I'm sure you already know, black tie, dinner at eight. I'll send you a reminder card."

"My escort's name—you did mean for me to bring an escort, didn't you—my escort's name is Franklyn Bassett."

Chapter 17

"TEST ELEVEN. *South Sea Adventures.* Franklyn Bassett. Take one," said the clapper boy, clapping his slate in front of the camera on stage eleven of Colossus Pictures. It was late. Ten actors had already tested for the role of Adam Troy, the seagoing wayfarer, as Abe Grossman and Jess Dragonet described the character in their revival of the television series *South Sea Adventures.* The crew was tired and sick of the scene and anxious to get home. Most of the dialogue was of a technical nature relating to latitude and longitude and Fahrenheit information, warning the natives on an island by wireless of an impending hurricane. There was an air of restlessness and let's-put-this-show-on-the-road on the set, and the already nervous Franklyn Bassett was aware of the rush he was getting.

"Listen, uh, Mr. Carey, I haven't had a chance to talk to you about the scene," he said to the director.

"Call me Phil," said the director, an old television veteran.

"Phil," said Frankie.

"Didn't you watch any of the other tests?" asked the director.

"No," said Frankie. "I thought it might confuse me if I watched any of the other guys."

"It's real simple. Just act natural. You'll be fine."

"Yeah."

"What, are you nervous?" asked the director.

"Yeah, I'm nervous," said Frankie. "All this longitude and latitude and Fahrenheit stuff. I keep getting it mixed up in my mind."

"Listen, don't worry about it."

"How come the crew keeps laughing?"

"They're not laughing at you," said Phil Carey. "It's getting late, and they're getting restless. That's all. They've been hearing the same stuff all day long."

"Yeah," said Frankie.

"Hey, quiet it down, fellas," Phil Carey called out. "Quiet 'em down, will you, Milt?" he said to the assistant director.

"Quiet on the set," called out Milt.

"How about if I just give you a personality test?" said the director.

"What's a personality test?" asked Frankie.

"I just ask you some questions in front of the camera, and we see how at ease you are. Stuff like, uh, where you're from, when you first knew you wanted to be an actor, where you studied, that kind of stuff. I mean, the lines don't matter."

"Did the other guys do all the lines?"

"Yeah, but it's not important."

"I'll do all the lines too," said Frankie.

"Okay, suit yourself. You're sitting here on this keg, talking to your dog. You can feel it, there's a storm coming up, and you're worried about the natives on that island which is in that direction, camera left. Bring in the dog, will you, somebody? Now, this is supposed to be the deck of your ship, the *Tiki* it's called. We're going to turn on a wind machine, to give the feeling of the approaching storm. That won't throw you, will it?"

"This tee shirt doesn't fit right they gave me from wardrobe."

"Don't worry about it. Looks fine. Is this your first time in front of the camera?"

"Second," said Frankie, hoping he wouldn't ask him about the other time.

"Everybody ready? Let's do one. Lights. Camera."

"Test eleven. *South Sea Adventures*. Franklyn Bassett. Take two," said the clapper boy, clapping his slate.

"Action," said the director.

Later, at home, Mona asked, "What was it like?"

"What was what like?" asked Frankie.

"When he said, 'Lights, action, camera,' and the lights came on and the camera started to roll?" asked Mona, wanting to know every second of his experience.

"You really want to know?"

"Yes, I really want to know."

"When the lights came on, and the camera started to roll, I felt like I was going to get a hard-on. That's what it felt like."

"I knew you were going to be a natural," said Mona.

"Only then I fucked up the lines," said Frankie.

Mona Berg went to the couturier called Danny Damask to get a dress made for Sylvia and Marty Lesky's party for Faye Converse. She told Danny Damask that Sylvia Lesky had told her about him, conveying the impression that she and Sylvia were girlfriends together. She didn't know how to dress yet. She told Danny she didn't know what to wear, and she'd like to put the matter into his very capable hands. He looked at her, the ampleness of her, and recommended the fullness and flow of a chiffon caftan. She was hoping he'd have an idea other than a caftan.

"My boyfriend always calls them muumuus," she said, letting him know that she was not an unwanted woman.

"Calls what muumuus?"

"Caftans."

"Are we dressing for your boyfriend, or are we dressing for Sylvia Lesky's party? That is the question," said Danny Damask, pursing his lips, his slender ringed fingers playing with the gold chain around his neck, his pale blond eyebrows arched in disdain.

Such a queen, thought Mona to herself about Danny Damask, furious that his waist appeared to be no more than twenty-eight.

"I think that's a wonderful idea about the chiffon, Danny. I see what you mean about the fullness and the flow. I know, uh, I'm, uh, overweight—"

"Why don't you try the Schick Center?" said Danny.

"What's that?" asked Mona. She was particularly sensitive whenever her weight was mentioned, and she knew it was about to be mentioned.

"It's for weight control, at a serious level. They give you shock treatment."

"I'm on a diet. I only had cottage cheese and two Ry Krisp for lunch today," said Mona, hating the conversation, wanting to get out of it.

"And I bet you had a double scoop of chocolate chocolate chip at Baskin Robbins later as a reward," said Danny, who was looking at her and drawing the dress on a sketch pad.

"Don't get too smart, Mary," said Mona, a touch of deadly in her tone.

"I knew you were thinking like that, and see how I brought

it right out of you? Now listen, you need to lose some weight, and everybody's probably too intimidated by you to tell you that. I'm not intimidated by you. I don't care if you come to me or you don't come to me. Wear muumuus for the rest of your life. Now, if you'll excuse me, I have an appointment with Taffy Grossman."

"I don't want to wear muumuus for the rest of my life," she said, a note of contriteness in her voice.

"I could give you a look if you'd pay some attention to me," he said.

"What kind of a look?"

"You're a little bit like Joan Crawford in *Mildred Pierce*. I might put you in a turban, out of the same material as the caftan, with some panels flowing in the back. And listen, you've got to do something about your hair."

"What's wrong with my hair?"

"Let Yushi tell you. I've said enough already."

"Yushi. Isn't that the little Jap all those people use?"

"Make sure you say that when you call for the appointment."

"I didn't mean it that way. I just meant Sylvia Lesky was talking about him at lunch the other day. Is that the same Yushi?"

"That's her," said Danny Damask, and they both laughed, having become allied in the first stages of Mona Berg's transformation.

After the fiasco at the AFI dinner, Marina Vaughan went to a couple of AA meetings in Malibu, but being a movie star took the anonymous out of Alcoholics Anonymous for her, and she didn't go back after her picture appeared in the *National Enquirer* emerging from one of the meetings. She did stop drinking, however, except for white wine, and taking drugs, except for a little grass and the occasional toot, as she called it, of cocaine. She went down to Palm Springs to stay with Babette Navarro for a few days while Nando was off playing in a celebrity golf tournament in Pebble Beach.

"It's one of the number one rules, darling," said Babette with exasperation in her voice for unbecoming conduct.

"What's one of the number one rules, darling?" asked Marina.

"You don't bring home anyone to ball whom you just picked up at a bar when you're a house guest. At least not in this house. Nando would be furious, and I know he'd ask you to leave."

"Oh, Babette, for God's sake."

"That's not the kind of house I run."

"All right, darling. I won't do it again. I promise. Anyway, there's no harm done."

"The maid's salary is missing from beneath the toaster."

"I'll pay it back."

"It's not the money, darling. It's bringing people like that, who take things, home with you. Something's happening to you. There's a feeling of coming apart at the seams about you."

"What do you mean?"

"Darling, you're screwing several times a day with different men. Mona Berg told Sylvia Lesky you were the kind of girl who sucked off men at parties."

"I have never sucked off a man at a party," said Marina with a note of indignation, as if to set the record straight on that score.

"It's the image you're projecting."

"I hate Mona Berg."

"Mona Berg's not your problem, darling. You're your problem."

"I know. The other day I let five guys fuck me, Babette. Over in some crappy little apartment in Venice."

"How do you get yourself into a situation like that?"

"Don't ask."

"But why?"

"I can't get enough. It's like the only thing that makes me forget."

"Forget what?"

"That I'm in the first stages of being washed up." It was a subject that embarrassed people in their crowd. It was what they most feared.

"What was it like with five guys?"

"Listen, Babette, do you think Nando could use me on the Amos Swank show?"

"Darling, talk to Nando about it. I make it a rule never to get involved in Nando's business."

"Let's have a joint," said Marina, walking over to look out at the pool.

"Maisie, would you roll Miss Vaughan a joint please," Babette called out to her maid.

"What are you going to wear to Sylvia and Marty's party?"

"How many are coming to this party for Faye?" Marty Lesky asked his wife a few mornings before the day of the party. He had shaving cream on his face and walked into the bedroom from his dressing room and bath as if it were a matter he had been giving thought to in front of the mirror.

"Six tables of ten," answered Sylvia Lesky, not looking up from the society pages of the Los Angeles *Record*. She was in her Porthault-linened bed with her Porthault-linened breakfast tray in front of her. In the side basket of the tray were the *Hollywood Reporter, Daily Variety,* and the morning mail, still to be dealt with. "I hate this picture of me at the opening of *Mercury in Retrograde.* I look about a hundred. I specifically told Dolores I didn't want her photographer taking my picture."

"There's a couple of people I want you to ask to the party," said Marty Lesky, not even glancing at the picture she handed him.

"Who?" asked Sylvia, an icy tone in her voice.

"Abe and Taffy Grossman."

"Taffy Grossman! Not on your life!"

"She's a very nice woman. She's writing a book."

"She's a climber. And I'm already stuck with Mona Berg and some actor. What are you trying to turn this party into?"

"It's business."

"It's always business with these people. This is supposed to be a party for Faye. She doesn't know the Grossmans. Or the Bergs either, for that matter."

"She knows Abe Grossman all right. She did thàt TV show for him last year, where she was in the iron lung."

"That's the best reason I ever heard not to have the Abe Grossmans. Faye was too big a star to do TV. It was a disaster."

"We're going to have them, whether you like it or not, or I'm not going to be here," said Marty, starting back into the bathroom.

"Why?" asked Sylvia, not about to give up so easily. "I can't stand that television crowd. It's a whole different thing than the kind of people we know."

"Because Abe Grossman's television unit makes more money for Colossus than anyone else on the lot. That's why.

181

And I don't want him taking his business anywhere else."

"Then have them over for a movie some night."

"He's got his own projection room, Sylvia. Bigger than ours."

"Have your secretary call and invite them. I'm not going to."

"You call and invite them, Sylvia." Their eyes met for a minute. The conversation was over. The last word was his. Abe and Taffy Grossman would be coming. That was it. A fact of life. First outwitted by Mona Berg. Second foiled by Taffy Grossman.

"It's not such a bad picture," he said, referring to the photograph of his wife in the paper.

All day long Mona Berg had been in a nervous state. The screen test for *South Sea Adventures* had been three days earlier, and she had heard not a word on the subject, which did not seem like a good omen to her. She had seen Jess Dragonet at the Polo Lounge that day at lunch, but he did not come over to her table and left the restaurant before she could stop by his, which filled her with more than a bit of anxiety on the subject that was closest to her heart. No other on her gilded client list mattered to her as much, in the matter of business affairs, as the inexperienced hitchhiker whose destiny she had undertaken to change in exchange for services rendered.

In addition, it was the night of the Leskys' party for Faye Converse. The hairdresser Yushi had not been able to take her because of the demand for his time by his regular customers. The dress from Danny Damask had not arrived until six o'clock in the evening. She had gone to the Beverly Hills Hotel to have her hair and nails done and nearly missed the messenger with the dress box.

"Do I look all right?" asked Mona, unsure of herself in matters of fashion, looking at herself in the mirror.

"You look fine. I told you that already," said Franklyn Bassett.

"Do you like the dress? It cost me an arm and a leg. Danny Damask designed it for me."

"Beautiful. I already told you. How do I look? I never wore one of these tuxes before."

"Not tux. Dinner jacket," she corrected him as Marina Vaughan once corrected her. "You look beautiful."

"Should I wear a carnation in my lapel?"

"No. We better go. We can't be late at their house. You sure I look all right?" Frankie had never seen her as nervous.

The telephone rang. If she hadn't stopped to adjust her turban once more, she might have been behind the wheel of her yellow Mercedes, and not even heard the telephone, but she did stop to adjust her turban and check the flow of the panels, and the minute she heard the tone of the telephone bell, she knew it was bad news. Being a lady who spent a great part of her life on the telephone, she knew a thing or two about what was going to come over a telephone.

"I'm not going to answer that," she said.

"I heard that one before," said Frankie.

"The service will pick up."

"You fired the service, or the service fired you, depending on whose version of the story you choose to go with," said Frankie.

The telephone kept ringing. Whoever was on was not about to be discouraged.

"Hello," said Mona.

"I knew you were going to do that," said Frankie.

"Miss Berg?" said the voice on the other end of the wire.

"Who is it?" asked Mona, not committing herself, knowing it was a mistake to have picked up the telephone.

"This is Mae Toomey, your mother's nurse at the rest home," said the voice on the other end.

"I'm just on my way out the door. I'll call you tomorrow," said Mona.

"I'm sorry to tell you, Miss Berg, that your mother expired at six-o-two this evening. She was a wonderful woman, Miss Berg, and her last words—"

"I'll be in touch with you in the morning. Good night, Miss Toomey," said Mona, and hung up.

"Everything all right?" asked Frankie, who had been listening to Mona's side of the conversation while adjusting his black tie in the mirror.

"Why do you say that?" asked Mona.

"You sounded funny for a minute. I don't mean funny ha-ha. I mean funny, uh, something," said Frankie.

"No, no, it was just an accountant about somebody's contract. It was nothing that couldn't have been handled just as easily in the morning as right now," she said. Waves of strange feelings were going through her. She had never gotten down to the home to see her mother, but she knew her mother understood how busy she was. She was glad that Bill had remembered to send an arrangement of flowers from her on her birthday last week. Bill. Bill. That was the answer.

"I have to go to the bathroom," she said.

"We're going to be late," said Frankie.

"I'll only be a minute," said Mona.

There was no way she was going to back out of going to the Marty Leskys' party that evening. She knew she'd never be invited back if she backed out of going at such a late hour. She knew what a stickler Sylvia Lesky was for place-carding

184

her tables and the wrath she heaped on people who chucked at the last minute. She knew there was nothing more she could do for her mother that night, as she was dead already. She decided to delay any mention of what had happened to Frankie until morning, as if she had just heard it then.

She called Bill from the telephone in the bathroom, with the taps running, so Frankie couldn't hear what she was saying, and asked Bill to go over to the rest home where her mother died, and make all the arrangements with the funeral home. She asked him to pick out the casket, sky's the limit, she said, and that she'd be there in the morning at the funeral home to make arrangements for the service. "You do think I'm right in going, don't you?" she said to Bill, meaning going to the Leskys' party, the tone of her voice commanding him to believe that she was making a sacrifice, in the name of her career, in forcing herself to go through with the disagreeable but necessary task. And Bill did agree with her, and tell her she was doing the right thing, because that was the game they played together.

"Listen, darling," Mona said to Bill, there in her bathroom, with both taps running. She always called him darling in moments like this, when he told her she was right in the deceptions that became more and more of her reality. "Don't say anything about this to Frankie. He doesn't understand this business the way I do. I mean, if I back out of Sylvia Lesky's now, I'll never get invited there again. You don't know what I had to do to get there this time. I know I told you she insisted I come, but I had to practically back her into a corner. Listen, darling, I've got to go, or I'll be late. Tip that nurse, what's her name, Miss Toomey, tip her fifty bucks."

"You okay?" Frankie said to her when she came out of the bathroom.

"I'm fine," said Mona, looking at herself in the mirror again, pinching her cheeks for color. "Just nervous, I guess."

"Well, all right, Ms. Mona, now cheer up, ya hear? We're stepping out in high society," said Frankie, rising to the occasion of what was ahead of them.

"Now listen, Frankie, no cocaine, no matter who offers it to you, and no four-letter words, even if they use them."

"Don't worry, Mona, I'm not going to embarrass you."

Chapter 18

DOLORES DELONGPRE, the gossip columnist, quoted Sylvia Lesky as saying, "It was a dinner for a few chums," but to the social world in Hollywood that followed such things with a microscopic eye, the dinner for sixty in honor of the beloved film star Faye Converse was the party that counted that night, that week, that month, that season. When the Leskys threw open the splendid gates of their Palladian villa in Holmby Hills for a party, it was an event taken seriously.

"Black tie," the reminder cards read. It conjured up the picture of the night to come. Gilt chairs. Round tables. Place cards. Flowers. Maids in black silk and white aprons. Butlers, waiters, bartenders, parking boys. A real party.

"It all starts with the guest list," Sylvia Lesky often said when she was quoted in the papers about her parties. Her circle was a hard circle to crack, a world of people who had arrived, beyond the reaches of people on the make. She did not make herself available to social climbers, and it galled her, as she was seating her tables, doing her *placement,* she called it, that Marty had made her ask Abe and Taffy Grossman, of the Grossman-Dragonet Grossmans, for business reasons. It galled her even more that she had been outmaneuvered by Mona Berg succeeding in getting herself invited. It was her intention to put them all together at the same table, along with Faye Converse's hairdresser, whom she insisted on having, and the wife of a producer and the husband of a movie star who didn't possess quite the same charisma as their mates. Lump them all together at one table, people like that, was her theory. She loved seating tables. Secretly she thought she understood how to seat a table better than anyone so that the right person sat next to the right person for the purpose of conversation and laughter, to create the sound of a party that told her people were having a good time.

"I want you to put Abe Grossman next to Faye Converse," said Marty when he walked through the dining room, where she was placing the place cards an hour before the party.

"What's with Abe Grossman?" cried out Sylvia in a fury. "I am not going to put Abe Grossman next to Faye."

"It's business, Sylvia," said Marty quietly.

"What kind of business?" she asked in a tone of voice that implied monkey business. "Listen, Marty, I don't tell you how to run the studio. You don't tell me how to seat my dinner parties."

"I'm asking you a favor, Sylvia," said Marty patiently.

"He's in some kind of trouble and you're covering up for him, right?" asked Sylvia, looking at Marty. "Right?" she repeated.

"Something like that," he said.

"You forget I grew up in this business," she said.

"No, that's one thing about you that I never forget," said Marty as he moved out of the dining room to finish dressing.

"Who are you seating me next to?" asked Cecilia as she wandered into the room.

"Now don't you start with me," said her mother. "Here," she said, handing her a place card. "Put Jane Fonda next to your father on the left, and here, put Amos Swank on the other side of Jane. Faye is on your father's right, and, ugh, Abe Grossman is on Faye's other side."

"Who's Abe Grossman?" asked Cecilia.

"Oh, television," said Sylvia in the dismissive tone she used for television people.

"Who are you putting me next to?" Cecilia asked again.

"Robbie Slick. He's the new head of Liberty Studio. Single. Just divorced," said Sylvia.

"He sounds hand-picked by Marty for my second husband," said Cecilia.

"You better go up and get dressed, and have Yushi do something about your hair, Cecilia."

"Who's Franklyn Bassett, on the other side of me?" she asked, picking up the other place card and reading it.

"Mystery guest," said Sylvia. "A client of Mona Berg's from New York who's out here to test for the lead in some TV series." She put on her glasses and proceeded with her task.

"Candy Bergen here, Jack Nicholson here, then Babette, then Myron Kahn, then Marina Vaughan, and then Count Stamirski, and SanDee Dietrick . . ."

No detail was left to chance at one of Sylvia Lesky's parties. It was never a matter of a telephone call to Chasens to do the food, or to Las Floristas to do the flowers. Never, not at her house. The food was cooked by her chef, in her kitchen, with her staff, and extras added. The flowers were

189

from her greenhouse. The crystal and porcelain were from her pantry.

"I thought we'd start with a shrimp and scallop soup," she said to Victor, her chef Victor, a week before the party. "Then I thought curried chicken breasts with coconut-sprinkled pineapple, and marvelous vegetables, all marvelously arranged the way you do them, Victor, and then salad, and a brie, and then, maybe, a chocolate bombe, with chocolate sauce. How does that sound?

"I'm going to want a Pouilly Fumard for the first course," she said to Theodore, her butler Theodore, a week before the party. "Then I thought a Lafite Rothschild for the main course. And Dom Perignon with the sweet. How does that sound?

"I think we'll use the Flora Danica for the soup and the main course," she said to Mae, her maid Mae, a week before the party. "And the Lowestoft with the dessert. And that glass, and that glass, and that glass at every place. And be careful. They're Waterford.

"I want the six round tables covered in green moire and then overlaid with white organdy," she said to Perry Rifkin, her decorator and friend, on whom she doted. He could talk about pleats and tucks and cut-on-the-bias. He could remember who sat next to whom at last night's dinner party. He knew about Flora Danica, Porthault, Rigaud, and Baccarat. "Then I thought rubrum lilies from the greenhouse for the centerpieces. And masses and masses of delphiniums everywhere. Don't you think it sounds divine?"

Outside, on Delfern Drive, the gates were wide open. Two guards with guns in holsters and the Doberman Pinscher guard dog flanked the wide driveway and waved the cars through after the names were checked on a list. It was only

190

on party nights that the huge Palladian villa was lighted up outside, and the effect was startling as the cars turned from the driveway into the courtyard that fronted the house. A crew of parking boys dressed in black artfully lined up the cars, grills out, Rolls after Mercedes after Rolls, like a temporary sculpture. The fountain played in the center of the courtyard, and cymbidium plants in immense profusion flanked the black lacquered door that was opened by a maid waiting within before the bell could be rung.

The butler knew most of the guests and greeted them by name inside the door.

"Good evening, Miss Vaughan," said the butler.

"Good evening, Theodore," said Marina Vaughan.

"Good evening, Mrs. Navarro," said Theodore.

"Good evening, Theodore," said Babette Navarro.

It was thought to be a mark of one's acceptance as a regular guest of the imposing home to be so greeted.

"May I take your fur?" asked the maid.

"Please sign the guest book," said the butler.

"Your table number, for when dinner is announced, is on a card inside this envelope," said the secretary.

Guests were always asked to sign the guest book at the Leskys'. They had twenty-five years of guest books, made in England, filled, thousands of pages filled, with signatures of everyone who ever mattered in movies, plus Marty's friends in big business and political life, and Sylvia's friends in the jet set, the Greek tycoons and Italian countesses and English lords who frequented her home. Someone always said, sotto voce, out of Theodore's hearing, and the maid's, and the secretary's, that Marty used his guest books for income tax purposes, to deduct his friends as business expenses.

Jewels and haute couture were the order of the evening.

Sylvia Lesky received her guests at the entrance to her drawing room looking, as she knew she did, to the manor born. It was the thing she had that none of the others had. She would have liked her daughter to stand next to her and receive the guests with her, in the same way that she had stood next to her mother at her parties and received, for the look of it, handing on the mantle, but Cecilia remained indifferent to the glittering world of Hollywood society. She had still not come downstairs, although more than half of the guests had arrived, a matter of the utmost annoyance to her mother.

The art-filled, candle-scented rooms began to fill. Film stars. Social figures. Studio heads. Producers. Directors. Tycoons. Titles. Columnists. Hello, darling. Hello. I love your dress. I love yours. Do you know Count Stamirsky? May I present Faye Converse. Would you like some champagne? There's caviar in the library. Hello, darling. Hello. Where's Cecilia? She'll be down. Hello, Candy. Hello, Liza. Hello, Jane. Hello, Marina. I love your dress. I love yours. Hello, Ryan. Hello, darling. Hello. Hello. There's Marty, under the Monet. Where's Cecilia? Look at Faye's ring. Hello, Babette. Hello, Pearl. Hello. Hello. Hello, darling. . . .

Marty Lesky was sometimes with Sylvia at her post greeting new arrivals, more often not. He could never stand in one place for an hour receiving people the way Sylvia did, saying exactly the right thing to each of them, in her gracious hostess manner. Marty liked to move around, acting in an open friendly manner, a joke here, a joke there, a way he rarely appeared to those who saw him only at the studio. He took Warren Beatty over to look at the new Van Gogh, which Sylvia had given him for his birthday. He took Rex Vaughan outside to the sculpture garden to show him the new Henry Moore, where Cecilia's playhouse used to be. There was always something new to look at. A painting. A piece of sculpture. A Coromandel screen. When Marty's fortune multiplied into nine figures, his business advisers urged him to "get into art," as a means of diversification. He enjoyed the acquisition period he was in and liked explaining his purchases.

Dom Belcanto, the legendary singer, talked to Faye Converse, the legendary star. Marina Vaughan kissed Warren Beatty, with whom people said she'd once had an affair, and Ryan O'Neal, with whom people said she'd once had an affair, and Jack Nicholson, with whom people said she'd once had an affair. Dolores DeLongpre, notebook and pencil in hand, wrote down the names of all the people, without looking at her pad, while carrying on a conversation with Robbie Slick. Perry Rifkin took an Italian countess over to look at the Monet.

"I think she's hung it too low," said the countess.

"It has to be that height," said Perry, who had hung it himself only that afternoon, "because the Cinemascope screen comes down over it when they run films, which is practically every night." He wasn't about to have his work criticized by some Italian passing through town. "Who are those people who are staring at us in awe?" he asked, holding his glasses lorgnette-style to his eyes.

He was looking at the late arrival of Mona Berg and Franklyn Bassett. Sylvia Lesky had vacated her post to attend to a hostess duty, and they stood there in an awkward way, not sure whether to enter or wait. There was a look about Mona, as if she were wearing a dress that she had bought especially for the occasion, that it cost more than she had ever spent for a dress before, and that she was holding herself in a position that was not natural to her, in order to live up to it. There was no person in the room who wanted to be at that party more than Mona Berg. She had manipulated her way to get into it, and she had postponed dealing with her mother's death until it was over.

She had her arm in Frankie's, as if they were a couple. There was possession in her look and attitude, as if she felt enhanced by the association with his extraordinary looks. The story that went the rounds of the party about him was that he was a hot new actor, with credentials, whom she had just brought to the West Coast to test for the lead in the television revival of the old series *South Sea Adventures*. As he stood in the archway of the Leskys' splendid drawing room, there was on his face the look of someone watching a marvelous movie, and enjoying the experience of what he was seeing, smiling at the spectacle that it was instead of pretending he wasn't impressed.

"Lordy, Lordy," he said under his breath, for her ears.

"Shhh," said Mona, who did not want it to appear that she was not used to the society of the house she was in. He knew how to be impressed without feeling lessened himself. He didn't envy what he saw. He was just glad, if all this existed, that he was seeing it. This was a group of people who were long past the point of wonderment at their life style.

During the course of the evening, Frankie said he'd never been in a house with an atrium before. In fact he'd never heard the word before. He remarked that the greenhouse was like a set in a movie, with the rows and rows of thalianopses in bloom. He asked the butler if he should keep his knife and fork after the fish course. And he whistled when the Cinemascope screen lowered from the ceiling, obliterating the Monet, and the Picasso at the rear of the room rose electrically to reveal the projection booth behind it.

Everywhere Mona looked were faces she had seen in the

194

papers. Rita Belcanto, the daughter of Dom Belcanto, the legendary singer. My God, she thought, there's Dom Belcanto himself. Her heart skipped a beat at the sight of him and Faye Converse talking together, two of her favorite stars. More than anything else she wanted to know what they were saying, people like that, what sort of things they said to each other. Dolores DeLongpre, the movie columnist. Otto Ottoman, the society columnist. Warren Beatty. Jack Nicholson. Shirley MacLaine. Jane Fonda.

She watched the room. There were three studio heads. There was the head of William Morris. There was the head of ICM. She was in a hall of power, where she always wanted to be. There was Reade Jamieson, the multimillionaire, and his beautiful wife, Elena, who was at that moment kissing Marina Vaughan. And Diana Ross talking to Abe Grossman. And Amos Swank telling a funny story to Pearl Silver and SanDee Dietrick, who were laughing uproariously. And Perry Rifkin the decorator, staring straight at her, holding his black-rimmed glasses lorgnette style. She knew he could tell she didn't belong.

"Good evening, Mona," said Sylvia Lesky, returning from her hostess duty.

"Sylvia!" said Mona, in a voice that bespoke friendship. "I'm sorry we're late, but the telephone would not stop ringing." Business, business, business was the impression she conveyed.

"It's all right," said Sylvia, who liked her guests to be on time. "The Pecks still aren't here."

"I'd like you to meet Franklyn Bassett," said Mona. "This is our hostess, Mrs. Lesky."

"I'm pleased to meet you," said Sylvia Lesky.

"Same here," said Frankie. "This is some crowd."

"Who's that trying on Faye Converse's earring?" asked Mona.

"Taffy Grossman," answered Sylvia.

"Abe Grossman's wife?" asked Mona, immediately identifying her. "I didn't think she'd be so young. Look at all those diamond bracelets."

"One for each of Abe's series, she told me," said Sylvia. "I suppose she wants Faye's earrings next. Oh, there are the Pecks. Would you excuse me? The bar's that way," said Sylvia. "Or Theodore will take your order." She moved away to greet the new arrivals. "Veronique," she said. "I love your dress."

"Do you see Dom Belcanto?" asked Frankie.

"Don't stare!" said Mona under her breath.

"I'm not staring. I just said did-you-see-him?"

"I saw him. What do you suppose he and Faye Converse are talking about?"

"There's Marina Vaughan," said Frankie. It had never occurred to him that he would run into anyone he knew, especially from the part of his life when he met Marina Vaughan. He wondered if she would recognize him.

"That cunt," said Mona, who did not know that Frankie knew her.

"It was you who made the rule about no four-letter words," said Frankie.

"Are we supposed to stand here, or shall we mingle?" said Mona, who wanted more than anything else to look as if she belonged.

Dolores DeLongpre, pad and pencil in hand, work-work-work every minute, was talking to Rex Vaughan, who was trying to bolster the sagging career of his daughter, Marina. Dolores loved playing grande dame at parties. DeLightful.

196

DeLicious. DeLongpre. The ladies of the group said about her that her shoes were never right for the evening dress she was wearing, or that her shoulder strap was pinned with a safety pin, or that her hair was dyed much too black, but they never said that to her. They liked too much to read about themselves in the paper, and they gave her seats of honor at their parties. She usually got a film star on one side of her and a studio head on the other.

"She's going to do this TV special. What's it called, Marina?" Rex Vaughan asked his daughter.

"It's called *Marina: She Sings, She Dances*," said Marina, dutifully. "A colon after Marina."

" 'Marina, colon, she sings, she dances,' " Dolores said and wrote. "I was surprised to hear you were doing TV."

"There's not enough good roles for women these days," said Rex, who seemed more concerned than Marina on the subject. "This special is going to be great for her."

"I was surprised to hear you'd sold your beach house," said Dolores to Marina. "Why'd you do that?"

"Every time I drove down the Pacific Coast Highway, those good-looking Malibu cops busted me, as you kept reporting in your column, Dolores," said Marina. "I was beginning to get a bad reputation."

Her father gave her a look to be careful. Dolores turned away to speak to Faye Converse, who told her she was thinking of moving back to California, after all the years in Europe, and was already looking at houses. Then Marty Lesky asked Dolores to please not use the word heiress when she wrote about his daughter, Cecilia, in her column. Then Mona Berg told Dolores who Franklyn Bassett was.

"Franklyn's a new client of mine, Dolores," she said. "The last name's Bassett. B as in boy, a, double s as in star, e, double t as in terrific." She looked to see how Dolores wrote it, leaving nothing to chance. "The Franklyn's l-*y*-n, not l-i-n. He studied with Stella Adler, and I brought him out especially to test for *South Sea Adventures*. Any plug you could give him would be greatly appreciated, darling. And remind me later to tell you what I heard about Christopher Reeve and Bianca Jagger."

"Well, I must say," said Dolores DeLongpre, about Franklyn Bassett, "he has a certain *je ne sais quoi.*"

"I don't know what that means," said Frankie, "but it sounds good to me," and they all laughed. It amazed Mona how easily he fit in. "I always read your column, every morning," he went on. "May I get you another drink? Scotch mist, wasn't it?"

Dolores was charmed by him. "Aren't you sweet?" she said, loving it when young men flattered her. "Lovely manners, in addition to all his other attributes."

"Who's that with Mona Berg?" asked Marina Vaughan.

"His name's Franklyn Bassett," said Sylvia Lesky.

"Looks familiar," said Marina.

"Actor. New York. Here to test," said Sylvia.

Marina looked at him again, across the huge room, and he looked away at the moment their eyes met.

Franklyn Bassett walked to the bar in the library, walking sideways through the people, everyone talking, waving, laughing, inching his way through. All the beautiful faces so close that he had watched on the screen. So this is what they're like, he thought. This is how they spend their nights. Lordy, lordy.

"A scotch mist," he said, putting Dolores DeLongpre's glass on the bar.

"Okay, Frankie," said the bartender, "and take this vodka rocks over to Rex Vaughan."

They looked at each other. He was Rusty the pool man. Rusty who had gotten him the bartender's job he was on his way to on the afternoon he met Mona Berg.

"I'm not working this one, Rusty," said Frankie. "I'm a guest."

"No kidding," said Rusty, and they roared with laughter at the curiosities of life.

At that moment Marina Vaughan, not wanting to be where Mona Berg was, came into the library with Perry Rifkin.

"Scotch mist," said Rusty, handing Frankie the drink he was fetching for Dolores DeLongpre, and Frankie moved on.

"That guy looks familiar to me," said Marina about the departing Frankie.

"He's an actor from New York whom Mona Berg brought out here to test for a new television series," said Perry Rifkin, who always knew who everyone was.

"I heard all that," said Marina. "Doesn't ring a bell."

"What we call hot-looking," said Perry Rifkin.

"Just what was running through my mind," said Marina Vaughan, and they both laughed, and so did Rusty the bartender.

Frankie went out of the library with Dolores DeLongpre's scotch mist, not wanting to encounter Marina Vaughan face to face at that moment, when he hadn't had a chance to tell Rusty what his new name was. He had a feeling that she recognized him but didn't remember where from.

The structure of the house was such that he had to cross through the hall to get back to the living room. Coming down the imposing stairway, one hand loosely touching a banister, was the girl in the white Porsche, as he had come to think of her since the day of their meeting on Sunset Boulevard. Their eyes met at the same moment. Each was stunned to see the other. They stared at each other. She was the youngest girl at the party and the only one not covered with jewels. Her dress was pink and strapless. Her arms and neck were tanned from tennis. Her hair was short. Her eyes were gray-green. She walked down the stairway as if she'd walked down it a thousand times before.

"Funny," she said, the beginning of an elfin smile on her face.

"What's funny?" he asked.

"I wouldn't have taken you for a drinker of scotch mists."

"Beer out of the bottle. That's probably what you thought."

"Something like that."

"It's for Dolores DeLongpre."

"DeLightful DeLicious DeLongpre."

"You walk down those stairs as if you lived here," said Frankie.

"I do," said Cecilia Lesky.

"I was afraid you were going to say that," he said.

"Which one of us is going to say 'small world'?" she asked.

"I will. Small world."

"I got the black eye. Just like you said I would."

"Listen," he said sincerely, "I'm sorry about last time. I was way out of line jumping into your car like that. I've thought about it a lot. I'm sorry."

"I know. You said that then when it happened. You even had tears in your eyes, which was nice. It was my fault too. I've thought about it a lot too, why something like that happens."

"Why?" he asked. She was lovely. He had never met the kind of girl that she was, and he stared at her in a fascinated way, as he did on the day he had gotten into her car.

"I haven't figured it out yet," she said.

"Aren't you curious to know who I am, and why I'm here in your house?" he asked her.

"I know who you are and why you're here in this house," said Cecilia. "I helped my mother with the place cards, and I got the run-down from her. What I didn't know until this very moment was that Franklyn Bassett, the new discovery of Mona Berg, and the hitchhiker at the red light, as I have come to refer to you in my mind, were one and the same. You don't look like a Franklyn Bassett."

"I don't even know your name," said Frankie.

"Cecilia."

"I never met a Cecilia," he said.

"A night of firsts," she said.

"What do you do?" he asked.

"The newspapers call me an heiress."

"I never met an heiress before either."

"It's not all it's cracked up to be."

Then Mona arrived, huffing and puffing a bit, keeping her eye on her man at all times. "Franklyn, I've been looking for you everywhere," she said. "Dolores DeLongpre said you went to get her a scotch mist and vanished into thin air."

"The mist seems to have melted," he said.

"Oh, you must be Cecilia," said Mona, the slight tone of annoyance toward Frankie in her voice evaporating in the presence of the privileged young woman. "I'm so glad to meet you finally. I've heard so much about you from your father. I'm Mona Berg and I see you've met Franklyn."

All her life Cecilia Lesky had seen people make up to her because of who her father was, and who her grandfather had been. She had a built-in wariness about people who befriended her to curry favor with her father.

"There's such a good picture of you in *Interview* this

month," Mona gushed on, always effusive with the up-to-date compliments she showered on people who were already where she wanted to be.

"Don't mention that picture around this house," said Cecilia in her quiet voice. "They called me a millionette, and you can imagine how that went over with my father. He'll assign me a bodyguard next. I think we're going in to dinner."

The pale green dining room was lit by candles. Crystal and silver gleamed. Maids passed. Waiters poured. Conversation buzzed. White wine with the fish. Red wine with the meat. Champagne with the sweet. Gossip. Deals. A night at the top.

"You do this better than anyone, Sylvia," said the decorator Perry Rifkin, on whom she doted. He was talking about the spectacle that it was, a dinner for sixty.

"It's a lot of hard work," said Sylvia, "that's what it is, doing these parties. I mean this person doesn't speak to that person, and that person doesn't speak to this person. Do you know how long it took me to seat these tables? I thought I'd go *mad*."

"Tell me something, Sylvia," said Perry.

"What?"

"Tell me about that hot number seated next to your daughter."

"Some discovery of Mona Berg's. Don't get me started on *her*. First she almost blackmailed me to get invited here, and then she changed the place cards and seated herself next to Marty, where Jane Fonda should have been, and poor Jane's between SanDee Dietrick's brother and Faye Converse's hairdresser."

"N.O.C.D.," said Perry, about Mona, meaning not-our-class-darling,

"You said a mouthful," said Sylvia.

"Why don't you start?" asked Cecilia Lesky of Franklyn Bassett.

"I was waiting for you to start," said Frankie. "I don't know which fork to use."

"That one," she said, pointing to the one on the outside. "Work from the outside in. God help you when they bring the finger bowls."

"Did it take you long to learn all these things?" asked Frankie.

"It comes with the upbringing," said Cecilia.

"Mine was strictly a one-fork upbringing," said Frankie, and they both laughed. "What happens with the finger bowls?"

"Listen, Marty," said Mona Berg to her host Marty Lesky, on whose left she was seated. "I hear you saw the tests for *South Sea Adventures.*" Nothing more mattered at that moment in her life than for her to get Frankie the part in the series. She talked in a low intense kind of voice, that indicated seriousness of purpose in the midst of frivolity. Marty Lesky didn't like to talk business at the table, and especially not in hushed tones, as if to indicate how important the matter was, to the exclusion of his other guests nearby. "I can't get that putz Jess Dragonet to tell me a thing."

"Look, Mona," said Marty, "I don't like to talk business at the table. I was just looking at Marina Vaughan. She seems to be pulling herself together. I hear she's doing a special."

"She's probably on lithium," said Mona. "She's a loser. Listen, Marty, just tell me if you saw his test or not."

"This is not the time or the place, Mona," said Marty.

"Can't you at least tell me if you've made a decision?"

"Your friend can't act, Mona," said Marty.

"So?" asked Mona. "How many of those guys on TV can? Look how he looks. That's all that's going to matter on that series. Some guy talking to a dog on the deck of a ship in the Pacific Ocean better be good-looking."

"There's a lot of good-looking actors who can also act," Marty said.

"Look around this room, Marty," said Mona. "There's not a woman here who can keep her eyes off him. Including your daughter. And a couple of the fellas also. Even Dolores De-Longpre said he had a certain *je ne sais quoi*."

"Which means?"

"Which means hair below the belly button, Marty, sex in capital letters. Whatever it is that turns people on, he's got it. You strip him down in every episode, and you'll have every woman and every gay in America tuned in just to catch his body. I have an instinct about things like this, Marty."

"You don't let up, do you?" said Marty, looking at her, seeing himself in the early days, before he married Sylvia. Hungry. Yearning. Wanting to be in. Then he smiled. "You're getting to be a good agent, Mona."

"I'm getting to be the best, Marty," said Mona. "Now, how about Franklyn Bassett?"

At their table, Franklyn Bassett and Cecilia Lesky had not stopped talking to each other throughout the meal. Neither had spoken to the person on the other side.

"It's not so great being a rich kid," said Cecilia. "You grow up without any friends. They tell you every girlfriend you have is secretly jealous of you and every boyfriend you have is after your money."

"I always thought if you had money, you didn't have any

problems left," said Frankie. "You ought to move out. Have your own life."

"Tell that to Marty Lesky," said Cecilia.

"Uh-uh," said Frankie as the butler put the finger bowl in front of him. "This must be the finger bowl. Do I wash up?"

"First you put the spoon and the fork on the side," said Cecilia, doing the same for his benefit. "Then you pick up the bowl with your right hand, and you pick up the doily with your left hand, and you put the doily on the table there, and you put the finger bowl on top of it."

"What do you do with the plate?" asked Frankie.

"That's what you have your dessert on," said Cecilia.

"I wonder how Mona's handling all this," said Frankie.

Marty Lesky rose and tapped on the side of his champagne glass with his fork, silencing the conversation in the dining room.

"Now what?" Frankie whispered to Cecilia.

"Toasts," Cecilia whispered back.

"I feel like I'm in a movie," whispered Frankie, and they both laughed. It was the first time she had enjoyed being home.

Marty Lesky made a toast to Faye Converse. He talked about all the years they went back together. He said that Faye had been a bridesmaid when he and Sylvia eloped, and that Faye was under contract to the studio when Sylvia's father was still running it. Then Rex Vaughan made a toast, and said charming things about Faye Converse. Then Dom Belcanto, the legendary singer, rose and paid his compliments to the great star. The champagne flowed. Then Faye Converse rose, and gave her speech about old friends and coming home and feeling welcomed. There was a tear in many an eye in the lovely room. Big-time people behaving in a big-time way in a big-time house.

"Let's all move into the living room for coffee and liqueurs," Sylvia Lesky said after Faye Converse finished, but there was the sound of a Georgian fork hitting the side of a Waterford glass, and the room fell silent once again.

Mona Berg rose in a shy and respectful manner, with her champagne glass in her hand, just as Marty Lesky had held his, and Rex Vaughan held his, and Dom Belcanto, and Faye Converse.

"I feel so honored to be here in the presence of so many people whom I have so long admired," she said. "If anyone ever told me that one day I would be sitting down to dinner in the same room with Faye Converse and Dom Belcanto, my two most favorite movie stars ever, and Rex Vaughan, and Jack Nicholson, and Warren Beatty, be still my heart, I would have said—"

"Who is this broad?" asked Dom Belcanto, not inaudibly, nor kindly.

"The one who took over Warren Ambrose's agency," whispered his wife, Pepper.

"The nerve of her," said Dom.

"I'd like to ask everyone to rise and join me in a toast to our wonderful hostess, Sylvia Lesky, who gets my vote as the First Lady of the Industry," said Mona, enchanted with herself that all eyes in the room were on her. "The perfect hostess. The perfect wife. The perfect mother." She finished in a modest and self-effacing manner and sat down to mild applause.

"Thank you, uh, Mona," said Sylvia, tight-lipped. "*Now,* let's all move into the living room for coffee and liqueurs," and she led the way out of the dining room.

206

"Inappropriate," said the septuagenarian blue-haired Delphine Kahn.

"Unctuous," said Babette Navarro.

"Pushy," said Pearl Silver.

"Ass kisser," said Marina Vaughan.

"She'll be running this town one of these days," said Abe Grossman.

At some level of himself not yet arrived at, the newly named Franklyn Bassett realized that Mona's toast was considered out of place, and he dropped his eyes rather than witness the eye contact that was going on among the ladies of the establishment, knowing which side his bread was buttered on as he did.

"Tell me about Mr. Beautiful you were sitting next to," said Marina Vaughan to Cecilia Lesky as they went upstairs to the ladies' room.

"His name is Franklyn Bassett, and he's out here because he's tested for—" said Cecilia.

"I heard all that," said Marina, interrupting her.

"Then what do you want to know?" asked Cecilia.

"Is he the private property of, uh, Miss Berg?" asked Marina.

"She certainly checks up on him all the time," said Cecilia, although the possibility that theirs was more than a business relationship had not occurred to her.

"He doesn't look like a Franklyn Bassett to me," said Marina.

The inevitable happened. Try as each did to stay in a different room from the other, Marina Vaughan and Mona Berg passed close enough to each other so that it was impossible not to speak when the living room was being rearranged for the film that was about to be shown.

"Hello, Marina," said Mona, as if nothing untoward had transpired between them.

Marina nodded, without acknowledging Mona vocally.

"May I present Mr. Bassett, Miss Vaughan," said Mona, as if she were Sylvia Lesky herself doing the introductions. Their eyes met, Marina's and Frankie's, as they said hello to each other, and it was then that Marina remembered who he was, the substitute pool man to whom she had paid a hundred dollars for services rendered. A different hairstyle. A different look, but unmistakably someone other than whom Mona Berg was passing him off as being.

Franklyn Bassett stood there waiting for the exposure that he felt was inevitable, feeling the antagonism that existed between the two women.

"Hello," she said instead, extending her hand to him.

"Hello," he answered, shaking her hand.

"Do you miss your beach house?" asked Mona, trying to engage in the sort of social conversation at which Babette and Pearl and Delphine and Sylvia were so good, that had nothing to do with making deals or manipulating for invitations.

"What?" asked Marina, shifting her eyes from Frankie to Mona, as if she had not heard her, which she had.

"I said, Do you miss your beach house?" asked Mona again.

"Yes, I do," said Marina, and then added, quite unnecessarily, "Do you miss your typewriter?" She turned and left the room.

"Cunt," said Mona Berg for the second time that evening.

The Cinemascope screen was lowered electrically from the ceiling, completely obliterating the Monet at one end of the handsome room. At the other end of the room, a small Picasso and a small Van Gogh rose electrically to reveal the windows of a projection booth behind. Plates of candies and chocolate pretzels were placed on the tables by the maids.

"Wooooow. Look at that, Mona," said Frankie, thrilled by what he was seeing. "The Cinemascope screen's coming right down from the ceiling."

"Don't keep acting like you've never seen anything like it before," said Mona in a low voice meant to dampen his enthusiasm.

"I never did," he answered quite truthfully.

"Now listen," she said. "I want you to talk to Sylvia Lesky before the picture starts. Compliment her on the food and the house. She gets off on that, and she could have a big say about the test."

"Would you like a liqueur?" asked the butler Theodore.

"Where's the men's room?" asked Frankie.

"Down that hall," answered Theodore, pointing. "Turn right at the Rouault."

The bathroom door was locked when he got there. Then it opened.

"I'm sorry," Marina Vaughan said. "I didn't realize there was anyone waiting." Then she recognized who it was.

"You know," she said, "I rather think we know each other."

"Yeah," he said.

"Don't you have a tiny little butterfly tattooed, right, down, *there?*" she said, pointing to the left cheek of his rear. "Don't you like to talk dirty? And take poppers? Stop me when I'm warm."

"You could fuck this whole thing up for me," he said.

"The minute I saw you here tonight, I said to myself, I know that man, and I said to our hostess, Who is that perfectly divine creature that La Berg has in tow? He's some new actor everyone's talking about, she said, just out from New York, to do a screen test. But none of that rang a bell for me at all. Excuse me if I'm talking nonstop. I just took a little blow, as we call it in the picture business, and it makes me talkative," said the film star, blow being the slang word of the moment for cocaine. "Like a little?"

"No thanks," said Frankie, acting like Franklyn Bassett.

"Yes, you do, darling," said Marina. "I can see it in your face. It'll loosen you up a bit in front of all these swells, help you get the part. Come into my mirrored lair."

"Listen, uh, I have to take a leak," said Frankie, stepping inside.

"Heavens, don't let me stop you, darling. Go right ahead. You can toot while you pee," and she followed him back into the bathroom and locked the door. She took out her accoutrement—the brown glass vial, the golden spoon—and put an ample portion of the white powder under his nose. "First one nostril," she said, "that's a good boy, you sound like a horse, and now the other one, there you go."

"That was one of the hottest afternoons I ever spent," he said, snorting, peeing, looking at the tableau of the two of them in the mirrored walls, becoming excited by the madness of the danger. Their eyes met in the mirror.

"How'd you like to get blown by a movie star at your very first Hollywood party?" she asked. "I mean, since it's already out."

"Jesus," he said. He was fully erect. "Someone might come."

"That's part of the rush," she said, falling to her knees, taking it into her mouth. He put his large hands behind her head and pulled her toward him. They picked up each other's rhythm.

"Oh, my God," he said. "Oh, my God."

There was a knock on the door, a sharp and meaningful knock.

"Are you in there, Franklyn?" It was Mona Berg. "I've been looking everywhere for you. Franklyn?"

"Listen, I'll be out in a minute, Mona," said Frankie.

"What's going on in there?" asked Mona from her side of the door.

"Listen," said Frankie, finishing. "I got the runs. Leave me alone. Okay? I'll be out in a minute."

"Probably the lobster," said Mona. "Should I ask Sylvia if she has any Pepto Bismol?"

"No."

"They're about to start the movie," said Mona. "I'll save you a seat."

"I'll be there in a minute," said Frankie.

"Another night in Hollywood," whispered Marina.

"You're one hot lady, Marina," he whispered back.

"Tramps, darling. That's what we are. Tramps."

"White trash."

"Of which there is no trashier."

"Let me go out first, in case she's still there," he said. "Listen, it's been memorable."

"Frankie," she said, stopping him.

"What?"

"I hope you get the part."

"What was Franklyn Bassett's screen test like?" Cecilia Lesky asked her father.

"Why?" asked Marty Lesky. The picture was about to start.

"Just wondered," said Cecilia.

"That's the first time I ever heard you ask a question about my business," said Marty. He ate a chocolate pretzel.

"He's awfully good-looking," said Cecilia. "Everyone's talking about him."

The film was in progress for the people who wanted to watch it. Frankie entered the room and took his place on the sofa where Mona had saved a seat for him. In the relative darkness of the room, lit only by the film on the screen, Mona moved closer to Frankie in a romantic way.

"I think I got you the part," she whispered in his ear.

"They liked the test?" he asked, stunned.

"I didn't say that," she whispered. "I said I got you the part."

He looked over and saw that Cecilia Lesky was watching him, watching them, and he felt embarrassed for the first time at the way his relationship with Mona Berg must appear to others.

"I'm going to make you a star, Frankie," Mona continued, her head on his shoulder.

"I would have thought he could have done better than that," whispered Marina Vaughan to Cecilia Lesky when she saw her young friend watching Frankie Bassett and Mona Berg during the screening of the film.

Cecilia, who was embarrassed to have been caught looking at them, turned to Marina, shrugged her shoulders, and whispered back, "Hollywood."

"How about going out on the town when this up-tight party is over?" whispered Marina.

"Where?"

"I know a good party, given by a gangster. We'll dance the night away."

"What about my parents?"

"Oh, darling," whispered Marina, exasperation in her voice.

"Okay," said Cecilia. "I'll go."

Chapter 19

DIZZYING. It became an oft-used word to describe the events of Mona Berg's life in the months that followed Marty and Sylvia Lesky's party. People said about her that she was a dynamo. There was story after story after story about her. Her deals. Her jokes. Her pushiness. Her toughness. She was the most talked about woman in Hollywood. They talked about her more than they talked about stars. Even her detractors knew that she could no longer be overlooked.

She wanted it all, and she wanted it quickly, and there was no stopping her. At the same time that she was turning Franklyn Bassett into a star and holding center stage for every important deal of the Ambrose-Berg Agency, she bought herself a million-dollar house in Beverly Hills, gave her first Hollywood party, and, most startling of all, transformed herself, through surgery, into the kind of woman she always wanted to be.

Bill, Mona's secretary Bill, always thought it was Marina Vaughan's joke about her, hilarious at the time of the telling, not so hilarious when it was printed in a gossip column, to the consternation of all, that motivated Mona to take the drastic steps she took in undergoing the operation that changed the shape of her body.

"I read in Dolores DeLongpre's column that your father was offered the lead in *The Thorn Birds*," said Amos Swank, the talk show host, to Marina Vaughan at a dinner party at Babette and Nando Navarro's.

"He turned it down," said Marina. She was a little drunk.

"That's supposed to be a great part," said Amos.

"He didn't want to spend six months in Australia," said Marina. "Pour me another glass of wine, will you, darling?"

"What is it about Australia?" asked Amos. "No one wants to go to Australia."

"Australia," said Marina, thinking about it, as if she had something profound to say on the subject, getting the attention of the table, taking another sip of her wine, "Australia is like Mona Berg's cunt. Everyone knows it's down there, but no one wants to visit it."

There were shrieks of laughter. Her remark was the success of the evening. No one found it more amusing than the decorator Perry Rifkin, who laughed and laughed, and couldn't wait to repeat it. Later that night, after he'd taken Pearl Silver home, he ran into Otto Ottoman, a new columnist beginning to make his mark, to the consternation of Dolores DeLongpre, at a late night party in the Hollywood Hills, and repeated it to him.

"She's hilarious," said Otto Ottoman, about Marina Vaughan. "Was she stoned?"

"Does the Pope wear a dress?" asked Perry.

Irrepressible Marina Vaughan's remark about Australia being like Mona Berg's bleep is the laugh of the Bel Air circuit.
                    —from Otto Ottoman's column,
                        "Our Town," *Hollywood Chronicle*

"Jesus, Marina, you must have some kind of death wish," said her father, the film star Rex Vaughan, on the morning that Otto Ottoman's column appeared.

Marina didn't know what to say, so she remained silent. It occurred to her that every time she drank too much she said funny things that weren't funny the next day. Oh, God, she thought to herself, give me a break.

"You have to call Mona and apologize," said Marty Lesky in a separate call to her that morning.

"Let me tell you exactly how it happened, Marty," said Marina. "I was at this party, at the Navarros', and I was sitting next to Perry Rifkin, and Amos Swank said to me, and, uh—"

"Yeah," said Marty. There was a coldness in the tone of his voice that she had not heard before.

"I mean, I didn't know Perry was going to repeat it to Otto Ottoman, like it was the latest camp of the week," said Marina with a trace of hysteria in her voice.

"My advice to you is to call her and apologize to her," said Marty. She wanted to say that Mona had not called her to apologize after spreading the word that she was a drug addict, but she didn't. Nor did she call Mona.

From the time Mona Berg met and fell in love with Franklyn Bassett, she began taking diets of every description, none of which she was able to maintain, in an effort to deal finally with the overweight that had plagued her life. Diets were too slow for her, and the day-by-day was torturous for her. She went to Overeaters Anonymous but became impatient with the food stories of the unhappy people there and never raised her hand to share her experiences. She preferred diet pills and went to Dr. Denniston, whom she had mocked for coming to surgery in a dinner jacket, and got prescriptions for Eskatrol and Dexamyl, but the pills made her frantic and mean, and Frankie told her she was difficult enough without what the pills added to her personality. Then she had her jaws wired together to keep her from eating anything other than liquids, but she could not conduct her business, or her social life, or her sex life, and she became more frantic than ever, and that process was abandoned.

Then Marina Vaughan's remark was published in Otto Ottoman's column, and she was devastated. She postponed the revenge she knew she would get in time for the more immediate task of dealing with the problem of the shape of her body. She wanted to be slender, and she wanted it instantaneously. What will power could not perform, surgery could. "May I speak to Dr. Denniston, please. This is Mona Berg."

"What this operation does, Mona, is reroute the passage of food through your body." Behind him on the wall of his office on Rodeo Drive was a chart of the body to which he was pointing. "It's called an intestinal bypass. What it means, quite simply, is that the intake of food no longer will go through the digestive process."

"What happens to it?" asked Mona.

"You see, your intestine will be tied off. You eat, and then you shit, if you'll pardon the expression, and the fattening foods will not get into your system," said the doctor.

"Is it a guarantee of slimness?" asked Mona.

"Well, there's the problem of the excess flesh that will

216

have a tendency to hang off you after the vast weight loss that will occur."

"Is there a solution for that?"

"Yes."

"What?"

"The excess flesh can be cut off surgically, leaving only a very slight scar across your stomach."

"Will I be able to wear a bikini?"

"Well, maybe not a bikini, but certainly a two-piece bathing suit."

"A size eight dress?"

"Yes, I'd say so."

"I want it. I want to do it."

"Well, let's see now on my schedule," he said, putting on his granny glasses, opening the Gucci appointment book on his desk.

"I want to go in tonight. I want to start it right away."

She made no secret of it. She did it as a public thing, for all to know about and talk about. Dolores DeLongpre kept all up to date, not only on her amazing transformation but on the deals for her clients that she made from her bed at Cedars-Sinai.

In a matter of four weeks, Mona re-emerged on the scene, much like Bette Davis in *Now Voyager*, as she likened it to, as a slenderized woman of striking appearance, pointed out and stared at in public situations for what she had put herself through.

"My God, you'd never know it's the same woman," said Abe Grossman.

"You know what you'll do for love, darling," said his wife, Taffy. "As the old song says."

She spent a million dollars for her new house in the flats of

Beverly Hills. It was the area she had always liked best, from the first time she took the movie star tour of the stars' homes. She never forgot that Jimmy Stewart and Lucille Ball and Jack Benny lived next door to each other, and she could think of nothing more wonderful than living on a street where every house was owned by someone famous.

She decided to buy the house during a brunch at Jess Dragonet's house one Sunday. There were lots of beautiful bodies, and lots of marvelous food and drink. And there was a swimming pool and a tennis court and a Jacuzzi. And there were Chinese servants. And music playing. And it was simply too lovely, she said to Dolores DeLongpre.

"Where else in the world does anyone live like this?" said Mona, lying back on a chaise, wearing a large straw hat and drinking a banana daiquiri, which Jess Dragonet said was his *specialité*.

"Nowhere, darling," said Dolores DeLongpre. They both knew that people who longed to be elsewhere than Hollywood never really made it in Hollywood, and they never stopped complimenting it.

"This is the sort of house I should have," said Mona. "I have to start entertaining. I could give marvelous parties." She wanted a setting for herself that befitted her own celebrity.

She didn't have a million dollars, but she knew that you didn't have to have a million dollars to live in a million-dollar house. All that you had to have was the down payment, and the ability to keep up the payments. Mona had no fear about being able to keep up the payments, but she didn't have the capital for the down payment. In the end she got a house for free. She went to Warren Ambrose, who was still recovering from his stroke, and suggested that the agency buy the house for her.

"Now listen, Warren," she said to him during her weekly meeting with him to discuss agency business. "I don't have much time today. I have to meet Rebecca Kincaid at the Polo Lounge at five-thirty. I think it's only fair to tell you, Warren, that I've had another offer from the William Morris Agency that it's going to be awfully hard for me to turn down."

It was a way she had, of telling him about other offers, knowing that he could not do without her. She let him mumble and stumble a bit.

"What Mona needs, Warren," she said about herself, "is a big house in Beverly Hills. So I can start to entertain. You can't expect Marty and Sylvia Lesky, and Abe and Taffy Grossman, and Robbie Slick to come up to that little dump I live in in Laurel Canyon, can you?"

"But, but—" Warren started to say.

"It's important for the agency that I start to entertain in my own home, Warren," Mona went on. "You used to do a lot of business entertaining in this house. You know how important it is."

She knew he would come around. In the long run there would be no other choice for him. He needed her to run the agency. He was partially paralyzed, and his speech was impaired, and she knew that he knew that she was running the agency better than he had been running it for the past few years. She was getting sick of the time waste needed to cajole him into compliance each time that an outlay of money was needed for her advancement.

"If you don't think I'm worth a million-dollar house, Warren," she said with a hint of exasperation in her voice, "I can guarantee you others will."

She got her house. It was a near mansion, white and pillared and impressive, with a curved driveway in front and a swimming pool behind. A beloved comedienne was her neighbor on one side and a famous singer was her neighbor on the other. Everyone said about the neighborhood that it was the safest.

"Are you keeping someone on the side, Abe?" asked Marty Lesky.

"No," said Abe Grossman.

They were walking on the back lot of Colossus Pictures, which they did several times a day to discuss the affairs at hand between them, away from all possibilities of being overheard.

"Are you being blackmailed?" asked Marty.

"No," said Abe.

"Are you a secret gambler?"

"No."

"Then what the fuck's the matter, Abe? You're one of the richest men in Hollywood, and you're stealing money," said Marty.

"It's just so fucking easy to do, Marty," said Abe.

"They say there's so much money you're keeping it in your wife's hat boxes."

Abe merely shrugged.

"You know something, Abe?"

"What's that?"

"If your unit didn't make so fucking much money for this studio, I'd blow the whistle on you."

"Are you altogether lily white in the money department, Marty?"

"We're not talking about me. We're talking about you."

Inside her new house Mona Berg took the decorator Perry Rifkin on a tour of the empty rooms. He said he wanted to reserve judgment on whether or not he'd take on the job until after he'd seen the house, making Mona more determined to get him than ever.

"The house was built by Florence Eldridge and Fredric March in 1937," said Mona to Perry, very much the proud possessor, giving the history of her house, enjoying the newness of the experience. "Later, Freddie March sold it to Tyrone Power, after he divorced Annabella and before he married Linda Christian, and *then*—"

"What's in here?" asked Perry, opening a door to another room. His eyes caught every molding, every dado, every dimension. He was getting the feeling he got when he knew he was going to take on a job with someone new, expanding his circle of expensive clients by one more.

"That's the library," said Mona. It was the first time she had ever had a room called a library, and she liked the way it felt when she said it. "I'd like it the way you did Sylvia Lesky's library."

"Wrong," said Perry, singing the word as if it were a note.

"What do you mean wrong?" She was always sensitive when her taste was being questioned.

"That's called old money, that look," said Perry, "and let's face it, Mona, you're rags to riches all the way. You're what they used to call *nouveau.*"

"Better *nouveau* than never, I always say," said Mona, just on the edge of bristling.

"Now you're talking," said the fashionable decorator. "Let me tell you how you should do this house. Early Joan Crawford. Satin and mirrors and black and white marble. By the time I get finished with this house, you'll expect Joan herself to walk right down those stairs in an Adrian gown with padded shoulders."

"I like it. I like it," said Mona, who never knew what was right for her until someone told her.

"Say," said Perry, looking up at the stairway as he moved back into the hall, as if something about it were familiar to him.

"What?" asked Mona. Her eye had gone outside to the pool, where Frankie and Rusty were running their lines for the next day's shooting. Mona couldn't stand Rusty. She didn't like anyone who knew Frankie from before.

"Isn't this the house where Johnny Stompanato was murdered?" asked Perry.

"*Sssshhhh!*" said Mona, frantically indicating Frankie outside. "Don't let him hear that. He'll give me all that crap about bad karma and tell me I shouldn't have bought it."

"He fell right down that stairway when she killed him," said Perry, reliving it all. "They called me later to replace the carpet. Blood everywhere. What a *mess!*"

Outside, Frankie put his script aside, stepped to the edge of the pool, dropped the towel around his middle, revealing tight white buttocks that contrasted with the deep tan of his back and legs, and dove into the pool. It was a tableau of Hollywood life that was not lost on Perry Rifkin, like watching a painting by Hockney come to life was the way he described it to Jess Dragonet later.

"I'll take the job," said Perry, referring to Frankie, and smiling. Mona loved to hear people make sexual references to Frankie. She had never had anything before that was coveted by other people.

"Show me upstairs," said Perry. "Who's that other guy out there?"

"That's his stand-in," said Mona in the dismissing manner she used for people who had jobs like stand-in and prompter. "He prompts Frankie on his lines."

"His name's not Rusty, is it?" asked Perry.

"Yeah, his name's Rusty. Do you know him?" asked Mona, always on the alert to collect information, especially about people she didn't like.

"He's a hustler," said Perry.

"How do you know him?" asked Mona.

"First-hand experience," said Perry. "Now, are you and Frankie going to get married? Give me the scoop on you two. This is like Joan Crawford and John Garfield in *Humoresque*."

They went upstairs.

The house was rushed to completion, or a semblance of completion, as Perry Rifkin called it, in time for Mona to give her first Hollywood party, for which she got a turn-out of power that amazed most of the observers and chroniclers of the Hollywood scene. Events were working in her favor.

The party that Mona Berg gave that attracted all the powerful was in honor of Taffy Grossman, the wife of Abe Grossman, of Grossman-Dragonet Productions, on the publication of her book *Spendthrift*, a shopping guide for rich women, on where to buy what, in matters of fashion, beauty, exercise, and life style. Abe had it ghostwritten for her, to satisfy what she told him were her creative urges. That Mona should be the hostess of such an occasion—the two women were no more than nodding acquaintances prior to a few days before the party—was due to circumstances that came to light regarding "questionable financial transactions," as they came to be known, in the television empire of Abe Grossman and Jess Dragonet.

"What's that all about, Marty?" asked Mona Berg of Marty Lesky about Abe Grossman.

"It's nothing," said Marty Lesky. "It's like the time Benny Doberman got into his financial jam. A little excitement for a few months, and then everything passes. Don't talk to anybody about it. Keep the lid on. If anyone asks you about it, say it's not true."

And, of course, she said it wasn't true when she was asked—which she was, being known more and more as a confidante of Marty Lesky—and her virtue was rewarded.

Because of the financial irregularities that had started to be gossiped about in the circles in which they moved, the publication of Taffy Grossman's book, dealing with extravagance as it did, came at an inopportune time, if anyone who thought about such things tied together the alleged misappropriation of funds on the one hand and a book dealing with spending as an art form on the other. Taffy, however, did not want to be denied her publication party, which she looked upon as her very own moment in the sun, and Abe, after consulting with Marty Lesky and Myron Kahn and a few others in the rulers' circle, decided that not to have the party would appear to take seriously the alleged irregularities, which they thought to be inconsequential, nothing more than errors of bookkeeping, part and parcel of the business in which they excelled.

All agreed that Taffy's publication party should not be given by Abe, and the question then became who would have the party. Sylvia Lesky told Marty in no uncertain terms that she would not give a party for Taffy Grossman in her home. Coming from a rulers' circle family as she did, Sylvia never quite accepted any of the television crowd as equals, even though their wealth was often in excess of the movie hierarchy's. On top of which Sylvia Lesky thought Taffy Grossman's book was "the tackiest thing I've ever heard of," and she was not going to let reporters in her house to advance the cause of Taffy Grossman's literary career, thank-you-very-much. When Sylvia added thank-you-very-much to any of her pronouncements, she retreated into the privilege from whence she came, as Marty once described it to Warren Ambrose, and he knew not to persist. "I had them at my table at the AFI dinner, and I had them at my party for Faye Converse," said Sylvia to Marty about the Grossmans, letting it be known that she had more than done her duty in their behalf.

Myron Kahn said that he and Delphine were going to be in London and couldn't give the party either. Neither Pearl Silver, who could always be counted on to give a party, nor Babette Navarro, who was also known to be a party enthusiast, seemed inclined to be the hostess. The matter was thought to be solved when Jess Dragonet, the partner of Abe Grossman, offered his newly decorated Bel Air mansion as a setting, but Taffy Grossman despised her husband's partner, although she pretended not to for the sake of business, and the excuse was given to Jess that the party should be given by someone outside the firm. It was Marty Lesky who came up with the idea for Mona Berg to give the party.

"Mona Berg?" said Taffy Grossman, disappointment in her tone, fearing a diminishment in importance of her moment in the sun.

"She's getting to be a very important woman in the industry," said Abe Grossman to his wife, taking the same approach to the selling of Mona as Marty Lesky had taken with him earlier in the day.

"Doesn't she live in that little dump up in Laurel Canyon that she's too ashamed of to let anyone see?" said Taffy, not liking this idea at all.

"She bought the old Lana Turner house on Camden Drive," said Abe patiently, "and Perry Rifkin's doing a rush job to have it completed in time for your party. You just make up your list, and get it over to Mona's secretary, and she'll send out the mailgrams."

"None of the good people will come to a party of Mona Berg's," grumbled Taffy Grossman, a bit of a sulker when she felt thwarted in her ambitions. By the good people, she meant the crème de la crème, Dolores DeLongpre's famous list of who mattered in social life.

"You'll have every studio head there, I guarantee you," said Abe, who'd been through this whole conversation with Marty Lesky.

"With wives?" asked Taffy.

"With wives," said Abe. "And the stars from all my series. And all Mona's clients, and that's not exactly chopped liver. There will be plenty of people to photograph, don't you worry." He wanted to have the matter settled and over with.

It didn't bother Mona Berg a bit that she was the sixth choice to hostess the party in honor of the publication of Taffy Grossman's book *Spendthrift*. She knew from all her years with Warren Ambrose that whenever there was a suspicion of financial irregularities in the upper echelons of power, the moguls stuck together in a show of solidarity, giving public support one to the other, knowing that the same support might be needed back if their own business practices came under too close scrutiny by too scrupulous an eye.

What Mona knew was that people who never would have ordinarily gone to a cocktail party for the publication of a shopping guide for rich women would go to this one, and she as hostess could only benefit from the association. She also knew that the tab for the party would be picked up by Abe Grossman. There wasn't a thing she skimped on.

The flowers from Las Floristas, or Bruce and Barry, as

Mona now called them, were much commented upon, as were the five-pound tins of Russian caviar that were opened one after the other, and the case after case of Dom Perignon champagne, and the five-piece orchestra, and the chorus of singers in top hats, white tie, and tails who sang Cole Porter songs in the background. She wanted people to say about her, "That Mona Berg sure knows how to give a party," and that was exactly what they did say.

Mona gave a toast. Ever since the Leskys' party, she became enchanted with the idea of giving toasts, liking to be up in front of people, liking to be noticed and talked about, liking to receive applause.

"Ever since I came to this town, Abe and Taffy have been like family to me," she said in a manner so convincing that even Abe and Taffy believed it. Behind her the chorus of singers sang the song "Money" from *Cabaret*, in which the lyric was the single word money repeated over and over. "You may think of Taffy as the lady with all the diamond bracelets on her arms, but I am here to praise her literary accomplishments, and her keen eye for being able to spot exactly the right thing in matters of shopping—"

Flashbulbs flashed and strobe lights strobed, and Taffy Grossman wept, and Abe Grossman beamed with pride, all the time piling high the paté de foie gras on the pumpernickel bread, denying in attitude to the film community that there was a whiff of scandal in his television empire.

Marina Vaughan, who had heard the whispers, watched and wondered. "Money, money, money," sang the singers. "Money. Money. Money." She turned and left the party, not waiting for her father to arrive, whom she had promised to meet there. She was experiencing feelings of unrest that she did not understand.

Dolores DeLongpre was there, of course, notebook and pencil in hand, busy, busy, busy, and Otto Ottoman, and the *Times* and the *Examiner* and the trade papers, and *Women's Wear Daily*, and *Beverly Hills People*, and Grace St. George, the society publicist, the one who had guided the social advancement of Warren Ambrose. She saw to it that all the right pictures were in all the right papers and magazines; and in time, so frequent were her mentions, the party came to be remembered more as Mona Berg's party than Taffy Grossman's publication party, much to the annoyance of both Grossmans, authoress and underwriter as they were.

Mona Berg's party set the protocol for the social behavior regarding Abe and Taffy Grossman during their period of unwanted celebrity resulting from the "questionable financial transactions," as they came to be called in the press. The Leskys had them to their dinner for the ex-governor and his wife. Babette and Nando Navarro had them to their dinner for Amos and Marianna Swank and Dom and Pepper Belcanto at Trader Vic's. Delphine and Myron Kahn had them to the dinner dance they gave at Chasens for two jet-set lesbians who were passing through the city.

Her slendering operation, her newfound friendships with socially advanced people in the industry, the success of her party for Taffy Grossman, the improvement of her appearance by the couturier Danny Damask and the hairdresser Yushi, the constant mentions of herself in the trade papers and social columns, and the feeling of love for the actor Franklyn Bassett that filled her system, all combined to give Mona Berg a new confidence in herself, making it less necessary to resort to subversive dealings in her day-to-day life to get what she wanted.

She began to discover for the first time that she had a sense of humor. Her mother had never laughed at things she said, nor had Warren Ambrose in her years of servitude for him. He only smiled tolerantly or nodded his head in acknowledgment of an amusing line from a subordinate, although he was known to repeat it as if it were his own at whatever table he happened to be lunching or dining. Marty Lesky was the first important person to laugh at her stories, and she took it to be an acknowledgment of equality, and that safe feeling allowed her to go further in the elaborate detail of her stories. Soon other people of Lesky rank began to appreciate and repeat. She was beginning to feel that, after all the years of never fitting in anywhere, she was finally starting to belong. At the very top of the heap.

Chapter 20

IN TIME FRANKIE became used to having his name in columns and his picture on the cover of magazines, but in the beginning, when it was all new to him, he savored every word of it and wondered always if the priests back in St. Joseph's Home for Boys, where he grew up, were reading about him, and realizing that Franklyn Bassett and Frankie Bozzaci, for whom they had once predicted a dim future, were one and the same.

Shortly after the Leskys' party for Faye Converse, when it became official that Frankie had won the coveted lead in the revival of the television series *South Sea Adventures*, beating out all others in the highly publicized nationwide talent hunt, Dolores DeLongpre carried the story as the lead in her column.

> When I was a young girl in this town, feeding items to Hedda Hopper, she used to say to me, "The same stories happen over and over again. Only the stars are different." A new star is being born in our town and will soon burst forth for the world to see. His

name is Franklyn Bassett. He has just been signed by studio topper Marty Lesky, of Colossus Pictures, Executive Producer Abe Grossman, and Producer Jess Dragonet, for the much-sought-after lead in *South Sea Adventures*, immediately going into production for mid-season replacement. Watch for him, ladies of America. He's divine.

"How do you like them apples?" asked Mona of Frankie in the bedroom they shared in her palatial new home, having read the item aloud to him, holding the paper as if she were presenting him with a marvelous gift of her own creation, which, of course, was exactly what it was.

"I hope they read that back at the home," said Frankie.

"Enough with the home," said Mona, a bit of impatience in her voice. She was never interested in hearing about that part of his life. For her, his life started on the day she picked him up on Sunset Boulevard. "There's more."

"Go on," said Frankie.

Mona went on reading from Dolores DeLongpre's column as if she were reading it for the first time, as if she hadn't fed all the information to Dolores herself. Her attention was rapt. "'Already people are calling Franklyn Bassett the next Al Pacino, the next Bobby De Niro, the next John Travolta. My prediction is this: Franklyn Bassett is the next Franklyn Bassett! He's the personal discovery of superagent Mona Berg, the girl with the golden touch, and it is she who is grooming him for stardom.'"

"Wow," said Frankie.

"Is that all you can say? Wow?" said Mona, putting her hand on his stomach.

"The next Travolta better get his ass in gear and get to the studio," said Frankie. "Work, work, work."

He pulled himself out of the bed, naked, and leaned over to pick up the newspaper that Mona had tossed on the floor. She

231

was never able to look at him undressed without craving him. She began kissing his back and putting her hand around to the front of him, reaching for his center, wanting to kneel in front of him, wanting to empty him, so all thoughts of that nature would leave him while he was away from her.

"Hey, what's this?" he said, reading further down in Dolores DeLongpre's column.

"What's what?" she asked, hanging on to him, kissing his buttocks.

" 'A further note from Hollywood,' " he read from the column. " 'The highly touted television special *Marina: She Sings, She Dances*, which was to have been the television debut of Marina Vaughan, was abruptly canceled yesterday afternoon. There are conflicting reports. Insiders believe the beleaguered star is going through a period of personal problems and is unable to meet the strenuous demands of the schedule.' How come you didn't read that part?"

"I didn't see it," she said, kissing his legs, working her way around to the front of him.

"What happened with Marina?" he asked.

"How should I know what happened with Marina?" she asked.

"You seem to know everything else that goes on in this town," he said, pulling away from her. "I don't like to be mauled like this."

Work, work, work. It was true. He worked morning, noon, and night. He was being made into a commodity. There was shooting, sometimes twelve hours a day, and learning lines, and an acting coach. There were sailing lessons. There was picture taking, and posing for magazine covers to coincide with the series going on the air. There were interviews. There was looping. There was going on location.

Sometimes they talked about him in front of him as if he

weren't there. There were a few people who said he was simple, so rarely did he open his mouth during that period. There were a few more observant people who said he was wise. It was a period to be listening rather than talking. Posters began to appear of him at meetings stripped to the waist.

"The campaign should open this way," said Mona to Marty Lesky and Abe Grossman and Jess Dragonet. "Full-page newspaper ads in twenty-six cities, and half-page ads in three hundred and twenty more. Just Frankie. Fierce. Handsome. Stripped to the waist, and nothing but the words 'He's Coming Your Way!' And then, two weeks later, run the same ad in the same papers, only this time give Frankie's name and the name of the series. That way we start to build a curiosity about him. 'Who is this guy? Who is this guy?' everybody's going to be asking."

She had the campaign all mapped out. "And then this mysterious figure will suddenly appear on thirteen hundred billboards in sixteen cities around the country. By this time the curiosity about him is rising, rising, rising all over the country. Everyone will be wondering, Who is this beautiful man?

"As we get closer to air date, I visualize twenty-five thousand television spots of Frankie's face beaming into tens of millions of homes. One million photographs of the poster have been printed to be given away, with an order to hold for two million more.

"By the time this show hits the air, Franklyn Bassett's face and name are going to be as well known to the American public as Al Pacino and Bobby De Niro and John Travolta."

Sometimes he thought to himself, Where's the joy? Where's the fun? Is this what it's all about? He was isolated from everyone except Mona and a few others, like Bill, Mona's secretary Bill. Sometimes he wanted to see his old friends, or get loaded, or get laid, or do something that was of his own choosing, but there was shooting and learning lines and rehearsing, and the grind went on and on.

One day the studio driver assigned to him took him from the studio to an interview in Beverly Hills. As they drove down Wilshire Boulevard, he spotted a Porsche agency, in the window of which was a black Porsche, just like the white Porsche that Cecilia Lesky was driving on the day he got into her car on Sunset Boulevard.

"Stop here, Charlie," Frankie said to the driver.

"The interview's at the Beverly Wilshire," said Charlie the driver.

"I know," said Frankie, "but I said stop here."

"What's up?" asked Charlie.

"You can go back to the studio," said Frankie.

"How will you get back?" asked the driver.

"I'll drive myself," said Frankie.

"In what?"

"See that car in the window?"

"Yeah."

"I'm going to buy it," said Frankie.

He went into the showroom. It was calm and peaceful inside, and the automobiles were shiny and sleek and looked like works of art. The salesman wore a pink button-down shirt from Dorso, open at the neck, a blue blazer, gray slacks, Gucci loafers, no socks, and a gold chain. He looked at the young man in the tee shirt and the blue jeans and the cowboy boots who walked past all the models to the car in the window. He opened the door of the car, got in, and sat behind the wheel luxuriating in the feel of the luxury.

"Can I help you?" asked the salesman, a touch of snobbery in his voice. "We don't like people getting into the models," he added.

"How much is this?" asked Frankie, cutting right through the formalities.

"The price is posted on the windshield of the passenger's side," said the salesman, disdaining to quote the price himself.

Frankie looked at the salesman, got out of the car, walked around to look at the price posted on the windshield of the passenger's side, thirty-five thousand dollars.

"I'll take it," he said.

The man looked at him, not in total disbelief, only partial. It was Hollywood, after all.

"Come here," said Frankie, beckoning for the man to come around to his side of the beautiful car. The man did. He pointed outside, through the plate glass window of the showroom, up high to a billboard overlooking Wilshire Boulevard.

"See that?" he asked. It was Frankie. Fierce. Handsome. Stripped to the waist. Looking just the way Mona had said it would look. "He's Coming Your Way!" read the teaser. "Tuesdays, 9–10, ABC."

"That's me," said Frankie.

"Franklyn Bassett," said the salesman, reading the name off the billboard.

"This is the kind of car I always wanted," said Frankie.

"You make my job easy," said the salesman, realizing he was serious about buying the car there and then.

"I only want it if I can have it right now," said Frankie, taking his checkbook from the back pocket of his jeans and writing out a check. "Is there gas in it?"

Later, after his interview, he stopped by the Ambrose-Berg Agency on Sunset Boulevard to show Mona what he had bought. It was a bit of independence on his part that she did not approve of. She liked to be the one who fulfilled his fantasies for him, but he would not allow her to dampen his enthusiasm.

"There's no guarantee the series is going to be a hit," said Mona. "You're going to be up against some very stiff competition."

"All the more reason to have something to show for it," said Frankie. "Look, Mona, it's what I wanted, and it's the first time I spent a nickel since I started making all this money."

"You're not making all that much money," said Mona.

"Compared to cleaning other people's pools and tending bar and doing a few other things I won't go into here, I'm making a lot of money," said Frankie.

"I could have gotten it for you on a lease," said Mona, "and worked the payments into the budget of the series. These are things I know about."

"I didn't want it on a lease," said Frankie, "and I didn't want it paid for by the budget of the series. I never bought myself a present in my whole life before, and I wanted to buy myself a present. Without any strings attached to it."

"I got an idea," said Mona, knowing when to give in on a point, but still getting in the last word. "We'll put the time slot of the series on your license plate."

One night on the news, an entertainment columnist ran a videotape of Frankie signing his contract at Colossus in Marty Lesky's office, as part of the hype that was being generated in advance of the debut of the series. It was a backstage view of a new star's life, an idea of Mona's, showing Marty putting his arm around Frankie's shoulder, in the old Louis B. Mayer–Clark Gable tradition, welcoming him to the studio, clowning a little for the camera. Then a piece of film from his screen test—in which he had removed on camera the tee shirt that hadn't fit correctly—was shown.

"Did you ever see anything so beautiful in your whole life?" said Mona to Bill about the undressing. "Do you know something? If he hadn't taken off that tee shirt, he wouldn't have gotten the part."

During the commercial break, the telephone rang, and it was the columnist, wanting to know how it had sounded.

"I thought that would be her mother," said Frankie to Bill. "How come her mother never calls anymore when her name's on TV?"

"She died," said Bill. "Didn't Mona tell you?"

"No, she didn't tell me. When?" asked Frankie.

"The night of the Leskys' party," said Bill. Frankie remembered the telephone call, when they were on their way out the door.

"You went to a party the night your mother died?" he said to her, the orphan in him shocked.

"I did it for you," said Mona, quick to her own defense. It was her house, and his life was her creation, and she wasn't interested in hearing any critiques from him about her after what she had done. "You ended up with the lead in a series they didn't even want you for because of that party."

He let it pass. He wanted what she was making available to him. Growing up in an orphanage, he had learned how to accommodate himself to other people in order to get what he wanted, and he accommodated himself to her, and questioned less and less the things about her he did not like.

"Let's do something that costs a lot of money," she said. It was a way she had of making up after there had been a tense moment between them, as if she had to keep providing him with wonderment to hold his interest.

"Like what?" he asked. Her spending binges fascinated him.

"Let's charter a jet, and fly to Vegas for Pia Zadora's opening," said Mona, "and we'll be back here by midnight." She liked to do extravagant things at the drop of a hat.

Between the time of the Leskys' party and the time that his series went on the air and he became the love idol of American television, Franklyn Bassett and Cecilia Lesky met on only two occasions. It was as if each understood that the stirrings of inner feelings for the other were taboo. Mona, who was ever alert to the possibility of a flirtatious glance in her lover's direction, never considered that the shy heiress harbored secret feelings for him, or that Frankie ever gave a thought to her.

The first time they met was at Jess Dragonet's Sunday brunch, when Mona decided she had to have a house of her own in Beverly Hills to begin to entertain. They were the only two people to use the swimming pool to swim. Others used it to lie around for the sun, but no one went in it except Cecilia and Frankie.

She was wearing the kind of bikini her mother hated her to wear, brief in the extreme. Frankie did not notice her until she was getting out of the pool and he was on his way to the diving board. She was deeply tanned, and her hair was wet, and her body glistened in the noonday sun, and his heart reacted. He was wearing the briefest of bikinis himself, the kind that Mona loved him to wear, as if the sexiness of him enhanced her, whose possession she thought he was.

They spoke in passing, but did not stop, as if each realized the other was forbidden fruit.

"That bathing suit's positively indecent," said Cecilia.

"That's the whole point," said Frankie, and they both laughed. Their eyes met for an instant. "You've got a beautiful body," he added.

"Thanks," she said, warmed by his compliment. "Yours is beautiful too."

He climbed to the top of the high dive and did a show-off dive for her benefit.

"Franklyn," called Mona, from the pavilion that separated the tennis court from the swimming pool. "Jess is serving lunch."

"Coffee?" Cecilia said to him at the buffet lunch when she got up to get herself some.

"Only half a cup," said Frankie, looking up at her.

"What's the matter? Don't you like my coffee?" asked Cecilia.

"It's not the coffee. It's the caffeine I can do without," said Frankie, shaking his head.

"This is Brim *decaffeinated* coffee."

"This is Brim?"

"Yes!"

"Well, if it tastes this rich, I don't want half a cup. Fill it to the rim."

"With Brim?"

They laughed and laughed, and looked at each other, and laughed again. It occurred to each of them that they rarely laughed in the glamorous lives they were living.

Sometime later, after Mona bought the house on Camden Drive in Beverly Hills, the doorbell rang one Sunday afternoon when Frankie was studying his lines for the next day's shooting outside by the pool.

"Answer that, will you, Frankie?" called Mona out the window from the second floor. "It's probably the guy from the burglar alarm system. Tell him I'll be down in a few minutes."

Frankie pulled a towel around his waist and went to the front door to let in the man from the burglar alarm system. Instead, it was Cecilia Lesky holding a package. Each was startled to see the other.

"Cecilia," said Frankie.

"It never occurred to me you'd answer the door," said Cecilia, wondering if her feelings were showing. She handed him the package she was carrying. "This is from my father for Mona. I suppose it's a house present. He asked me to drop it off."

"I saw you at the studio the other day having lunch with your father," he said, not wanting her to go.

"I saw you too," she said. "You're getting famous. Everybody's talking about you."

"I'm getting nervous too. All this hype. Suppose it turns out I can't act?" said Frankie, looking at her in the eye. "I never have anyone to talk to. How come you stay away from me? How come you act like I'm not even there most of the time?"

"Is that the man from the burglar alarm?" called Mona from upstairs to Frankie. The sound of Mona's voice and the look in Cecilia's eyes at the same moment gave him the answer to his question.

"I have to run," said Cecilia. "Bye, Frankie."

"Bye, Cecilia." She looked at his new black Porsche, like her white Porsche, that was parked in the curved driveway.

"Copycat on the car," said Cecilia.

He smiled at her because she had noticed.

"Gross on the license plate," she added, getting into her car.

240

"That's my time slot. Tuesday, nine to ten. It's part of the hype," called Frankie. She backed out of the driveway and was gone. He always felt ashamed of his relationship with Mona in front of her. She had never once thrown herself at him, or even sought him out for conversation, but he had a feeling about her always that the moment would come for them, in the natural order of things. The beginning of their relationship was too momentous, with its connections and coincidences, and he sometimes thought in terms of fate.

"So you're the lover I have waited for. The mate that fate had me created for." It was what was playing on Cecilia's car radio, and on Mona's portable radio as she joined him in the hall.

"Was that the man from the burglar alarm system?" she asked.

"No, it was a house present from Marty Lesky," said Frankie, handing her the box.

"Oh, that's not a house present. It's a pistol Marty sent over, now that I'm a house owner in Beverly Hills," said Mona.

"A pistol?" asked Frankie, an incredulous note in his voice. "What's Marty Lesky sending you over a pistol for?"

"You know how hipped Marty is on protection," answered Mona, putting the box with the pistol on the table in the front hall. "He probably didn't want the chauffeur to know he was carrying a gun, so he said it was a house present."

"It wasn't the chauffeur," said Frankie quietly. "It was Cecilia."

"Say, why don't we drive over to the Sunset Strip and look at your billboard," suggested Mona. "Perry Rifkin says it's causing a traffic jam."

Chapter 21

IT WAS NOT the best of times in the life of Marina Vaughan, nor was it the worst. She was in the transition period of going from the former to the latter. She remained a vivid figure in the film community, because of who she was and who she knew, and for this reason her fall from grace and favor was tolerated longer than most.

She made her unfortunate remark about Mona Berg, funny in the instant of telling, not so funny when it was quoted in Otto Ottoman's column, and repercussions followed.

Before the end of the week the television special *Marina: She Sings, She Dances,* which was to have been her comeback from this bad luck period she was going through, was canceled in the first week of rehearsal. She heard the news when she read it in Dolores DeLongpre's column. Dolores wrote that there were conflicting reports.

"But why?" cried Marina over the telephone to the producer of the special.

"I don't know any more than you do about it, Marina," said the producer.

"Tony Charmoli said I was wonderful," said Marina, not making any attempt to hold back her sobs.

"I thought you were wonderful too, Marina," said the producer.

For a time following the cancellation of her television special, Marina Vaughan dropped out of sight. She stayed home behind closed doors, not drinking, not drugging, just looking off into space, wondering what was happening to her.

"Take the phone off the hook, will you, Juanita. I don't want to talk to *anybody*," she said to her maid.

"You're allowing your behavior to prove her point," said her father, Rex Vaughan, when he stopped by to see her. He was talking about Mona Berg, on whom he felt his daughter was obsessing. "You've let yourself become her victim."

"I want to ask you a question," said Marina. "Do you think I would have made it if I hadn't been yours and Mom's daughter?"

"All that I ever did was open the doors for you," said Rex. "You had to take it from there. Come on, Marina. Why are you laying all these trips on yourself? You're a proven star."

"When I did that play on Broadway, people used to say you made up the deficit every week so it would last out the season," she said.

"And where the hell am I supposed to have gotten that kind of money?" said Rex.

"Whatever it was I had, I've lost," said Marina. "When I had it, I never took it seriously, because deep down I suppose I always thought I lucked into it, but now that I'm losing it, I realize how much I want it. You know, I've been thinking a lot about Mom lately."

"So have I," said Rex. "That's why I'm so concerned about you, Marina. The circumstances aren't that different. She got a reputation for drinking too much, and nobody would touch her, and she lost her nerve and she kept getting into trouble, and then she bit the dust one night."

"I'm not going to bite the dust, Daddy," said Marina, getting up to get herself a drink.

He picked up the photograph of Montgomery Clift in the silver frame on the table next to her sofa. "The glass is broken on Monty's picture," he said.

"Mona Berg knocked it over one night," said Marina. "That was the beginning of my troubles, now that I think of it. Oh, Daddy, what am I going to do?"

Then she danced with Cecilia Lesky at a disco party, as a joke, as a madcap thing, and someone started a rumor that something occurred in the love-that-dare-not-speak-its-name category, when nothing of the sort had occurred, or had been intended to occur, and again repercussions followed.

"Guess who's diking it up?"

"Don't make me guess, for God's sake."

"Marina Vaughan—"

"So what else is new?"

"You haven't let me finish. Annnd—"

"And who?"

"Promise you won't tell?"

"Promise."

"Cecilia Lesky."

"Cecilia Lesky!"

"You promised."

Sylvia Lesky sat in the back seat of her chauffeur-driven Rolls-Royce, on her way to Magnin's to try on hats for the opening of the Santa Anita race track. Beside her was her daughter, the increasingly restless Cecilia Lesky, staring out the window.

"Is it true you were dancing at Miss Garbo's with Marina Vaughan?" asked Sylvia, critically adjusting her make-up in the mirror of her gold and diamond powder box.

"Heiress news travels fast, I see," answered Cecilia, surprised that her mother would have heard.

"You won't be an heiress much longer if your father hears about this," said Sylvia, continuing her ministrations.

"I'll manage," said her daughter.

"Is it true you were drinking champagne out of the bottle?"

"Dom Perignon, Mother. At least you should approve of that."

"I mean, it didn't go any further than dancing, did it, with Marina Vaughan?"

"Oh, Mother, for God's sake. We were just having some fun."

"I hope it doesn't get in the papers."

"How did you hear?"

"Mona Berg."

"That piece of shit," said Cecilia, disgust in her voice.

"Oh, that's nice talk," said her mother, concerned with the impropriety of the language.

"How did Mona know?"

"Apparently her secretary, Bill, tried to cut in on you." Cecilia laughed.

"Oh, darling, Marina's such a tramp," said her mother.

"If they do this to Marina, Marty, they'll be putting the final nail in her coffin," said Rex Vaughan to Marty Lesky, in

Marty Lesky's office at Colossus Pictures.

"The show's already been canceled, Rex. There's nothing I can do," said Marty.

"You can call this dame off her back, Marty," said Rex.

"Whatever's going on is going on between those two ladies, Rex. I don't have anything to do with it."

"What does this Mona Berg have on you, Marty? Dirty pictures? Little girls? Forged checks? Abe Grossman?"

"You're way out of line, Rex," said Marty, beginning to shuffle through some screenplays on the table behind his desk.

"She's got some hold on you, Marty, or you wouldn't be dancing to her tune," said Rex Vaughan, turning to leave the office.

"Say, Rex, there's a script here I'd like you to look at. It's a new version of *Dodsworth* I'm thinking about doing. Let me know if it's something that might interest you."

Marina couldn't get any of the top agents to represent her and settled for a relative unknown called Joel Zircon. He was young and brash and using her, and she knew he was going to let her down. If she hadn't been on her way down, and he hadn't been on his way up, they probably wouldn't ever have been in the same room, but she was, and he was, and they were. Once her confidence in herself was shaken sufficiently, she began to set herself up to fail, although she would not have accepted that as a correct prognosis at the time. She knew that she'd been blackballed, that she was tarnished and smeared, and no one wanted to use her.

When people said to her, "What are you doing these days?" more and more tentatively, as it was apparent she was doing less and less, she started to say, "I'm writing a book," as if that were the thing that she most wanted to be doing rather than pursuing the stardom that was slipping away from her.

"What's it about?" asked her friend Babette Navarro.

"Me," Marina answered.

"Like Joan Crawford's kid, you mean?" asked Babette.

"No," she answered quietly. It was hard for the people in her group to see past the current flop of her, as if what had been and what was going to be no longer mattered.

"Are you going to Pearl's on Wednesday?" asked Babette, diverting the conversation to more agreeable areas.

"I'm just a tiny bit mean to Pearl in my book," said Marina, knowing it would get back. If she knew how to write it, she would be mean, but she felt she didn't know how to write it. She talked about it as if it existed, as if there were a growing stack of typewritten pages in her work room, and quaking-in-the-boots on the part of certain people could be expected, but the fact was the ideas in her head had not yet gotten to the typed page, and it soon became apparent that it was one of those books that get talked about and talked about but probably never written.

When I was a little girl, I never visualized myself as the kind of woman who got married three times before she was thirty, but that's what I did, wrote Marina Vaughan as a first line to the autobiography she started to write. Warren Ambrose, who used to be her agent before the stroke that felled him, always told her that if she ever wrote her story just as it happened, movie star daughter of movie star father sort of thing, telling it all, about her mother's suicide with her head in the toilet bowl, and her father's affair with Montgomery Clift, he could get her an advance, "in the six figures," as he put it.

But in those days she was still operating. She'd made four

pictures in four years and thought she was on a merry-go-round she was never going to get off. It wasn't a period for reflection then. That was what she was in now. Her new agent, Joel Zircon, told her he had publishing connections in New York and promised her he'd "shop the idea around."

"Let me get this straight," said Joel Zircon, taking a second line of cocaine. "Why was your mother's head in the toilet bowl?"

"You see, she'd had her hair done, and her nails, and she was wearing a beautiful satin nightgown, and there were wonderful sheets on the bed," said Marina, looking off into space as she told him the story. "She wanted to look beautiful when she was found, but she got sick, you see, from the Seconal and the vodka, and she threw up and choked on her vomit, and that's how I found her, with her head in the toilet bowl."

"I can sell that," said Joel.

Her father was beginning to feel differently about her. It was a reality that she became aware of, and allowed to happen, in that she did not say the words of protest that might have stilled the criticisms that had replaced the delight he used to feel in the events of her life. His return to the pinnacle, from which he had once toppled, signaled a return to a more conservative way of life than he had espoused during his lean seven years. After a lifetime of avoiding the social circuit, he had started to play the game, the drawing-room game, which he once denounced. More, he was enjoying it, his new role in the scheme of things, since the AFI dinner in his honor, of younger elder statesman of the industry, following along in the golden footsteps of Cary Grant and Gregory Peck and Jimmy Stewart and Dom Belcanto.

All that she had to do was turn in three chapters, and a

publisher Joel Zircon had discovered was going to give her fifty thousand dollars in advance money, which she needed badly as the adverse state of her economic life worsened. Her father told her right off when she told him the news, thinking he would be thrilled for her, that he didn't want her using that old story about him and Montgomery Clift.

"Listen, Marina, I don't want you using any of those old stories about Monty and me," he said to her. They were having dinner at La Scala at the time, and the unstated accusation that she might wounded her.

"What do I know about Monty Clift, Daddy?" Marina replied, choosing her words. "He dropped me at my christening. I'm going to write about that, of course. And he used to always come to my birthday parties when we still lived in the house on Walden Drive, but I never saw him again after the car crash at Elizabeth Taylor's, and I was only six or seven when that happened. That's all I'm going to write about Monty, what I remember about him."

"That story about Monty and me hung on and on, and there was never a word of truth to it," he said, not letting go of what she had assured him was not to be.

"You used to tell me it didn't make any difference, that story," she said. "I used to tell you I thought it made you a more interesting man."

"I told you, Marina, I don't want you to use it," said Rex.

"And I told you I had no intention of using it," Marina answered.

"How about your mother?"

"What about mother?"

"You're not going to tell that story about her dying with her head in the toilet bowl, are you?"

"I'm the one who found her, Daddy," said Marina. "It remains as one of the most vivid moments of my life. Of course I'm going to write about it. It's my autobiography."

"The story we gave out at the time was that you learned about your mother's suicide when you read about it in a movie magazine," said Rex Vaughan. "It sounds so much better, Marina."

"But it's not the way it happened," answered Marina with the beginning of a sharp note in her voice. They sat in silence for a moment.

"This fettucine stinks. Let's get out of here," said Rex. "Give me my check, will you, George?"

"Here you go, Mr. Vaughan," said George, who had been calling Rex Vaughan Mr. Vaughan for twenty-five years. "I liked you on the Amos Swank show the other night."

"Thanks, George," said Rex, signing the check, using the moment to cool the anger he was beginning to feel. "That Amos Swank's a master of making you feel at ease. I hadn't told that story about the White House dinner to anybody, and here I was on TV telling it to millions of people. It sounded all right, huh?"

"Great story," said George. "Poor Marilyn."

"Yeah, poor Marilyn. I think about her a lot. The last time I ever saw Marilyn, she was sitting right at that table there," said Rex. He had gotten to the point where he liked to reminisce about olden times.

"That's right. The night before it happened," said George, who was prepared to continue the conversation about Marilyn, meaning Marilyn Monroe, and tell who she was with that night, and about a telephone call she had received during the meal on the private telephone that had been put in for the personal use of Dom Belcanto, the legendary singer.

"I think I'm going to go, Dad," said Marina, interrupting the conversation, having heard it before, not being interested enough to hear it again, feeling dispirited that the joyous news of her publishing coup had been received so joylessly.

She stopped talking to her father about her book after that. Whenever she tried to work on the three chapters that she needed to turn in in order to get the advance money that she needed so much to live on, she began wondering what her father's reaction would be to the stories of her life that she was telling. She began to change things in the actuality of them, keeping in mind sensibilities and proprieties, and they sounded not like she wanted them to sound, and then she became confused, and the fun that it started out to be turned into agony, and knots of anguish filled her stomach, and weeks went by, and the task remained unfinished, and the advance money remained unadvanced, and she threw away invitations to charities she had given to before, and cut her maid Juanita back to three days a week, and allowed to expire magazine subscriptions that were expiring.

Then she was disinvited at the last minute to Pearl Silver's dinner for Elena Jamieson, after Mona Berg said she wouldn't attend if Marina was going. It embarrassed her that it still mattered so much to her. It embarrassed her more that, when given such a problem, Pearl Silver had picked Mona as a more attractive addition to her table than Marina, especially as Pearl had told her when she invited her that Elena Jamieson had asked especially to see her.

It was going to be fourteen people, of the group that she no longer saw, or who no longer saw her, and she wanted to go. She wanted to be seen in that group, to show herself as bearing up under pressure. She did things she did less and less those days: she went to Yushi and had her hair done, and she went to Danny Damask and got herself a new dress.

Right there should have been the clue that the evening was not to be. The saleslady, who was Taffy Grossman's mother, told her that her MasterCard was no longer valid, and reported that the verification operator had said she should cut the card in two. She paid for it with an American Express card, which passed muster, but it gave the dress a bad aura, and she never liked the way it fit. Then Pearl Silver called her and canceled her out with a manufactured story of seating difficulties in her dining room.

"What's happened, Marina, is that everyone's got house guests. The Kahns have those two jet-set dikes, and now I've got too many women, and I can only seat fourteen, and you're *such* an old friend, I felt that you'd understand," said Pearl.

"You mean you'd like me to back out from coming," said Marina.

"You understand, don't you, about the table and the seating?" repeated Pearl.

"Of course," said Marina, who didn't understand.

"You're such a good friend for doing this," said Pearl, as if she were bestowing an honor, "and, you know, we'd love to have you in after dinner. I hope you're not one of those people who feels funny about coming in after dinner."

"Let's play it by ear," said Marina, knowing she'd never go in after dinner, just as Pearl knew she wouldn't and felt safe suggesting it. Marina didn't let on that she minded at all, although she took it as another demotion.

It wasn't until she read about the evening in Dolores De-Longpre's column and saw that Mona Berg was a guest that she realized what the true situation had been. When the wife of a producer she had once worked with called to ask her if she had any clothes she wanted to donate to a celebrity auction for a worthy cause, she sent over the new dress, which made her think of Taffy Grossman's mother every time she looked at it.

Marina Vaughan was drinking a lot of champagne, and taking a lot of cocaine, and going to a lot of parties with a new younger group that she liked to tell people were a lot more fun than Pearl Silver and the Leskys and the Navarros and the Kahns and the Swanks and so on and so on, where she seemed to be invited less and less.

"I'm a young woman," Marina was heard to say. "What am I going around with all those old people for? That's my father's crowd, for Christ's sake." The fact was she liked to be in that crowd. She liked to be the youngest one in the older crowd. She liked the special attention that went with it from people who had known her all her life. She felt much less sure of herself with people her own age. Somewhere within her lurked a suspicion about herself that she got where she was by being who she was, and that people her own age resented her.

"How'd you like the script of *Dodsworth*, Rex?" Mona Berg asked Rex Vaughan at Pearl Silver's dinner for Elena Jamieson.

"I liked it fine," said Rex. "Why?"

"My client Lambeth Walker wrote the screenplay, and Marty Lesky told me he gave it to you," said Mona.

"Oh, yeah?" said Rex. He had felt strange being seated next to her, expecting her to be different from what she was being.

"It would be such a great part for you, Rex," she said. She knew all his pictures, even the remote ones not many people remembered, and he was flattered by the detail with which she remembered certain of his scenes.

"I always thought Greg Peck was going to do the part," said Rex.

"Peck-Schmeck," said Mona. "You were born to play this part, Rex. You're just the right age. Did you ever see Walter Huston do the original version?"

"A couple of times," said Rex.

"You'd be better than Huston," said Mona.

"You think?"

"I know. Who's your agent these days?"

"Well, I've been thinking of making a change," said Rex.

"Why don't we talk? I'll give you a call tomorrow."

"I'll be home all morning."

"These vegetables are scrumptious," Mona said, helping herself to more. "Tell Ling he's a national treasure."

"Tell who what?" asked Rex.

"No, no, I was talking to the butler," said Mona.

Marina Vaughan called Jack Crawford her very own Gatsby. He had a jet, and a couple of Rolls-Royces, and a mirrored and marbled house. He had dark and mysterious connections and he kept a loaded gun next to his bed. His bedroom had a mirrored ceiling and a bed that undulated. He liked to get stoned on cocaine and watch her blow him. She never knew where the money came from, and she never asked. She knew he was using her to get in with the movie crowd, but she liked being back with one guy again, and the sex was good, and the drugs were plentiful, and the excitement was high, and he was young and good-looking.

"You're the first guy with a hairy back I ever got hung up on," she said to him.

"Just suck that dick, baby," he said to her, "and play with those nuts."

"My very own Gatsby," she said.

"My very own Linda Lovelace," he said.

254

Her father gave her some money. It paid off all her bills, and took away for a while the stress that was growing and growing within her about the desperate economic mess her life was. She hated taking money from her father, and it increased the strain that was building between them, because she no longer felt she had the right to come to her own defense when he slighted her, which she felt that he was doing more and more.

"I signed with Mona Berg," he told her one night at La Scala when they were having one of their once-or-twice-a-month dinners together. She felt betrayed by him for having gone into a business arrangement with the woman she felt was the enemy of her life.

"How could you do that?" asked Marina.

"She didn't do anything to hurt your career," said her father.

"How can you say that to me?" she asked him.

"Let's keep the voice in the lower decibels," he answered. "I asked Robbie Slick to ask her."

"You asked him to ask her if she blackballed me?" she asked her father in an incredulous tone.

"Mona's a good friend of Robbie's and she would have told him, and he said she said no, it was all a figment of your imagination," said Rex.

"And that was good enough for you," said Marina, not as a question but as the answer to the question.

"She's not the one who got drunk at the AFI dinner," said her father in an easy fatherly manner that covered the sting of the remark. It was the first time he had ever mentioned it to her.

Chapter 22

THE BEVERLY HILLS HOTEL for lunch was Joel Zircon's idea, not Marina Vaughan's. He liked being seen there, in one particular part, at the rear of the Polo Lounge looking out on the garden, but he wouldn't have been seated in that part if he hadn't been with Marina Vaughan, and she knew it, and he knew that she knew it; but she let him outpower her, and they went there rather than to a place where she wouldn't have run into so many people she didn't want to see. He had a habit of table-hopping, sometimes to tables of executives who didn't speak to her, leaving her alone for periods of up to ten minutes. She had started to despise Joel Zircon, although she pretended not to. It wasn't just that he always had bad news for her in the matter of employment. It was a habit he had developed of imitating the voice of the person who had rejected her, for whatever part, giving her the word-for-word of it, to deflect the fault.

" 'That unreliable drug addict,' " he said, contorting his face, modulating his tone, with great exactitude, into the

sneer and rejection of Jess Dragonet describing Abe Grossman's reaction to the idea of her playing a guest star role in
an episode of one of his television series.

"I got it," said Marina, not wishing him to elaborate on his
performance. She never allowed him to see how deeply she
was hurt when he did this.

"I said to him, 'Listen, Jess, this girl hasn't had any powder
up her nose since I took over her management,'" said Joel
with protectiveness in his voice for his role in the scene.

"You have a way with a word, Joel," said Marina, realizing
that yet another avenue was closed to her. She had thought
that they would leap at the opportunity to get her, movie star
that she was, or had been until recently, for one of their television episodes.

"He ate it up," said Joel, as if he had Jess Dragonet and
Abe Grossman eating out of his hand, which he did not. Selling Marina, or trying to sell Marina, had been the wedge that
had finally gotten him into their office for the first time, and
direct contact had been made for future dealings with other
clients in his stable.

"But he turned me down," she said flatly. Money was on
her mind. Money, money, money. What am I going to do for
money if I don't get some work soon? was what she was
thinking but not saying.

"I meant, you know, for the future," said Joel.

"*Quelle* future?" said Marina in a bittersweet tone that
was creeping more and more into her voice.

"*Listen,*" said Joel, as a new thought occurred to him, a
delicious bit of gossip of the industry variety, waiting there in
storage to deflect the conversation away from the direction of
money and problems that he knew it was taking. "I *knew* I
had something to tell you."

"That sounds like your divorce-news or dike-news voice," said Marina.

"I got the scoop on the Abe Grossman story. He did some creative accounting on Faye Converse—a million bucks' worth," said Joel, with his put-that-in-your-pipe-and-smoke-it look on his face, for having produced what he would call the scoop of the year when he table-hopped and repeated the story to people on a higher rung than he, for the attention that it gave him.

"How?" asked Marina, who knew hot news when she heard it.

"Do you remember that movie of the week that Faye Converse made for Abe Grossman a couple of years back when it was still a big deal for Faye Converse to be on television?"

"When she played the whole thing in the iron lung?"

"Emmy nomination, the whole bit. Zilch in the ratings."

"Where does the million dollars come in?"

"In order to get her to do it, they offered as an extra added attraction part of a piece-of-shit pilot that they thought was never going to sell."

"You've got my full attention," said Marina.

"The pilot was *Sally, Irene, and Mary*," said Joel.

"Hit of hits," said Marina, following his story.

"Three seasons and no profits, is what he told Faye. He said the show was operating at a loss," said Joel. They were all people on a level above him, and he loved to talk about them and hoped they would be caught, but knew he would do the same thing as they did under the circumstances.

"I saw him talking to Faye at the Leskys' one night as if they were the best of friends," said Marina. "And all the time she didn't even know, and she's trying to sell those diamond and pearl earrings of hers to maintain her standard of living."

"Would you excuse me just a minute, Marina. I see Laddie

over there. I'm in the middle of a deal with him, and I want to catch him," said Joel.

"It's so tacky to table-hop, Joel," said Marina.

"It's business," he said with perfect logic, as if it sufficed.

"You don't see Laddie doing it," said Marina, "and it's the third time during this lunch that you will have done it, and I'm not just crazy about sitting alone at a table in the Polo Lounge being treated like an actress on the skids."

"Miss Vaughan," a voice called out. "Miss Marina Vaughan."

"There's someone paging you," said Joel.

"No one knows I'm here," said Marina.

"Right here," said Joel, waving to the midget in the bell-hop uniform.

"Hello, Miss Vaughan," said the bellhop.

"Hello, Danny," said Marina.

"How's your dad?" said the bellhop.

"He's doing a picture at Colossus," said Marina.

"He never stops," said the bellhop. Affectionate moments between the classes puzzled Joel Zircon. He was always rude, or overfriendly, with people who worked in positions of service, and felt more in control of the situation when the size of the tip determined the degree of friendliness.

"Who wants Miss Vaughan?" he said to the bellhop, handing him a closed fist with several dollars in it.

"No, thank you, sir," said the bellhop to Joel, waving away the money. He never took tips from the people he'd known all their lives, the old families who knew how to do things right and always gave him a big check at Christmas, but he didn't bother to explain this to Joel Zircon.

"There's a gentleman in the lobby who'd like to see you, Miss Vaughan," said Danny.

"Why doesn't he come in?" asked Marina.

"He said it's kind of a surprise," said Danny.

"Do you want me to go out and see who it is?" asked Joel, wanting to be involved with whatever was happening, feeling excluded from their duologue. He's like Mona in drag, thought Marina about her new agent. Why do I always get hooked up with people like this?

"No, no, I'll go," said Marina. There was something about Danny coming to fetch her, making a moment with her, treating her as of old, that made her feel she should handle the matter herself. "You go table-hop and repeat your gossip."

"There's a tight lid on that gossip, Marina," said Joel. "If that gets heard coming out of your mouth."

"What are you trying to tell me, that the offers will stop pouring in?" said Marina, getting up, knowing people were looking at her. On her way out, following the bellhop, she looked straight ahead toward the exit all the way, as if she did not see Mona Berg at a table with Abe Grossman, and Pearl Silver at a table with Delphine Kahn, and Marty Lesky at a table with Scotty Warburg—of the brokerage house of the same name, which underwrote the stock of Colossus Pictures—with whom she'd once had an affair.

"It's the gentleman right across the lobby, the one looking in the fireplace, with the raincoat on," said Danny. They were standing in the lobby outside of the Polo Lounge.

"This is like Watergate," said Marina to Danny, and they both laughed. She walked across the lobby.

As she got to the fireplace, the man turned around, put out his hand, and said, "Hello, Marina. Do you remember me?"

"I'm not sure. Kind of. Help me out," she said.

"I wrote a piece on you at the Cannes Film Festival once," he said.

"When I didn't show up for the award that I won. I remember," she said. "You were the only one who was nice to me. One of those bitches wrote I was locked in a suite at the Hotel de Paris in Monte Carlo with Marcello Mastroianni. Is that the surprise?"

"That was just to get you out here. My name's Johnny Griffin, in case you forgot, and I'm now with the *Washington Post*," said the man. He was thirty, or thereabouts, Irish-looking, dressed in prep school fashion, of the flannel and tweed and button-down-collar variety.

"The *Washington Post* has an austere sound to it," said Marina. "I'm more accustomed to the *National Enquirer*."

"I'm beating around the bush," he said.

"Yes, you are, and my cold lunch is getting warm," she said.

"My boss, Mrs. Graham, Katherine Graham, Kay Graham," he said.

"Yes, yes, yes, I was with you from the first one," she said.

"She had a tip from a very good source about some gross financial irregularities in the Grossman-Dragonet television empire. I mean, it's a red-hot story if there's anything to it, and I can't get anyone to return my telephone call. I was wondering if you could be of any help to me," he said.

"How did you happen to pick me for this honor?" Marina said, turning around to see if anyone was watching her.

"I saw you go into the Polo Lounge with that guy who was kissing everyone in the lobby," said Johnny Griffin.

"That's my agent," said Marina.

"What happened to Warren what's-his-name who was your agent in Cannes that time?"

"Ambrose. Warren Ambrose. He had a stroke. Let's not get off the track here," she said.

"That's all there is to it. I saw you go in. I remembered our experience together. You wrote me a nice note after I wrote that article about you. You said you appreciated what I wrote. You always seemed like a nice lady to me, and I thought I'd ask you if you could help me out."

"Madcap. You were the first one to call me madcap. Unfortunately, it was a word that stuck, although it sounded awfully nice and glamorous when you wrote it," she said. "I don't know anything."

"You know who all the people are. You know all the private telephone numbers. If I can catch people off guard, I can get my story."

"I know all the numbers all right. Town. Beach. Desert. Ranch. And chalet. Several of the principals of your cast of characters are seated right in the Polo Lounge at this very moment."

"You'll help me?" he asked.

"I better get back to my table," she said. "My agent ought to have finished table-hopping by now. When we shake hands, there will be a card in my hand with my address and telephone number on it. Why don't you call me this afternoon, and we'll arrange a time."

"Are you still at that fabulous house in Malibu I used to read about?" asked Johnny Griffin.

"I gave that up. I'm living in an apartment in Beverly Hills now," she said. "Just off Wilshire Boulevard. Anyone can tell you where it is."

"Who was it?" asked Joel Zircon when she got back to her table in the Polo Lounge.

"Oh, just an old friend," said Marina.

"Who?"

"Nobody famous. You wouldn't be interested. How was the table-hopping?"

"Laddie said to say hi."

262

* * *

Blackballed. No one would touch her with a ten-foot pole. Her money was running out. Her living was not easy.

"What happened to all the money?" It was a question a lot of people asked at a lot of dinner parties when her name came up, and the answer always was, quite correctly, that she'd always spent more than she earned, and she'd never saved a penny for the proverbial rainy day, because she never thought the rainy day would ever come.

She felt a lot of hostility toward a lot of people. She hadn't arrived at the point where she understood the extent of her own involvement in her downward mobility, as she described it to her friend Babette Navarro, and she directed the blame for the sad events that were befalling her to others, none more strongly than Mona Berg, whom she blamed, not to herself only, as the architect of her destruction. And there were others. Pearl Silver, for disinviting her to her party at the last minute. And Abe Grossman. She was deeply hurt by Joel's imitation of Abe describing her as an unreliable drug addict, especially since Joel practically lived on Quaaludes and cocaine. She remembered Abe at the publication party for Taffy's book *Spendthrift,* when the rumors were first starting to circulate of financial malfeasance, piling the paté de foie gras on the pumpernickel while the chorus sang "Money," as if all were right with his world. She remembered her feelings of unrest at the time.

She wanted to talk to Cecilia Lesky, to tell her about the reporter who wanted to meet with her, to ask her what she thought she should do. But Cecilia was Marty Lesky's daughter, and everyone knew of the close bond that existed between Marty Lesky and Abe Grossman. And Marty and Mona Berg. She decided against calling Cecilia. She was trying to attribute noble motives for opening her door to a reporter from the *Washington Post*, hell-bent on getting a story on a cover-up of corruption at the highest level, but revenge more than matched the nobility involved.

"If I hadn't been there at that exact moment, it never would have happened," Marina explained to her father, when she told him what had happened to her in the lobby of the Beverly Hills Hotel that day. "That particular reporter, at that particular place, at that particular time."

"Are you attributing mystical significance to this meeting?" asked her father, and there was in his voice a newfound tone of not taking her seriously, in the mockery of fate that it suggested.

"Please don't make fun of me, Daddy," she said.

"I'm not making fun of you, Marina. It's just that you've had one unhappy session with the press already in the last few months," said her father. He was referring to the story about Mona Berg that she had told at a party that was repeated word for word in Otto Ottoman's column, with devastating aftereffects. It was a delicate and sore subject between them.

"That was not my fault that it appeared in that column," she said very defensively, as if it were a subject they had been through before, with differing points of view.

"What I meant was, Why get mixed up with people like that? It seems to me you're in enough hot water already in your life in this town," said Rex Vaughan.

"But Daddy, they're screwing Faye Converse blind with their financial shenanigans and they're keeping it out of the newspapers," said Marina.

"That's Faye's problem," said Rex. "It doesn't have anything to do with you. Take my advice, Marina, and stay out of it."

"What about the right and wrong of it?" asked Marina.

"What about it?"

"You're getting different now that you made it again."

"Pyrrhic victories are for the birds, Marina."

"Goodbye, Daddy."

"You're not going to see him, are you?"

"No."

"Promise?"

"Promise."

When the telephone rang a few minutes later, she knew it was going to be Johnny Griffin from the *Washington Post,* and it was.

"I was wondering when we could get together?" he asked.

"How about right now?" said Marina Vaughan.

Chapter 23

IT WAS NOT until Cecilia Lesky returned from Italy to live with her family, after five years of being on her own, since the annulment of her marriage to the social figure Cheever Chadwick, that she realized how deep her resentment was toward her parents for having talked her into going through with the wedding ceremony in order to avoid the embarrassment of canceling it. Although she acquiesced, she was unaware at that time of her life that other options besides compliance were available to her.

It was particularly irksome to Marty and Sylvia Lesky that Cecilia's brief bridesmaid acquaintance with Marina Vaughan of five years earlier should develop into a full friendship in the months following Cecilia's return to the film capital. It accounted to them for the defiant attitude and the craving for an independent life away from her parents that had crept more and more into the conversations between mother and daughter.

The Leskys were dining *en famille*, as Sylvia put it, a rare occurrence in the family those days. Marty was always at the studio since the first rumblings of the scandal involving the "unauthorized business transactions" began to appear in the press.

Sylvia Lesky liked to find new places to sit, and the table was set in the atrium, surrounded by cymbidium plants in clay pots, with candles in Waterford hurricane lamps. It reminded her of a picture she had seen in *Vogue,* and she relaxed in contentment in a bamboo chair, surveying the beauty of her setting as Cecilia and Marty droned on about the Grossman scandal.

"People say he's guilty, Marty," said Cecilia Lesky to her father.

"You've got to be logical about it, Cecilia," said Marty Lesky in a voice filled with infinite patience, a way he had developed when being called upon to come to terms about this matter.

"Mae, would you pass the eggplant soufflé again," said Sylvia to her maid. "I'm mad about that color."

"If he was going to steal some money, he wouldn't steal a lousy million dollas. If Abe Grossman needed a million dollars, there's any of a dozen people he can call to get it in an hour's time if need be. It don't make sense for a man with that kind of money to steal a million dollas," said Marty.

"Don't say it don't, and don't say dollas," said Sylvia Lesky. The bad grammar that her husband sometimes affected, or reverted to, as Sylvia put it, was like fingernails on a blackboard to her.

"Marina Vaughan said that Abe Grossman has a secret life," persisted Cecilia.

"I don't have any interest in hearing anything Marina

267

Vaughan has to say on any subject," said Marty Lesky, who had heard that Marina Vaughan was seen talking to a reporter from the *Washington Post* in the lobby of the Beverly Hills Hotel. He'd also heard that Marina Vaughan and Cecilia had danced together at a gangster's party. The idea that tongues had wagged in that direction, as Mona Berg put it to him, filled him with a rage toward Marina Vaughan, a rage made more fierce by having to absorb the rage he felt toward Abe Grossman for not having covered his tracks sufficiently.

"Marina Vaughan don't know shit from Shinola," said Marty, his bamboo chair making a sharp scratching sound on the terrazzo floor as he pushed it back away from the table and walked out of the atrium.

"What's the matter with him?" asked Cecilia. "Don't I have the right to discuss what everyone else in town is discussing?"

Never talk in front of the servants was one of the cardinal rules of the Lesky household. "Wouldn't this make a pretty color for a uniform?" said Sylvia to Mae, about the eggplant soufflé that was being passed for the second time.

"I don't like purple," said Mae.

"It's not purple, Mae," said Sylvia Lesky in a weary voice. "It's aubergine. I have such a terrible headache."

"Why do you suppose Marty gets so up-tight about Abe Grossman?" asked Cecilia.

"When did you get interested in all this?" asked her mother in reply to her question. "You never used to even listen to the conversation at the table."

"I asked you a question, and you're not answering me."

"Oh, I never pay any attention to these things. Everyone gets so excited about them, and blood pressures go up, and hearts get strained, but they all have a way of passing, and no one's ever really the worse for the wear," said Sylvia. "In my father's time, they went to jail, and now they don't."

"Why?" said Cecilia. "I'm sure he stole the money. If he was poor, he'd go to jail."

"Oh, please, let's not start that old chestnut, if-he-was-poor-he'd-be-in-jail. I'm just not up to injustice talk. Mae, would you ask Mr. Lesky which picture he's running first," said Sylvia. "Now be careful of that hurricane lamp when you blow it out. It's Waterford."

"They say that Daddy's afraid that if they find out anything on Abe Grossman, they'll come after him next," said Cecilia.

"I wish you'd stop seeing Marina Vaughan," said her mother.

At first, when the subject came up about Cecilia moving to a house of her own, it was dismissed as unfeasible. It made perfect sense to Marty Lesky that the pavilion between the tennis court and the swimming pool be rebuilt into living quarters for her that would have total privacy as well as all the advantages of the estate, including the impeccable security that was almost an obsession with the family. He was not used to having what he said on any subject questioned. It was the way things were to be, and that was that. It particularly annoyed him that the subject kept coming up, and he put the blame on Marina Vaughan, who was blameless in the matter.

"I don't like being treated like I have no say in the matter," said Cecilia to her mother, not politely. "I'm twenty-four years old and I have an annulled marriage behind me and I want to be listened to. I'm sick of doing it your way."

The last remark was the latest in a series of references to

the ill-fated decision to marry Cheever Chadwick.

"Let's not start up that conversation again," said her mother.

"If his name had been Hymie Cohen from the William Morris Agency instead of Cheever Chadwick from the Social Register, there wouldn't have been a wedding in the first place," said Cecilia.

Sylvia Lesky was deeply stung by the insinuation of her daughter's remark and slapped her face. It was a well-known fact about her that, were she given her choice in such matters, Episcopal is what she would have picked for herself.

Perhaps it was the remark. Perhaps it was the slap. Perhaps it was the combination of the two. They began to look at houses, assisted by Chico Gonzales—the youngish, as Sylvia described him, real estate agent with the rich wife—who had found the perfect house for Faye Converse.

"He understands about people like us, how we live," said Sylvia about him to her daughter, explaining why she had picked him.

Sylvia Lesky didn't like any of the houses that Cecilia Lesky liked, and Cecilia Lesky didn't like any of the houses that Sylvia Lesky liked. Chico Gonzales, the real estate agent who drove his clients around in a Rolls-Royce, never let his impatience show as the weeks went by and mother and daughter continued not to see eye to eye on a proper residence for the young heiress.

"I think this house satisfies what you're both looking for," he would say to them over and over as he pulled his Rolls up in front of another beautiful home.

"Too big," said Cecilia, looking at the house from inside the car.

"Wasn't this the house Elizabeth Taylor was living in

when Mike Todd was killed in the plane crash?" asked Sylvia.

"Yes," said Chico, never sure with Sylvia Lesky if her historical information on the houses of Beverly Hills would work as a plus or a minus in the potential sale.

"I don't want to live here," said Cecilia.

"She doesn't like this, Chico," said Sylvia.

"The old Debbie Reynolds manse on Greenway's on the market again," said Chico, starting the Rolls.

"Isn't that where that gangster had his finger cut off by the mob?" asked Sylvia.

"Pass on the old Debbie Reynolds manse on Greenway," said Cecilia.

"This house would have been perfect, but I just sold it to Mona Berg," said Chico, pointing out the white and pillared mansion they were passing.

"Wasn't this the house where Lana Turner's daughter killed Johnny Stompanato?" asked Sylvia, staring out the window.

"Yeah," said Chico.

"Say, Chico," said Cecilia.

"Yeah?" said Chico.

"Don't show us the old Sharon Tate manse if that comes on the market," said Cecilia.

"Most people love that shit," said Chico.

"We aren't most people and don't say shit," said Sylvia.

"There's a house over on Sunset that doesn't look too big," said Chico.

"Whereabouts on Sunset?"

"Charing Cross. Behind the fence, that one."

"Didn't one of Jack Warner's daughters live there?"

"That's the one."

"That sounds all right. How much is it?"

"A million two."

"She can't go over a million her father says."

"We can work that out," said Chico. "Let's see if you like it."

"I don't want gates," said Cecilia.

"Listen, let's go home. I have a terrible headache," said Sylvia.

"Mona came up with a pretty good idea," said Marty Lesky to Abe Grossman on one of their walks on the back lot of Colossus Pictures.

"What's that?" said Abe, who was beginning to show the first signs of nervousness as the publicity about the case continued.

"Dr. Rose," said Marty.

"Who's Dr. Rose?" asked Abe.

"The shrink," said Marty. "They say he's the best shrink in the city."

"I don't need a shrink," said Abe. "I need someone to call off that fucking reporter from the *Washington Post*."

"Mona says if you go to him three times a week for a couple of months, he'll give a report to the Grand Jury, if it should come to that, or to the District Attorney, that it was a temporary aberration, the whole thing, the taking of a million dollars, when a million dollars don't mean anything to you," said Marty.

"Temporary aberration, huh?" said Abe, thinking it over.

"Yeah," said Marty.

"Sounds good," said Abe.

"That way you don't sound like a common crook. It's like you got guilt feelings about your success. That's why you did it."

"Okay," said Abe. "I'll see him."

"Listen, Abe, one more thing," said Marty, looking at his watch. "How many kids do you have working in your production company now?"

"Well, let's see," said Abe, starting to count on his fingers. "The head of the network. I got two of his kids as junior executives. I have Myron and Delphine Kahn's grandson as a production assistant on *Sally, Irene, and Mary*. I have Pearl Silver's son working as an assistant to Jess Dragonet. And, let me see, uh, who else?"

"I want you to hire Cecilia," said Marty.

"Cecilia?" asked Abe. "I'd be proud to hire Cecilia."

"Maybe have Taffy ask her if she'd be interested. So it don't look like it came from me," said Marty.

"I could put her on *South Sea Adventures*," said Abe, "as a production assistant."

"Keep her busy," said Marty. "She's spending too much time with Marina Vaughan."

Chapter 24

CECILIA LESKY moved out of her parents' Palladian mansion in Holmby Hills, and into her own Santa Barbara–looking house in the hills of Beverly Hills just in time, before a clash occurred between her mother and herself. The situation between them had become intolerable. She could not stand the perfection that her mother demanded, and she moved into her new house, with only a bedroom and sitting room completed, to take over the rest of the decorating herself. Months went by, and people in working capacities came and went, and did this and that toward bringing the house to completion, but progress did not occur, and there was no improvement in the state of the house, a fact that gave credence to Sylvia Lesky on the disorganized state of her daughter's life. Cecilia hired a decorator that she had heard about, someone other than her mother's beloved Perry Rifkin. But she made herself unavailable whenever a decision had to be made, and work stopped, and the decorator was blamed for inefficiency, and the first one was fired, and the second one was hired, and the same thing happened again.

"There's a Vasarely around here somewhere, I don't know where," the young heiress said to one of the decorators, about a painting she wanted hung in a certain place.

She didn't know what she wanted. She didn't know what look suited her. She couldn't wait until she started to work on her new job so that she could absent herself from the decisions of making her home a background for her life. A thirty-foot-high scaffolding stood in the middle of the two-story living room with a view that looked out on the city below. Everyone agreed who saw it that one day it would be spectacular, one of the best rooms in the city, but the walls were never painted, and the bookcases never completed, and the yellow drapery for the vast window never draped, and the thirty-foot scaffolding remained in its place as a permanent fixture.

For a while her friends would roar with laughter at her eccentricity, of living out of boxes and staying huddled in the two rooms that were completed, but as it became apparent that incompletion was a permanent state, her friends found it less amusing and quite uncomfortable, and her behavior in the matter more strange than eccentric. Some people said it was because her mother was such a perfectionist in matters of decoration and life style. Some people said it was because she never really had a home, despite the splendor of the houses in which she had been reared. Some people said she didn't yet know who she was.

Having achieved her goal of having a home of her own, there were aspects of her independence that were terrifying to Cecilia Lesky. All her life the fear of kidnapping had been implanted within her, for the real possibility that it always was. There were times when she was frightened at night in the house, and she became manic on the subject of locks and alarms. She would never admit it to a soul, least of all her parents, but she missed the guard with the gun and the Doberman Pinscher called Pal that patrolled the grounds of her parents' estate.

She lived in only two rooms of her ten-room house, and every time she was within, she locked herself first in one and then in the other, in addition to activating the alarm system on every door and every window. She understood every aspect of the complicated alarm system, and worked the lights and switches and signals with the look of one who has done it always. She had been taught to be afraid, because of her privilege, and often she wished she had a friend that she could share her home with.

"We have made inquiries with executives of Colossus Pictures regarding Abe Grossman. We have heard rumors from the press of potential criminality, but there is no formal investigation at this time."

Van Endicott
Assistant District Attorney

"What do you think they'll give me?" asked Abe Grossman. He and Marty Lesky were walking on the back lot of Colossus Pictures.

"I think we can talk them into letting you make a picture on the evils of angel dust, or free basing, something that hasn't already been done," said Marty Lesky.

A mock police car drove by from one of Abe's television series that was shooting on the back lot New York Street, with

276

an actor in police uniform behind the wheel as if on his way to make an arrest.

"Here comes my car," said Abe, in the gallows humor that he had assumed toward the predicament that he was in. Marty didn't laugh. They didn't feel compelled to laugh at each other's jokes.

"How's Taffy taking the whole thing?" asked Marty.

"She says the most embarrassing thing for her was when that guy wrote I didn't actually go to Harvard, like I always said I did," said Abe Grossman.

"I never understood why you told everyone you went to Harvard," said Marty.

"You told everyone you went to Andover, and you only went to Andover High," answered Abe. "What the fuck's the difference?"

"Is Taffy going to stick it out with you?" asked Marty, meaning was she going to stay in the marriage.

"She's going to stick it out," said Abe.

"How much?" asked Marty, meaning how much was Abe going to have to pay Taffy for her not to divorce him.

"What do you mean how much?" asked Abe, with irritation in his voice for the rudeness of the question.

"You know fucking well what I mean how much," said Marty.

"Five million. In her name," said Abe. "And she wants Faye Converse's earrings."

Cecilia applied herself with diligence to her job as production assistant on Grossman-Dragonet Productions. She wore jeans and a tee shirt, and brushed her hair straight back, and was the first one at her job every morning, and the last one to leave every night. She knew that people knew that she got the job because of who her father was, and she knew that she had the credibility problem of the rich person in the working world to contend with, and she performed her functions in a manner that succeeded in overcoming what she felt were her liabilities. She worked as a girl Friday in all areas and carried a clipboard with notes on things to be done. She had a pleasant manner, and people liked her and were pleased when she called them by name, and they said about her to other people that she was Marty Lesky's daughter.

Her commitment to her job gave her the excuse that she needed not to have to deal with her house, or her mother, or the rumblings of love for a man committed to another that were beginning to stir within her. "Don't bother me here at the studio," she'd say to whomever called her about whatever decision had to be made. "I'll look at the colors over the weekend and let you know," but she wouldn't look at the colors over the weekend, and she didn't let anyone know, and eventually all work ceased on her home, and all communication ceased with her mother, and the love that she felt for the star of the series remained unspoken and unacknowledged.

She left her home very early in the morning and came back very late at night. She went for an entire summer without seeing her mother, working always as she was, sometimes seven days a week, never having time. She would have gone without seeing her father, so as not to appear to capitalize on the relationship, but sometimes he sent for her, to go to his office in the Administration Building immediately, and she dreaded the moments when she was paged on the set for that reason. The meetings between the two were always difficult.

"How come you haven't seen your mother?" asked Marty. He was on the telephone, having been put on hold by Jane Fonda, while a scene was being shot on the set where she was working. "She was expecting you Sunday night, and she said you didn't even call to cancel."

"Daddy, I'm working seven days a week, thirteen hours a day. I don't have time to go to Mother's parties. I haven't had a weekend off for five weeks," said Cecilia.

"Are you complaining?" asked Marty. "Half the country's out of work. You're lucky to have a job." It was a fact of their relationship that he never took her seriously in her endeavors, and she displayed to him an indifference to his indifference.

"Your mother said it was the same when you took up horseback riding. Seven days a week, all day long, ride, ride, ride, and then you got sick of it and never looked at your horse again," said Marty.

"I can just hear Mother say that," said Cecilia. "Leave it to her never to pay a compliment. I thought you'd be proud of me, how hard I'm working."

"Listen, I don't work seven days a week, thirteen hours a day, and I run the goddamn studio," said Marty, with the implication that she was doing something wrong in the managing of her time card.

"I have to get back to the set," she said quietly.

"Shhh," said Marty, holding his hand up for silence as Jane Fonda came back on the telephone, her take having been completed. There was never a moment of the business of making pictures that did not consume Marty Lesky. The business at hand was to inform Jane Fonda of the successful sneak preview of her latest film for Colossus that had taken place the night before.

Cecilia had listened to hundreds of calls like it over the years—other stars, other directors, other producers. It was a thing her father was expert in. She didn't understand why he never brought to his home and his family the charm and the wit that were so celebrated in his work. She had never managed to catch his interest enough for them to have the kind of moments together that are commonly associated with the relationship they shared. They were a disappointment to each other. She walked out the door of her father's office, slightly dispirited.

On the way back to the set, the agent Joel Zircon introduced himself to her, knowing who she was, that she was Marty Lesky's daughter.

"Hi, Cecilia," he said in the exaggeratedly friendly voice he used when he wanted to make an impression on someone important. "I'm Joel Zircon. My client Marina Vaughan is always talking about you, in the very nicest kind of way, and I know she would have wanted me to say hello to you and introduce myself."

She hated when people did this to her. She knew that if she weren't Marty Lesky's daughter, this latest smart operator in town wouldn't have stopped her to be charming.

"How is Marina?" asked Cecilia.

"Comme ci, comme ça," Joel Zircon said, waving his hand in the gesture that signified Marina Vaughan was less than so-so.

It was not a conversation she wished to pursue with him. He was seizing on the intimacy of the topic to advance his own cause in her eyes, by the solicitousness he intended to show for the state of Marina Vaughan's life. He was a type she understood totally.

"I'll give her a call," said Cecilia. "I'm turning off here. I'm going to the set."

"How's *South Sea Adventures* going to be?" he asked, not wanting to let her go.

280

"Everyone's excited about it. It goes on the air next week," said Cecilia. "Goodbye."

"How's Mona Berg's trick?" he said, as a joke, meaning the actor Franklyn Bassett, about whom there was such an immense amount of talk. The words did not come out in the way Joel thought they were going to, in a way that would make her laugh at the audacity of him. She kept going toward the set.

"I'll get Dolores DeLongpre to ask you if you ever contemplated suicide," said Mona Berg to Abe Grossman, about a television interview on Dolores DeLongpre's show that Mona thought would be a good idea in clearing up forevermore, in the eyes of the industry, any lurking suspicions that Abe might not have paid his debt to society, nor that his atonement was not complete.

"She's going to ask me if I ever contemplated suicide?" said Abe. "On the air, you mean?"

"On the air," said Mona Berg, who had taken over the public relations of the embezzlement affair.

"What do I answer?" asked Abe.

"You pause a bit," said Mona, "as if a pain is going through you at the memory of it, and then you whisper, in a voice you can hardly hear, 'Yes,' and they'll hate Dolores for the tough bitch that she is, and for overstepping the bounds of good taste by asking you a question like that, and then they'll admire you for your guts and courage in admitting it, that you almost took your own life, and the whole matter will be cleared up before the premiere of *South Sea Adventures.*"

"You're sure Dolores won't slip in any questions I don't know about?" asked Abe Grossman. "I don't want to get caught with my pants down."

"Dolores will do what I tell her to do," said Mona about the famous gossip columnist who had created Mona's own legend, naming her Ms. Mona as she had, creating the word superagent for her, making her a household word, at least in the kinds of households that read her columns and watched her telecasts.

Chapter 25

MARINA VAUGHAN was broke. She was living in a thousand-dollar-a-month apartment—on two floors, with two terraces, and some lovely furniture that she'd inherited from her mother or picked up during her marriages and on her travels when she was on locations making movies—but she was at a point in her finances where coming up with the rent money was becoming a constant worry in her life. She went to a jeweler in the downtown Magnin's who used to make jewelry for her mother when her mother and father were still married and popular stars and gave each other glamorous gifts. She brought him a brooch with gold and diamonds and pavé sapphires, splashy in a way that her mother had liked things splashy. She thought he would have an artist's pride in his work, from the peak of his popularity, and would offer her enough money so that rent would cease to become a factor for at least a year.

It was not a pleasurable meeting. Marina told the jeweler

that she had been in her safe deposit box at the bank and looked at the piece for the first time in years and decided that as long as she never wore it she might as well sell it. The actress in her, and her pride, would not allow him to see that she was desperate for the money, nor did she allow him to see how shocked she was at the little bit of money that he offered her—for his own work.

"It was a nice piece in its day, Marina, but that's a very fifties kind of look in jewelry design that I'd have a hard time unloading today."

What he offered her would only have paid for one month's rent, and seemed to her a shabby slight on her mother, and she told him she decided not to sell.

There was no way she could bring herself to go to her father and ask him for more money. He had already lent her money, which he never mentioned and probably wouldn't have cared if she ever paid back, but it had been the cause of a change in the dynamics of their father-daughter relationship, and the closeness that had always been between them was diminished. They talked to each other on the telephone and saw each other once every week or two, but he talked only about his own life and accomplishments, in the successful period that he was in, and asked her less and less about her own life, and sometimes answered in silences if she brought up her own problems. His attitude about them was that they were of her own doing, and so they fell into a pattern of pretending things were better than they were.

To have had money always and then to have none was the position she found herself in. It was a fear that paralyzed her more than anything else. There was not a person with whom she could discuss it except her maid, Juanita, who used to live in when she had the big house in Malibu, and who now only came once a week, and sometimes wouldn't take the thirty dollars that Marina paid her on the one day a week that she came. Her own life was in tatters and shreds at the time, with a husband abandoning her, with a sick child and money problems of her own, and on several occasions the two ladies wept together and hugged each other, and did not need to pretend they were not the failures they thought they were.

She was surrounded by rich friends. She knew powerful people. But she could not bring herself to discuss her plight with anyone who could help her. She expended a great deal of energy in pretending that things were not as they were, because she couldn't bear to think that people were saying about her that she was broke.

"Do you know who's broke?" she could imagine them saying about her at the dinner parties she was no longer invited to.

"Who?" she could imagine everyone at the table answering almost in unison, because it was the thing they all feared the most.

"Marina Vaughan" was the answer, from whomever said it, and she could imagine the feeling of satisfaction and the secret smiles of her enemies, like Mona Berg, and her former friends who had given up on her, like Pearl Silver and Delphine Kahn, and the embezzler Abe Grossman, whose story she had helped bring to the front pages, and various and sundry people to whom she had been rude or thoughtless during her heyday.

It was too painful for her to dwell on, but dwell on it was what she did, and it depleted her, and she wrote little on her autobiography. When she told her agent, Joel Zircon, that she wasn't going to use the story of finding her mother's head in the toilet bowl, having choked on her own vomit from the overdose of pills and vodka that she had taken, he told her, in the faintly mocking tone of voice that he had begun to use when he talked to her, that the head-in-the-toilet story was just about the only thing he'd be able to get her an advance on from a publisher, autobiographies of losers not being in very high favor that year.

Then, when it was getting toward the end of the month and the rent was about to be due, she wrote a letter to Jack Crawford, whom she once called her very own Gatsby, and told him she had squandered all her money and was in dire straits. She asked him if he could help her out with a loan, which she would repay when she finished her autobiography, which she knew would be a great commercial success.

While she was writing to him she felt a certain affection for her former lover. He was now part and parcel of the inner sanctum of the Beverly Hills–filmland party set that she had first introduced him to, and which she was no longer part of, and she liked the fact that it was she who had created the Gatsby image for him. When she wrote him the letter asking him for the money, she smoked a joint first, and took a bit of cocaine.

She told him that she'd always spent more than she earned, even when she was earning big bucks. She told him she'd never saved a nickel for a rainy day. In her imagination, she thought he would be absurdly touched by the honesty of her approach. She thought he would open his Louis Vuitton briefcase, and take out a big packet of money, and have his chauffeur deliver it to her, and send his love, and wish her well.

She always had a tendency to romanticize people, and it was a bitter and shameful blow to her when he did not reply to her letter, which became apparent when the days went by and no answer was forthcoming. It had not occurred to her that he would not accommodate her for the start that she had given him, for the fun that it had been between them. Waves of shame overcame her for having written a letter in which she exposed herself so totally, only to be ignored. She wondered if he would read it around town at dinner parties. It was one more thing that she wished she'd never done.

The telephone rang. And rang again. She wasn't going to answer it. She spent more and more time sitting in her apartment looking off into space, smoking marijuana to numb the fear that was enveloping her for the state of her life.

"Hello," she said finally, her voice dull and flat.

"Marina?"

"Yes."

"It's Cecilia."

"Oh, Cecilia." Her voice warmed.

"You sound awful," said Cecilia.

"You know something, Cecilia?" asked Marina.

"What?"

"Every time someone like my father or my agent or Babette Navarro asks me how I am, I always say, 'Fine,' or sometimes I even say 'Great!' with an exclamation point; but I ain't fine, and I ain't great. I am awful, just like you said I sound."

"That's what I heard," said Cecilia.

"What did you hear?" asked Marina. "Did Jack Crawford read you the letter I wrote him?"

"I didn't know you wrote a letter to Jack Crawford. What did you write a letter to Jack Crawford for?" asked Cecilia. "I heard from your agent, a slimy little number he is, and from Franklyn Bassett that you were having a rough time."

"Where'd you see Franklyn Bassett? And what does he

know about me except the Mona Berg version of my life?"

"I'm working for Grossman-Dragonet Productions."

"No wonder I haven't heard from you," said Marina.

"Frankie said it in a very caring way about you, as if he liked you a lot and was concerned about you," said Cecilia.

"I knew him when."

"I knew him when too."

"You never told me that."

"You never told me you knew him before either."

"Small world," said Marina. "Tell him hi. Tell him thanks. Tell him I'm great. Oh, Cecilia, I wrote the most embarrassing letter to Jack Crawford asking him for money, and he didn't even reply. I feel so embarrassed I could die."

"Why did you ask him for money?" asked Cecilia.

"Because my rent's due on Thursday, among other things," said Marina.

"As bad as that, huh?"

"Worse."

"You ought to sublet that apartment and move in with me," said Cecilia in a sudden flash of thought.

"Are you serious?" asked Marina, immediately aware of the possibilities of the idea.

"It would be perfect. Just between you and me, I get scared to death living alone now that I got what I wanted. It would be doing me a favor to have you here. And there's plenty of room for you to write your autobiography. I better warn you, though, there's only two rooms decorated so far, my bedroom and sitting room, so you'd have to sleep on a pull-out bed in my sitting room until the guest room gets finished."

"I wouldn't care about that," said Marina. "I would love to sublet this apartment, make a little profit to live on while I write my book, and drop out of sight for a while."

"I leave at the crack of dawn for the studio and don't get home until long after dark, so I've dropped out of sight, too," said Cecilia. "We sound like the perfect couple."

"What do you think your parents will have to say about that? They don't seem to be big fans of mine," said Marina.

"I don't give a shit what my parents have to say about anything," said Cecilia Lesky, verbalizing openly for the first time the hostility she had begun to feel for her parents.

"This is a new Cecilia Lesky I hear talking on the other end of this phone," said Marina, her spirits rising at the show of friendship displayed by the lonely young Lesky heiress. It was the happiest she had been in a long time.

"Darling, what about this house?" asked Marina Vaughan one night after she had been living there a week.

"What about it?" asked Cecilia.

"Well, I mean, uh, do you like that scaffolding in the middle of your living room like that?"

"Don't you start on me."

"I'm not starting on you. I was offering to finish it for you, if you'd like me to."

"I thought you had to write a book."

"I'll write the book in the morning and decorate in the afternoon. Do this room in terra cotta, why don't you? And hang your Kenneth Noland there, over the sofa, and your Vasarely over the fireplace. Cover all the furniture in the same blue-and-white Valentino print. And use those bamboo chairs your mother gave you in the dining room."

"You make it all sound so easy. It's been the most awful problem for me to put any order into this house," said Cecilia.

"I wish I could write a book as easily as I can decorate a room," said Marina.

Chapter 26

"HELLO?"

"Miss Berg?"

"Who is it?"

"Miss Mona Berg?"

"Who is this?"

"My name's Uriah Jerome."

"How did you get this number? This is an unlisted number."

"I've got more than your unlisted number, Miss Berg."

"I'm going to hang up."

"I wouldn't if I were you, Miss Berg."

"What do you want?"

"Does the name Frankie Bozzaci mean anything to you, Miss Berg?"

"Bozzaci, did you say? I'm not sure. Why?"

"I have a videotape of Frankie Bozzaci that I thought you might find interesting."

"Why would I find it interesting?"

"Because it looks an awful lot like a client of yours named Franklyn Bassett, of the about-to-premiere *South Sea Adventures.*"

"What, uh, sort of videotape, Mr. Jerome?"

"It's called *Rhapsody in Blew.*"

"I don't know why that would be of any interest to me."

"It's spelled b-l-e-w blew, if you get my meaning."

"Yes, I get your meaning. Where do we meet? Where do we discuss the details?"

There was a great deal of talk about Franklyn Bassett. He was the name on every lip. He had received what *Time* magazine called the star build-up of the decade. He was Jane Russell. He was Marilyn Monroe. He was Raquel Welch. He was Farrah Fawcett. His picture was on billboards across America stripped to the waist. By the time of the premiere of the television series *South Sea Adventures,* Franklyn Bassett's picture had been on the cover of sixteen magazines. He was handsome. He was sexy. He had charisma. There was immense curiosity about him for the unknown quantity that he was.

All credit for the lavish campaign went to Mona Berg. "She orchestrated every move of this build-up brilliantly," said Marty Lesky to Abe Grossman and Jess Dragonet, the producers of the series, about Mona, in her defense, when they complained to him constantly of the aggravations she caused.

The fact is, Mona had them all by the short hairs, a term she was fond of using when she talked about the situation, which she did from time to time. Either they were deeply indebted to her for things she had done in their behalf, or she had something on them. She was letting Marty Lesky use her house in the afternoons for an affair he was having. She was the one who came up with the term "temporary aberration" that was believed to have been the single most important factor in having the charges against Abe Grossman dropped. And she had witnessed, quite by accident one night at a nightclub, a humiliating episode for Jess Dragonet, when Dom Belcanto, the legendary singer, paid the captain a hundred dollars to knock off Jess Dragonet's hairpiece as a joke for the amusement of his table. Jess Dragonet always knew that Mona would not hesitate to repeat the story at a meeting, in the baroque fashion she had for telling stories, if she were crossed. He could not bear that that might happen, and so allowed her to get away with things that he ordinarily would have blocked, like hiring a very expensive writer to rewrite the first six episodes, which was the latest thing that she had demanded.

"Strip him to the waist in every episode," said Mona about Franklyn Bassett, the man she loved. She marketed him as the sexual object that he was. Mona understood Frankie from the moment she met him. She knew what she was creating. She understood his talent before he understood his talent.

What he always knew was that there was something in him that was destined for greater things, and that sex would be the way to it, but he didn't know what the something was, and he might have settled for much less than what he became if he had not met Mona Berg. She saw him as a sex star, pure and simple. She told him that the look of wantonness on his face when he ejaculated was the look that would make him a star. She changed the entire concept of his series from action adventure to romantic adventure, and each episode included a beautiful woman and a love scene as sexually explicit as television would allow. Dolores DeLongpre wrote about him that he had "crotch," the way Hedda Hopper once wrote that Ann Sheridan had "oomph," and the word crotch was a word that stuck with him. "He's got crotch!" *People* magazine said in its cover story.

The six months between the time Mona Berg picked up Frankie Bozzaci on Sunset Boulevard and the night the first episode of *South Sea Adventures* went on the air were dizzying times for the young man. Everything was new to him.

Including his relationship. The live-in lover of the most powerful woman in Hollywood. Sometimes Frankie thought he was going to burst if he couldn't talk about it all with somebody, but he couldn't ever really find the one to talk to. He looked up his old friend Rusty who used to get him jobs like bartending and odd-job carpentry and the occasional hustle if money was tight and the price was right, and he got him the job as his stand-in on the series, and occasional bit parts. He didn't have to pretend to be the brand-new-person Franklyn Bassett in front of Rusty. In addition to his new life, Mona had given him a new name and a new background, and he had not settled into his new identity sufficiently to feel at home in it.

"Do you fuck her?" asked Rusty, during one of their talks, about Mona.

"Sure," said Frankie. "What do you think?"

"I mean, uh, do you have to? I mean, uh, is that part of the deal?" asked Rusty.

"There's no actual deal," said Frankie. They were lying out by the swimming pool at Mona's new house. It was Sunday afternoon, and they had played tennis and swum, and it was the time to study the lines for the next day's shooting,

293

with Rusty reading all the other parts and prompting Frankie when he could not remember the lines.

"It's still a hustle," said Rusty, "only instead of getting a hundred bucks a trick you're getting a TV series."

"That's just the give and take of life, Rusty," said Frankie. "Look what she's doing for me. Putting out doesn't seem to me too heavy a price to pay for what I'm getting."

"Is she in love with you?"

"Yeah."

"You're not going to try and tell me you're in love with her?"

"No."

"Is it hard work?"

"I never met the person yet I couldn't get a hard-on for if the returns were right," he said, after a pause.

"That would sound great in Dolores DeLongpre's column," said Rusty.

"I think we've carried this conversation to its limit," said Frankie, picking up the script with the blue cover and the pink pages entitled, "*South Sea Adventures*, Episode 6, 'The Rains of Ranchipur.'"

Franklyn Bassett's black Porsche, with the license plate TUE 9-10, the time slot of his series, pulled up in front of the all-night newsstand at Hollywood Boulevard and Las Palmas. Row after row after row of magazines had Franklyn Bassett's picture on the cover. On *Life* magazine, behind the wheel of his ship. On the cover of *People*, raising sails. On the cover of *Sailing*. And movie magazines. And television magazines. And gossip magazines. He looked up and down at the rows of pictures of himself, from his car. A sight he had been brought to see by Mona.

It's like a set, he thought to himself, all dressed for the day's shooting, in a movie about a star's encounter with his stardom. When he first saw the billboard of himself on Sunset Boulevard, stripped to the waist, eighteen feet high, which was causing traffic jams and accidents, which might have to be moved to a different location in the interest of safety, he had had the same feeling, that none of it was real.

Mona hopped out of the car with a sprightly step, as if she herself were an actress in that very movie about the star encountering his stardom for the first time. In a neatly choreographed continuing movement, she indicated in a grand gesture the row upon row of pictures of him, as if it were yet another in the seemingly endless fantasies she was fulfilling for the young man. She filled her arms with magazines, two of each, one for her, one for him. She paid the old man who ran the newsstand much too much money, and didn't wait for the change.

"Keep the change," she called behind her, not wanting it to go completely unacknowledged, so he would remember. It made a better ending for the scene, she thought. Showed her lighter side. Not good to always be tough. Audience sympathy.

She should have ended with "Keep the change," got in the car, and gone off. But no. She never could end on a subtlety. It became important for her that this news vendor know who they were; as if the whole thing would have been wasted if the vendor hadn't been informed of the moment of wonderment they shared. It was one of the things about her that Frankie had begun to despise.

"Do you know who this is?" she said to the news vendor, taking him over to meet Frankie. The series wasn't even on the air yet. Of course he didn't know who he was. But she told him. The time slot. The network. She got Frankie to sign an autograph for him. "Dear Vin. Good luck always, Franklyn Bassett." She said she'd have an eight-by-ten glossy with an inscription sent over the next day from her office. She dispensed largesse. Frankie could not understand her need to identify herself in every situation as the important person she felt she was.

When they drove off, he didn't deal with the moment. He didn't tell her he didn't want the kind of praise that had to be generated. He didn't say to her that she didn't even have to say, "Keep the change."

"Suppose they say I stink after all this big hype?" he said instead, looking through the magazines on his lap, with his own image looking up at him.

"So?" she said in an insolent manner, as if the matter were of no import.

"What do you mean, so?" he said. And then he imitated the way she said it. "So?"—adding a soupçon of gross to the tone. Not lost on her. The beginning of rebellion.

"What difference does it make? Do you want me to tell you about Paul Newman's notices on *The Silver Chalice* when he first started? It didn't hurt him. And it's not going to hurt you. You're going to be a star. That's all that matters. And every woman in America is going to want what I have every night on my Porthault sheets."

She moved over closer to him, snuggling in to him. She slipped her hand into his open shirt, through the hair that she so loved to touch, and began to fondle his nipple in the rough manner that she knew he enjoyed. In a moment reminiscent of the single flash of violence in Cecilia Lesky's white Porsche all that time ago, he grabbed Mona's wrist so rapidly that a slap sound was heard. He thought Cecilia Lesky had snubbed him, high class to low class, and he thought Mona Berg had violated him, low class to low class.

"If there's a pass to be made, I make it. Understand?" Frankie said in a deadly serious tone.

She met his look. Eyeball to eyeball. She knew how to put down an insurrection. "Don't ever forget what side your bread is buttered on, Frankie," she said to him as if his new life was only built on a hill of sand after all. "You better understand that."

There was silence for a moment as they stared at each other. The match was a draw. Then she changed the subject completely and returned to the jaunty mood. "Now, let's go home," she said, "to our new million-dollar house and read about ourselves in all the magazines."

In the midst of all the hype around him, he was lonely. Rehearsals. Shooting. Interviews. That was his life. People, people everywhere, and not a friend to talk to. One night he went walking in the streets of Beverly Hills in the area called the flats. Jimmy Stewart's house. Lucille Ball's house. Jack Benny's house before he died. Except he wasn't looking at movie stars' houses. He was just walking after midnight, a lone figure in jeans and jacket, deep in thought. A young man experiencing changes within changes.

A Beverly Hills police car coming from the other direction passed him, then made a U-turn, lights blinking, and pulled up next to him. Two officers jumped out, hands to holsters.

There were enough times in Frankie's early life when just this thing had happened. Being frisked. Suspicious character. Wrong place at the wrong time. He thought that as they frisked him, but he offered no resistance and made no instant self-identification. He hadn't done anything wrong.

"Do you have any identification?" asked one of the policemen.

"I don't," said Frankie. "I couldn't sleep, and I decided to come out for a walk."

"Don't you know there's an ordinance in Beverly Hills that prohibits walking on the streets after midnight?" asked the other cop.

"I read that in a movie magazine once," said Frankie, "but it slipped my mind."

"Where do you live?" asked the first cop.

"What's your name?" asked the second.

"I'm new in the neighborhood," said Frankie. "I'm a, uh, house guest at Mona Berg's at 814." He couldn't think of another way to identify his relationship. "My name's Franklyn Bassett."

"I thought I recognized you, Frankie," said the first policeman. "I'm really looking forward to the show, man. When's it on now?"

The second policeman answered for him. "Next Tuesday. Nine to ten. ABC. Right?"

"That's right," said Frankie.

"They almost had a riot on the Strip where your billboard is," said the first policeman in admiration.

"I heard. They're going to have to move it," he said, and started to laugh.

"Jim Garner got me a walk-on as a cop in his series," said the first policeman.

"Listen, Frankie," said the second policeman, "I'd be careful about walking on the streets at night. There's been reports of a prowler in this neighborhood for the last week or so, and everybody's getting a little jumpy."

298

Chapter 27

THE NIGHT CAME. Night of nights. The premiere episode of Franklyn Bassett's series, *South Sea Adventures*. It was their night. The two of them. To spend together. Dinner on a little table in the library set up expressly for the occasion, the way Sylvia Lesky did it. A bottle of Dom Perignon in a silver ice bucket with a bow and a card. A half-pound tin of Beluga caviar resting in ice in a silver bowl. A night of celebration for the road they had traveled together.

"The bottle of Dom Perignon came from Bill," Mona said, meaning her secretary Bill, "and the caviar came from Perry Rifkin." She was nervous. She was rambling on. "I bet you never thought when you were a kid in that Home that one day you'd be getting caviar and champagne and roses from the head of a studio." She spooned out some caviar and put it on a cracker. The chopped egg white. The chopped yolk. The diced onion. Just the way Sylvia Lesky did it. The squeeze of lemon. "Here, try some of this."

He was looking at the TV set, which was on without sound, the lead-in program before his.

"I never tasted this stuff before," he said, popping the caviar into his mouth, the whole of it. He chewed a couple of times and hated the taste of it. "Yecccchhhhk," he said, not wanting to swallow.

"Don't drip it on my lavender satin," she screamed at him, as if it mattered, as if it were desecration.

"Where do you think I was brought up? In a Home?" he asked quietly. "Gimme a napkin."

"Oh, darling," said Mona, handing him one of her new Porthault napkins. "I'm so sorry. I didn't mean to yell like that. It's just that I'm nervous and—"

"That's the first time I've ever heard you say anything like that, Mona. You're always so cocksure of yourself."

"All this build-up, all this anticipation," she said. "I mean, think about it. Six months ago you were hitchhiking on Sunset Boulevard, and tonight millions of people are sitting home waiting for you to come on television."

"I have been thinking about it, Mona," he said. "Thinking about it a lot. You know, I always knew something like this was going to happen to me. I didn't know I was going to be the star of a TV show, but I knew something special was going to happen to me. It's what got me through all those years in the Home. And now, here it is."

"Yeah," she said. "Here it is." She flicked on the sound.

"Stay tuned for the mid-season premiere of *South Sea Adventures,* starring Franklyn Bassett," said the announcer, over the famous picture of Frankie stripped to the waist behind the wheel of the ship.

"I love you, Frankie," said Mona, her excitement building as the theme music started. "I know I've told you that before,

300

but I've never told you how much. I love you with all my heart and soul and body and mind." Excessive. Unanswerable. "And here comes the main title. Good luck, my darling."

"Listen, Mona," he said, as if he had something to say too at this moment that they had worked toward for so long.

"Shhhh," she said, her eyes glued to the set.

"I just wanted to say thank you for everything you've done for me."

"Last night, on this very network, television history was made," said Dolores DeLongpre, reporting the news from Hollywood on her new television segment on *Wake Up America.* "The man with the biggest publicity hype in years proved, without doubt, that he is the most romantic leading man to hit the screen in years. Franklyn Bassett is the name. Wake up, Hollywood, this is a man crying out for the big screen! He's tough, and he's gentle, and the combination is irresistible. Bassett plays Adam Troy, skipper of the schooner *Tiki,* home port Tahiti. Premiere episode dealt with Troy rescuing island princess, fetchingly played by Karen Valentine, from the hands of evil gun runner Axel Garth, menacingly played by special guest star Ed Asner, in a departure performance. But the evening belonged to Franklyn Bassett. He glowed in his own starlight—"

"Get to the ratings, get to the ratings, Dolores," said Mona Berg, snapping her fingers at her television set. "Tell them how we clobbered everyone! Tell them how we took the time slot! Tell them how the switchboard was flooded. Bigger than *Roots.* Get to the good stuff! We're a *hit!"*

Franklyn Bassett hit, and hit big. The way Travolta did after *Saturday Night Fever.* Everyone knew his name. The studio reported that he got ten thousand fan letters a week. After the obligatory shy period following that kind of success, Frankie began to feel his oats a bit. Then Travolta, who was Frankie's idol, sought him out about appearing in a picture with him, where they would play brothers in love with the same woman, when the series went on hiatus. Travolta dropped by his trailer on the back lot of Colossus one day and gave him a script to read. It wasn't something that Mona had manipulated. Mona didn't even know about it until he told her later.

It was Frankie's first indication that his career had a life of its own, that he didn't have to be beholden to Mona for every moment of it, as if without her ministrations in his behalf everything would collapse under him.

As a gag, Travolta agreed to do a walk-on in the episode they were shooting that day, dressed as a coolie carrying guest star Suzanne Pleshette's luggage aboard the *Tiki* to Captain Troy. It was thought to be a good omen.

"It's breaking my heart what's happening to Marina, Rex," said Marianna Swank, the wife of Amos Swank, the talk show host, "but I don't know what I can do to help."

She was seated next to Rex Vaughan at Delphine Kahn's dinner for Count Stamirski.

"You could suggest that she sing at the SHARE Boomtown party," said Rex Vaughan. "That way everyone in the industry could see that she's got her act together again."

"Well, you see, we already have Dom Belcanto on the program, and Amos is master of ceremonies, and there's the dancers, and that doesn't leave much time for anyone else—"

"Yeah?" said Rex. "You're the chairperson, aren't you?"

"Yes, well of course. I'll look into it, Rex."

* * *

Mona didn't pursue the subject of marriage until after
Frankie's series became a success. She loved him madly, but
she probably wouldn't have married him if he had flopped in
the series and become nothing more than one of those actors
who appear in the occasional episode of this series or that as a
token gesture. Nor did she wish to appear to have a gigolo on
her hands either, as if that were the most she could hope for.
In the social set to which she aspired there was no tolerance
for failure. The men of the group, in particular, felt more
comfortable in social situations with successful men they
might despise in business than with nonentities or light-
weights or, worse still, flops, who made them nervous.

On the other hand, as far as the women of the group were
concerned, Mona knew that her only hope of full-time acceptance was as a married woman. It wasn't that they feared
that she would take one of their men away from them. They
didn't. Single women were a nuisance in social life. There
were never enough extra men to go around, what with the
widows, and the tables were thrown off balance. Or, worse
still, they brought their hairdresser or accountant, and the
men hated it when they did that. It had to be marriage, and it
had to be marriage to the right person. When Frankie became a star, the die was cast. Mona envisioned the two of
them as a dazzling duet in social circles, with his beauty and
fame and her astonishing success.

What seemed not to be considered, in the rush of events,
was what Frankie had to say about the whole thing. At some
point he began to feel trapped in the situation that he was in.
During the build-up period, whenever there were differences
between them, she always had the upper hand, because she
was in charge of the transformation of his life from hustler to

star, and he would never have endangered that metamorphosis. He let things pass that should have been dealt with. The horizon was cloudy between them. He had no intention of marrying her, and she had every intention of marrying him.

Chapter 28

"IT'S THE HOUSE of my dreams," said Mona Berg to Barbara Walters, on the Barbara Walters special, *Women of Hollywood*. Faye Converse, the star, and Edwina Calder, the writer and intellectual, had preceded her in the hour. "I knew it the first time I walked in here."

She told Barbara that it had been built by Fredric March and Florence Eldridge in 1937, and that Tyrone Power had lived there, "after Annabella and before Linda Christian." She spoke about Ingrid Bergman, "who was living here when she met Roberto Rossellini," and Natalie Wood, "who put in the sunken bathtub." She skipped over the part about the murder that had taken place there.

"Tell me about the first time you met Warren Ambrose," asked Barbara Walters.

"That, Barbara, was a perfect example of learning how to take advantage of a situation," said Mona. She told the story of backing her car, "my old crate of a car," into Warren's Rolls-Royce, in the parking lot of Schwab's, and ending up with a job as his secretary.

They were sitting in the living room side by side on one of Mona's new lavender satin sofas, career girls together, women at the top talking about getting from there to here, reliving anecdotes.

"Now what exactly do you say to a man after you've put a six-hundred-dollar dent into the side of his Rolls-Royce?" asked Barbara Walters.

"I walked up to him," said Mona, smiling at the recollection of it, as if it were a story that she had told many times in her life, "and I said, 'Oh, Mr. Ambrose, I was looking out my rear window, but I didn't see you. I probably should have honked.' Barbara, he was *furious!* Purple!"

"How did you know what his name was?" asked Barbara Walters.

"What?" said Mona Berg.

"I mean," said the interviewer, "if he was a total stranger to you, how would you have known that his name was Warren Ambrose?"

"Well, maybe I didn't call him by name," said Mona, in a revision of her text, so as to eliminate the implication that she had backed her old crate into his splendid vehicle on purpose to create an introduction. Then they went on to talk about Franklyn Bassett, because that was the point of the interview anyway.

"This is certainly an exciting time for you, Mona," said Barbara Walters. "You've reached the pinnacle of success at an early age. You have this beautiful Beverly Hills mansion. This is how Joan Crawford must have lived at her peak."

"Funny you should say that," said Mona, wearing her

Danny Damask copy of the Adrian dress with the padded shoulders that Joan Crawford wore in *The Women*, and the ladies laughed.

"Franklyn Bassett," said Barbara Walters, getting down to brass tacks, girl talk over. "Does that name mean anything to you?" she asked, and they laughed again, for the obvious joke that it was.

"You picked for stardom America's newest love idol. How is that done? How does that happen? Where did you meet him?"

"Everyone asks me that," said Mona, smiling, with the look on her face of getting ready to tell another of the milestone stories of her history. When Dolores DeLongpre asked her that same question on her segment of *Wake Up America*, months ago, Mona answered, "I first saw Franklyn do a scene at Uta Hagen's acting class in New York, and I said to myself, That boy has a certain *je ne sais quoi.*" That was an early story she had made up in the beginning, when the studio said he couldn't act, to give him credibility. Uta Schmuta. She abandoned that one. Bore-*ing*, she thought to herself about the Uta Hagen story. The only part that still worked was the "I said to myself, That boy has a certain *je ne sais quoi.*" She liked the sound of it when she said that.

"I've never told this before, Barbara, because it sounds so preposterous," said Mona, "as if I were horning in on Mervyn LeRoy's story about discovering Lana Turner, but the truth of the matter is, I discovered Franklyn Bassett at the counter of Schwab's, and do you know what he said to me, Barbara? He said, 'Are you going to eat your pickle?' Zing went the strings of my heart, Barbara. I said to myself, This boy has a certain *je ne sais quoi.*"

"And how right you were, Mona," said Barbara Walters.

"He's getting more mail than Marilyn Monroe got at her peak, Barbara," said Mona.

"Is there, or is there not, a romance going on between you and Frankie Bassett, the love idol?"

"We've kept it awfully quiet, Barbara," said Mona, "because of his new show, and because I've been in mourning for my mother, but the truth is, yes, there is a romance between myself and Franklyn Bassett, or Frankie, as I call him. I suppose this is as good a time as any to let you be the first to see this."

She held up her ring hand, on which there was an immense diamond ring on the fourth finger.

"What a beautiful ring," said Barbara Walters. "He must love you very much."

"Thank you, Barbara. I feel that I'm a very lucky woman."

In a trailer on the back lot of Colossus Pictures, Frankie Bassett sat in a chair in front of a mirror while his make-up man, Maurice, applied scrapes and blood to his face for the close-ups of a fight scene that had just been shot with doubles. It was night. In the mirror Frankie watched the television set on which Mona Berg was being interviewed by Barbara Walters.

"I suppose this is as good a time as any to let you be the first to see this," said Mona on television, holding up her left hand, as if she were Faye Converse showing off the enormous diamond.

"Holy shit," said Frankie Bassett.

Frankie and Mona were in the back seat of their chauffeur-driven limousine on their way to the SHARE Boomtown Party at the Santa Monica Civic Auditorium, a party with a cowboy and Indian theme. She was dressed as Pocahontas, Indian princess. Frankie was dressed as an Indian brave, or undressed for the most part, with war paint on his body. The atmosphere was tense. The silence was strained. They looked out different windows.

"Did you put on the alarm system?" Mona asked. She knew the alarm system was on. She was trying to start the conversation before they got to the party.

"Yeah," he said.

"There's supposed to be a prowler in the neighborhood," she said, pursuing.

"Yeah, I heard," he said.

"Look, Frankie, how long are you going to keep up this sourpuss act?" asked Mona, as if she'd had enough.

"Look, Mona," he said, and there was anger in his voice. "I did not ask you to marry me, and I did not buy you that engagement ring you were flashing around on television last night."

"I didn't actually say we were engaged," she said.

"I do not like my life to be manipulated by you," he said.

"Well, of all the ungrateful people," she said to him. Then she added the word "hitchhiker," in a tone of voice meant to get things back into their proper perspective.

"You know something, Mona?" Frankie said, looking her right in the eye, equal to equal. "I'm getting a little tired of being grateful. Especially on demand. My bag of gratitude is just about empty. I deserve a little of the credit, which you seem to forget."

"I got the studio to take you when they didn't want you," said Mona, mean-voiced, reminding him again what was what. "Which you seem to forget."

"Well, they want me now, Mona. You don't have to do all

your stunts in my behalf anymore. I'm the one who's getting ten thousand love letters a week."

"Lower your voice," said Mona, indicating the chauffeur with her head, and closing the window between them.

The limousine arrived at the Santa Monica Civic Auditorium. The chauffeur said there were so many fans outside he was afraid the limousine was going to get tipped over when they recognized Frankie in the back seat, knocking on the windows, waving at him, chanting his name.

Mona pulled back from the fight. She still believed she was in control of the situation. She checked her make-up as the limousine pulled up in front of the entrance.

"It's called feeling your oats, what you're going through," she said in a calmer, gentler voice, soothing things over. "And a perfectly natural stage it is to go through too, but let me caution you, before you feel any more oats, that a certain pornographic film has reared its ugly little head. *Rhapsody in Blew*, I believe it's called, in which you co-starred with a certain Miss Leigh, and I don't mean Vivien."

It was one of the things he wished that he'd never done, the pornographic movie that he made. He was taken aback for a moment by the disclosure. "I hope this doesn't come back to haunt me," he had said to the producer at the time, a black guy from San Francisco called Uriah Jerome who weighed three hundred pounds, and only paid him three hundred of the six hundred he had been guaranteed.

"Now smile," said Mona, smiling at him, as if to show him how. "There's about a thousand photographers out there. Don't make me look for you when the party's over," she said to the chauffeur. "You be right here at the entrance. I don't want to wait one minute when we come out of here." Then she looked back at Frankie. "Just look at it this way, darling.

At this moment in time, you and I are going to be the most photographed couple in the world."

They got out of the car, and the fans went wild. Frankie. Frankie, they screamed. He smiled and he waved, dressed like an Indian brave. Lift it up. Lift it up, the fans yelled about the loincloth that covered the front of his private parts, or the loincloth that covered the rear of his private parts. He was beefcake. There hadn't been beefcake on the screen for a long time, and the screen was ready for beefcake again. Frankie! Frankie!

Mona entwined her arm in his and looked up at him. Indian princess and Indian brave. A phalanx of photographers walked backwards, taking their pictures as they made their way to the door. They smiled and waved as if they were happy, and at that moment, in the wildness of acclaim, they were.

All the big stars performed at the SHARE Boomtown Party, a yearly benefit with a Western theme for a clinic for emotionally disturbed children. Show business people entertaining other show business people in a show business atmosphere, all in the name of charity. It was thought to be a triumph for Babette Navarro and Marianna Swank, of the committee, that both Dom Belcanto, the legendary singer, as he was always called, and Amos Swank, the talk show host who needs no introduction, as they always introduced him, were scheduled to appear on the same program, although they were known to be cool to one another in private.

It was another of those nights in Hollywood where "everyone" was there, as Dolores DeLongpre liked to say, and Mona Berg liked to say. The charity exceeded itself in gross receipts, raising more money than it had ever raised before.

Ebullience was rampant in the atmosphere. And no one was more ebullient than Mona Berg.

"Hello, darling . . . Hello, darling . . . Hello. Love your costume. . . . Hello, darling. There's Angie Dickinson. Hi, Angie. Hi, Raquel. Hi, Candy. Hi, Jaclyn. . . . Do I want a drink? Of course I want a drink. I want a double drink. . . . Hi, Ryan. Hi, Tatum. Hi, Farrah. . . . Look, there's Charles Bronson and Jill Ireland. In the gold sheriff's outfit. . . . You look adorable, Stephanie. Hi, R.J. Frankie'd love to have you guest on his series. . . . I just wanted to say, Warren, I read your script for *Reds*, and I loooved it. Thanks. Hi, Marty. Hi, Sylvia. Where's Cecilia? Did she stay home again? Hi, Goldie. Hi, Jack. Hi, Angelica. . . . Oh, my God, there's Marina Vaughan. Danny Damask told me her check bounced for that costume she's wearing. . . . Hi, Tuesday. Hi, Valerie. I just want to run over and say hi to Liza. . . ."

"She knows everyone."

"Yeah."

"Do the photographers bother you?" said Sylvia Lesky to Franklyn Bassett, at the Lesky table, which was ringside. The regulars were there.

"Hi, Pearl," said Mona. "Hi, Babette. Nando, darling. You look so macho in that hat. . . . Hi, SanDee. Hi, Delphine. Good evening, Myron. Hi, Taffy. Oh, you're Pocahontas too, huh? Wait till I get my hands on Miss Damask tomorrow. Did you see the Nielsens, Abe? Number one in the ratings."

"I didn't hear what you said in all this noise," said Frankie to Sylvia Lesky.

"I said do the photographers bother you?" she repeated.

"No," said Frankie in a disarming way. "I suppose you get used to it, and it gets to be a pain in the ass, but I'm still in the enjoying-it period." They both laughed.

312

Hi, Frankie. Hi, Frankie. Hi, Frankie. Hi, Frankie. Hi, Frankie.

"I can't believe all this is happening to me."

"What?"

"I said I can't believe all this is happening to me." Thanks. Thanks. That's very nice of you. Thanks. Sure you can have my autograph.

"Did you always want to act?"

"As a matter of fact, I don't know anything about acting. All that crap Mona tells about discovering me in some acting class in New York is just Mona-talk."

"You mean you just learned?"

"You see, when that guy claps the board in front of my face and says 'Take one,' I get a charge through my body that feels as good to me as sex," said Frankie Bassett to Sylvia Lesky.

"My word," said Sylvia Lesky, retreating from this conversation.

"And then whatever happens on screen happens."

"I hate this chicken-in-a-basket kind of food, don't you?" said Sylvia Lesky.

Say hi to Dom Belcanto. And his wife Pepper. And his daughter Rita. Say hi to Amos Swank. And Marianna Swank. Say hi to Gregory Peck. And Veronique Peck. Say hi to George Burns. Say hi to Cary Grant. . . . This is a pleasure, sir. This is a real pleasure for me, sir. I'm very honored, sir. Oh my God, Rex Vaughan. Pleased to meet you, sir.

"He wants his own company, Marty," said Mona Berg to Marty Lesky about Franklyn Bassett. "He's hot, *hot*, HOT! He wants a three-picture guarantee, and he wants final cut and director approval. Now, about the merchandising—"

"This is a fucking party, Mona," said Marty Lesky. "Can't it hold till Ma Maison tomorrow?"

"Just hear me out, Marty, while the hearing's good. Hi, Dolores. Hi, Faye. I came across this screenplay, Marty, two Italian brothers, one of them just out of the seminary, in love with the same woman. Then I got Travolta locked into the project. Frankie plays the ex-priest. We can shoot it during the hiatus, Marty. He's crying out for the big screen, Marty. Hi, Rock. Hi, Clint. Hi, Paul. Hi, Joanne. Think of the two of them, Marty. Frankie and Johnny. They'll ignite the screen, Marty."

Another drink? Sure. Drink for you too? Sure. How about you? A double. Did you hear Jack Crawford got busted? Did you hear Delphine Kahn wet her cowgirl pants? Did you hear Robby Slick's picture's a bagel? You won't *believe* who's diking it up. . . . Who's got some cocaine? Ask Marina. Don't ask Marina anything. She's a wreck. She's going to sing tonight. After Dom Belcanto. And Amos Swank. Her father, promise you won't tell this, Rex Vaughan went to Marianna Swank and asked her to put Marina on the program, and Marianna didn't know which way to look. Here, I've got some coke. Come on in the ladies' . . . Oh, Pepper, you must be so proud of Dom. He was great tonight. Great, Dom. . . . Never heard you better, Dom. Dom's got a new hairpiece. Looks like Jimmy Stewart's. . . . Drink? Drink. Drink? Drink. . . . Want another snort? I never say no to another snort, darling. Don't let anyone see. . . . Amos, I never heard you funnier. In all the years I've known you, I've never heard you as funny as you were tonight. When you tap-danced with SanDee Dietrick, that was pure Keaton. Buster, not Diane. Great, Amos. Great show, man. That tap dance with SanDee Dietrick. I mean that'll go down in the annals. Drink? Drink. Drink? Drink. . . . Ladies and gentlemen, Miss Marina Vaughan. What?

"And now, ladies and gentlemen, Miss Marina Vaughan,"

came over the loudspeaker. I hear she's on the skids. I hear her father went to Marianna Swank to get her on the program. I hear her check bounced at Danny Damask's. Poor Rex. I feel so sorry for him.

Marina came on the program late, after Dom Belcanto and Amos Swank had wowed the crowd, and after the SHARE ladies had tapped tapped tapped their way into everybody's heart, four times. Then the raffle. Then came Marina's turn at the mike. . . . Oh, God, let her be good, thought Babette Navarro, who always liked her. Give her a break, God, thought Rex Vaughan, who was her father. Remember when she fell down the stairs at the AFI dinner? Shhhh.

There was a fanfare, and Marina walked out to the spotlight. She sang a song called "People Like Us," meaning them, people like them, who lived the way they lived. She was in good voice, although an astute observer would have noted that a certain spark she once had was missing. It was simply that it was too late in the evening, and everyone had had too much to drink and was sated with stardom, and no one listened to her. She sang on gamely, in trouper fashion, as if to atone for the fool she had made out of herself at the AFI dinner in honor of her father.

Then the sound system at the Santa Monica Civic Auditorium gave out. Jinxed, isn't she? someone said. A hideous electronic whistle pervaded the hall, piercing and painful to the eardrum. People turned to look at her, as if she were its source. She made a gesture to the audience in a funny manner, as if to say, "It ain't me, gang," and got a little laugh, and a little weak applause.

"Ladies and gentlemen, we're having technical difficulties," said the announcer's voice, over a bullhorn. "We'll ask Marina Vaughan to come back up again as soon as we get the system working. A big hand for Marina, everybody!" Clap. Clap. Clap.

If she had been alone, she would have cried, but she was not alone. She knew how to assume a nonchalant look. She walked across the stage and down the steps as if to rejoin her table, good humor and show business bravery in her attitude. There was her father. He stood to greet her.

"Another flop, Daddy," she said.

"It wasn't your fault," said Rex Vaughan, relieved almost that there was something to blame it on.

"If it wasn't the sound, it would have been something else," said Marina very quietly. "I seem to be living under a shadow these days."

"Did I ever tell you about the time Sonja Henie came out of retirement to ice-skate one more time at a big charity event like this one?" asked Rex. He always came up with a parallel story from twenty-five years earlier.

"And Sonja fell right on her ass? Right? Yeah, you told me that one," said Marina. "Are you making a parallel?"

"No, I'm not making a parallel," said Rex defensively. "They'll get it fixed. You can still do your number."

"I'm not doing any number," said Marina. "I'm going home."

"You okay?"

"Right as rain, Daddy."

"Call me. We'll have dinner."

"Sure."

Within her was a malaise of the spirit. She made her way through the tables to the exit, not stopping to speak to the people who reached out to her. Sorry, Marina. Rough, Marina. Poor Marina. Jinxed, isn't she? Loser. I feel sorry for poor Rex.

Then she ran into Franklyn Bassett between two crowded

tables on his way back to his table. He had been upset when people talked through her number. He felt a loyalty to her for not having told what she knew about him, at a time it could have kept him from getting the part that had made him famous. It was the first time they had seen each other since the night at the Leskys' party. She had been a star then, and he wasn't. Now he was a star, and she wasn't.

"Hello, Mr. Gorgeous," she said.

"Hey, I'm sorry about the sound," he said.

"Another night in Hollywood," she said, as if it didn't matter.

"Are you upset?"

"The way I look at it is, it'll be a good chapter in my autobiography, if I could ever get my autobiography written," she said, sounding weary.

"Are you sure you're okay?" he asked.

"Listen," she said, snapping herself out of her mood. "You've got me glued to my set every Tuesday night from nine to ten. I think it's great what's happening to you."

"You knew me when."

"I'll say. You look hot, Frankie. I was always hoping I was going to hear from you."

"I didn't know your telephone number," he said, enjoying the blatant flirt that her unpredictable mood had switched to.

"I wrote it on the bathroom wall," she said.

"In lipstick, I hope," he said.

"Do you call that thing a loincloth that's hanging around your center?"

"Yeah, that's a loincloth."

"I'm thinking about putting my hand under it." They both laughed. Each of them had a slut streak. It was what drew them together.

317

Mona Berg made a beeline across the room when she saw the two of them talking together.

"Good for you for not falling down the stairs again," said Mona, moving in on the conversation, taking Frankie by the arm. "Our fingers were crossed."

"Hey, Mona—" said Frankie.

"Such a shame about the sound, Marina. And you were doing so well," she said, going on. "Frankie, Dom Belcanto wants to meet you, darling."

"I already met him," said Frankie.

"I hear you're going to marry her, Frankie," said Marina in answer to Mona's remarks. "Forgive me if I don't say good luck. She's not one of my favorite people."

"Go have a few drinks, why don't you?" said Mona in her talk-to-a-failure voice. "With the sound and all, you've got a real good excuse to tie one on. Come on, darling, let Harriet Has-Been get to the bars."

"Hey, Mona—" said Frankie, upset at the way the conversation had turned.

"She doesn't bother me, Frankie," said Marina. "I could take this guy away from you, Mona."

"You lay one finger on him, you coked-out drunk," said Mona, "and I'll make sure you never work in this town again."

"You seem to forget, Mona, you've already done that."

"No, honey, you've done it to yourself."

"A lot of people hate you, Mona."

"They're just jealous."

"Hey, ladies, this isn't the time or the place for this conversation," said Frankie, breaking in at just the moment Dolores DeLongpre, dressed as a rhinestone cowgirl, arrived with her cameraman, with camera rolling and lights blazing,

318

covering the star-studded event for her morning telecast.

"And here's an exciting trio," said Dolores, microphone extended, centering herself amongst them, the doyenne of newshens doing her job, covering the news. "America's newest sweetheart, Franklyn Bassett, oh, my dear, I hope they won't censor you out on TV, more naked than dressed he is, beefcake is back, America, and this is the lady who is responsible, superagent Ms. Mona Berg, a woosome two-some, a duet, a love match, ah, and Marina, Marina Vaughan, in a bordello costume of yellow sequins by Danny Damask, bad luck about the sound, Marina, we were all rooting for you, ladies and gentlemen, the sound went out in the middle of Marina's number—"

"Dolores, Franklyn and I are going back to our table," said Mona. "We don't want to take any of the spotlight away from Marina. She's been away from the cameras long enough."

And they were gone. Back to Sylvia and Marty. And Babette and Nando. And Myron and Delphine. And Amos and Marianna. And Dom and Pepper. The couples at the core.

"It has been a long time, Marina," said Dolores De-Longpre to the beleaguered star. "Any plans for coming out of retirement?"

It had been one long rotten evening for Marina Vaughan. Her check had bounced on the costume she was wearing. She found out backstage that her father had arranged to get her on the program. Then the sound went out in the middle of her number. Then Mona Berg called her Harriet Has-Been. And now she was on television with Dolores DeLongpre, being asked for a statement on her crumbled career.

"Oh, I'm not in retirement, Dolores," said Marina, the reckless in her taking over. "Retirement's just a Hollywood word for being out of work. That's what I am, Dolores, I'm out of work. And I've been out of work for two years. Actually, it's been two years and three months, if it's exactitude you're after. As for my career plans, isn't that what you asked me about, Dolores?"

"I loved you in *The Day Before Lent*," said Dolores, signalling her cameraman to move in closer.

"Well, there aren't any," said Marina, going on, "career plans, that is. Singing here at this charity for free was supposed to remind the industry that I'm still around. Do you know what Mona Berg called me tonight, Dolores? She called me Harriet Has-Been, like the doll of the same name, you wind it up and it flops."

Chapter 29

MARINA SAT IN HER BED in the recently completed guest room of Cecilia Lesky's house and watched herself on Dolores DeLongpre's morning television segment of *Wake Up America*. She held the telephone receiver in her hand as she looked at the video tape of herself from the SHARE party of the night before.

"*Retirement's just a Hollywood word for being out of work,*" she said on the screen.

"Oh, my God," she said.

"Jesus," said her father on the other end of the line.

"It gets worse," said Marina.

"*Actually it's been two years and three months, if it's exactitude you're after,*" she said on the screen.

"It's like instant replay," said Rex Vaughan.

"Don't give me instant replay," said Marina.

"*As for my career plans ... there aren't any,*" she said on the screen. "*Singing here at this charity for free was supposed to—*"

"Why do you do these things to yourself, Marina?" asked her father.

"I've really blown it, haven't I?" said Marina. "I wouldn't even hire me."

She hung up the telephone. She turned off the television. She looked off into space. There was a tap on her door.

"Are you okay?" asked Cecilia from outside.

"I'm fine, Cecilia, really I am," said Marina.

Rex Vaughan had developed a way of looking away when Marina's name was mentioned in conversation, as if it were something too painful for him to discuss. His eyes were moist, people would say about him. People felt sorry for him, for what he was going through, rather than for Marina, for what she was going through. The fact is, his embarrassment exceeded his sorrow.

"Thanks for bleeping out my name on the Harriet Has-Been line, Dolores," said Mona Berg on the telephone in her office. She was covering her tracks, afraid she had gone too far. Frankie wasn't laughing at her jokes anymore the way he did in the beginning. "You know I only meant it as a joke. Marina's a great artist, and you can tell anyone I said that."

Then they went on to other things. Parties. People. Deals. This star. That star. "Have you heard about this female impersonator at Miss Garbo's . . ."

Bill, Mona's secretary Bill, and Perry Rifkin were in Miss Garbo's, purely by happenstance on the night Marina Vaughan went to see Brucie, as he was called, just Brucie, do his, or her, imitation of Marina on Dolores DeLongpre's segment of *Wake Up America.*

Brucie didn't like to be called a female impersonator, as Mona Berg told Dolores DeLongpre he was, and Dolores had thus described him in her column. He called himself a comedienne, a light comedienne, an interpreter of women. He sang. He tapped. He played the piano. He camped. He could imitate any movie star. With great exactitude. Not just Bette Davis, or Tallulah Bankhead, or Katharine Hepburn, or Miss Joan Crawford, as he always called her. He liked to get into remotesville, he told his audience, and asked them to call out their favorite to him, and he would comply. Gale Sondergaard, someone called out, and Brucie knew how to do Gale Sondergaard. And Iris Adrian. And Brenda Joyce. And Mara Corday.... No, no, I won't do Frances Farmer. Or Jean Seberg. Or Carole Landis. Next. You. You there, with the big basket, Rula Lenska, is that who you want? Yes, I can do Rula. Here's Pia Zadora. How about Judy, or are you sick to death of Judy? Somewheeeere ov-ver the rainbow, all right, okay, next, next, who do you want, Yvette Vickers, Barbara Eden, you name it, how about Marina Vaughan? Marina Vaughan! Did you see her on Dolores DeLongpre's program? Did you see her! It was like a movie. It was like that time Bette Davis took the ad out on the back of the *Hollywood Reporter*, and said she was out of work, and broke. This was the vidtronic version. She had on this yellow sequin number with the boobs up to *here* . . .

It was all part of the act. He pulled out a yellow sequin top and pinned some gardenias in his hair, the way Marina Vaughan always wore gardenias in her hair.

"Oh, I'm not in retirement, Dolores," mimicked Brucie, becoming Marina, a little bit stoned, a little bit drunk. "Retirement's just a Hollywood word for being out of work. That's what I am, Dolores. I'm-out-of-work."

The room loved the act. Failure jokes never miss with the gay crowd, Brucie told his agent.

"And I've been out of work for-two-years."

"Two-years!" called back the audience, imitating Brucie imitating Marina.

He was funny and sad, and he worked his way into it, deeper and deeper, like an actress taking on an identity.

"Actually, it's two years and three months, if it's ex-act-i-tude you're after . . ."

He was into it. He had the boys rolling in the aisles. Even Bill, Mona's secretary Bill, who always loved her, and Perry Rifkin, who had been a friend of her mother's.

"Singing here at this charity for free was supposed to remind the industry that I'm still around. I'm Harriet Has-Been, like the doll of the same name. You wind it up, and what happens to it?" he called out to the audience.

"*It flops,*" called back the entire audience.

"I can't hear you!" yelled Brucie.

"IT FLOPS," the audience called back again.

"Psssssst." Someone waved from backstage to Brucie, and there was a momentary huddle in the wings.

"What? What's that you said? Where? Oh, lady and gentlemen, I have an announcement to make. I understand Marina Vaughan is in the room. Won't you please stand up, Marina? It was all meant in good fun. I'm one of your biggest fans. Really I am. I've seen all your pictures. Where are you? Shine the spotlight around the room. I loved you in *The Day Before Lent*, playing Faye Converse's daughter. There you are, at last. It was all meant in good fun."

She was movie star anonymous, in huge dark glasses and a turban. She rose and waved to the crowd, drinking champagne out of the bottle. The boys in the room rose and applauded her for the good sport she was. She was drunk. She was at the end of her rope. She was playing her last scene of putting up a front.

"Do you suppose she knew he was going to do her? That's why she came?" said Bill to Perry Rifkin.

"She's like her mother all over again," said Perry.

"When they do the movie of her life, this will be a great scene," said Bill.

"Fine," said Perry, "but what happens between now and then?"

She sat down at her table. She wanted to get out of there. Check, please. No check. Brucie's guest. Thank you.

"Hey, that was great," said a young man to her.

"What was great?" she asked.

"You. Standing there with your bottle of champagne, waving to everybody. What was that movie he was imitating?"

"That was no movie. That was my life. Who are you?"

"Just a fan."

"Who hasn't seen any of my pictures."

"I wouldn't mind a sip of that champagne."

"Be my guest." She pushed the bottle toward him.

" 'I've got an appointment in Samarra,' " sang Brucie, back to being himself again, seated at the keyboard, playing one of his own ditties.

"I feel great, sitting here, drinking champagne, with an ex–movie star," said the boy.

"Thanks," said Marina.

"How many movies did you make?"

"Nine."

"What are the others?"

"What do you do?" asked Marina, shifting the conversation.

"I'm a waiter at the Palm."

"Do you want to talk about bussing tables?"

"No."

"I don't want to talk about my old movies."

"You wouldn't happen to have a Quaalude, would you?"

"You zeroed in at the right table," said Marina, looking into her purse, finding what he wanted, giving it to him.

Bill and Perry saw them leave together, Marina and the waiter from the Palm. She was used to being picked up by men. There was a wantonness in her, there always had been, that people on the prowl could sniff out.

The boys made a path for her as she left the nightclub. She held her head high, as she had held it high when the sound went out on the stage of the Santa Monica Civic Auditorium, and smiled at the people who spoke to her, but she did not remove the dark glasses that hid her wounded eyes. In her hands she held the half-empty bottle of Dom Perignon.

Some of the boys spoke to her. I loved you in this picture, I loved you in that. They remembered things her friends didn't. Thanks, she said to one. I wish you were running MGM, she said to another. Excuse me. Thank you. I'd like to get through here. Thank you, darling, thank you. You must be one of the ten people who saw that one. Excuse me. Will you get my car please?

She knew it as a fact about herself that she would be remembered more for her exploits than her talent. Madcap. Irrepressible. Those were the words that would follow her. Her brief marriages. Her many affairs. They would be more talked about than her films. Hers was a talent undefined, as she was undefined at the core of her as to who she was and what her role in life was really supposed to be.

"That was like *This Is Your Life*," said the waiter from the Palm. He had a motorcycle. She had a car. They decided on her car.

"Can I drive?" asked the boy.

"Sure," said the lady.

"Can I put the top down?"

"Sure."

"Beautiful night."

"Yeah. Beautiful."

"Full moon."

"Empty arms."

"What?"

"Old song."

"Where to?"

"Out Sunset."

"To the beach," he yelled.

"To the beach," she yelled back.

It was a fabulous night. They drove out Sunset Boulevard. The boy was in an exuberant mood. From time to time she handed him the bottle of Dom Perignon, and he drank from it and handed it back to her. The car radio was on. Music was blaring.

They turned onto the Pacific Coast Highway when they got to the beach. The moon was on the water. The highway was almost empty. She watched the speedometer as it started to rise, and then stopped watching it. She didn't care. She knew what was going to happen.

"See that house?" she asked, pointing across the highway to a brick wall covered with purple bougainvillea.

"What about it?" asked the boy.

"I used to live there," she said, looking at it as they passed it. "Goodbye, house," she called out.

The boy let out an Indian war whoop. "My 'lude just hit," he said. "I feel so good, movie star."

She leaned her head back against the seat of her car, looking up at the moon and the starry night. She took off her dark glasses and turned and looked at the handsome stranger next to her who was having such a good time driving her car at ninety-five miles an hour.

"It used to be I couldn't drive down this highway without getting pulled over by one of those good-looking Malibu cops," said Marina.

"What?" said the boy. "Talk louder."

"You know something, handsome?" she asked. "I don't even know your name. And that's what makes it so perfect."

"What?" he said, turning to look at her.

The boy, his Quaalude having hit, lost control of the car. It crossed the center divider, going ninety-five miles an hour, and hit a telephone pole. There was no scream. There was only silence. And then an explosion.

Her body was thrown from the car before the explosion and hurled against the stone gates of the record impresario Zeus Istan, who was having a party at the time.

The accident made headlines for weeks, in the seamier kind of newspapers. "Broke and Washed-up at Thirty-one!" "She Blew Her Opportunities."

The waiter from the Palm, who lost an arm but not his life, gave out several interviews after his recovery. For quite some time after it happened, he achieved a minor celebrity, at a new restaurant where he worked, as the maitre d'.

"See that guy?"

"What guy?"

"With the one arm."

"What about him?"

"He's the guy who was driving the car the night Marina Vaughan was killed."

"No shit!"

Chapter 30

THERE WAS A vast throng of people outside the Church of the Recessional at Forest Lawn Cemetery in Glendale, a forty-minute freeway ride from Beverly Hills. There were more of the curious outside the church—as well as media attracted by the scandal of the star's demise—than there were mourners inside the church. There were secretaries and assistants and publicists who pointed out to the ushers the riff from the raff so that only friends and acquaintances were seated inside. Dolores DeLongpre reported in her column that Marina Vaughan's funeral was S.R.O., meaning Standing Room Only.

"I hope it won't be an open casket," said Babette Navarro, getting out of her limousine.

"I shouldn't think so," said Nando. "I heard it was tomato soup time."

"Poor Marina," said Babette. "Ill-fated, wasn't she?"

"Poor Rex," said Nando.

"Oh, my God," said Babette, seeing someone unexpected.

"What?" asked Nando.

"There's Warren Ambrose."

"Where?"

"In the wheelchair, being pushed by the blonde in the black angora sweater." They stopped to wait.

"Hello, Warren," said Babette. "It's so nice to see you again."

"Hello, Warren," said Nando. "What a surprise."

"It's Babette and Nando," said Babette, helping him.

"Babette," said Warren slowly.

"Isn't it a shame it takes something like this to bring everyone together again?" said Babette. "Hello, I'm Babette Navarro, and this is my husband, Nando," she said to the blonde in the angora sweater.

"Hi," she said. "I'm Laurel Leigh, Babette. I'm Warren's fiancée."

"I put Marina in her first picture," said Warren Ambrose, talking slowly and with great effort.

Laurel Leigh continued to wheel him into the church, right in the middle of one of his long sentences.

"Did she say she was his fiancée?" asked Nando.

"He'll be around when the rest of us are all dead and buried," said Babette.

"That was some wig he was wearing," said Nando.

The flowers on the altar had been coordinated by Las Floristas, or Bruce and Barry, in colors of pink and red and white, so that all the arrangements sent by friends and studios blended into a scheme. Vast camellia trees in full pink flower dominated the altar. The casket was covered in a blanket of pink roses. Already seated in the first row was Rex Vaughan, accompanied by Faye Converse.

"Bruce and Barry did a beautiful job with the flowers," said Perry Rifkin to Bill, Mona's secretary Bill.

"Look, there's Warren Ambrose," said Bill.

"He looks about a hundred," said Perry. "Who's the chickie?"

"Her name's Laurel Leigh," said Bill. "Wait'll Mona hears this."

"I don't see your boss here," said Perry.

"And you won't either. They didn't like each other, those ladies."

"There's Cecilia Lesky."

Poor Rex. Poor Rex. Rex Vaughan was the drawing card at his daughter's funeral. "We came because of Rex," people said. "It's so awful for Rex." "He did everything he could for her." "She was ill-fated. Just like her mother."

"Everyone in Hollywood's here, Rex," whispered Faye Converse. "It's a beautiful tribute to Marina."

"Too bad they couldn't have been there when she needed them to give her a job," said Rex.

Faye turned to look back at the congregation. "I see Warren Ambrose," she said.

"Warren came, huh?" said Rex. "Warren put Marina in her first picture. Who else?"

"Babette and Nando. Delphine and Myron. Pearl Silver. Perry Rifkin with someone I don't recognize. Dolores DeLongpre. Do you remember when Marina used to call her DeLightful DeLicious DeLongpre? I see Cecilia Lesky. All alone. She's always alone, that girl."

"Who else? Liza? Candy? Jane? Do you see any of her other old friends?" Minnelli, Bergen, Fonda, he meant. The daughters of Hollywood.

"No," said Faye. "I know Candy's on location, and Liza's in New York, and I don't see Jane."

The minister walked to the center of the altar and said, "Please rise."

331

Marty Lesky did not want to give the eulogy for Marina Vaughan. He didn't like Marina Vaughan. He hadn't liked her for a long time. He resented the fact that she had been living in his daughter's house. But to have turned down the request from his old friend Rex Vaughan would have caused an awkward situation, especially as they were in the middle of shooting the remake of *Dodsworth* at the studio, so he agreed, reluctantly.

"Lambie," he called Lambeth Walker, the English screenwriter, on the night before the funeral.

"Yes, Marty?" said Lambeth Walker.

"Listen, I need you to write something for me quick," said Marty.

"What's that?"

"I need to give the eulogy for Marina Vaughan's funeral tomorrow, and I'm up to my ass in production problems, and I wondered if you'd write it for me."

"Poor Marina," said Lambeth Walker. "She's the one who should have played Iris March in *The Green Hat.*"

"Yeah, well, don't put that in the eulogy," said Marty, a little testily. "I want about five pages. Double spaced."

"Double spaced. Double time."

"That's right."

Outside the church, his limousine was waiting. He had to meet Mona Berg at Ma Maison directly following the service.

"She grew up in it," he read from the five pages, talking about fame. "Movie star daughter of movie star parents. The glitter and the glamour that are so often written about were normal to her eye. She never knew any other life. Fame was second nature to her. And she knew, more than most people, how the joys of fame can turn to agonies, when the publicness of defeat can cause despair—"

332

Up the center aisle, late, during Marty Lesky's eulogy, walked Franklyn Bassett. Alone, no Mona. He had a feeling within him that Mona was responsible in some way for the sad events that had happened. He'd always liked Marina. She never told about him that he'd been a hustler, and he never told about her that she'd blown him at a party at the Marty Leskys'. It was a tacky bond that had held them together, but it was a bond nonetheless. Honor among wantons.

He genuflected, in the Catholic manner, and crossed himself, in the abbreviated fashion of a former altar boy. Name of the Father, Son, Holy Ghost. He entered the pew. It was the same pew in which Cecilia Lesky was sitting. Alone. She was always alone, people said about Cecilia Lesky. Her mother hadn't come. She had an appointment she couldn't break, and besides she hated funerals, and Marty was going to be there anyway. She was glad her mother hadn't come, because her mother would have been furious with her at that moment, because she hadn't brought a handkerchief. An imperfection of grooming, she would have called it, right there, during Marty's eulogy, as if it took precedence over the grief that Cecilia was feeling.

"Here," whispered Frankie, handing her his handkerchief.

"The Marina that we will remember is the beautiful young star with the sad eyes, whose nine films will live on forever as a testament . . ." It occurred to Marty as he was reading that Marina died in the same way Iris March had in his remake of *The Green Hat*, the part that Marina said she was born to play.

A record started to play. It was Marina singing "People Like Us," the song she had sung at SHARE, previously recorded, in case she ever got her material ready to do an album. "They did this at Jeanette MacDonald's funeral," whispered Delphine Kahn to Pearl Silver. It was piped outside for the fans to hear and the media to tape, for the news coverage.

The casket was removed for cremation. Rex Vaughan walked down the aisle, accompanied by Faye Converse. Aisle after aisle filed out. I'm awfully sorry, Rex. I'm awfully sorry, Rex. I'm awfully sorry, Rex. I'mawfullysorry.rex. Thanks, Marty. Thanks, Myron. Thanks, Abe. Thanks. Thanks. Thanks.

"I put her in her first picture," said Warren Ambrose, in his slow stroked voice, in his first appearance since the heart attack, or stroke, or heart attack/stroke, felled him in the Jacuzzi.

"Awfully sorry for your trouble, Rex," said a beautiful blond girl in a black angora sweater who was pushing Warren Ambrose's wheelchair. "I'm Laurel Leigh, Warren's fiancée."

"Did she say she was his fiancée?"

"Pearl's having everyone for lunch, back at her house. I know Rex would want you to come. Tell Babette. And Delphine."

Inside, the church was nearly empty. The pink, red, and white flowers were being sent to the Cedars-Sinai children's wards. The camellia trees were being sent to Westlake School, where Marina had attended when she was a little girl, for the May Day program.

Still seated in their pew midway down the aisle, unnoticed and unmissed, were Cecilia Lesky and Franklyn Bassett.

"Thanks, Frankie," said Cecilia, handing him back the handkerchief he had lent her to blow her nose and dry her eyes.

"Feel better?" asked Frankie.

"I still can't believe it happened," said Cecilia. "She didn't care anymore. A couple of weeks ago she almost jumped in front of a train in Santa Barbara. This funeral cost more than she had in the bank."

They sat there in silence, thinking their thoughts, oblivious to the florists at their work inside, oblivious to the confusion of limousines and chauffeurs and traffic jams outside.

"It's a strange place, this town," said Frankie. "Last week nobody wanted her. Then she got killed, or let herself get killed, and now she's a legend. And next week someone will announce they're going to do her life story. And they'll get Liza Minnelli or Goldie Hawn to play the part. You know something, Cecilia, I don't know if I'm cut out for this place. I don't know if I'm that tough."

"When I first met you, I thought you were the toughest person I ever met," said Cecilia, looking at him.

"That was just my orphan asylum coming out," said Frankie. "That's not how I am."

"I knew that, Frankie. I even knew it when I thought you were tough," said Cecilia. They smiled at each other.

"Do you ever stop to think how it all ties together? If I hadn't given you that black eye, your mother wouldn't have called Mona to fill in for you at the AFI dinner, and I wouldn't have gotten the part in *South Sea Adventures.*"

"I wish you weren't getting married, Frankie," said Cecilia, gathering up her things. She said it in a way that let him know what her feelings would have been for him if he weren't.

"I'm not getting married, Cecilia," said Frankie. "I knew from the moment I heard about Marina's death, I wasn't going ahead with that. Listen, Cecilia, I've got the rest of the afternoon off. How about taking a drive up the coast to air out after all this?"

It started as a drive up the coast, to air out after the sad events that had befallen their mutual friend Marina Vaughan. It was a perfect California afternoon. The sun sparkled on the Pacific Ocean. The sky was blue. The sea was green. A painting. Painted especially for the DeBeers collection. That kind of painting.

They left through the rear of the church, behind the altar. They had been driven in the back of Las Floristas truck to Cecilia Lesky's white Porsche, parked away from the privileged and private and roped-off areas, in the public lot. No one saw them leave except the driver of the truck, who thought he was helping Frankie avoid the fans, and for an instant of his life felt part of it all.

Frankie drove Cecilia's car. He'd come to the funeral direct from the set in a studio car with a studio driver. There was no sense of destination about the way he drove. It was an afternoon-drive kind of driving.

"I feel like I'm playing hookey from school," said Frankie, unloosening his tie, unbuttoning his collar, starting to relax.

"Me too," said Cecilia. "From my life."

"How long before someone's going to miss you?" said Frankie.

"Let's not think about it for a couple of hours," said Cecilia. "How about you?"

"Let's not think about it for a couple of hours," he said.

They looked at each other and smiled.

They'd never really talked before, other than of-the-moment kind of talk on the several occasions they had seen each other. She told him all about her life. He told her all about his. The things they never talked about, because neither ever had the right person to talk about them to.

She told him Gary Cooper came to her christening. She told him she'd had a playhouse called Tara, with white pillars, and a soda fountain inside. She told him her parents were always afraid she was going to be kidnapped. She told him about her marriage that never was to Cheever Chadwick.

"Now tell me this," he said to her about the event, wanting to get the complete picture. They were sitting at a hot dog stand at a beach they happened to pass, eating hot dogs and drinking soda pop. "You went through with the marriage ceremony knowing there wasn't going to be any marriage because the guy was still married to someone else?"

"That's right. All those people were there. From all over the world. My mother's kind of friends, and my parents were too embarrassed to call it off, and we went through with it."

"Did you walk down that winding stairway in your parents' house?" he asked. He followed every detail of what she said, fascinated by her kind of life. Fascinated by her.

"Oh, yeah," said Cecilia. She liked the feeling of having someone listen to what she was saying. "Down the winding stairway, veiled by Galanos, a ten-foot train behind me, on my father's arm. Music playing. Here comes the bride. All dressed in white. Marina was one of my bridesmaids. It was what's known as a major event. Six hundred people. A tent. A marquee my mother called it. Peter Duchin's orchestra, with Peter Duchin himself, flown in for the occasion—"

"Who's Peter Duchin?" asked Frankie.

"Doesn't matter."

"Tell me this."

"What?"

"When you were upstairs, before the wedding started, just you and your father in the room, waiting for 'Here Comes the Bride' to start, what did you talk about?"

"We didn't say anything. What was there to say? We just sat there waiting for it to start, in silence."

He told her his father kicked his mother in the stomach, and she died. He told her he grew up in a home for boys. He said he didn't know where his father was, if he was even still alive. He told her he'd had a dicey kind of life.

"Let's talk about dicey," Cecilia said.

"I used to hustle," he said to her.

"That means doing it for money?" asked Cecilia.

"That's right."

There was a silence.

"Used-to are the operative words," he said, in atonement, interpreting her silence for disapproval.

"I wasn't being disapproving," she said.

"I knew from the time I was a teenager in that home that my looks were my only asset," he went on, as if in justification. "Oh, listen, I've had a real low-down past, if you want to know the truth. I even made a dirty movie. Trash. Tramp. That's what I've been. Until all this happened to me, what's happened to me, the stardom. You don't do that if you don't have to, and I don't have to any longer."

She told him about her parents. "I feel like I'm a constant source of disappointment to them," she said to him. "My father's always threatening to cut me off without a cent. He thinks that's a big threat to me. . . . My mother always found something wrong with the way I looked. Even at my fake wedding, when I was standing there at the top of the stairs, in costume, as I call it, the last thing she did before she went down the stairs in her mother-of-the-bride outfit was to tell me I was holding the bouquet the wrong way."

"What do they want for you?" he asked her.

"Live in the ruling class with them. Marry some nice studio head. Carry the strain another generation. Be on all the committees. Run a big house. Be a hostess. Have fittings. Have my hair done three times a week."

"To an untrained ear, that doesn't sound like a fate worse than death," said Frankie.

"I'm only interested in how it sounds to my ear," said Cecilia. "I've seen it too close to be dazzled by its glamour."

They couldn't stop talking to each other. He told her all about Mona. About the first time he met her, or remet her, on the same day he first met Cecilia. He told her how beholden he was to Mona for everything she had done for him, but that he grew to feel trapped and enslaved in the relationship, as if his life had been taken away from him. He said he felt he'd been taken out of the gutter and put in paradise, but he'd lost his free speech along the way.

"If you get out of line with those people, they can ruin you, you know," said Cecilia. "I've seen it firsthand, what my father's done to people." They talked as if they had been uncorked, all the things inside of them that they never got to talk about.

They walked on the beach. The sun was setting, squatting, orange, on the Pacific. Desire, as yet unspoken, was buzzing from their untouching bodies. It felt young and innocent between them. People who realized they were embarking on a major moment.

"You know, you're beautiful," Frankie said to Cecilia.

"No, I'm not," said Cecilia. "Interesting-looking. Almost pretty. Those are the adjectives that are applied to me."

"You've got to stop listening to your mother. I think you're beautiful," said Frankie.

"Say it again, Frankie. This is a first for me," said Cecilia.

"You're beautiful."

"So are you."

"I'm having a real nice time, Miss Lesky."

"Same here, Mr. Bassett."

"Oh!"

"What?"

"There's something I've been meaning to tell you. The name's Bozzaci."

"You know, Frankie Bozzaci, for the love idol of American television, you take an awfully long time to get around to the first kiss."

"I was never so shy in my whole life. Oh, Cecilia, I love you. I love you." Feelings of love, of the pure kind of love, when the right people meet at the right time, at the right place, burst from his body as he said the words, enveloping them.

"I love you, Frankie," she said. "I've loved you for so long. Oh, kiss me, Frankie. Kiss me, Frankie."

"Cecilia?"

"What?"

"Let's disappear. Let's not think of any of the problems there's going to be. Let's just be together for a few days. We may as well face the fact, Miss Lesky. We're a hot couple. We're front page news. Let's just enjoy each other to the fullest. In the privacy of a motel room."

"That sounds so lovely to me," Cecilia said. "They vanished into a motel room on the Pacific Coast Highway."

"Vanish," he said, repeating her word. "Nice word, vanish. Let's vanish."

Behind all that, where they lived, where they were expected, where they had obligations, there was consternation. The few people who knew that Franklyn Bassett was missing and the few people who knew that Cecilia Lesky was missing did not connect the fact that they might be missing together, and the consternations were separate.

"Do you mean to tell me you never even spoke to your own daughter at the funeral?" said Sylvia Lesky that night to her husband, Marty Lesky, in the tone of voice she used when she meant to imply dereliction of duty. They were watching a movie at the same time, remaining calm, reconstructing what might have happened.

"I arrived at the church just in time to give my eulogy, and I had to leave right after, as soon as I paid my condolences to Rex Vaughan, to be at Ma Maison by one fifteen to keep a very important appointment with Mona Berg about a very important picture. I just didn't see her. I didn't *not* speak to her. I didn't run into her."

"You should have looked," said Sylvia. "This picture stinks."

"You should have been at the funeral, where you belonged, and all this wouldn't have happened," said Marty, eating a chocolate pretzel.

"I had a very important appointment that I couldn't break," said Sylvia.

"You had a very important appointment with your hairdresser, Sylvia—Yoshi, whatever the fuck his name is—that's what your very important appointment was that you couldn't possibly break."

"Yushi was leaving for Hawaii for a week's vacation, and it was the last chance I had to see him," answered Sylvia, furious, laying out her justification. "And don't eat any more of those chocolate pretzels. That's your third one."

"See this actor?" said Marty, pointing to the actor on the screen, the star of the film. "He's a fag. The director fell in love with him during the picture. That's why all the loving close-ups."

"Call Dolores DeLongpre, Marty," said Sylvia. "Give her the scoop. I don't give a goddamn."

"Neither do I," said Marty slowly.

"Where could she have gone?" said Sylvia.

"You don't think she's a dike, do you? Skip to the last reel, will you, Wilbur?" he said over the intercom to the projectionist in the booth.

"Of course she's not a dike," said Sylvia.

"Remember that time she was supposed to have danced with Marina Vaughan at somebody's party?" said Marty.

"Marty, she's not a dike. Period on that conversation. All right? What's the other picture after this one? Do you know what I think? I think she's in love. I think she's been in love for a long time, with someone who's not in love with her. Do you think we should call the police, Marty?"

"Do you remember that time some guy gave her a shiner? You don't think she picks up strangers, do you? I don't even know what she thinks about, Sylvia."

"Every advantage, and nothing's right. I never understand it."

"That's what you were always telling her, Sylvia, how lucky she was, after you told her her slip was showing."

"I can play that game too, Marty," said Sylvia.

"Yeah, I know," said Marty wearily.

"Do you think we should call the police? If it was a kidnapping, we would have heard something by now. I don't want to watch the other picture. I'm in no mood for pictures. Marty, I think we should call the police. I think something must have happened to her. I know I pick on her. I try not to pick on her, but she always does something that drives me maaaaad, and then I pick on her. The other day she had on stockings that didn't even match. She knows how crazy that makes me."

"You can go, Wilbur. Good night," said Marty to the projectionist.

"Good night, Mrs. Lesky," said Wilbur.

"Good night, Wilbur," said Sylvia Lesky. "How long was Wilbur standing there? Do you think he heard what we were saying? They all talk. All those people."

"Wilbur talks, Wilbur gets fired, Sylvia."

"You know what it's like, Marty? It's like that time at her wedding when we made the wrong decision and went ahead with it."

"I thought we made the promise that we never discuss that again."

"It's just that we don't know what to do this time either."

In the second house of consternation, Mona Berg was in a frantic state. The man she loved, craved, worshiped, adored, to excess, had not been heard from in two days. It was a matter of pride with her that she could not bring herself to tell Bill, her secretary Bill, who was loyal to her, that Frankie had moved out of her bedroom into a different bedroom in the house, when he was asking her questions as to what might have happened, as if there could not have been a connection between the two.

She made exotic speculations. Kidnap. Violence in the air. Dangerous times. Mad people. She looks awful, Bill was thinking to himself about her while she was talking about gun control. She had on the same caftan for two days. Her hair was all over the place. Behind her dark glasses, her eyes were all puffed up from sleeplessness and crying.

"I told him he should have a bodyguard," said Mona. "Travolta has a bodyguard. Erik Estrada has a bodyguard. Does Bassett have a bodyguard? Oh, no. I-don't-need-a-body-guard, he says."

"Bullshit, Mona," said Bill. "You're not planting a story in Dolores DeLongpre's column. This is life."

"Don't you start on me, you little faggot," she said. It was a way they sometimes spoke to each other in moments of truth.

"You're bullshitting yourself. He wasn't kidnapped, Mona," said Bill, cutting under her insult, getting to the facts. "You smothered him, Mona, and he ran away. Let's get down to what the facts really are, and start to deal with it from there."

"Okay. But don't say he ran away from me," said Mona.

"And don't call me a faggot again," Bill said, "or I'm going to walk out, just like he did, and you're not going to have anybody left, Mona."

"I'm sorry. I didn't mean to call you a faggot. You know I don't give a shit. Ever since you took the Advocate Experience you're so touchy."

"Let's start at the beginning. He was driven to the funeral in a studio car by a studio driver. When he didn't appear after the service, the driver assumed he got a ride and left," said Bill.

"I don't understand how nobody, nobody, could not see him leave," said Mona. "He's the most famous face in America this week, on the cover of *Time*, and nobody notices him leaving the church."

"What are you going to tell the studio, Mona?" asked Bill. "I can't keep stalling the studio. How long can his migraine headache last?"

"What I want you to tell the studio is this, tell them Mr.

Bassett is suffering from exhaustion. And tell them he's under doctor's orders to remain in seclusion for several days," said Mona.

"You know the studio's going to send over their own doctor. They have to, for the insurance. The show can't shoot without him," said Bill. "Jess Dragonet says it's costing 37,221 dollars a minute. What happened, Mona?"

"Nothing," said Mona.

"Something must have happened, Mona," said Bill. "To just disappear like this is not his way of doing things."

"Nothing happened," said Mona. "He became an overnight star, and he's a little overwrought. That's what the trouble is."

"Did it have anything to do with the engagement announcement on Barbara Walters' program?"

"Of course not."

"His make-up man said the first Frankie heard of it was on television."

"I've got enough problems without her opinions," said Mona.

"Did it have anything to do with Marina's death?" Bill persisted.

"No!" said Mona, feeling trapped. "He's gone. That's all we need to deal with."

"At what point do the police get called in?" Bill asked.

"Oh, God, I don't know," said Mona, starting to cry.

Chapter *31*

THE PACIFIC COAST HIGHWAY. Night. Early dark night. On the way back from where they had been. Three nights of bliss behind them. Turmoil ahead of them. Floating in contentment. Filled with love. The white Porsche. Heading back. Purpose in its sleek movement.

"You know something, Frankie?" Cecilia said, turning to him, a smile on her face.

"What?"

"Marina Vaughan once told me she went to Acapulco with Jack Crawford, and they didn't get out of bed for three days. And do you know what I said to her? I told her I thought she was cheap."

They roared with laughter.

"How do you feel?" he asked her.

"Sated," she replied, moving closer to him. "In the love-liest sense of the word. How about you?"

"Contented. In love," he said. "Those were the best three days of my life."

"Look what we've got ahead of us," said Cecilia a short time later as they got closer to the city. It was what was on their minds. "My parents. Mona. The press. Imagine what the headlines are going to be. 'Love Idol Marries Movie Heiress!' "

" 'TV Star and Boss's Daughter Hitched!' " said Frankie. "I'd feel much purer about the whole thing if you weren't so rich."

"At least they can't say you married me for my money," she said. "They'll cut me off without a cent when they hear I'm Mrs. Bozzaci." They roared with laughter again.

"I love you, Mrs. Bozzaci."

The large white house, with the pillars, on Bedford Drive in Beverly Hills was in darkness. The white Porsche of Cecilia Lesky moved slowly past the house by one and pulled to a stop. Frankie hopped out of the car and shut the door silently as Cecilia moved over into the driver's seat. They talked in low voices.

"I'll tell Mona. I'll get some clothes, and I'll meet you at your house in an hour," said Frankie in a final recap of the plans they had talked through over and over. "And then we'll call and tell your parents."

"I'm scared," said Cecilia.

"I love you."

"I love you."

A Beverly Hills police car, in nocturnal vigilance, slowed as it passed them, saw the kind of people they were and the kind of car they were driving, and moved on.

The car drove off. Cecilia Lesky, Cecilia Bassett, Cecilia Bozzaci, went home to her house. She did all the things a bride would do on a bridal night. She took a bath. She put on a nightgown. She changed the sheets on the bed. She lit a scented candle. She put music on the stereo and champagne on the ice. She even went out in the garden, at that hour of the night, and picked some roses for the side of her bed.

Franklyn Bassett walked down the curved driveway toward the darkened house. Past his black Porsche, with the license plate TUE 9-10, the time slot of his series. Past Mona's new Rolls-Royce, with the license plate MS MONA, the name Dolores DeLongpre gave her, back in the beginning, when it first started to happen to her. He looked up at the impressive house, the manse, as Chico Gonzalez described it, that Fredric March built, that Tyrone Power once lived in, that Johnny Stompanato was murdered in, that Mona Berg told Barbara Walters was the house of her dreams. What a dark night it is, he thought. He opened the front door of the house and was surprised that the alarm system wasn't on.

He turned on the lights in the hall, and the glittering showplace glittered. It looks like a set, he said to himself. He always thought everything looked like a set from a movie. This is the set where the most powerful woman in Hollywood lives. In this scene I am about to play, I am exiting her life, like John Garfield in *Humoresque* exiting the life of Joan Crawford.

He walked across the black and white marble floor to the library. He noticed that the new Magritte had come and been hung, all in white, to match her room. He opened the door of the room and walked in. The television was on, with no sound. Only it wasn't the television. It was the Betamax playing over the television. A pornographic movie, starring himself in an earlier career, called *Rhapsody in Blew*, with the luscious Miss Laurel Leigh, the fiancée of the stroked and heart-attacked Warren Ambrose, whose agency Mona now owned.

348

Mona Berg was lying with her back to him on one of her lavender satin sofas, the one he spat the caviar on. She was intent on the film, in excitement, in desperation, in loneliness, in love, her caftan pulled up to her waist, her hands working herself in frenzy. "I love you, Frankie. . . . I love you, Frankie. I love you, Frankie. I love you, Frankie," she said over and over again, as in a litany, to the beautiful young man on the screen as he withdrew, wet and wanton, and ejaculated in great quantity over the beautiful breasts of the future Mrs. Warren Ambrose.

If he heard her bring herself to climax, watching him do the same, he gave no indication of so doing as he crossed the room and turned off the set.

"Not one of my finest hours," he said.

She shrieked in fright. "Oh, my God, you scared me, Frankie. I didn't hear you." She grasped her heart in terror, for the scare it was to her. "Wasn't the alarm on?" She pulled down her caftan and raised herself to a sitting position.

"Even the creeps who made that said I had star quality," said Frankie, referring to the pornographic film. He didn't care anymore if the alarm was on or off. It was no longer to be a chore of his existence.

"Oh, Frankie, I knew you'd come back. I knew it. Oh my darling, Frankie, I've been so worried about you. I didn't know if there was anything really the matter, if I should call the police, or what had happened to you." She was crying. "The only thing that matters is that you're back here."

Her relief was overwhelming. She thought everything was back on course again. She thought he had come back to her. She began to pull herself together. "I must look a fright," she said, puffing out her hair with her hands. She gushed forth her plans for him. The picture with Travolta was *set*, at Colossus, to be shot during the hiatus, where they would play two brothers in love with the same woman.

"And I got you first billing," she said, her arms and hands making her magnanimous gesture, as if there were no limits to where the two of them could go together. Movies. Big screen. She knew how to hold a man.

"I have a few things I want to tell you, Mona," Frankie said quietly, in charge of the situation, not wanting to talk about what was going to happen during the hiatus, wanting to talk about that moment they were living, wanting to get to the point of the scene.

"Listen," she said, forestalling, forestalling. "I'm sorry about announcing the engagement on television like that, on Barbara's show, but you know what Barbara's like when she starts questioning you, how she gets, pushy, won't let you off the hook, push, push, she promised me she wouldn't bring up your name . . ."

She always uses important people's names in her lies, Frankie was thinking, as if giving verisimilitude to them. Above-your-station kind of people. To be free of it all. The monopoly she had on his life.

"Mona," he said quietly, wanting to get on with the matter at hand.

Forestall. Forestall. "It was just that I love you so much, and I felt you were growing away from me," she said, hearing in her ear the beginning of panic in her voice. She was the most famous deal maker there was, and she knew when she wasn't making a deal.

"What happened between us has been extraordinary," said Frankie, in the manner of a man giving credit where credit was due in a farewell address. "You took me from nowhere to prime time in just under a year."

He wished he hadn't said nowhere to prime time. It was in

one of the thousand or so magazine articles about him.

"Look what I had to work with!" she said, with an exclamation point, as if compliments might change the course that the conversation was taking.

"And I'm very grateful," he said, continuing his thought, not allowing digression, "which I've already told you, and showed you, during the time we were together." Were together. Past tense. Past tense in present time. "But that time is over, Mona. I'm moving out."

"Oh, darling," she said, getting up, overriding, going on. "We're both tired. We've been under this terrible strain. Let's go to bed now and talk tomorrow. Wait till you see the new sheets I just bought for you."

"Listen, Mona. *Listen,*" he said to her. "There is no tomorrow. There's no tonight even. I just came back to tell you, and to pick up a few things." He turned and walked back to the hall and headed for the stairs.

Silence. A time for strategy. A change of tactics. Business. Contracts. Obligations. Money. Big money.

"You can't walk out," she said to him, using her voice with the sneer in it, bringing the meeting back to order, getting down to the realities of the business situation. "You're under contract!" She screamed the word contract at him as if it would make him stop dead in his tracks, Harry Cohn to Kim Novak, Jack Warner to Olivia de Havilland, Louis B. to Judy G. You're under contract!

"I didn't say I was walking out of the series, Mona," said Frankie. He was reflected in the smoke-mirrored walls as he walked up the winding stairway with the new white carpet to get his things. "I said I was walking out on you."

He looked down at her, from where he was, looking up at him.

"I don't like you, Mona. I don't like what you did to Marina. I don't like you for what you didn't do for your mother. You think life is all about buying more stuff. You think if you buy more stuff than anyone else has, than the Leskys have, than the Grossmans have, that your way is the right way to be."

"Oh, I see," said Mona, straightening the all white Magritte. "A lesson in morality from the star of *Rhapsody in Blew*. Listen, you cheap hustler, without me, you'll end up back on Santa Monica Boulevard peddling your ass for bucks, like your friend Rusty." Belittlement in her voice. And contempt.

"No, I won't," Frankie said with simplicity, for the truth that it was, and proceeded up the stairs to the bedroom where he had been sleeping since he moved out of her room, and closed the door.

And, of course, he wouldn't end up on the streets again peddling his ass for bucks. As she heard herself say the words, she knew it wasn't true. He'd gone too far. He'd gotten too famous. She gave him a name. She gave him a history. She gave him a character to play. She made him a commodity to be reckoned with. But. He took it from there. That was what she didn't have control of. He gave to the character that became a commodity a life force that was his alone. Bigger than the small screen. Crying out for Cinemascope. Just like Dolores DeLongpre said.

A madness of rage flooded her system. And the old feelings of being passed over, left out, the only one in the class not to get a valentine, the only one not asked to the party, get the coffee and close the door behind you. But she'd shown all those people. She was everything she ever wanted to be. She was the most powerful woman in her industry. Pointed out and stared at in public situations. A possessor of things. An incipient collector. A patroness to be. At the vortex. In. Wanted. Belonging. Part of it. With the most handsome and famous young man of the moment to complete her perfect picture of her perfect life, for the world to see.

She has it all. She has everything. That's what she wanted them to say about her. Not he left her. Did you hear? He left her. Did you hear? Frankie left Mona. He left her. He left her. He walked out on her. He didn't buy that ring. She bought it herself. No. No. No.

Ruin. That was the word that came to her mind. Ruin. "I'll ruin you," she said to herself, in rehearsal. Her heart was beating fast within her ample bosom. She knew about ruining. She knew how to ruin. She knew about taking the pornographic film that she had just masturbated to, the wetness drying stickily on her fingertips, her mind racing with vengeance. Whom should she show it to for maximum destruction? The head of the network where his series aired. The head of the advertising agency that wanted him to do the Wheaties commercial. Travolta! Travolta wouldn't touch him with a ten-foot pole. She thought about Dom Belcanto, the legendary singer with the underworld connections. I'll get his fucking legs broken, she said to herself. Marty Lesky! Her heart leapt as this latest thought occurred to her. Marty Lesky. He knew how to take care of people so they never worked again. Leaving no traces.

"I'll get Marty Lesky to *ruin you!*" she screamed up at him.

The door to the bedroom opened. Frankie came out carrying his bags, the plain Gucci bags, without the G's all over them, that Mona could never understand why he preferred.

"Did you hear me?" she asked imperiously, as if she had all the cards in her hand. "I said I'll get Marty Lesky to *ruin you,* as only Marty Lesky can ruin you, so you'll never work anywhere again. He'll put out the word on you. He'll put that cum shot in every sleazy magazine in the country. No studio or network will touch you when Marty Lesky's finished with you."

Frankie started to walk downstairs, a bag in each hand, walking out of her life, as if the words she was yelling at him, about ruination, his ruination, and destruction, his destruction, held no power over him. "Marty Lesky's going to be all primed to do that anyway, Mona," said Frankie in a reckless moment. If she hadn't mentioned Marty Lesky, he wouldn't have mentioned his marriage, not then, not until later, keeping issues separate, as the plan had been. "You see, I married his daughter in Tijuana this afternoon."

She looked up at him walking down the stairs. Stunned at the words he told her. A possibility that had never occurred to her. TV Idol Weds Movie Heiress. Cecilia Lesky, born with a gold spoon in her mouth, with a playhouse called Tara, and a snobby manner, who all her life had everything given to her. She felt as if she had been slapped, and slapped again. She, who never lost, realized that she had lost irretrievably the only person she had ever loved.

In a dazed state she moved to the hall table and looked at herself in the vast smoked mirror that reflected the staircase he was descending. Reason had abandoned her. On the table, still in the box in which it was delivered, was the gun that Marty Lesky had sent over, by way of his daughter Cecilia, as a present, for protection, when she moved into the house. "Let's hope it never comes in handy, Love, Marty," was written on the card which was still on the box. She opened the box and saw the glint of silver inside.

It was the first time she had ever held a gun in her hand. It was hard and metallic and compact. Her finger found its position on the trigger. Her arm raised it and pointed it at the man she loved. Even then at that instant he continued his movement out of her life, purpose in his gait, other fish to fry on his mind, as if what was happening was not happening.

She fired. A roar exploded in their ears. Blue fire flashed in their eyes. The bags dropped from his hands and rolled over each other down the white-carpeted stairs.

He looked at her unbelievingly, that she would take his life away from him, that she would rather have him dead than lose him. He felt the sledgehammer blow as the bullet entered his body.

"Oh, my God, Mona, what have you done?" he gasped. For an instant he remained frozen in position, midway on the white-carpeted winding stairway. He grasped the railing with his left hand as the pain in his chest intensified. He placed his right hand against himself and felt his hot blood seeping through his shirt and jacket.

"Oh, God," he said, in pain and in prayer, shutting her out in his last moments, reverting to the altar boy in the orphanage that he once was. He could feel his life begin to drain from him.

"Oh, Cecilia," he whispered. Then his body crumpled under him, and he began falling as consciousness left him, spewing blood on each of the white-carpeted stairs. He landed face up on the black and white marble floor. There was silence in the mansion. Dead silence.

Chapter 32

THE GUN WAS HOT in her hand. The heartbeat within her went from high speed to low. Thumping slow. She could feel the blood begin to drain from her face. Her mouth was dry as she sucked in air to keep from fainting. She couldn't faint. There was no time for fainting. Conflicting thoughts of self-preservation flooded her brain.

She didn't go to Frankie to look at him where he had fallen. She knew if she looked at him, blood coming from him, she might fall apart at a moment in her life when she needed to be in full control. The deed was done. She couldn't undo it. And the rest of her life was at stake.

Calm. Calm. Calm is the word to remember. Cold water on the face. She went to the powder room off the hall. Black marble sink. Gold-plated dolphin fixtures. Proofs of her success, even then, in that kind of moment. Who did Lana Turner call? Who did Claudine Longet call? Before they called the police, she meant, who did they call? Who did Ann

Woodward call? Who wrote their scenarios for them? She had to have a scenario. She had to have a part to play.

Mona picked up the telephone. It wasn't the police she dialed. It was Marty Lesky. The head of Colossus. The most powerful man in Hollywood. The defender of the embezzler Abe Grossman. The father of the bride of Mona Berg's slain lover. On his private line.

It was one o'clock in the morning. The telephone rang in the bedroom of the Palladian villa of Marty and Sylvia Lesky. They leapt awake. Their daughter, whom they neglected, had been unaccounted for, for three days.

"What?" It was the way Marty Lesky answered the telephone at one o'clock in the morning, expecting a kidnapper to discuss ransom.

"It's Mona, Marty," Mona said. There was a deadness in her voice.

"What's the matter?" asked Marty.

"You better get over here, Marty," said Mona.

"What's the matter?" he asked again.

"Somebody's dead. I know. I know," said Sylvia Lesky. "Someone's dead."

"Frankie's dead," said Mona. Silence.

"I can't come over there," he said.

"Do you want your daughter's name all over the papers, Marty?"

"What's Cecilia got to do with it?" The first counterconnection.

"Cecilia," whispered Sylvia frantically. "I knew it."

"You better get over here, Marty," said Mona.

"I want to come with you," said Sylvia Lesky, starting to get up from her bed as she watched her husband pull on a pair of trousers and a cashmere sweater and put his feet into

357

the pair of velvet slippers with his initials on them that were at the side of the bed.

"She don't want you to come," said Marty.

"She didn't say that," said Sylvia, for once not correcting his grammar.

"Then I don't want you to come," said Marty.

"Why?"

"You stay here. When I find out what happened, I'll call you."

Marty Lesky knew—before he arrived at Mona Berg's house, before he knew what his daughter's involvement was in the death that had taken place—that there were plans to be made, a script to be written, innocence to be proclaimed, investments to be protected. Time was of the essence. At some point the police would have to be called, and they would be able to pinpoint to the minute almost the time of expiration. What he didn't need was a hysterical wife to further complicate a complicated matter.

"But what about Cecilia?" asked Sylvia.

"I don't know what about Cecilia. That's what I'm going to find out," said Marty.

"I'm going to call her," said Sylvia. "I'm going to find out what's happened." She pushed the buttons of the push-button telephone.

"You don't think she's home, do you?" asked Marty, not having considered the possibility. "We must have left a hundred messages with her service in the last three days."

"Shhhh. It's ringing."

One ring. Two rings.

"Frankie! Where are you?" came the voice of Cecilia Lesky on the other end, loud enough for Marty to hear standing where he was near the door of the bedroom. Sylvia Lesky could only stare at the telephone, not knowing how to answer

her daughter, as if she had caught her out in something secret.

"Frankie, is that you?" repeated the voice of their daughter. There was a trace of apprehension in her voice.

Sylvia Lesky looked at her husband. She held out the receiver, not knowing what to do, the beginning of panic in her face. She put her finger on the disconnect button and collapsed back on her pillows.

"Whatever happened, she don't know anything about it. She don't even know he's dead," said Marty.

"I didn't even know she knew him," said Sylvia.

"That fucking ginney," said Marty, beginning to put together the pieces of the puzzle, realizing that an involvement had occurred between his daughter and Mona Berg's lover. "I better get out of here."

"I always hated Mona Berg," said Sylvia Lesky quietly.

"I'll call you," said Marty. "You better get dressed."

"Marty."

"What?"

"Keep Cecilia's name out of the papers. Please."

"I'll do what I can."

"I don't know how she could do this to us."

He walked into the six-car garage. There were the two Rolls-Royces. He decided against either of those. Too noticeable on the streets at that hour of night if someone he knew might be coming home late. There were the two Mercedes, the station wagon and the small two-door convertible. There was the chauffeur's car and the maid's car. He decided on the small two-door convertible Mercedes, the kind that was a dime a dozen on the streets of Beverly Hills, that no one would turn around to look at. He was aware of the need to remain inconspicuous in the hours to come.

He drove carefully the three miles that it was from his

house in Holmby Hills to Mona Berg's house in Beverly Hills, never exceeding the speed limit, not wanting to risk being stopped by a police officer hidden from view on a side street waiting to pounce on a traffic violator. When he came to the big white house on Camden Drive, he did not pull into the curved driveway behind Mona's new Rolls and Frankie's black Porsche. He went around the block and stopped the car finally at the cross street at the side of Mona's house, parking it a quarter of a block away. He got out, closed the door quietly, and walked the few hundred yards to the front door. The door was slightly ajar and Mona was standing inside waiting for him.

"Where the hell have you been?" she said. "I thought you'd never get here."

"I'm here now," said Marty, looking at her standing in the partially open door, her make-up washed off her face, her skin a sickly color, her hair awry, her tiny eyes puffed and red behind the violet lenses of her thick glasses. "I wasn't sitting up waiting for your call. You going to let me in, or are you going to tell me what happened out here on the stoop?"

Mona opened the door wide enough to let him in. "I didn't mean to use that tone of voice. I'm just a little frantic here all by myself."

"What happened?" he asked. He closed the door behind him. Like the exterior, the interior of the house was in near darkness.

"He's dead, Marty. Frankie's dead," said Mona. She pointed her hand behind her to the foot of the stairs, but she did not turn around to look where she was pointing.

Marty walked around her to the spot where she was pointing. The house was so quiet that the sound of the heels of his velvet slippers on the marble floor of the hall seemed deafening. There, lying in a pool of blood, was the lifeless body of the most famous face and name of the television season. The thought went through Marty's mind of the millions and millions of dollars in syndication billings for Colossus Pictures that had ceased to be, but he was sure that she knew that as well as he knew it, and it seemed not the moment to articulate the thought. Instead, he said simply, "Jesus Christ."

Frankie's eyes were open, staring straight up. His lips were open, the lips that had mouthed the name Cecilia as the last word of his life. Even in death there was a beauty about him. His corpse was a commanding presence.

"I can't touch him, Marty," said Mona. She had come over to the place where Marty was kneeling beside the body, but she kept her head averted from the tableau.

"What do you want to touch him for?" asked Marty.

"I want to get that piece of paper that's sticking out of his wallet pocket," said Mona, pointing but not looking at what she wanted.

"What's my daughter got to do with all this?" asked Marty. "She don't even know he's dead."

"Get me that piece of paper, Marty," repeated Mona.

"I'm asking you about Cecilia."

"You pull out that piece of parchment, and I think you're going to find your answer."

He didn't want to touch the body either. He wished he had a pair of tongs, but it seemed inappropriate to ask for tongs, and he made a pick at the paper and pulled his hand away, and then another pick, and the paper came loose, and the third time he reached for it he pulled it out.

"Give it to me," she said, grabbing at it from him, knowing what it was going to be, wanting to see it before Marty. The paper was stiff like the parchment it was, and folded in three sections, and when she opened it, the writing was in Spanish.

"That fucking little cunt," she said.

"Who?" asked Marty.

"Your daughter. That's who. Sixty-five million plus what's on your walls wasn't enough for her."

"What are you talking about?"

"Here!" she said, handing him the Mexican marriage license. "She married my fiancé in Tijuana this afternoon."

"Jesus Christ," said Marty for the second time in a few minutes. "We didn't even know she knew him, except in a casual way." He used the newel post of the stairway to pull himself to his feet. There on the bottom step of the stairway was the murder weapon where Mona had dropped it.

"Isn't that the gun that I sent over as a house present?" he asked, recognizing it, knowing it was registered in his name.

"Yeah," said Mona.

"Jesus."

"It's a regular family affair."

Lest Marty Lesky have any misconception about his own involvement in the scandalous affair, Mona Berg ran on her Betamax the last few minutes of *Rhapsody in Blew*. The withdrawal, wet and wanton, and the ample ejaculation.

"Why am I looking at this?" asked Marty Lesky.

"This is your daughter's late bridegroom," she said.

"Jesuschrist," said Marty.

Marty called Sylvia and told Sylvia what to do, what arrangements to make, whom to call, about what had to be done. The jet had to be made ready. Clothes had to be packed. Sit there. He would call her.

They figured it all out in an hour. Like at a script conference, when they had lunch together at Ma Maison and discussed this script and that script. There must be no mention of Cecilia Lesky. A given.

"I won't mention your daughter, and you'll take care of me," said Mona.

"Right," said Marty. "Now listen to me, Mona. I think I have it now. The solution for this is in the prowler. The prowler. The prowler. You thought it was the prowler. A very well established prowler, in your back story. You told your hairdresser. You told your manicurist. You told your secretary. You told me. I sent you this gun. For protection."

"I've got all the back story, Marty," said Mona.

"And you were extra jumpy tonight because the new Magritte had just arrived, had just been hung, was not wired to the system, was not insured, and your fiancé was away, and there was a prowler in the neighborhood."

"Frills, frills, Marty. Ross Hunter time," she said. "Let's get to the plot. I know how to dress it up."

"Your fiancé, the famous television star, on the cover of *Time* this very week, a love idol, like Valentino. Like Travolta."

"Frills! Back story! I know all that," said Mona.

"He's been away. A couple of days of R and R after the exhaustive rigors of his television series and the adjustments to fame. Off by himself. Fishing. Camping. Woods. That's what he was really like, you'll say. You weren't expecting him until the day after tomorrow. We'll find out later, from someone where he was, that he missed you so much he decided to come home early and surprise you."

"Okay," said Mona, picking up on the plot. "So I put on the alarm and fell asleep in the library watching television."

"He came in the house and went upstairs looking for you in the bedroom to surprise you, carrying his luggage," Marty went on.

"And I hear a noise in the library and wake up," said Mona, continuing on his story line.

363

"That's right," said Marty. "You go outside into the hall, look up at the top of the stairs, which is in semi-darkness, and see this guy there with two suitcases."

"I think it's loot."

"That's right."

"Panic grips me."

"That's right. There on the hall table is the gun that I sent you for your safety and, get this, that Frankie taught you how to use in case of an emergency," said Marty.

"Oh, Frankie," said Mona, starting to cry. "You know, Marty, when he turned after the bullet hit him, up there at that stair by the curve, his eye caught mine. Oh, my God, how could all this have happened?"

"Save all that for the police," said Marty. "Mourn on your own time. I've got my own problems."

"You're tough, Marty," said Mona.

"You're tougher, Mona," said Marty. "Now, listen, wear your engagement ring. Look at it. Touch it. Suffer with it. It was what he gave you. And pull yourself together. You look like shit. That caftan's got cum on it. Lose the dirty movie."

They went into intricacies. This position. That position. A rehearsal. He told her the importance of courtesy.

And he reiterated his chief concern. "Under no circumstances is Cecilia's name to be brought into the case. Understand?"

"Understood," said Mona.

"I'll find out from Cecilia where they were married in Tijuana and have all traces of it removed. What's his real name?"

"Bozzaci."

"Jesus."

"Now, listen, Marty," said Mona.

364

"I have to get out of here," said Marty.

"Don't be in such a hurry," said Mona.

"What?"

"There's a couple of things I want. In return."

"Like what?" He could smell a deal coming on. Even then. In those circumstances, with the body of her lover staring up, bearing witness.

"I want to be the head of the studio, Marty."

There was a pause. "What studio?"

"Colossus," she answered.

"I'm the head of the studio, Mona."

"You can become chairman of the board."

"Nothing doing."

"Sylvia's not going to like seeing her little baby's name all over the front pages."

"I'll think about it," he said quietly.

"There's no time to think about it, Marty. We gotta call the cops before rigor mortis sets in. I'm not easing you out, Marty. I'm just enhancing the setup. Think what kind of a studio we could run together."

"Okay," he said. He didn't know if he meant it or not. He wanted to get it over and done with and get out of her house.

"Okay what?" she asked.

"It's a deal," he said, getting up. "Now I have to get out of here so you can call the police."

"There's a couple of more things, Marty," she said.

"Like what?"

"The salary."

"For God's sake, Mona. We can work that out."

"I want a million a year, Marty, for the first year, escalating up to—"

"All right. All right."

"And a million dollars for art acquisitions for the length of my deal."

"Mona, for Christ's sake, you have to call the police."

"I'm scared, Marty."

"Now, remember. It was an accident. You thought he was the prowler."

"What's going to happen to me?"

"You'll be bigger than ever. Now I want you to start to cry, Mona," Marty said, "and when you're really out of control, I want you to call the Beverly Hills police station, ask for Captain O'Neill, 275-0900, tell him you just shot your fiancé, weeping, weeping, hysterics, by accident, tell him you thought it was the prowler. And when I hear you make the call I'm going to leave you, and you're on your own."

"I'm scared," said Mona.

"Cry, Mona, work yourself up into a real state. You killed the only person you ever loved, Mona. I'll lead you in there. I'll get you hysterical. You killed the only man you ever loved, Mona. That ten-inch dick with the quart of jism that you used to brag about, that you had it every night on your Porthault sheets, Mona, bye-bye, bye. Forever. He's gone, Mona. He's gone. If you hadn't killed him, he was going to leave you. He didn't want you anymore. He had enough. He was sick of you. Here's the phone, Mona—275-0900. Captain O'Neill. Out of control. Get out of control."

"I thought he was the prowler!" "I thought he was the PROWLER!" "I THOUGHT HE WAS THE PROWLER!"

It was a shriek that went around the world, from headline to headline.

Chapter 33

CECILIA LESKY BOZZACI was awakened by the chimes. Mournful-sounding, she thought as she awakened on the sofa still. She had lived behind alarm systems all her life. She never opened doors without looking out the peephole first, but she ran to her door and opened it wide to welcome her husband.

Marty Lesky was standing there. It was four o'clock in the morning. She noticed he was wearing a sweater without a shirt underneath, as if he had dressed in a hurry. It was not a way she was used to seeing him. Emergency was in the air.

"Is mother dead?" she said to him.

"No, your husband is," he said to her, walking past her into the house.

It was not a call of condolence, to tell her how sorry he was that her bridegroom was dead. He never allowed her a moment of mourning, as if her sadness, her grief, was of secondary importance.

He told her to pack. He told her she was leaving the country. He told her he didn't want there to be any connection between her and the events that had happened.

There was a degree of plausibility in the story that the sleeping Mona shot her fiancé in the mistaken belief that he was the publicized prowler who had been reported in the area. The degree of plausibility with that story would be lessened if it came to the fore that the victim had been married on the afternoon of the shooting to someone other than the woman whose fiancé he was reputed to be.

Then Sylvia arrived. Even in circumstances like that, at four-thirty in the morning, spiriting her daughter out of the country to avoid scandal, Sylvia looked perfect. Red Adolfo suit, hat to match, and a sable coat. She was carrying a mink coat for Cecilia to wear on the long flight on their private jet. She said it was only a loan, she wanted it back.

"What about me?" asked Cecilia.

"We'll talk about you when you get to where you're going," said her father. "I don't want you to be here when the shit hits the fan."

"I want five minutes," said Cecilia. "I have some things I want to say."

"You have to pack," said her mother.

"You pack," said Cecilia. "That way you can get everything that matches, the right shoes for the right suits and the right blouse for the right skirt."

"This is hardly the time for you to be insulting to me," said Sylvia.

"My husband is dead, and you haven't even told me how he died."

While her mother was packing her clothes, and her father was on the telephone with an assistant about going to Tijuana and eliminating her marriage certificate, Cecilia wandered

368

through the rooms of her house, sensing somehow that she would never return to it, that her time in that location was over. She had never gotten used to the newly decorated rooms that Marina Vaughan had completed for her, with their terra-cotta walls and chintz coverings. She thought to herself that she had never given a party in them. She thought to herself that Frankie had never seen them. She looked outside at her red brick terrace and her swimming pool and beyond at the spectacular view of Los Angeles with its millions of twinkling lights. She felt numb inside herself. She had not cried or screamed out that her happiness had been so short-lived. She knew only that she did not believe what her father had told her, that Mona Berg had mistaken Frankie for a prowler.

"Don't forget your passport," her mother called to her from where she was in the bedroom. "Marty, tell her not to forget her passport."

"Get your passport," her father called to her, looking up from his telephone conversation, and then he returned to the business at hand. "Bozzaci, the name was," he continued. "B-o-z-z-a-c-i."

Cecilia went into the den, which her mother preferred to call the library. The bookcases were filled with books, many of which she had never gotten around to reading, that Marina Vaughan had organized for her and supplemented for her. She thought how warm and cozy the small room looked. The fire in the fireplace that she had lit for the arrival of her husband was nearly out, but the small flame that remained flashed on the brass rungs of the fireplace bench that Marina had given her, that had once been in Marina's house in Malibu. She went to the desk to look for her passport which she remembered being in the center drawer. On top of the desk was the small electric typewriter that Marina had used to write the book that she wanted so desperately to finish. Marina. Marina. The evidence of her was everywhere. The impression she had left as a visitor was more lasting than the impression left by the heiress whose possession the house was.

Cecilia opened the drawer. Her passport was there where she had placed it, worn and stamped with the usage of nearly five years of travel between her first one-day marriage and her second one-day marriage. Next to it was an unfamiliar package, a large manila envelope of several inches in thickness. She picked it up. There was no marking on either the front or the back of it. She pushed together the two-pronged clip that held it closed, opened it, and pulled from within what she immediately recognized to be the manuscript of Marina's book. *"Candles at Lunch,* by Marina Vaughan," the title page read. She hadn't any idea that Marina had written so much. She thought, as so many people had thought, that Marina's book was one of those books that get talked about but never written.

She began to flick through the pages. *When I was a little girl, I never visualized myself as the kind of woman who got married three times before she was thirty, but that's what I did,* the first line read. She saw names she recognized. Warren Ambrose. Rex Vaughan. Montgomery Clift. Faye Converse. She began to put the pages back into the manila envelope. She thought she would ask her father to send the manuscript on to Marina's agent, what was his name, who had treated her so shabbily. Joel Zircon, she remembered. Then something caught her eye toward the end of the manuscript. She saw her father's name, and Mona Berg's name, and Abe Grossman's name. She read the line *"Dolores De-Longpre will write what I tell her to write,"* said Mona Berg to Marty Lesky.

"Did you find your passport?" asked Marty Lesky, entering the room.

"Yes, yes, it's right here," said Cecilia, shoving the pages back in the manila envelope and turning around to him with the passport in her hand.

"What's that?" he asked, referring to the package.

"I was just gathering up some magazines to read on the plane," she answered, looking in his eyes as she lied to him, the way he had looked into her eyes when he lied to her.

"We better get going," he said. "It's going to be light soon."

She followed her father into the hall where her mother was waiting with two packed bags. She was looking at herself in the mirror of her gold and diamond compact, rubbing her little finger back and forth to even the lipstick on her lower lip.

"Help me close that suitcase, will you, Marty?" she said to her husband.

"I'll do it," said Cecilia. She knelt in front of the canvas bag and tossed the manila envelope into it, then brought the cover down and closed the suitcase.

"You got your magazines?" said Marty to Cecilia from the front door.

"Oh, the hell with them," said Cecilia. "I don't feel like reading magazines anyway."

"I brought *Vogue* and *Town and Country*," said Sylvia. "They're in the station wagon."

They moved out of the house, Marty carrying one of the suitcases, Sylvia carrying the other.

"Use the *alligator* bag, Cecilia," said Sylvia, trying to conceal the note of exasperation in her voice as she saw her daughter pick up the worn black leather one she carried to work each day. "I transferred all your things."

"Remember to put the alarm on," said Marty from the station wagon where he was putting Cecilia's luggage next to Sylvia's in the back.

Cecilia turned back to the house, stepped into the hall, and made the adjustments on the burglar alarm system. "Goodbye, house," she said, tears in her eyes, tears in her voice, looking back from the front door. And then she added, "Goodbye, Frankie."

Chapter 34

FOR SEVERAL MONTHS Cecilia Lesky did not read, or even remember, the manuscript of Marina Vaughan's book that she had taken with her on the night of her husband's death when she was whisked out of Los Angeles by her parents.

She stayed in a house in the English countryside belonging to her friend Antoinette Kingswood, with whom she had gone to school, with whom she had shared an apartment after the annulment of her marriage to Cheever Chadwick, with whom she maintained a long-distance friendship.

"The only thing is, Vyvyan and I are going to be in Sardinia for the month," said Antoinette shortly after her arrival. Vyvyan was her husband, a lord, a restless lord. They traveled constantly.

"That's all right," said Cecilia.

"You could come with us," said Antoinette.

"No," said Cecilia. "I just want to stay here."

"It'll be boring for you."

"No, it won't."

"What happened out there in Hollywood, Cecilia?"

"My friend Marina died."

"Yes, I read that. Awful."

"Awful." She didn't tell her anymore. She didn't tell her the rest of it. She hadn't sorted out her thoughts. She hadn't allowed herself to experience her grief.

They left, Antoinette and Vyvyan. Cecilia stayed in the lovely house, in the solitude that she craved. She watched Frankie's funeral on the television news in England. She saw the madhouse it was, the thousands and thousands of weeping fans, women of all ages. "Not since Rudolph Valentino's funeral has there been such an outpouring of grief for a love idol," said an announcer on television. She watched the heavily veiled Mona Berg collapse on his casket and call out his name. She read over and over again the headline that went around the world: I THOUGHT HE WAS THE PROWLER.

She followed the details of the story from where she was, six thousand miles away from where it was happening, as they appeared in the press. Frankie Bassett had returned a day early from a fishing trip, it read, to surprise Mona Berg, his discoverer, his mentor, his fiancée. He had run upstairs to greet her, not realizing that she was asleep in the library downstairs. She had awakened, hearing the sound of someone upstairs. It was late. The house was in near darkness. She had seen a shadowy figure at the top of the stairs carrying two suitcases. Mistaking him for the prowler, she had fired the fateful shot. Mona Berg was neither indicted nor charged. The death was deemed a tragic accident.

As for Cecilia, her part had been eliminated from the plot of the story. She had been left on the cutting-room floor.

374

Weeks passed. A month. Two months. The Kingswoods returned. She decided it was time to move on.

"You don't have to go, you know," said Antoinette. "You can stay on as long as you want."

"I know," said Cecilia.

"Are you better? You seem better."

"I'm better."

"Are you going back to Hollywood?"

"Oh, I don't think so," said Cecilia. "I thought I'd go back to Rome for a while."

"That lady who killed the television actor became the head of your father's studio," said Vyvyan, reading from one of the morning papers. "Woman to Head Studio," read the piece.

"What?" said Cecilia, shock in her voice.

"You didn't know?"

"No. Let me read it."

"Funny they didn't tell you."

That night, when her bags were brought for her to pack, she found the manuscript of Marina Vaughan's book that had been left inside.

When I was a little girl, I never visualized myself as the kind of woman who got married three times before she was thirty, but that's what I did, read the first line. She read on. The stories she already knew. Montgomery Clift, a little drunk, dropping her at her christening. Faye Converse catching her. Her mother's suicide. Her first picture, when she was eleven, starring with her father. A children's birthday party at Cecilia Lesky's, who had a playhouse called Tara with a soda fountain inside. My friend Cecilia Lesky, she called her, *sad always, separated by her privilege from the rest of us.*

She read on. Being kicked out of Westlake School for marijuana and boys. Making movies. Warren Ambrose. Her father. Making movies. Getting married. Going places. Doing things. Getting divorced. Making movies. It was all there. A movie star's life. No better, no worse than any of a dozen biographies of movie stars that were on the market.

She read on. Mona Berg. The secretary to her agent, Warren Ambrose, helping her out of a jam with the Malibu police when Warren was in Brazil. Warren's heart attack. Mona Berg. Mona Berg. The name became more frequent in its mentions. Her friendship with her. Her betrayal by her. Her loss of the part that she felt she was born to play because of that betrayal. The story of a substitute pool man called Frankie who was to become the television star Franklyn Bassett.

She read on. Her downfall. Her inability to get work. The blackball of her because of the drug story that Mona had spread about her. It all began to read like a hard-luck story.

One day I was having lunch in the Beverly Hills Hotel with my new agent, Joel Zircon, when I was paged by the bellboy and told that a person wished to speak with me in the lobby, the new chapter started. Johnny Griffin. A reporter with a lead on a hot story about financial corruption and a skillful cover-up at Colossus Pictures.

"Keep out of it, Marina," my father said to me when I told him of the meeting with the reporter who had once written kind things about me after I had failed to show up for my prize at the Cannes Film Festival. I had only to be told to keep out of something for me to get involved. Besides I wasn't working and had nothing else to do.

Cecilia read on. Abe Grossman. Marty Lesky. Mona Berg. The names were repeated over and over. *This was not really a story about a cheesy producer called Abe Grossman who* had diverted huge amounts in profit participation from the film star Faye Converse, my godmother, to his already well-lined pockets. At stake was the control of a five-hundred-million-dollar corporation, Colossus Pictures, and the huge profits that Marty Lesky stood to derive from the sale of the stock if the Grossman scandal were not brought to light.

Lordy, Lordy, as Frankie used to say. An atmosphere was created that Colossus Pictures was going to collapse if Abe Grossman was forced to leave the studio. Marty Lesky and Mona Berg spread all the stories, that Lesky himself would leave the studio, that Jess Dragonet would leave the studio, that Rex Vaughan, Rebecca Kincaid, and even the robbed Faye Converse would never appear in another picture for Colossus. The atmosphere was that there wouldn't be a studio left to run.

Cecilia read on. Then, inexplicably, Johnny Griffin, whose source had been within the ranks of the studio, vanished. I went to the Beverly Crest Hotel where he was staying, and he had checked out the previous night. There was no forwarding address. The Washington Post said he was not with the Washington Post. I never heard from him again. At that time I was asked to sing at the SHARE Boomtown party, and I thought that it would be a chance for me to make a comeback for myself and began devoting myself to preparations for it. . . .

That was all. There was no more. It was what Marina once told her, what she had repeated to her mother, that Marty was afraid if they got to Abe Grossman they would start looking into him next.

"I wish you'd stop seeing Marina Vaughan," her mother had said to her at the time.

"I have your ticket for Rome," said Vyvyan Kingswood to Cecilia the next morning at breakfast.

"We hate to have you leave," said Antoinette. "Maybe we'll come and visit you there once you get settled."

"I'll let you know what my plans are," said Cecilia. "Thank you for everything."

"You seem much better," said Antoinette.

"I think I am," said Cecilia. "You know I didn't tell you everything when I came here."

"I didn't think you had. That's all right."

"I loved someone, and he was killed, on the same day I married him, and I couldn't bring myself to talk about it."

"Cecilia," said Antoinette, hugging her.

"I'm not going to Rome," said Cecilia. "I'm going back where I came from."

"To Hollywood?"

"I thought I never wanted to go back there, but there's a few things I want to look into. You can't solve your life by running away from it."

"Do you want to call your parents?"

"Oh, no. I want to surprise them," said Cecilia Lesky.